STEPHEN G. KIRK

AND MIDNIGHT CAME TO CALL

Stephen G. Kirk

AND MIDNIGHT CAME TO CALL

US Copyright © 2016
ALL RIGHTS RESERVED
ISBN - 978-0-9937959-0-9

The author gratefully acknowledges
the cover's photograph generously provided by
Ashley Lepard

Contents

Just Curious…

Ever wonder what its like to be dead? Really dead… and I don't mean like winding up in heaven if you're good, hell if you're not, or maybe limbo for all those who prefer to sit on the fence. Com' on! Give it some real thought.

Could it be you are one of those types that think you can just come and go (from goodness or badness knows where) and simply visit this earthly plain on a whim after you're gone? Here's an interesting idea; you could leave little calling cards to let your friends know you've been around. Like leaving the smell of your favorite cigar or perfume floating about, maybe not a good idea if they have allergies, but hey, maybe you never really liked them all that much in the first place. How about moving their sentimental keepsakes from one place to another; say a favorite coin or maybe an antique… a real expensive one; it'll drive 'em nuts! Ok, on the positive side maybe you could save them from getting hit by a bus or warning them of a natural disaster … or even giving them the winning numbers of the lottery!? Wait, not that last one, after all, there are rules, apparently even on the other side.

Yeah, rules for the dead, can you imagine that? You can do this but not that. You can help but only so much. You can't hinder good people, only the bad and then only enough to thwart their evil intent, never to really kick their ass like everyone would really like to see happen. Sorry folks, but that's left up to the Big Guy himself.

Perhaps you're one of those "Captain and Mrs. Muir" types. You know, those folks that like to think that after you croak you can hang around for half a century waiting and watching the love of your life, a good friend or a favorite relative bumble about, just so you can make a flashy entrance when they finally buy it, leaving together hand-in-hand for the

Promised Land. Tough luck if they followed the high road to heaven while you took the lower detour, if you catch my drift.

Let's take a moment to split a few religious hairs, not that it would bother me, I happen to be a baldy. "Ok, all you Dogans into the center, Jews over there to their right, Muslims to their left, oh and who is that back there? You... yeah you reincarnation types... Hindus, Buddhists; for Christ sake, you're in the wrong building altogether; the recycling depot is around the corner. As for you Satanists? Sorry the Almighty isn't an equal opportunity employer... to Hell with you all."

Naw, I don't believe in those fairy tales. None of it, not a word of that stuff is true! You might ask how I happen to know, well that's because I'm dead and not here to tell you, that's how. Pardon me, is that a raised hand I see in the audience? "Ok, you... yes you... how did I die? Let me tell you."

"It happened last Tuesday while a friend and I were hiking in the Catskills. This bear wandered up; after all, he had heard the bells we wore and naturally assumed it was dinnertime. Now when I was alive I could move pretty fast if I had to, just not quite as fast as my friend and unfortunately, nowhere near as fast as the bear. This said, I'll spare you the "grizzly" details... sorry folks, just couldn't resist."

Anyway, following a rather exciting ending, things just sort of faded to black, and I mean absolute pitch. And nothing, and I mean nothing, has happened since. As for me? I'm just lying here, well here and there, and ok, well maybe over there... but hey, wait, what is that?

Forget what I just said, I think I'm finally seeing the Light!

Tenant

"In Memory of Shae"

He awoke before the alarm. Turning to the digital clock by his bedside, he saw it was 5:15 am, February 29, a leap year and coincidentally; the same date on which he had retired from the Chase pulp and paper mill exactly twelve years earlier. He lay back, sinking into the soft mattress and considering the time that had since passed. Twelve long years, or in retrospect, maybe only three years ago; just three if you happened to relate to the folks who having been born on that particular date now insisted in celebrating their birthdays only once every four-years.

Jim had little need to rise early today, or any other day for that matter, but habits can be difficult to break, especially for those of the older set. As he put it, habits were akin to putting on thick socks, a well-worn pair of shoes, and a woolen sweater on a cool Saturday morning in late fall, in fewer words, habits were simply comforting.

He sat on the edge of the bed, eyes half closed; going through the list of things he ought to take care of today. Sensing the clock would sound within seconds, Jim leaned over to the nightstand preempting the alarm before rising and shuffling his way to the bedroom window. He tugged gently on the roll blind's cord, then squinted into the early morning light as the Venetian rose up to reveal what promised to be a fine day.

He always made sure he had things to do, every single day. Some months before Jim Evanston left the mill, he had overheard his fellow workers discussing recent retirees who had fallen stone dead within only a few short years of leaving. When death had come to visit, the cause had seldom been accidental, nor had they been in poor health. Instead, the group seemed to conclude that without anything meaningful to accomplish the fellows just seemed to fade and wither away. With his own retirement looming before him, Jim became determined that the same fate would not befall him.

Jim prepared himself for that day by spending his Saturday afternoons in the Chase Public Library, pawing through books that bore titles like "Making the most of your Retirement" or "Active Living for Seniors." Jim found little in any of the books that related to his specific interest until he came across a book authored by one Amos Petty. "Rules to live by, till you Die."

Jim had skimmed through the first several pages and liking what he read, flipped to the back cover and the writer's short bio. Jim figured the guy must have something going for him. The gent was already eighty-three years of age when he first wrote the book. In this latest edition, a photograph showed Amos blowing out ninety some odd candles on an immense birthday cake surrounded by friends and family. Jim signed out the book, reading it cover to cover in only a couple of evenings and gleaned several rules he felt applied directly to his situation.

1. Always have a reason to get up.
2. Have hobbies, some outside interest, even a part time job.
3. Never _ever_ become unsociable!

The first two rules he had already considered, but to the third, he hadn't given any thought to at all. This said Amos most certainly had. In fact, he dedicated nearly twenty pages to the subject. According to Amos unsociable quickly translated to lonely.

That was especially true if your spouse was audacious enough to pass on before you, or if you were divorced or single, as was the case with Amos. Jim had engaged to marry many years ago, but she had called it off for reasons she had never made clear. Since then Jim had become a confirmed bachelor.

When he hit his early fifties, Jim thought it might be time for a more permanent arrangement, but found that these came attached with a lot of baggage; in fact, a lifetime's worth in his age group. Jim concluded the pros didn't outweigh the cons. To be sure, he had struck up casual relationships with women, but over the last twenty years or so, those had become rather infrequent. While Jim rather expected a decline in this part of his life, he hadn't expected to see the number of his buddies dwindle so rapidly.

First, he hadn't realized just how many of his friends actually fell into the "work associates" category. After the first six months of retirement, he had lost touch with most of the guys from the mill. Before leaving, Jim swore never to become one of those old codgers that made pests of themselves by hanging around the lunchroom boring the guys with "do you remember when?" stories.

Secondly, the fellows he regularly used to see at his favorite pub didn't show up as much anymore, not even for baseball or football playoffs. Jim found that even his best friends seldom came over to visit anymore and he felt uncomfortable just dropping in on them. Turned out their wives, children, and grandchildren now took up most of their time. Jim was finding that following Mr. Amos Petty's rules were proving a whole lot tougher than he first thought. Jim had considered a part-time job, but the mill was the only real employer in town and he didn't want to be a Wal-Mart greeter, but not for the reasons you might think. He actually thought he'd enjoy the job, but knew what friends he had left would tease him unmercifully owing to the stereotype.

Jim had to force himself to take extra steps to be sociable. He would walk the five blocks down to The Caboose café each Wednesday and Saturday timing his arrival to coincide with the departure of the lunch crowd. He'd have a good yak or play a game of checkers with a couple of other old-timers that frequented the place and sometimes flirt with Julie, the young fifty something waitress.

He rose from his side of the double bed and walked toward the bathroom, his bare feet slapping the cold hardwood floor. He showered, brushed his teeth, and combed his thinning hair. Remembering to take his heart medication, he dressed then made his way downstairs to the kitchen.

The sun was just peeking above the horizon and the thin white shade that covered the kitchen window glowed with the soft pink it borrowed from the dawn sky. Jim reached up, pressed the "on" button atop a small radio that sat atop the fridge. An overly cheerful weather girl summarized the days expected weather. A few moments later, a Hank Williams tune twanged out on the classic country station and he walked over to the countertop nearest his sink. Picking up his old stovetop percolator, he loaded it with ice-cold water and dark ground coffee he scooped from a large red Hill's Brothers can.

His was a typical kitchen, unchanged from the early sixties when he bought the house. Small white wall tiles framed the stove, fridge, and countertops. Interspaced among the plain tiles were another half dozen or so accent tiles featuring colorful vegetables, teapots, and the obligatory big red rooster. A small round wooden oak table with two matching chairs sat in the center of the kitchen atop a worn and yellowed linoleum floor.

Atop the kitchen entrance archway hung a large green and white "bird clock," while to either side was a column of Bradford Exchange collector plates, each showing colorful songbirds set in different poses. The clock itself had pictures of resident songbirds spaced regularly about its round face, each positioned next to a corresponding numeral. At the top of each hour, a loud birdcall would sound matching the species associated with that particular hour.

Jim set the coffee percolator on the stove's front burner, turned the control to "maximum," and walked over to his kitchen window. Hands on his hips he arched his back while gazing at the pretty sunrise taking place in his backyard. The morning sun lifted itself above the earth, flared briefly only to disappear into a bank of gray clouds hovering near the horizon.

He stood motionless before the window lost in thought before the percolator's energetic bubbling and impending boil yanked him back into the present. He ambled over to the stove removing the pot from the red-hot element just before the steaming liquid spewed forth. Later, finishing his second cup of coffee, he stole a glance at the bird clock. He'd better get a move on if he was to obey Petty's first rule, "always have a reason to get up."

Normally Jim walked, but if the weather was bad or if he ran late, he would drive his old Ford half-ton to the local gas station and purchase a copy the morning newspaper. It was important to ensure he arrived before seven-thirty. Any later and the odds were certain that the five or six measly copies of his favorite tabloid would have already been sold off to the passing motorists that fueled up at the station. If he failed to obtain the publication, he would have to make do with an old copy of the weekly Western Family Review while he sat on the john awaiting the arrival of his morning constitutional. A less pressing although wholly legitimate reason for rising early in the morning had to do with the second of Amos Petty's rules for achieving near eternal life; his hobby.

In the first summer of retirement, Jim had taken Amos' advice. He'd taken up golf and would have two or three games a week at the local nine-hole pitch and putt, but by July, his arthritic knees sidelined him. Working in his vegetable garden kept him active during the summer months but winters proved difficult. He found himself spending more and more time inside the house watching television, worse yet, daytime TV. Nearly ten autumns previous, Jim felt the walls closing in on him and for the first time in his life realized he was depressed. In neglecting Amos Petty's rules, he had quickly become glum and surly. Then early that same December, he had received a large package from New Jersey. His sister had come to his rescue sending him a nice pair of 10x70 binoculars and Sibley's Guide to Birds as a Christmas present.

He wasn't too sure if he'd take to bird watching or ornithology as the hobbies avid aficionados referred to it, but within several weeks, he found himself taking an active interest in whatever bird might alight on the back fence, the old oak tree, or shed roof. In the early spring, Jim's budding interest in the new hobby caused him to purchase several additional birding books as well as a bird feeder. With the hanging of the feeder came a myriad of small birds that Jim had never noticed before. Soon Jim began to take walks in the nearby aspen forests searching out songbirds, watching prairie hawks soar upon the summer thermals or patiently sitting among the bulrushes beside shallow sloughs, binoculars and camera in hand, awaiting the arrival of the fall ducks, geese, and other migratory fowl.

As the various seasons and years passed, Jim added small trees and berry bushes guaranteed to entice different species of birds to linger about his home. In time, his front and back yards contained no fewer than six feeders of various design and purpose as well as numerous nesting boxes and colorful birdhouses that hung from fences, trees, the shed, and even the walls of his home.

Jim looked out the window, the late March sun hid itself behind a wall of light gray clouds while a light breeze stirred about the yard reminding him to put on a coat. "You missed rule four Amos," he said aloud, "don't catch a cold." At the age of seventy-two, you could not afford to take any chances catching your death from something as simple and avoidable as a spring cold.

Why, just last month Bill Ashford passed away after battling pneumonia for three weeks. Jim visited Bill in the last several days, toward the end Bill had to use a ventilator to breath. Jim saw Bills' frightened watery eyes, the way he lifted and turned his head weakly when Jim came into the room. Bill couldn't talk, but he didn't need to. He looked like a drowning man who caught in a sudden flood, stared desperately at a distant boat knowing it would never arrive in time to save him. Bill finished drowning in his own fluids a couple of days later. "Rule #5, never go on a ventilator!" Jim muttered and walked out the back door toward the shed where he stored the birdseed.

Over the last winter, Jim hadn't built a single house or feeder in the little workshop in the basement he had set up for that specific purpose. In fact, he hadn't set a foot downstairs with the exception of short visits to the deep freeze and once last fall when he replaced a weak breaker that inconveniently tripped whenever he turned the toaster and microwave oven on at the same time.

Jim entered the basement in the late afternoon and spent a full ten minutes bending over the large deep freeze trying to figure out what he felt like eating for dinner. Eventually deciding upon turkey, he rummaged amid the freezers contents as flakes of white frost showered down from every angle. He made himself a silent promise to defrost the appliance later in the week while pulling his dinner out from of a disordered stack of thin red and white rectangles near the bottom. He reclosed the chest lid setting the Hungry Man TV dinner down on its' top.

The freezer's cold had penetrated his hands. He rubbed them together and blew into his palms trying to warm them. Jim finally placed each hand under the opposing armpit then turned slowly looking about the basement where his gaze wandered and fell on the workshop where he had spent so many enjoyable hours building feeders and birdhouses. Suddenly he felt the old urge to build something return, but not just anything. He had built nearly every birdhouse design he thought possible. If he were going to motivate himself to return to the workshop, he'd need something entirely new. He made a mental note to check around and see what he could find in the way of new designs. Pulling on the string of the bare light bulb swinging above his head, Jim grabbed his dinner and headed back up the stairs.

Jim was well into middle age when the information age dawned and the internet changed the world forever. He had held off buying a computer but having finally done so Jim now wondered how he had gone through the last twenty years without one. He sat at a small desk before the monitor and keyboard. It seemed to take forever before the system booted up and the familiar Windows theme appeared. Going straight to the internet, Jim hit the search button and typed in "bird house plans."

Before him was an interminable list of sites selling birdhouse plans. Many offered a wide variety of plans for purchase but in the end, Jim found none of them to be of particular interest. After an hour, he was nearing the end of his patience. Another half hour after that, with his eyes tearing and his mouse hand cramping, he figured he had had enough. Without closing the search site, he simply stabbed down on the tower's power button uttering a variety of choice cuss words and several irreverent phrases.

Jim was surprised by the level of the frustration that he suddenly felt, the anger it invoked and the words he used to express those feelings. Now Jim wasn't overly religious; in fact, he hadn't set foot in a church since Bill Ashford's funeral, but he was a quiet sort and not prone to the casual use of blasphemy, cursing or vulgarity. He closed his eyes sitting motionless in his chair.

Jim sat in that position for several minutes reflecting on the sense of loneliness that had too often enveloped him as late. As the melancholy slowly subsided Jim opened his eyes staring down at the white letters and numerals on the black keyboard then slowly pushed it away from him towards the base of the monitor. His eyes glanced up onto the screen. The screen displayed a website that he had not seen before during his search.

Uncle Nick's Aviaries and Domiciles

Friend, are you tired of the "same old, same old" when it comes to avian domicile design?

Do you feel that the full range of your woodworking skill remains untested by the limited originality of designs offered by other sites?

Simply put; are you ready for a Devil of a challenge?

Jim! You needn't look any further; our designs are first rate, completely original and thoroughly tested by fire to ensure that you get exactly what you deserve…

Wait a second; Jim's eyes scanned back to the previous sentence;

Friend! You needn't look any further; our designs are first rate, completely original and thoroughly...
He rubbed his eyes. He had obviously spent too much time on the machine but continued to read on.

... original and tested by fire to ensure that you get exactly what you deserve when it comes to a first rate Uncle Nick blueprint. One more thing, each domicile carries a full guarantee to breathe new life into your hobby by attracting highly unusual species!

Now our plans are not cheap and while we realize that you don't want to sell your soul, you only ever really get what you pay for don't you?

Jim moved his cursor to the side of the page and let it hover above **PRICING** before pressing it having already decided that he wasn't going to pay an exorbitant sum for any damn birdhouse, no matter how fancy. The screen flickered then displayed a single sentence.

*Try before you buy! Download or Print a free set of blueprints **Now!***

Jim muttered, "Well, that's more like it." Warned about the dangers of downloading free material, he selected the Print option. Nothing happened. Then he remembered that he had to turn on the printer... a few moments later the printer began to spit out Uncle Nick's free set of plans and continued until no fewer than thirteen sheets of paper lay in the printer tray. As the last sheet slid into place, the printer ceased to hum and the computer screen faded to black.

Jim played the mouse over the blank screen wanting to bring up the site and save it to his favorites but nothing came up. It was only after another minute or two that he realized that the computer had somehow turned itself off after printing the plans. Another thought raced across his mind for just a moment before he immediately discarded it... or perhaps it had never really been on?

He spent the evening pouring over the instructions and blueprints. The tolerances of the cutting work were exacting and Jim wondered if his equipment was up to the challenge. The materials list called for a number of different woods required in its construction. The instructions explained the differences in the hardness and flexibility within each wood was essential if the house were to fit together without glue, nails, screws, or fasteners of any sort whatsoever. The house was similar to that of a wooden ball puzzle. To say that the project was challenging would be an understatement of epic proportion, and it might not be cheap.

While most of the wood called for was readily available, some of the harder wood was likely difficult to come by if not impossible to get locally or even regionally. A high-quality scroll saw and special blades would be required when cutting the hardest wood; the African Blackwood, a wood almost legendary and believed by some to have been the original ebony mentioned in the bible. Jim would also need wooden templates and jigs that he would have to construct prior to beginning the actual work on the project itself.

Exhausted, Jim went to bed at nearly 1:30 am and immediately fell into a restless sleep. His subconscious mind was still in overdrive as he dreamt of the project and confronted the unique difficulties that each step presented. He awoke in the morning at first feeling rather spent, but quickly realized that for the first time in years he was genuinely excited, a part of him felt like a kid who suddenly realized that Christmas was just around the corner.

Jim spent that day and several more on the phone or computer tracking down what he needed for the job. He would borrow some of the equipment, including a small lathe and scroll saw from a previous co-worker at the mill. He would rent the saw blades and clamps from a tool shop in Townsend, a larger center located not far from Chase. These specialized tools would hold, bend, and twist the softer woods into the odd shapes and angles called for in the blueprints.

Jim was pleasantly surprised to find the local DIY store had a small but suitable quantity of African Blackwood in stock. The store had ordered the wood for a customer several years back but the customer never arrived to pick it up. Once in place, this special material was to form the heart of the structure acting as its bulwark by restraining and supporting the other wooden pieces.

All of the material and equipment were on hand in his shop within a week. While waiting for the deliveries, Jim had used the time to clean and rearrange the entire shop adding additional lighting and even building a specialized oak workbench. Jim drilled multiple rows and series of holes into the bench's surface. Inserting the hardwood dowels referred to as "dogs" into the selected holes, he would establish the necessary anchor points used to bend and mold the soft wooden pieces into shape. All was ready; he would start tomorrow morning.

To call the project advanced would understate the level of difficulty. By following each step of the instructions meticulously and with great diligence, Jim continually amazed himself finding that he was meeting and overcoming each obstacle slowly but surely.

The task took the better part of a month to complete. After the first two weeks, Jim had yet to join any two pieces of the house together; his time occupied cutting then soaking or steaming the softer woods, a process that allowed him to carefully bend, twist, and mold each piece. Jim doubted that he would have been able to attempt the task at all if it were not for his previous work experience at the mill.

In the third week, he began cutting the rock hard African Blackwood into the required shapes and thicknesses that would provide the considerable strength and rigidity to bind the other wooden members in place. Sometimes even if you have a considerable array of modern power tools at your disposal, it can be easier to use time-tested methods to accomplish the desired result, in Jim's case this was a bench chisel.

He had started working early in the morning and hadn't stopped for lunch. It was now nearly seven in the evening. Jim used a razor-sharp chisel to shave then notch the final piece of Blackwood held firmly within a wooden vise on his workbench. Working the wood at this angle was difficult and the hardness of the material required him to place considerable pressure on the edge. Jim placed his left hand behind the slender piece of wood to add additional support and provide himself a better angle of attack. In reflection, Jim should have known better.

It happened in an instant. One moment the chisel was in the wood, the very next it was through his hand. The razor sharp edge of the three-eighths inch wide blade had bit into his palm, easily slicing through and reappearing on its opposite side. He sat dumbfounded for perhaps thirty seconds holding the wrist of the injured hand up before him, a part of him wondering why it didn't hurt as much as he thought it should. A thin trickle of blood was only now seeping out where his flesh and the cold steel of the chisel met. The trickle was soon to become a veritable flood.

Jim carefully grasped the tool's handle and began carefully removing the blade from the wound. As he did so, he could feel the cool steel gliding and sucking on the meaty tissue of his hand, grating slightly when it met shards of severed bone and tendon. Continuing to retract the blade, the blood flow started to increase, then came much faster before finally spurting out across the workbench in a rush when the leading edge of the blade finally left his hand.

The flow and amount of blood very quickly began to alarm him. With a curse, Jim tossed the offending tool down atop the workbench. Grasping the wound with the fingers of his right hand, he crossed the basement floor and climbed stairs leaving a trail of splattered blood to mark his passing. Arriving in the kitchen, he wrapped the painfully throbbing hand in a tea towel then headed out the door to where his old truck sat parked. Using his good hand, and praying he would not pass out from lack of blood, he sped off toward the medical campus in Townsend.

Back at the workbench, the spatters and pools of congealing blood trembled in place where they had fallen from Jim's injured hand. The quivering continued for some time in the dark silence of the workshop, then by some ungodly means the droplets of blood grew animated. Transforming themselves into a horde of wriggling red maggoty things, they slowly inch wormed their way toward the pieces of Blackwood strewn across the workbench. Upon meeting the wood surfaces, they were immediately absorbed.

He arrived back home in the late afternoon two days later. The blade's passing had severed a tendon and nicked several bones in his hand requiring immediate surgery to repair the damage and avoid loss of use. It appeared that Jim wouldn't be returning to the project anytime soon as his surgeon cautioned against significant exertion of the hand for at least a month. He made himself a sandwich, grabbed a beer, and settled down in front of the television for the night.

Generally a good sleeper, Jim tossed and turned the entire night. Experiencing unaccustomed waves of night sweats, he would awake in a daze finding that the dampened bed sheets had conspired among themselves to form makeshift strait jackets. The night was long and miserable and his hand throbbed constantly. The odd itching sensation, together with sparks of sharp pain sporadically thrown in for good measure refused to quiet even after he had downed the maximum recommended dose of painkillers. Just before dawn, he fell into a deep dreamless sleep.

Jim woke rather late the next morning and sat on the edge of his bed musing as to why his alarm clock had failed to ring. Reaching over, he examined the timepiece discovering that the alarm had in fact rang; the winding spring of the alarm was completely slack. "Wow, those painkillers must have finally kicked in" he said to himself.

He rewound the alarm, checked the main spring's tension for good measure, and placed the clock back on the nightstand. Getting up he walked across the bedroom then absentmindedly, took the bathroom doorknob in his left hand and gave it a twist; nothing happened. Sleepily he tightened his grasp on the handle and once again felt the knob slip and twist. "What the hell?" he muttered then looked down. Upon seeing his bandaged hand and remembering his injury, Jim quickly released his grip and awaited the expected sharp jolt of pain. The pain never arrived. Taking the knob into his hand once again, Jim squeezed tightly. Responding to the power of his grip the door swung in easily and opened into the ensuite.

Jim walked into the sunny bathroom. The cheery yellow walls basked in the midday morning sunlight that streamed into the room through its small window. He stood at the sink studying his bandaged hand and picking at an end of white tape that held the bandage gauze in place. He slowly unwrapped the wound watching the brilliant white strip slowly turn a faint rose then deepen into expected crimson. The end of the strip fell from a thick blood soaked pad that covered the wounds. He carefully peeled off the final protective layer … exposing the now unbroken skin of his left palm!

He examined the palm and back of his hand in detail, turning it over several times. His mouth dry, tongue playing over the lips of his drooping jaw his mind raced to explain the extent of healing he observed. Subconsciously Jim worked up the courage to touch the hand at the points where the chisel had impaled his flesh. There was no pain. He reached for a face cloth, dampened it, and softly rubbed away the film of blood from his palm and the back of his hand. Not a sign of either wound existed; the skin was unblemished.

Astounded, Jim's eyes widened as he clenched and unclenched his fist quickly wriggling his fingers that only yesterday afternoon painfully balked and complained when they moved only a few scant centimeters. He resisted the urge to call his doctor and inform her of the miraculous event, as he was still too unsure of his conclusions; besides what if this was some sort of self-medicated delusion?

He washed and dressed before heading to the kitchen preparing a light brunch of eggs and toast. While eating, he considered the strange situation and arrived at the unavoidable conclusion that the hand was healed and completely functional; time to get on with his day. It was already April 5th, he'd have to start getting the birdhouses ready. The little visitors would soon be arriving en masse looking for a place to call home. He spent a pleasant afternoon hanging the little houses about his yard and fences.

That evening Jim took in the six o'clock news over a fine repast consisting of canned meatball stew washed down with a light beer. The weather girl was finishing her spiel as he gathered himself up, found a bucket, mop, and other cleaning items then headed to the basement prepared to clean the nasty mess that he was sure awaited him in the workshop.

He decided to begin at the top of the wooden basement stairs leading down to the gun gray floor below. He had to rewet and brush out each of the droplets of hard dried blood that collected in every scratch, nick, and cranny in the old wooden steps. It took Jim a full fifteen minutes just to clean the stairs but things went more quickly as he mopped the basement floor to the point where it entered the shop.

Resting shortly while leaning on his mop, he surveyed his efforts. His gaze turned toward the shop, his eyes following the blood trail leading to his workbench. Wiping his brow and resolving to finish the job, he resumed guiding the mop slowly back and forth across the floor's surface. Upon reaching the workbench, he stopped and gaped, staring at its surface.
His bench and tools lay where he left them, including the offending chisel that he had tossed aside in the urgency of that evening, but there was not a drop of blood to be seen anywhere. Letting the handle of the mop drop to the floor, Jim began examining the surface of the bench. Picking up tools and pieces

of wood, turning them over this way then that, he sought but found himself unable to locate any sign of blood whatsoever.

Jim picked up the piece of Blackwood that he had been working on when he stabbed himself with the chisel. Surprisingly, it felt oddly warm, was it vibrating ever so slightly in his hand? The temperature of the air about him chilled abruptly; at the same instance, he felt the strip of Blackwood squirm snakelike within his grasp. Alarmed, Jim tossed the piece down onto the workbench and stared wide-eyed at the wooden form for several minutes where to his great relief it continued to lie motionless. Discomforted, he peered into the dimly lit corners of the basement then bent checking the shadowed floor beneath the workbench.

Jim had a strong sudden urge to leave the basement. He took a final glance about the room. As he turned off the shop's lights, a part of him instantly regretted having done so. Jim stood frozen and motionless as a sense of foreboding encased him. This feeling grew as his ears caught soft murmurings emanating from the now darkened shop. Startled and rather distressed, the old man crossed the basement floor with deliberation. As his foot hit the first stair, he found his unease replaced by abject fear. Climbing to the top of the stairs as quickly as possible, he reached the basement door. Relief came to him in a calming flood as he realized he had mounted the last three steps in a near panic. Slapping off the light switch, he slammed the basement door shut and leaned against it with his right shoulder breathing heavily.

Berating himself for acting like a frightened eight-year-old boy, Jim walked into the kitchen opened the fridge, and leaned on the door contemplating whether to grab a beer before closing the door. Instead, he walked over to a high cupboard where he kept the hard liquor and took down a partial bottle of twelve-year-old whiskey, pouring himself the first of several straight shots.

He awoke to the shrill chimes of the alarm clock, stilled the bell and lay back staring up at the off-white ceiling. Feeling off, he slowly rose and sat on the edge of the bed. A throbbing temple reminded him of the whiskey he drank the night before. Jim sat there for several long minutes reviewing and considering the odd circumstances of late. He had always considered himself a normal rational man and one who was unaccustomed to flights of fancy; maybe he was just getting old. He headed into the bathroom relieving his bladder and any remaining apprehension into the white porcelain bowl.

It was mid-morning when he made his way into the basement, determined to complete his project regardless of any ridiculous quirks his mind might suddenly decide to spring upon him. Two small somewhat grungy and crud covered windows in the upper walls allowed the sunlight to splash across the gray floor. Particles of dust glided and floated serenely within the bright streams of light. Any trace of residual trepidation Jim felt vanished in the ambiance of normality.

Jim worked the rest of the morning and into mid-afternoon without stopping for lunch. The work progressed more quickly than Jim had expected. By suppertime, all that remained was the final assembly. According to the instructions, there was no need for nails, screws, glue, or fasteners, nor would a paint or stain be required; the variety of natural woods provided both color and contrast. Jim considered leaving the final assembly for the following morning but after grabbing a quick sandwich determined to complete the project that night.

Following the detailed instructions, Jim positioned and connected each wooden piece in an exact and precise order but as he continued, he began to worry that he had made a mistake along the way. An hour later, he wondered if the plans themselves were in error. Either way, he stood back looking at an absurdity that should have been an attractive little bird house, but instead, the damn thing appeared badly skewed.

Having experience with the intricacies of avian domicile construction, Jim wasn't ready to concede that the problem resulted from a lack of quality workmanship on his part, at least not just yet. Disappointingly, after checking and rechecking every dimension, he arrived at the same miserable result. It was just after two in the morning when he finally left the basement, entered his living room, and dropped into his easy chair closing his tired eyes.

He leaned back into the comfortable chair and sighed, resigned that all the expended effort and expense had been for naught. He determined to find the offending website tomorrow morning, vowing to send them a well-deserved snot-a-gram. Reaching over, he turned off the floor lamp beside his chair and looked around the room, his eyes slowly adapting to the dim light. The artificial glow of sodium shone out from a distant streetlamp. Passing through the open drapes set to either side of the room's picture window, the enfeebled silvery gleam fell upon the well-worn carpet and pooled at his feet.

He closed his eyes emptying his mind and setting aside the evening's disappointment. He began to slip off, aware that he was on the verge of drifting into light sleep. He heard the comforting tick-tock of the grandmother clock that sat upon the fireplace mantle. Upon reaching the hour of 3 a.m., the timepiece softly chimed counting the hours. The echo of the third and final stroke faded, slowly diminishing into the silence surrounding the old man.

A deafening boom caused the house to shudder from joist to rafter. The thunderous report shocked Jim from his slumber and thrust him into full consciousness. He bolted from the chair, his mind already seeking a plausible explanation. He stole a quick glance out the living room window into the apparently calm still night before rushing across the still dark living room. Reaching the hallway, he used the palm of his hand to locate the wall switch, and then snapped it on.

The hallway walls, floor, and ceiling transformed from deep shadow to blinding white in an instant. Jim squinted and stood motionless as his eyes strove to adjust to the light. His ears were already pricked and alert to any new sound that might provide a clue as to what had or was still happening.

From this vantage, nothing appeared amiss. He began his investigation in the kitchen and continued throughout the main floor. As he made his way toward the stairs that rose to the second-floor bedrooms, he stopped and opened the door that led to the basement. Staring into the darkness he flicked on the light then sniffed the air for any indication of smoke before moving his inspection to the upper floor. His rounds ended back in the basement where he examined his furnace and hot water tank. Finding everything as it should be, Jim returned upstairs to the kitchen.

Still puzzled, Jim stepped out his back door and onto the narrow back porch studying the night sky for any sign of a rare spring thunderstorm. Not a single cloud drifted across the jet-black moonless sky while the backdrop of glistening stars stared back at him with cold unmoved detachment. He stepped from the porch walking slowly along the cracked concrete sidewalk that outlined the perimeter of the house. Having satisfied himself that the world wasn't ending anytime soon he secured his doors and made his way to his bed where he passed into a deep dreamless sleep.

The next morning saw Jim return to his daily routine. He walked down to the nearby gas station where he bought his morning paper then came home and read every page. Upon waking, he had made the decision to commit his project to the fire pit rather than waste any more time trying to remedy the situation. It was nearing ten in the morning when he went downstairs to clean the shop of sawdust and cuttings, organize his tools, and then return the items he'd borrowed or rented.

Reaching the bottom of the stairs, he heard odd sounds emanating from his shop. To his ears, it almost sounded like someone was cracking their knuckles; odd pops, clacks, and clicks punctuated a soft irregular discordance resonating in the background. Jim walked into the shop then stopped in his tracks and stared at the workbench where he had left the little house the previous night.

The miserable lopsided structure was in the process of being transformed into... well quite frankly if you had asked Jim to describe exactly what was before him he would have been hard put to do so. How do you describe something that was changing before your very eyes?

While the shape and size of the house often appeared to bear a vague semblance to his original construction, the color and texture of the surface details were constantly changing. The odd sounds that accompanied the twisting, bending and grinding of the wood surfaces were mixed with another sound... barely audible and indiscernible whispering. The later sent a chill up his spine.

One moment the little structure presented a rather natural surface sporting muted colors and tints, then in the next instance, the surface became thorny and warted, its colors vibrant. If you waited a few more minutes, any number of combinations would appear. The entranceway to the interior of the house itself had become an oblong shape that expanded then shrank in size, its surface glassy, its color the deepest black reminding him of obsidian. At times, Jim would detect a bright red swirl just below the black surface but more often, he just saw the stunned expression on his face reflected in its mirror-like sheen.

Although frightened and apprehensive, Jim stood motionless, his attention focused on the impossible scene before him. Within minutes, the changes in shape, texture and color of the little house seemed less pronounced and slowing. Its overall appearance began to resemble the original design of the birdhouse. Moments later all change and noise had subsided. The little structure had assumed a completely normal appearance. The swirling obsidian porthole had been the last of the peculiar features to disappear, now having become a rather ordinary looking hole.

It took Jim another five minutes longer to work up the courage to touch the house and did so as one might touch the burner on a stove suspecting it was hot. He picked the little house up turning it over in his hands and examining every side and detail. At first, he thought he felt a warm tremor held deep within the wood but this too faded quickly. He carefully set the house on the workbench and left the basement.

The birdhouse sat on his workbench where he had left it for nearly a week. Every morning Jim would go down to the shop and sit on his stool to stare at the unchanged little structure wondering if what he saw actually happened.

Whatever he thought he might have witnessed, there was no question that his little project appeared quite normal. No, better than normal actually, in fact, absolute perfection was closer to the truth. Where the wood surfaces joined, he couldn't even see a hairline between them. They blended seamlessly, one into the other, right down to the wood grain. Each aspect of the work whether considered by proportion, angle, symmetry or dimension was flawless. This alone should have convinced him that forces other than his own semi-proficient talents must have been at work.

Jim recognized the world's inclination toward the commonplace. He had observed its almost tedious routine unravel day after day over his past seventy-two years. Jim was unwilling to abandon its enduring commonality only to accept the fragile absurdities of recent events. There had to be some other reasonable explanation he had so far overlooked. Although in doing so Jim came to the unavoidable conclusion that if, these events hadn't actually happened, then his mind had and perhaps was continuing to play him false. Was he hallucinating?

He ruled out seeking psychiatric help, at least for now. That would be a last resort. Instead, he consulted the myriad of medical sites he found on the internet. Jim read that hallucinations could affect any or all of your five senses, the garden variety of causes brought on by abuse of alcohol, improper medication, or even getting too little sleep. He quickly ruled out all of these possibilities but going further down the list he found a long list of physical ailments he could not so easily discount, especially given his advancing years. In the end, he resolved to sit tight and go on with his life as before.

After supper, Jim walked down the basement stairs, strode into the shop, plucked the little house up and carrying it under one arm (so he wouldn't have to look at it too closely) made his way to the large oak that dominated the middle of his expansive backyard. In the deepening gloom of dusk, he lay the house down on the lawn beside the tools and the ladder that he would use during its installation. Looking at the darkening sky, he knew he'd have to hurry along. He stood back and evaluated a suitable spot to mount the house.

The tree was ancient, even back when he originally bought the property. The brown and gray of the dark gnarled bark and twisted trunk marked its passage through those many years. During its first decade of life, lightning had struck the main trunk of the tree splitting and stripping one of its two massive limbs away, all that remained was a three-foot stub in place of the arm. Jim decided that the fork would be the ideal place to mount the birdhouse. The location was high enough to attract the birds but still low enough to be seen when looking out his kitchen window or sitting on the porch.

Setting the ladder against the tree, he picked up the birdhouse, climbed the short distance to the fork, and placed the house against the tree holding it with one hand while fishing into his back pocket to retrieve a screwdriver with the other. That's when he remembered the screws he needed were still in the shed. He carefully balanced the house in the crook of the tree then nattered to himself as he climbed down the ladder and marched quickly off to the shed.

Several minutes later, he walked from the shed back to the tree. Setting a foot on the ladder's bottom rung and placing a hand on its side, he stole a quick upward glance before beginning his climb. He stopped and stepped down to the ground and back from the ladder, his eyes fixated on the crook of the tree. Jim broke into a cold sweat as a feeling of deep foreboding flooded into his belly. For an instant, his eyes left the tree and dropped down to his left hand that now began to smart and ache at the points where the chisel had penetrated his flesh. His heart raced and pounded in his ears as his eyes darted upward coming to rest once more on the birdhouse.

In the growing twilight, Jim could see a pulsating red glow surrounding the house; a glow that Jim quickly realized matched the rhythm of his own frantically beating heart. He stared as the glow brightened, blossoming into a yet deeper crimson. The thicker portions of the wispy glow gathered, assembling themselves into bloated tentacles that slowly probed reaching outward from the house and wrapping themselves about the limbs and trunk of the tree.

Jim knew the house was about to transfigure itself once again. The odd disquieting sounds he heard several days ago had returned and were slowly growing in strength and urgency, first creaking then building to a loud crescendo, the floor of the little house bent and warped downward until it met and conformed to the bowed shape of the tree's fork. Jim's hands flew to the sides of his head as he attempted to shut out the din and waves of noise that broke painfully against his eardrums. The little door hole of the house had become animated once again, but instead of the obsidian sheen Jim had previously witnessed, an eerie blue-green radiance shone outward onto the lawn. Blades of grass illuminated in that terrible light writhed back and forth, engaging in a creepy macabre dance.

Paralyzed with fear and dread Jim watched as the coagulating veins of red mist tightened about the trunk, penetrating then disappearing below the surface of the brown-gray bark. Whether it was the tree or the house, something screamed out in protest, the house sank downward, forcing its way ever deeper into the crook of the tree. Over the next few moments, the assault on his senses grew to a climax and he collapsed to the ground in a dead faint.

Jim came to his senses some time later. The night about him was dark and silent. The last quarter moon had risen above the east fence casting long dim shadows across his backyard. Jim guessed it was well after midnight as he slowly raised himself up into a sitting position and then leaned forward, his hands and knees resting in the dewy blades of the dark grass. He tried to stand but his balance was off and his legs refusing to bear his weight sent him sprawling. Rather than making a second attempt to rise, he crawled along the wet grass toward the wooden stairway at the bottom of his porch. Using the stairs to support himself, he raised himself to his feet then staggered up to the porch and into the house.

Jim locked the back door, turned out the kitchen light and stared out into the still and quiet night. His eyes slowly scanned the backyard paying special attention to the dark silhouette of the oak tree. Everything was as it should be. Suddenly immensely tired, he slowly climbed the stairs leading to his bedroom. Shedding his damp clothes, he left them lying where they fell on the bedroom floor. He turned back the bed covers and fell onto the mattress. Wrapping himself in the thick flannel sheets, he curled into a fetal position and passed into a deep dreamless sleep.

The short days of early spring lengthened and the natural world came alive with the warmth of the sun and the promise of summer. Jim pushed the mower through the long grass in his backyard whistling a light tune barely hearing himself above the din of the little gas engine. Jim thought this year's fine spring weather to be warmer and brighter than any he remembered back in the days of his youth when everything the world had to offer was still novel and exciting.

It had been a fortnight since he or rather the birdhouse, had hung itself in the tree. Jim had used the better part of those two weeks working up the courage to once again venture forth into the backyard, but would do so only in the light of midday. The huge oak tree stood as it always had, its leaves emerging from their sap soaked shoots drawing a severe though welcome contrast between the young green foliage and the drab browns and grays of the branches and twigs of the old tree.

The day he dared to re-enter the yard, Jim approached and stood a respectful distance from the old oak spending considerable time looking for, but failing to find any sign of the house itself. He scarcely expecting to, given his still vivid recollection of its unique nocturnal passage into the tree. Summoning the nerve to approach somewhat closer, he thought he noticed an unusual circular pattern within the bark, just beneath the crook of the tree.

He cautiously moved toward the tree leaning forward to get a better view. At first barely perceptible, the camouflaged outline of a small arched doorway became prominent. Measuring perhaps six inches wide and ten in height, he was certain he could even make out a small golden knob. Despite all efforts to disregard what his eyes revealed, Jim finally conceded the pattern in the bark indeed resembled a small doorway, but this was as far as he was willing to go. Backing away from the tree, he turned and left the yard.

Over the next two days, he conducted a round the clock surveillance of the tree and yard from his kitchen window but was unable to detect anything sinister lurking about; unless you considered the incredible explosion of new growth taking place within his shrubs and flowerbeds to be such. Jim felt a growing compulsion, an urge demanding reaffirmation of the doorway's presence and an explanation for the astonishing state of his yard and garden. Curiosity overcame caution; he determined to mount a return expedition.

That spring the verge burst forth with a vitality the like of which Jim had never seen before. The flowers and blooms of perennials and bulbs were vibrant and full, their perfume filled the yard with the aroma and essence of life. The apprehension surrounding the discovery of the door failed to deter him from spending time in the yard, his fear of its presence diminishing every morning since. As each day passed, Jim found himself more refreshed and rejuvenated than the day before. Earlier that morning he had awakened before his alarm clock yet again, he was eager to spend time in the yard. Today he would mow the lawn that was quickly becoming shaggy and overgrown.

By ten a.m. Jim had finished cutting a good third of the lawn. The mower's manicured swath was drawing ever closer to the center of the yard and of course, the huge oak. Since the night, the birdhouse had "become one" with the oak, he had given the grass growing near the tree a wide berth. Now it was only mid-April but already his dereliction was becoming an eyesore in what otherwise was, without a doubt, the finest and best kept yard and garden of any he had seen when strolling about town.

He stopped pushing the mower and turned off the engine. Slowly he walked into the ten-foot wide circle of long grass that outlined the no man's land boundary surrounding the tree trunk. With his eyes firmly affixed to the little doorway, he cautiously closed the space between himself and the tree, stopping only when he was no more than three feet distant.

"And how are we today laddie?" the voice asked in a distinctly Irish or Scottish brogue that seemed to emanate from somewhere in the tree's direction.

He just about jumped out of his skin. Jim's head snapped to the left and then right looking for the voice's owner who Jim assumed must be somewhere close by in the yard. Obviously, the visitor had entered unnoticed, his approach masked by the mower's engine.

Still looking around Jim answered "Uh, hello?" in a rather uncertain tone to no one in particular.

"No laddie, up here." the voice spoke yet again in a good-natured tone.

This time, there could be no mistaking where the greeting had come; Jim's eyes lifted and fell searching the lower branches of the tree finally coming to rest on a diminutive figure that stood in the crook of the tree. A little man was leaning against the right forked trunk, arms crossed and sporting an amused grin. Jim's reaction was to stand in slack-jawed awe with every muscle frozen in place. Only his eyes moved and they darted rapidly about the compact personage that greeted him so cheerily.

"I asked how you are today. Didn't you learn any manners as a wee child?" The little figure now had his hands on his hips facing the man directly.

"Err, yes?" Jim croaked, followed several seconds later with a hesitant, "good ... morning... what... um, who... are you?" His mind raced providing Jim the information he sought but wasn't ready to accept. The term Leprechaun leaped out of his subconscious and as it registered in his mind. His breath exhaled with a resigned "huh," as if punched in his stomach.

"I'm your new tenant of course!" The little man frowned but his eyes continued to glitter with a smile, the fellow obviously enjoying the larger man's discomfort, "and who did you suppose I was?" Jim hadn't moved or made any sound to this point, the little man continued. "You are right in the head aren't you... or maybe not the full shilling?"

"Ah, yes... but maybe not." Jim took in the image before his eyes. The small man wore a three-pointed hat, a red vest, a green jacket and matching pants, all set off with a pair of small square-toed dark brown shoes. His face, lined and wrinkled, his beard grayed, only his eyes denied the evidence of age and sparkled with youthful vigor.

Jim refocused on the conversation, finally deciding that he'd have to deal with the situation at hand, the word tenant seemed to demand an explanation. "Excuse me sir." It occurred to Jim that some degree of courtesy was in order, especially in the unusual case of one having to deal with a little man standing in ones' tree. "What did you mean tenant?"

The little man's face screwed up, "The one who rents your house of course." Noticing that the large man before him wasn't overly quick on the uptake, he continued. "Occupies a place 'e doesn't' own? Pay'n the landlord for its use?"

"What … house?" Jim asked and pointed to his own home. "That house?"

"No laddie, this house" pointing to the little archway in the bark of the tree.

"Oh dear…" Jim resignedly continued, "The bird… house."

"Look like a bird do I?" the little man then added; "You did build the house did you not?"

"Yes sir," Jim replied a little quicker, his mind finally adjusting to the odd situation.

"You put it up for rent?" the little man held his palms out waist high in askance.

"No, I put it up in the tree." Jim's voice had taken on a slightly peeved tone.

"And by doing so you put it up for rent!" The man continued, "Now I live here… and as you see I've been paying the rent." The small hands pointed about the beautiful greenery and blooms in the surrounding yard and garden.

Jim's head followed the little man's hands about the yard perceiving a delicate blush of radiance, a golden mist that went unnoticed before that very moment. He suddenly understood, or at least began to grasp that the little gent was responsible for the unusually vibrant spring taking place in his backyard. "I see what you mean… sorry, my name's Jim, and yours sir?"

"As a rule, I don't give out my proper name, wouldn't be fitting if you get my drift, but if you be needin' one you can call me Grady." His face became unreadable.

"Nice to meet you Mr. O'Grady," Jim replied and managed a small... very small smile.

"Just Grady, no O. Left that behind when I came over on the boat from the ol' land." The old man said matter of factly.

Jim's expression took on a pained and hesitant look as he asked the question that had been building in his mind since he first saw the little being. "Pardon me sir, but aren't you a... lep...a lepra"

"Leprechaun?" The elf finished the question for him. "No laddie, that's a nasty but well-deserved name given to some of my distant greedy cousins who live in dark grottos and caves... tricksters and thieves; can't trust 'em far as you can throw 'em." He paused briefly "No, I and my kin enjoy the sunlight, the smell of fresh earth, running sap and blossoms after a light rain and as I said, I don't ever give me proper name. Just call me Grady and you can drop the mister as well, we are common folk."

They spoke for several more minutes. Jim growing comfortable enough in that short space of time to overlook the fact that he was apparently now a landlord, renting a magical tree house to a garden gnome and conversing with same in his backyard on a sunny April morning.

The conversation slowed, the elf now wearing a somewhat bored expression. "As I said before you won't be seeing me very often, I'm not particularly fond of chit chat and no offense, but I like to keep to myself. After the first heavy frost, you won't see me at all 'til next spring."

"You fly south? Jim asked straight faced then grinned broadly seeing that he caught the old fellow off guard.

The elf grinned back, "no laddie we take our leave of fall and winter to walk in the springs and summers in the past, long ago when we and the world were still young."

"Oh sure... I understand" Jim said, suddenly glad he had watched The Lord of the Rings movie just last Sunday. Then on a serious note, he asked: "is there anything you require of me Grady?"

"I'm glad you asked. Just peace and quiet, I, in fact, demand it. Don't come knocking on my door, you won't get a polite response." The elf continued. "I chose your house from many others since you don't have the little noisy ones about or a busy body wife who would spoil things spilling the beans to her friends or leaving cupcakes and other goodies outside my door hoping to be invited in for a visit."

Jim looked thoughtful. "I can live with that, I'm not one who has to blab his business about the neighborhood" and under his breath continued; "besides I don't want to be thrown into the nut house either."

"Well laddie that should cover it. Enjoy your summer; we may speak again," The elf began to fade becoming semi-transparent and blending into the leaves and bark of the tree. He ended their conversation with "just remember about the peace and quiet and we'll do very well indeed." And with that, he was gone from sight.

Jim glimpsed the elf several more times throughout the summer, and always in the very early morning. On those few occasions, Grady was spreading what Jim figured was probably pixie dust or something similar about the plants in his yard. Whatever it was, it certainly worked. Jim had never before seen his vegetables growing so vigorously. If he could patent the stuff, he figured he'd be a millionaire.

If the growth witnessed in his garden was phenomenal, the birds visiting his yard were nothing short of a miracle. The common sparrows and swallows normally residing in his birdhouses disappeared, replaced instead by a multitude of songbirds and brightly colored finches. During that spring and summer, other unusual species of birds would occasionally appear. Some of these would defy Jim's attempts to identify them even when consulting his most complete and recent edition of the Birder's Bible.

Sunrise, mid-May, Jim stepped out onto the back porch and seeing the empty hummingbird feeders made a note to fill them later that morning. He stole a glance toward a large feeder hanging from the corner of the tool shed; it was doing a brisk business. A large flock of visiting Ruby Crowned Kinglets were busily swarming the feeder taking turns on its perches, flying to and from the fence and nearby bushes. What the diminutive birds didn't eat they'd spill. A constant shower of seeds fell to the ground below the feeder where many other birds scratched and pecked like miniature barnyard chickens. He'd have to replenish the feeder from one of the large seed bags he kept in the nearby shed but that too would have to wait until he had purchased the morning paper and made some breakfast.

He walked down the backyard's sidewalk to the high gate leading into the wide graveled alley. Jim's street was the last of the community's homes built at the edge of town decades earlier, those years when the town was still growing. Since then, the town like so many others in rural areas had seen their young people move to the larger centers. A fair number of older homes stood abandoned entirely, their elderly owners moving on or having passed away.

Taxes owed, the town had taken over many of the vacant though livable houses, selling them to urban folk seeking relief from the hot asphalt and cement environs of the nearby city, and tearing down the rest. A rising number of the new summer residents of Chase were enjoying the cool sparkling waters of Scandia Lake only a ten-minute drive from the town.

With their houses torn down, the newly vacant lots were scattered about the shrinking community. The remaining residents, many of whom were retirees like Jim and possessed of riding lawnmowers and time to spare, kept up the grounds and lawns. In fact, most residents agreed that the unintentional mini-parks gave the town a more pleasing appearance than ever before.

Vacant lots bordered Jim's home to either side, while a vacant house sat behind his home directly across the gravel alleyway. Somewhat of an eyesore, Jim figured the town would demolish the building in due course. He thought it ironic that he had originally wanted a small acreage on the outskirts of town but couldn't afford it back then, now years later, the acreage had come to him.

Having walked for about ten minutes, he approached a gas station. Two gas pumps sprouted from a thin concrete island sitting in the middle of an oversized lot, tufts of grass and weeds poked up from spidery cracks in the asphalt. A weathered sign advertising the "new pay at the pump" feature sat at the lot's entranceway in contradiction to the handwritten "pay at the pump not available" sign taped to the front of each pump.

The building itself was very dated having been built in the early 50s; the stations' wooden siding hadn't seen a new coat of paint in several decades. The glass windows in the overhead shop door sat coated with a dull uniform brown grunge; the lower wooden panels shed wide strips of lime green paint revealing the weathered bare wood below.

Chuck Brady, the station's current owner had bought into the business while it was part of a major chain twenty years before, but not being able to afford to keep the business up to corporate standards, he now operated the station as an independent.

Jim walked into the customer area through a faded green open door. Seeing the counter was unmanned he gave out a "good morning Chuck" in a loud voice that was immediately returned by a mumbled "be right with ya" coming from an inner door leading to the shop. The station's odor, an aged combination of gas, oil, and rubber greeted his nose with pleasing recognition. A moment later, a balding rather rotund older man with a pockmarked complexion walked in from the shop and took up a position behind the counter.

"Ah. It's you. I was expecting a paying customer!" Chuck used a paper towel to wipe a light coating of dirt and grease from his hands, balled up the paper throwing it toward and missing a small trash can set behind the till.

"Eight bits for this skinny rag you call a newspaper is probably the only sale you'll be seeing today." Jim scowled playfully at the man, and then winked. Jim looked down at the empty stand. "You still have a copy?"

"I haven't had time to put them out yet." Chuck reached down to the floor and yanked up a small packet of newspapers held together by thin plastic banding. Placing the bundle on the worn Arborite counter top, he cut through the tough plastic with a pocketknife that magically appeared from a breast pocket. "Here you go old man," Chuck handed Jim the top copy.

"Much obliged, and here you go sonny." Jim placed a buck on the counter and began reading the headlines. "Mmm… ain't much reading for a dollar anymore is there."

"No news is good news as they say," Chuck replied as a bell rang out several times in quick succession indicating a vehicle had arrived at the gas pumps. "Looks like a real customer, I'll be back in a minute." Chuck hung out of the front door, waved, and called out to a man who was trying to use the pay at the pump feature to gas up a large white cube van. "Sorry, that's out of order, but I can take care of you inside when you're done."

While the customer fueled up, Jim and Chuck discussed their health, the weather, and who might take the World Series in baseball. Saying their goodbyes, Jim shoved the folded edition beneath his arm and turned from the counter before being nearly bowled over by no fewer than three young boys that ran towards him, each jockeying for better position as they squeezed and fought their way through the open front door.

Judging from their looks, they were most definitely brothers, each sprouting a thick tuft of wooly carrot red hair that shot out from their scalps in every direction. Jim took the older two of the three boys to be twins, both were lanky, and tall, Jim placed them near twelve or thirteen. The younger boy was perhaps ten or so, and aside from his wiry red hair didn't share much in common with the other two, being overweight and moon-faced, but that didn't seem to slow him down at all. The three boys invaded the customer area in a rush striking the counter simultaneously, each loudly exclaiming that he had won the race. The little group split up as quickly as they had entered, each exploring the station like a group of wayward puppies.

The fat kid stuck his head and upper body in the shop's doorway. Sensing the child was about to step into the shop Chuck told him customers couldn't enter then glanced away to watch a man he and Jim each presumed was the father striding purposefully toward the front door of the station. A second later noticing that the fat kid had ignored his request not to enter the back shop Chuck left the counter and headed after the boy.

Jim smiled to himself watching as the twins concentrated their attentions on the small array of dust coated glass globes. Resembling giant lollypops, the candy dispensers arose from the dust-covered floor on thin metal stems. The boys small hands fingered the coin slot that promised to dump a small measure of unwrapped stale peanuts or candy following the insertion of a mere quarter.

A very large red haired man sporting a thick unkempt beard walked into the station, brushed past Jim and reached into the back pocket of his jeans taking out a large wallet secured by a chain to his thick leather belt. At the same time, Chuck came out of the shop area holding the fat kid's arm and upon seeing his customer notice his hold of the child explained that no one could enter the shop for safety and insurance reasons. Brusquely ordering the boy to his side, the father gave him a sharp cuff to the side his head. Jim didn't take the man as the type often accused of being overly friendly.

"That'll be thirty-eight fifty sir. Debit or credit?" Chuck asked.

"Neither." The man growled as he removed two twenties from his wallet dropping them on the counter. Chuck took the bills and made change placing the coins on the countertop.
Suddenly everyone's attention shifted to the sound of the twins arguing loudly and the rattle of hard candy on glass. A heavy metallic thumping on the linoleum floor began as the twins pushed and shoved one another while fighting for control of one of the candy-filled globes.

"Careful boys!" Chuck called out just in time to see the stand tilt crazily. One of the candy-filled globes came loose and fell to the floor with a loud crash. The contents of the globe, gumballs in this case, scattered and rolled outward in every direction, but somehow the glass globe remained intact.

The boys immediately stopped and looked back apprehensively at their father who now shouted angrily, "Get your asses out of here and back in the truck, now!"

"You too tubby!" the man said to the fat kid and shoved him roughly toward the door. The twins gave their father a wide berth as they and their brother slunk quickly out the door without apology or any acknowledgment to the station's owner.
Chuck in an attempt to ease the tension said, "Boys will be boys…" and was about to add something else when the man interrupted.

"I ain't paying for any of that…" Flicking an arm in the direction of the globe and the gumballs some of which had yet to come to rest on the dirty uneven floor, "you best keep that crap work'n proper for you get sued." The man turned and walked out the door with a scowl.

Jim and Chuck watched as the boys clamored and fought their way into the back seat of the cube van, the last and youngest of the trio rewarded with a hard swat from his father. The man slammed the door just after the boy entered the cab, the swinging door missing his fingers that had been resting on the center post mere moments before. Their father banged the side of the truck with his fist as he walked about the front of the vehicle. Entering the cab, the man started the engine, placed it in gear, and then gunned it. The van lurched from the pump island swaying from side to side and careening through the lot before swerving onto the main road.

Jim shook his head, "Pleasant sort wouldn't you say?"

Chuck walked toward the gumball machine holding a broom and dustpan. "Yeah, takes all kinds don't it."

"Need a hand with that," Jim offered.

Chuck waved a hand, "Uh? Oh no thanks Jim, it's not as if I have anything better to do just now. Take care I'll see you tomorrow."

The walk home was pleasant and Jim arrived home in good spirits. Entering the kitchen he went about preparing his breakfast that consisted of a large Italian sausage, two eggs, and toast; his favorite.

He finished his meal, refilled his coffee, and spread the newspaper out on the kitchen table. Jim was reading the classifieds when he heard a heavy sounding vehicle making its way up the alleyway. Figuring it was probably Monday's garbage truck, he tried to remember if he had put out the trash that morning before realizing it was Wednesday. Pulling back a curtain and taking a glance out the window, he saw the back end of a large vehicle passing behind his shed and trees. It didn't stop but continued driving down the alleyway. Jim went back to his paper.

Less than a minute later the vehicle returned drawing his attention once more. This time however, it stopped directly behind his house, Jim heard its transmission grind and complain before it slowly reversed. Jim stared as the white cube van rolled into the middle of the vacant house's overgrown weed-infested yard then stopped.

Three red haired boys bolted from the cab and immediately began running toward the house before engaging in an impromptu wrestling match while a large bearded driver slowly emerged from the cab. Yelling something at the boys, the man walked up and opened the back door of the house then walked in, the kids pressing at his heels. "Oh no…" Jim muttered as he stood up from the table and walked closer to the window, standing for several minutes and waiting for the group to reappear.

He didn't have to wait long. A minute later, the man came out and opened the back of the van. Reaching beneath the bumper, he grabbed a long steel ramp running it out and positioning an end on the lawn. Looking about but not seeing the children, he bellowed out something to the kids who were still inside the house. Whatever he said, it lit the proverbial fire under their butts. Quickly joining their father, the group disappeared into the back of the van. Jim continued to watch in disbelief as the group began moving furniture and other contents into the back door of the house. It took less than an hour to empty the van then the group piled back into the cab, driving out of the yard, and heading off down the alley.

Several hours later Jim was out in his yard filling up the bird feeders when he saw an older, rusted out Buick roll down the alley then pull into the yard of the no longer vacant house. Peering over the fence, he watched the same three boys leave the car and stand quietly at the back of the car. A moment later a thin scarecrow of a woman in a longish dark gray dress stepped out and walked to the rear of the car. Pulled back into a tight bun, her dark hair, prominent hawked nose and dark eyes accentuated a severe countenance. Jim figured that if the woman ever smiled her face would crack from the effort. Her movements were rapid, almost birdlike. Obviously a no-nonsense sort, she opened the trunk. Reaching in, she took towels, blankets and the like from its interior, distributing the items among her children before marching up to the house in quick short steps with her children trailing obediently behind her. Halfway through their second trip, Jim heard the loud drone of a powerful motorcycle in the distance.

It was getting closer. Occasionally, its operator would crack the throttle causing the bike to roar and accelerate along the pavement. Jim's ears could trace the Harley's course; down Main, up Third, then along Railway Street straight through the heart of the town's small industrial area. That's where the bike really opened up. A few minutes later, he heard it slow as it came into sight at the end of his alley. Its speed now reduced to a near crawl, Jim watched the bike and rider drive up, pull into the yard, and stop beside the Buick. The big bike sat idling for nearly five minutes. The Harley's characteristic "potato potato potato" echoed and reverberated throughout the neighborhood. The biker removed what Jim took to be an old kraut helmet from his head and turned off the bike; replaced by silence, the absence of the rumble was somehow disturbing.

Jim watched the man dismount his bike and join the others who had come out from the house and now waited in the yard. The family stood in the weed-strewn yard looking about their new surroundings, first at the weather-beaten house, then the yard, and finally across the alley, where all their eyes came to rest... directly on Jim. Realizing that he must appear to have been gawking, which of course he was, he was now feeling very conspicuous and even more self-conscious. He slowly raised an arm in greeting, his effort unconvincing, and his face wearing a feeble, sheepish smile.

The big man sneered, turned his back, and walked toward the house into the back door. One of the twins pointed to him, made some distasteful comment he couldn't quite catch. That caused the other twin to laugh unpleasantly then both turned away and returned to the Buick's open trunk. Meanwhile, the chubby kid stuck out his tongue at Jim and was in the process of making another face until his mother's well-practiced hand came down on the back of his head. The kid flinched but didn't cry out and ran to join his brothers at the back of the car.

The woman hadn't moved a muscle since first seeing him. She just stared at Jim appraising him as a hungry snake might a rat. Her eyes strayed behind him and he got the distinct feeling that she was evaluating his house and yard, though not in a good way. Her gaze turned back to Jim and their eyes locked. In that moment, Jim suddenly had the distinct feeling he was being sized up as a potential target. She cocked her head ever so slightly. Her eyes were ice cold as she formed her lips into something that nearly resembled a thin smile before turning and walking away.

The following morning, intending to refill the finch and hummingbird feeders Jim opened the shed door and came across the damage. The inside of the shed was a disaster area. The birdseed lay scattered and strewn about the floor, its bag now flaccid and limp sat in a corner, presumably bayoneted by the screwdriver discarded atop the empty sack. The normally well-ordered gardening tools previously hung upon wall hooks lay at his feet, his favorite unique bamboo grass rake was now a splintered wreck; its slender tines had been broken and twisted beneath the vandal's feet. The small window in the shed's back wall that faced into the alley was completely missing. Jim found the thin pane of glass in sharp broken shards lying among the stones of the alleyway.

Jim walked further into the shed, wondering who would have done such a thing, and then noticed how nicely the empty window framed the house that stood across the alley. Taking a step back, Jim's left shoe pushed down into something soft and squishy, at once the strong smell of human excrement wafted up assaulting his nostrils. Feeling his stomach threaten to turn, he cursed loudly and limped out of the shed's door while doing his best to keep the shit-covered shoe from tracking further along its floor. Now outside, he wiped the shoe clean on the grass.

No longer a young man, it took Jim several hours to clean up the mess and rearrange the tools in some semblance of their previous order. That afternoon he drove his old truck to the local glass store ordering an unbreakable Plexiglas panel to replace the broken window. Instead of waiting for his glass order, he drove down the block to Henry's Hardware buying several bags of birdseed, a cheap looking plastic grass rake, and three heavy-duty locks and hasps, one for the shed, the other two for each fence gate. He was nearing the checkout when he spied a motion sensor controlled yard light; he tossed that into the cart for good measure.

That evening he sat on his porch with a mug of coffee. Glaring across the alley into the neighbors' backyard, he watched his prime suspects as they took turns throwing rocks at beer bottles they had set up on a stump near the edge of the yard. Their younger brother, who they affectionately referred to as "Tubs," would replace the broken bottles with new empties he retrieved from several nearby cases. The game ended abruptly when one of the twins opened up on the targets just as Tubs set down a new bottle. The stone ricocheted off the younger boys head sending him reeling into the dirt. Rising to his feet, Tubs glared at the offending twin for a moment then ran toward the back door of the house, caterwauling loudly and holding a hand to the side of his head.

The carrot tops had already made their escape when Jim saw the mother bolt out the back door with a sobbing Tubs clinging to her side screaming out the names of the offending brothers. After several moments, realizing the twins wouldn't be appearing anytime soon the woman looked about and noticed Jim sitting on his porch. The woman sneered and spat into the yard while silencing Tubs with a swat upside the head. Spinning on her heel, she turned and headed back into the house leaving the screen door to slam angrily in her wake.

Jim began to feel badly for the younger brother who stood on the back steps crying. A small trickle of blood oozed from his scalp and slowly dripped onto his striped T-shirt. Sorry that was, up to the point the little beggar stuck out his tongue, flipped him the bird and quickly disappeared into the house after his mother.

It was a week later and Jim was in his garden using the hoe to clear some of the weeds that only lately had begun to grow. In other years, the weeds were always the first of the verge to appear in the garden and flower beds. He was just finishing hoeing the first row when he noticed a ball of bright yellow feathers near the base of a squash. He gave it a light poke with the tool and turned it over; it was a little finch.

He picked the bird up in a gloved hand wondering what had happened to the little fellow. Conducting his examination, he noticed a single, small bloody hole in the down on its breast. Judging from the size of the hole, Jim figured someone used a BB gun. He stole a glance upward and glared over toward the neighbors; "bastards!" he muttered. Using the hole to excavate a shallow hole, he laid the little bird to rest at the edge of the garden.

Jim found no fewer than four other downed birds of differing species scattered throughout the yard and decided he had to take action. The action would entail his speaking directly to the neighbors, something that given his recent observations, he was distinctively uncomfortable doing. Either way, he wasn't one to back down on his obligations as a bird lover or a resident of the community in good standing.

It was early afternoon, just after lunch, when Jim unlocked the back gate and walked over to the neighbors' back door. The Buick sat in its usual place among the knee-high grass and weeds, but the motorcycle was conspicuously absent, an observation that cheered Jim considerably. He hoped its owner hadn't simply parked it on the street at the front of the house. Summoning his courage, he walked up the three rather dilapidated steps leading to the small back door landing.

The screen door stood closed but the inner storm door was open. He rapped on the outer door several times and waited for ten seconds or so before knocking again. This time, he heard footsteps approaching.

One of the twins greeted him with a scornful "yeah," and a smirk.

"Your mother here son?" he said with as much cordiality as he could muster under the circumstances. The kid turned and left the door without a word then obviously met his mother on her way to see who was there. He heard the kid say, "old guy 'cross the alley."

A woman's voice called out loudly "just wait a sec." A moment later, the child's mother came to the door, hair disheveled and still in her bathrobe. Jim thought it odd that she wore a pair of sunglasses until he saw the cut on her lip and the bruising just visible on her cheek below the glass frames. "What do you want?" she asked placing an obvious stress on "you."
"I'm your neighbor, Jim Evanston. Mrs. ...?" He forced a smile.

"Ok Jim, I'm busy. What can I do for you today?" her tone dripped with something between boredom and annoyance. Even several feet away and the door screen between them he caught the odor of gin on her breath.

He stopped smiling and figured he should get right to the point. "I'm here because someone has been shooting birds with a BB gun in my yard." His eyes strayed to her neck where the bathrobe had parted slightly to reveal a set of angry bruises on either side of her neck, had the woman been strangled?

Taking notice of his gaze, she closed the top of the robe. "You saw... one of my kids shooting the gun?" she asked slowly.

Jim replied "no not exactly…" and he would have explained the reasoning behind the visit too if given the chance.

"Then screw off Jimbo or whatever your name is." and with that, the inner storm door slammed closed with a bang.

He stood there for a moment, a little shocked as to how quickly the conversation had deteriorated. He turned and walked down the stairway and out of the yard. Briefly, he concluded it was no small wonder the bitch came to get such a beating if she spoke that way to her asshole husband, but a second later castigated himself for such an uncharitable thought.

The phone call arrived on a Tuesday. A favorite cousin of his had passed away unexpectedly in her sleep. Katherine had been Jim's senior by nearly eight years but even so, Jim had figured the old girl had still been good for another five years during his visit with the family last Christmas.

Jim placed a single piece of luggage in the box of the old truck and hung his only dress jacket behind the seat; a dark blue blazer equally at home in any social occasion be they weddings, funerals, or something in between. A pair of scratchy gray flannel pants finished off the ensemble, the men's wear clerk insisting they complimented the jacket, even though they seemed to ride a little high in the crotch. He packed them at any rate thinking it would be a short service.

Stopping by Chuck's to gas up, Jim asked if he would mind "dropping by every once in a while" and check on his place then gave him a quick rundown of his recent troubles with the new neighbors. Jim made it to Willingdon by dinnertime; taking the new expressway had cut two hours off his driving time.

As funerals often go, it had gone well, sad and glad at the same time. He saw relatives that he hadn't spoken with for years owing to distance or just the ebbs and flows of life. One evening, several young nieces took him under their wings dragging him off to a barbecue get together with the younger set.

The fervor of the twenty and early thirty-something crowd had rubbed off on the old man bringing memories of his own youth flooding back to him. When the girls dropped him back at his motel he felt ten years younger, even hitting a nearby bar for a nightcap before turning in, something he hadn't done in many years.

Jim returned the following Monday, first dropping into Chuck's to refuel and catch up with the goings-on in town. After filling the truck's tank, he walked into the station. From the look on Chuck's face, he immediately knew something was wrong. Approaching the counter, he fetched his wallet from his back pocket, looked down, and pulled out his card, "ok, what's the word?"

Jim drove down the alley pulling onto the graveled parking pad next to his shed. Leaving his luggage in the truck, he went directly to the back gate. The lock was still there, a good sign he thought, as he turned the key. The gate swung open, as did his jaw, he felt his face redden with anger. The scene before him was far worse that his friend has described. Not a single feeder or birdhouse remained hung on the fences or porch. Instead, what was left of them lay scattered about in pieces on the lawn and in the flowerbeds.

Walking over to the garden, he discovered it to be an almost total loss. What the vandals hadn't taken with them, they had stomped into ruin. A quick look at the shed told him that they hadn't bothered with it, the door remained closed, the heavy padlock still dangled dutifully from its hasp.

Jim walked up the back stairs to his porch and rattled the back door knob, still locked, just as Chuck said it was. At least the house was ok. Getting out his key, he unlocked the door and stepped inside making a beeline for the phone punching in the numbers that would put him through to the town's police department.

Two and a half hours later a marked police van pulled up on the front street. Jim stood at the living room's picture window, arms crossed and brow creased as he watched the officer speak briefly into the radio's mike. The officers' close-cropped hair, clean-shaven chin, and the officious manner in the way he placed the cap on his head gave Jim some hope that the man might know his business. This hope vanished as he watched the officer step out, come around the van, and waddle up his sidewalk.

It wasn't just that the man was rather obese; he was…very. Instead, it was the sloppy manner of his dress. Draped carelessly about his bulk, the shirttails of his uniform shirt flopped and hung out above his Sam Brown. The wide belt, worn bare in places was in critical need of some polish and gave Jim the impression that the leather itself was desperately laboring to hold up the man's creased and wrinkled pants about their nonexistent waistline. Every second step, Jim could see a white sweat sock flash into view then disappear within a pair of unpolished, scuffed boots. Jim had learned many years ago that a man who prided himself on his overall appearance more than not also prided himself on his abilities. He wasn't wrong on this occasion either.

Over the next ten minutes or so, the police officer asked numerous questions, a few actually relating to the vandalism.

"Well Mr. Estavan," Officer Stuart started.
"Evanston" Jim interrupted then calmly corrected the man for the third time.

"Err, sorry Mr. Es, Evanston. Like I said without any proof I can't be making any arrests." He quickly jotted something down in his notebook below Jim's name, address, and phone number. "You should have called us earlier when you first noticed the damage; maybe we could have taken finger prints or something."

"I just got home three hours ago, besides that I don't really care about arrests, I just want this harassment to stop." Jim pointed a hand in the general direction of the neighbors' house. "Can't you just go by and talk to them, warn those kids to stay out of my yard and leave me alone?"

Like I said before, I have no proof it was them, and you don't have any other neighbors I could check with." Officer Stuart looked at the pained expression on Jim's face then added, "Look, I'll go by and speak with mom and dad, can't hurt can it. I happen to know the family, the Millers, they're good people."

Jim shook his head closing the door behind Officer Stuart watching the man hoist himself into the van and drive off. Jim walked into the kitchen just in time to see the van reappear in the rear alley and pull up behind his neighbor's home. The man now known as Mr. Miller was in the backyard working on his motorcycle, seeing Stuart arrive, the man stood up and walked over to the police van.

The two men spoke for a while, every now and again glancing over toward his house and laughing. The town cop shut the engine off, got out of the vehicle, and walked into the house with Miller. Jim grabbed the binoculars from the kitchen table and stood back from the window hiding as he trained the big optics onto what he assumed was the home's kitchen window. Every now and then, he caught a glimpse of Stuart and Miller, each laughing and sipping on a couple of Old Milwaukee's.

It was several days after Jim had returned from the funeral that he had the yard cleaned up. There was little point in trying to save the garden for the season so he had used his rototiller to break up and mix what was left of the plants into the soil. The feeders and birdhouses that he had mounted on the fences and trees were a total loss but he rummaged around in the shed and came up with several old plastic feeders that would do the job until he built some new ones.

Jim stood in the center of the yard near the oak tree and took a long look about, something was definitely amiss, but it took him several minutes to figure out just what it was. It finally hit him that the subtle warm glow that once graced his yard had completely vanished. Thinking back, he realized that he had witnessed it sputter like a candle in a quickening breeze over the last several days.

Walking up to the massive oak tree, he briefly studied the small arched door before working up the nerve to knock lightly. There was no answer. He'd never knocked on the door before today so he didn't know how long it might take Grady to answer the door or even if he and his kind actually answered doors. He knocked a little louder but got no response.

After trying the door a number of other times throughout the day, he concluded that perhaps the elf had decided to move on to a better neighborhood. Not that Jim could blame the little fellow. After all, lately he had considered doing the same thing himself, several times.

It was Saturday and as was his custom, Saturday morning meant grocery shopping. He picked himself up his usual selection of frozen dinners and a varied selection of vegetables, something he hadn't had to do in the late summer months for years, all thanks to the garden raiders. Saturday also meant a visit to The Caboose, a 24-hour diner that sat adjacent to Chuck's garage. Jim regularly mollified his sweet tooth with a piece of his favorite pie, pumpkin of course, served up with a little bit of whipped cream on top.

Arriving back home, Jim had already made a trip carrying the groceries in from the truck and was back to retrieve the sack of potatoes from the truck's box. He grabbed the potato sack and was closing the box when he heard a hubbub coming from where else, his neighbors house across the alley. He had heard this sort of thing before but never quite as loud. Pretending to disregard the commotion, he entered his yard laying the potatoes on the grass beside the gate. Jim turned facing the gate, lock in hand and clicking it shut when he saw the domestic argument spill out the Miller's back door and into the yard.

His hero, Hyrum as Jim had learned from his mail carrier, was in rare form this afternoon. Jim had seen him tinkering with his bike when he left that morning. By that time, he had already downed no fewer than four cans of Bud; the dead soldiers arranged in staggered file on the Buick's trunk near a rusted red toolbox. Now Jim figured the better part of a dozen empties littered the grass surrounding the bike.

Hyrum was chasing the little woman about the yard holding a beer in one hand and a thick belt in the other. At first, it appeared to Jim that Hyrum wasn't likely to catch the woman. Especially given the way she dodged first this way, then that in a manner reminiscent to that of a Thomson's gazelle escaping a cheetah, a drunken cheetah at that.

Unfortunately for his wife, she hadn't dressed for the occasion; her leopard skin flip-flop slippers would prove her demise. As the woman rounded the Buick for the second time, she lost her footing on the uneven dirt and tall grass, her ankle twisting as she went down with a cry.

Hyrum was on her in a flash. Jim watched as Millar ranted and raved while standing above her brandishing the belt before her terrified eyes. Crying and apologizing, the small woman laid on her side, holding up a defensive arm while pleading for mercy, a gift that wouldn't be forthcoming today. Jim watched Hyrum's belt as it rose and fell on the terrified woman's arms and back, each blow eliciting a high-pitched scream.

Jim yelled out to the man to stop his attack but whether Hyrum hadn't heard him or simply didn't care to, the beating continued. Jim rushed up the stairs to the top of the porch turning about and pausing for a second. The blows still fell on the prostrate form but thankfully, at a slower rate, the woman's piercing screams having now turned to loud whimpers. Jim gave a final glance. The twins and their brother had taken ringside seats on the porch; no doubt getting useful tips that would ensure future wedded bliss within their own homes. He entered his house and phoned the cops.

Thankfully, the cops arrived in the space of several minutes, the ambulance several minutes after that. The fat town cop that took Jim's complaint had been the first to rush over and try to restrain Hyrum from doing any more damage. Miller had given him a solid backhand to his jaw that sent the big man sprawling. The townie sat upright and rubbed his jaw but Jim could see the cop wasn't prepared to get back into the fight anytime soon.

Another car containing a pair of state troopers skidded in the thin gravel coming to a quick stop at the edge of the alley. These two looked to be all business as they marched over to where Hyrum stood over his now silenced wife. Upon their arrival, Hyrum got a lesson in street justice as a three-cell flashlight fell on the side of his head splitting his scalp wide open. A short roundhouse from the other trooper caught his face dead center, the thick closed fist destroying his nose and sending a bright red gush of blood spurting onto the lawn.

Jim watched while they handcuffed Miller then attended to his wife. Hyrum was belly down on the ground, his hands behind his back pushing himself forward like the maggot he was, his face laying down a trail of blood and snot along the weeds and blades of long grass.

About ten minutes later, the ambulance whisked the woman off to the hospital and the troopers foregoing any ceremony heaved Hyrum into the back of the cruiser and departed. A half hour later, a man and woman arrived in a large Ford. The town cop greeted them and together they walked into the back door of the Miller house. Jim figured it was probably social services, his guess was confirmed an hour later when the woman guided all three kids into the back seat while her associate and the cop brought up the rear carrying a couple of suitcases and several backpacks. The car left, disappearing down the alley spitting the odd stone of gravel from beneath the tires. Jim wouldn't see the kids or woman again.

The neighborhood had been dead quiet after the Millers' departure. Jim had been hoping that Grady might have returned but the elf's door remained unanswered and Jim's yard remained lackluster. Even so, Jim felt himself for the first time in several months. He hadn't realized how contending with those people had set him on a slow boil and now he could feel himself unwinding. This wasn't to last.

It was mid-morning; two weeks to the day Hyrum had gotten his comeuppance when Jim heard the now familiar and very much unwelcome sound of a Harley motorcycle, no make that multiple bikes, their engines reverberating and echoing up and down the alleyway. There were five bikes and all of them pulled into the Miller's yard parking beside the Buick and the motorcycle that Miller had been working on the day of his arrest.

Jim watched the group of men mill about while smoking and talking. Occasionally, one or two of them would look down the alley. Apparently, they were expecting someone. That someone was one of two men arriving on a large cherry red bike. The hog drove down the lane and pulled in beside the group of men, the passenger seated behind the operator looked vaguely familiar. Jim heard himself moan audibly when the man removed his helmet; Hyrum had returned.

An hour later, a large dump truck hauling a long flatbed trailer and carrying a front-end loader stopped in the lane. A few minutes later, several crew cab pickups arrived spilling out half a dozen or so workmen. Jim could see that the truck beds of each smaller vehicle contained metal poles and chain link fencing, and something else; "was that razor wire?" he asked himself. Hyrum and his buddies moved their bikes around to the front street as the front-end loader trundled off its' trailer. The heavy equipment took only several hours to clear off the grass and topsoil from the front and back yards while the workmen used a motorized post hole auger to dig holes around the perimeter of the yard. Just after 1 pm, the first of several large loads of gravel had arrived; the men quickly spread it about covering the yard.

Jim was amazed to see how quickly the yard changed over the space of the next several days. The yard was now a graveled compound surrounded by an eight-foot high chain link fence complete with a large sliding vehicle gate and an intercom system. The top of the fence was spiraled with evil looking razor wire.

The house had undergone some changes as well. A single heavy reinforced steel door had replaced the old back screen and storm doors while thick metal bars secured the ground floor windows. Security cameras and powerful automatic yard lights were mounted and positioned on the outer walls of the building. All in all, it gave the place the appearance of a prison, something Jim figured would make these types feel completely at home.

The fortress saw motorcycles, cars, and trucks coming and going at all hours of the day or night, but Jim seldom saw anyone outside the building except to enter or exit their vehicles. The building's yard lights came on each night at exactly ten, flooding his yard and banishing the stars with a harsh white brilliance giving the compound the look of a German stalag. Jim had trouble sleeping before he fit his upper floor bedroom and kitchen windows with heavy blackout cloth to block the invasive light.

It was like living next door to an all night truck stop, although Jim had to admit that during the day, and especially in the morning, things were pretty much as quiet as they had been before the Miller's had moved in. Jim contacted the town complaining about the unusual renovations to the house, but the proper permits existed and his concerns fell upon deaf ears. From his conversation with the town office, Jim got the distinct feeling that town management was only too happy that the bikers were taking up residence in one of the more secluded areas of town.

It had been a fine autumn day, an unexpected surprise since the killing frost had arrived earlier than normal this year, a perfect opportunity for Jim to start preparing his yard for the winter. The songbirds had begun their migration southward several weeks ago, now the ducks and geese were filling the skies as well.

Jim hadn't seen anything but Jays and sparrows at the feeders for the last several weeks.

He sat on his porch with his coffee looking out into his yard occasionally glancing at the fortress across the lane. The clubhouse was very quiet this evening, not a car or bike in the compound. The floodlights would activate in about another hour, someone hadn't yet adjusted their timers to take the shortening of the days into account. He looked up at the sky. The summer stars were out in force tonight, and Jim thought he hadn't seen much of them from his back porch this summer. Finishing his coffee, he set the mug on the deck railing and rose from the weathered rocking chair. Standing near the back door, he took a long look into the yard admiring the yard work he had accomplished earlier that day. That's when he noticed a subtle yet familiar pink radiance in the fork of the oak tree. Had Grady returned?

He walked down the sidewalk stepping onto the grass and standing several yards from the tree. "Grady! Nice to have you back" Jim said cheerily. The fork's pink glow swiftly transformed to a vivid crimson while in the same instant, the area about the tree had darkened perceptively. Above him, the stars dimmed and faded, cloaked as if within a dark shadow. "Grady?" Jim now questioned timidly; the air about him had grown distinctly icy. If it weren't so dark, he figured that he would have been able to see his breath. A moment later, the glow faded as quickly as it began. An unexpectedly warm and fragrant evening breeze swept across the yard banishing the frigid gloom but did little to reassure the man's sudden unease. Jim cautiously backed away from the tree then turning quickly abandoned the yard in return for the safety of his home.

Clear and cold, the wee morning hours of October 30 saw the last crescent moon riding high in the eastern sky. Jim hadn't been able to sleep well that night. Tossing and turning he finally concluded that sleep wasn't on the menu and got out of bed.

He'd eaten takeout from Taco Bell the evening before enjoying a spicy burrito, a treat he hadn't enjoyed in several years. Now with an upset stomach and a sleepless night he remembered the reasons for the burrito's absence. From inside the bathroom's medicine cabinet, he grabbed the bottle of Tums. He chewed up four of the tablets as he trod down the stairs to the kitchen intending to get on with his day.

As usual, the small light above the stove he always kept lit illuminated the kitchen with its soft yellow glow. The kitchen window's heavy blackout drapes hung closed blocking out most of the stray light spilling out from the compounds floodlights. Jim prepared a small pot of coffee placing it on the stovetop. He heard a vehicle approach in the alley then glanced at the wall clock...3:45 a.m.

Walking over to the window, he opened the heavy curtain just a crack and peered out. A full-size car had stopped outside the compound gate, the driver's arm reached out placing a key in the control box. The wide chain link gate came to life and slowly opened. Nocturnal visits to the clubhouse were hardly out of the ordinary and Jim was about to release the drape when the compound floodlights suddenly went out plunging the area into darkness. Thinking this might be interesting, he parted the drapes somewhat wider watching the vehicle enter the compound and pull up near the back door. Jim grabbed the large aperture birding binoculars from their place on the kitchen table and brought them up to his eyes.

Two men exited from either side of an older Lincoln town car and walked to the rear trunk opening it. At the same time, the back door of the clubhouse opened and a third figure emerged joining the other two. The trunk's interior light though dim was still sufficiently bright to allow Jim to see that the man that exited the house was Hyrum Miller.

Hyrum looked about quickly in the darkness and gave a nod. The first two men reached into the trunk and hauled something out letting it drop heavily onto the gravel parking lot. Hyrum closed the trunk lid while the others reached down and lifted a man to his feet. Half carrying, half dragging the limp figure, they made their way up the back stairs and in through the door. Jim let the curtain close to a mere slit just as Hyrum paused on the clubhouse landing and looked about, paying special attention to Jim's home. Satisfied that no one had been watching, Hyrum entered the house and closed the door. The floodlights came on a moment later as Jim poured his first of several cups of coffee and waited by the window watching the compound.

It was nearly six in the morning. The sky was still dark, but while the brighter stars remained, many others had already surrendered to the perceptible glow of dawn to the east. Jim's coffee had grown nearly as cold as his interest and was about to leave the kitchen and take in an early morning TV news program when the compounds floodlights were suddenly doused a second time. Once again, he picked up the binoculars and peered through a thin partition in the curtains. He remained confident that his actions were still imperceptible to even an attentive observer. As before, Hyrum opened the front door and walked down into the compound. Jim watched the man stroll about the lot for at least five minutes, the cigarette he smoked lending a casual suggestion to his early morning rambling.

Jim watched Hyrum walk to the trunk of the large car, open it, then give a slight nod toward someone still waiting in the building. The backdoor of the clubhouse opened and two men carried something wrapped in a dark blanket down the stairs and toward the vehicle. Jim watched an arm fall from beneath the gray shroud, its hand dragged in the gravel as the men struggled for a better grip at either end of what Jim had now confirmed was a body. Reaching the vehicle, they swung it like a sack of potatoes throwing it into the trunk. The back of the vehicle dipped as its shocks compensated for the added weight then Hyrum slowly closed the trunk lid. As the lid encountered the trunk's latch, he gave it a hard downward push locking the mechanism quietly into place. Hyrum pulled upward on the trunk lid testing the latch, it was secure.

The men that had placed the body in the Lincoln's trunk got in, started the engine, and then drove slowly out the compound's gate, turning into the alley and soon disappearing from site. Hyrum took a long final look about him then walked into the clubhouse and closed the back door.

Jim struggled between the choice of ignoring what he had seen or doing his civic and moral duty and reporting it to the authorities. You didn't have to look too far afield to see what sometimes happened to witnesses who came forward pointing an accusing finger toward organized crime figures. Jim thought this was especially true for an elderly man, living alone in a deserted community just a couple of hundred feet from a lair of killers.

It was only when he saw the televised news and the police spokesperson asking the public for tips about a missing husband and father of three that he made his decision. While he had no reason to believe the body he saw thrown into the car trunk might actually belong to the missing person, he didn't have any reason to believe that it might not either.

Around noon, Jim summoned up the courage to call the cops. Reading from the phone book, he punched up a number almost entering the last digit when he paused and hung up the phone. "Stupid!" he uttered aloud realizing that the number belonged to the town cops. What if they sent that fat crooked son of a bitch or someone else that was on a first name basis with Hyrum? He scrolled down the page and instead dialed the number of the state police.

When the receptionist at the police station answered the phone, Jim was unsure of who or even what department to ask for, so he stammered and paused before telling the woman that he might have information regarding the missing man from the television news. He didn't tell her about the body he saw dumped into the trunk. The girl explained that Detective Evans was looking after the case but he was in court for the remainder of the afternoon. Instead, she suggested she could send an officer to his home who would take the information, something Evans would probably have done at any rate. Jim gave her his information and hung up the phone.

A half hour later, the front doorbell rang. Jim went to the door and opened it. Two town cops stood on his front landing; one of them was Officer Stuart. Jim was suddenly thrown off balance with the unexpected change in events. The officers asked to come in and Jim obligingly showed the two into the living room. Jim sat in the middle seat on his long couch wishing he had taken any other chair in the room, especially as the cops now sat in chairs that flanked him on either side.

Jim watched as Stuart squeezed his bulk into the chair to Jim's left and having taken out his notebook was now busily searching his chest pockets for a pen. The other cop on his right, Higgins, as he introduced himself, began the conversation in earnest. Jim immediately felt that this fellow commanded a higher pay grade than Stuart.

"I understand you have information on a murder victim?" The officer smiled in a reassuring manner. "Just tell us about it in your own words and we'll ask any questions we need to afterward."

"Murder...victim?" Jim stammered slightly, "I called about the missing person" he added softly.

Higgins looked somewhat surprised and looked down at the clipboard in his hand. "We got a call from the state police in Chase asking us to speak to you about a Mr. Henry Stevens." Higgins expression changed to one of understanding. "The person in the news?" Higgins suggested.

"Yes, yes, husband and father of three." Jim heard himself repeat the newscasters' words verbatim and immediately felt a little foolish for doing so.

Higgins continued, "That's him. His body was found a couple of hours ago about five miles north of here." Higgins watched Jim's face fall. "Guess you didn't hear."

"No." Jim felt uncomfortable but allowed his eyes to glance over to Stuart who having found his pen now appeared to be doodling absentmindedly on a page in his notebook. Stuart's obvious disinterest gave him a little more confidence.

Jim paused and looked out the front window for a long moment considering if he should tell the cops what he had seen this morning or make something up. He glanced over to Stuart who was now looking at him expectantly and then to Higgins whose eyes locked onto his, fixing Jim's in their gaze.

"Your information sir…" Higgins sat forward in his chair; a professional at reading people he instinctively knew Jim could go either way. He wouldn't let it happen. "It has something to do with that clubhouse out back doesn't it."

Jim felt his head unintentionally nod in agreement then the entire story spilled out of him in a rush. At one point Stuart started to interrupt but Higgins silenced him with a single fierce look. Jim finished telling the cops everything he saw that morning. Higgins told Stuart to go out to the car and get an official statement form. When the other man had left the house, Higgins saw Jim relax somewhat.

"You don't like Dick much do you?" Higgins asked and saw the question in Jim's eyes. "Officer Stuart, Mr. Evanston" he clarified.

"I think he's a friend of Hyrum Miller, they drink beer together for Christ sakes" Jim answered.

"He may be, and Dick does like his beer. Both grew up in Chase and went to the same school together. So did I, but I never liked that prick." Higgins' eyes were clear and honest. "Look Mr. Evanston, may I call you Jim?"

"Sure, why not" Jim added.

"Call me Grant," the officer continued, "Jim you realize that by calling us and providing this information you may well have to give testimony down the road in open court?" Jim's head bowed downward, his eyes staring at his open palms. "Jim, I know Dick might practice poor judgment from time to time but he's not a bad cop. Dick's just a little less choosy about who he spends time with."

In the end, it wasn't Dick Stuart tipping off Hyrum, but a pretty clerk working in the state police office in Chase. Coming across Higgins' report and Jim's attached statement, she called her boyfriend, a striker seeking membership in Hyrum's motorcycle gang. Finishing the call the young woman hung up the receiver, walked over to the shredding machine, and turned it on.

The Halloween party in the clubhouse started mid-afternoon, the members starting to arrive just about the time Higgins and Stuart left Jim's home. Just after six p.m. Hyrum received the call from his striker telling him that Jim Evanston had just become a liability. Hyrum made several hurried calls to the club president and the master-at-arms, neither of whom had intended to come to the party.

While the gang appreciated Hyrum allowing his home to function as a clubhouse, the man was neither well liked nor well thought of. Bad tempered and not overly bright, Hyrum had a tendency to draw unwanted attention to himself and his brethren. This was especially true of the gangs' executive who desperately wanted to run under the cops' radar concentrating on legitimizing the dirty money they made importing drugs and running girls. Long gone were the days when the big boys would saddle up their steel chargers and ride through town doing their best impression of the "Wild Bunch."

At eight p.m., the leaders of the motorcycle gang arrived and stormed into the clubhouse immediately calling the emergency meeting to order. A half hour later the bosses left the compound, the engines of their BMW's red-lined and their tires creating rooster tails of gravel and dust that sprayed up in their wake as they sped down the alleyway.

The president had been livid upon learning that several of the gang's enforcers had beaten a "Joe average" citizen to death over a minor gambling debt. The president's orders were both simple and explicit. Jim Evanston had to disappear, and that would take place no later than tomorrow morning. Hyrum and the two soldiers would do what was required and bring Jim's body directly over to the farm for proper disposal, meaning that the body would be ground into hamburger and end up as hog feed. Any screw-ups and the president assured the three that they would join Evanston on Porky's menu.

Parties at the clubhouse normally wound into the wee hours of the morning, the last of the drunken revelers clearing out by dawn but tonight's Halloween party shut down immediately after the meeting. By ten p.m. only Hyrum's' bike, the big Lincoln and a low rider sat in the compound. Jim watched through the drapes of his kitchen window as the last of the visiting bikers drove away.

Jim was nervous, still worried the bikers had somehow found out what he had seen that morning. He wasn't sure if the early breakup of the Halloween party was cause for relief or concern. Higgins had given Jim a number where he could be reached at any hour of the day and promised that both the night cars would drive by his home at least once an hour to "show the flag". So far, Jim had twice seen a patrol car drive behind his house, as did the bikers who watched the cruiser crawl by their compound, the brilliant "alley lights" stabbing into the alley's shadows from either side of the vehicle during its pass.

Hyrum wasn't concerned. Tonight was Halloween, and he had friends in different parts of town that were going to make sure it a busy night for the bulls. Neither of the two night cars would reappear until well after two if they made it back at all. It was eleven forty when Hyrum killed the compounds' floodlights plunging the entire area into unaccustomed darkness.

Jim continued to survey the biker's clubhouse with his big binoculars through his kitchen window. As he scanned the building, he found himself taken aback when he noticed a figure in one of the darkened upper floor windows holding a set of binoculars apparently watching him watch them. Abruptly he let the curtain fall closed hoping they hadn't noticed him. He rechecked the front and back doors; they were still secure. He hadn't yet turned on a single light in the house that evening. He moved through its rooms with the help of a small penlight and made his way upstairs binoculars in hand. Reaching his bedroom and looking out the window he suddenly realized with a start that he hadn't bothered to turn on his front or back yard lights. He had gotten out of the habit a month or so ago ever since the compound's floodlights illuminated his yard equally well. The question was, he should do so now.

As Jim stood by the window, he caught a furtive movement just outside his back gate. A moment later, he spotted a dark outline moving further away in the alley; this figure was approaching a utility box. Rushing downstairs as fast as his arthritic knees and feet would carry him he flicked on the exterior front light switch.

Nothing happened. Hoping the light bulb had simply burned out Jim walked to the back door where the rear yard switch was located. When this too failed to light, he grew concerned. He hit the kitchen light switch, still nothing happened, and his concern became apprehension as he correctly concluded that someone had cut the power. He strode into the hallway, picked up the wall phone's receiver, and placing it to his ear heard the comforting hum of the dial tone. He punched in the first of two phone numbers scribbled on Higgins's business card and waited. One ring, two rings, and part of a third... the phone died. Suddenly Jim wished he had kept up with the times and got himself a cell phone when he had the chance. He was alone.

His mind raced as he sought an alternative to the very real possibility of his death. He would have to deal with whatever came through the doors or windows that night on his own. Jim expected the odds of his coming out on top were poor, a septuagenarian with a bad back, trick knee and a heart condition against God knows how many desperate men. If he were to have any chance, he'd need a weapon. He stole another quick look out the kitchen curtains.

The two men that he had seen in the alley minutes ago were no longer visible. The night was dark and clear, the quarter moon hung low in the west casting its feeble light into the back yard. A light mist was slowly enveloping the neighborhood, silently creeping along the earth, perfect for a Halloween night. Just not this night Jim thought, and then reminded himself he needed a weapon... fast! The shotgun!

He rushed to the front hallway closet, threw open the bi-fold doors and reached into its high overhead shelf. Urgently, his fingers pushed past hats, gloves, and scarves, stretching toward the back wall where they met the cold steel of a gun barrel. His hands yanked the shotgun from the closet shelf bringing with it a woolen avalanche that fell atop his head and shoulders. He opened the empty breech of the single shot twelve gauge knowing it wasn't loaded, but somehow hoping it was; now, where were the shells?

Remembering he had stored the shells in a cupboard along with his duck calls and a handful of mallard decoys. Beginning to make his way to the basement, he paused to peer out the small diamond shaped window set in his front door. A lone figure stood on the front street, just to the left of the house. The man was smoking. Jim saw the cherry glow of the cigarette brighten as the man took a drag then dropped the butt to the asphalt, presumably crushing it with his heel. Presumably, because the light mist had become a dense, low-lying fog that slowly eddied and swirled about the man's legs.

"Get the damn shells and quit gawking!" he chastised his delay as he rushed to the door leading down into the basement. Holding the penlight in one hand and the shotgun in the other, Jim hurried down the darkened staircase. He was half way down the steep stairs before his bad knee suddenly failed in an explosion of excruciating pain; his balance, never good at the best of times, evaporated completely. Pitching forward he let the flashlight fall from his hand and grabbed desperately for the railing but missed it completely.

Hyrum had left the front street, walked up the lawn, and stood at the south side of the house. Standing on his tiptoes, he looked over the fence and across the fog-draped yard to the back gate. Two figures stood behind the gate, he waved to the men and waited. One of the figures returned his signal. Having indicated that the coast was clear, one of the two men lay his hands on top of the fence and began lifting himself over.

Hyrum turned and walked along the front of the house, pausing to peer into the living room window, but it was of no use, the drapes covered the entire window. He continued to the front door and glanced through the door's small window, as expected all was in darkness. Even if they hadn't cut the power, Hyrum figured the old man had probably been in bed since nine that evening. Hyrum waited patiently by the door listening for the whistle from his buds that would indicate that they were ready for their entry at the back door.

The plan called for the men to simultaneously shoulder both the front and back doors and storm the house. The doors were thin and some fifty some years old. Two of the men would immediately find their way upstairs and check the bedrooms while the third would search the main floor just in case.

Hyrum had the only weapon, a small handheld stun gun that would make the old boy dance to any tune they cared to whistle. Besides, the other two men, powerfully built and well experienced, could singly overcome any resistance Jim was likely to offer. Hyrum had forbidden the others to bring along any weapons knowing that a weapon carried was one often used. That meant there would be a mess, and a mess wasn't anything you wanted left at a crime scene or worse yet take away with you. No, it was better to do your wet work elsewhere where you had the time to do things right, besides there was also a slim possibility of getting pinched by the cops. Busting into a home in the middle of a night carrying a weapon could add an additional five years onto whatever other sentence the judge might throw your way.

Hyrum waited by the front door but was losing patience; his men should have been at the back door by now. The bloody fog was nearly at his waist and was slowly rising higher by the minute. A solitary streetlight stood sentry a hundred yards down the block, its weak and sickly glow settled into a dim yellow pool atop the fog bank. He looked up and down the street checking for headlights, good, no cops.

The two men stood at the back gate, the taller of the two men returned Hyrum's wave, it was time to get this party started. The slightly smaller of the two men was the first to climb over the fence and lower himself down, his feet settling into the wet grass.

Reaching the ground Danny Groves looked around himself peering through the thick fog that obscured anything further than five or six feet away. He wasn't concerned; he'd grown up in a small fishing village on the east coast where mists like this were commonplace. When he still lived with his wife and family, he had once strung a rope leading from the back door to the outhouse for those occasions in the fall when a real "pea souper" would roll in off the ocean. Dan and his family had been glad for the rope more than once. Suddenly, he missed the smell of the ocean and realized that there was a definite odor in the air that he couldn't quite place, an unpleasant yet vaguely familiar smell.

His partner had climbed over the fence and stood beside him. The larger man gave him a sharp elbow then took the lead walking toward the back door about a hundred feet away. The big man was obviously uncomfortable walking in the foggy gloom; his feet invisible below the thick fog that parted before him only to fold in behind as soon as he had passed. Danny's partner moved forward with an agonizing slowness, extending first one leg and then the other, tapping and feeling his way along the earth with his feet as if he were blind.

The biker shook his head, noting the other man had barely crossed twenty feet in the last couple of minutes. Looking down he saw the fog had nearly risen to his chest, almost the same height of the yard's fence. Danny thought it strange that the thick fog filled the yard to the top of the fence then spilled over and outward, floating downward into the vacant lot that bordered Jim's yard.

It reminded Danny of a particular Halloween, his aunt had concocted a witch's brew for the kids. She added dry ice to some colored water causing a fine mist to bubble out of the bowl and spread out on the table. This fog, like his aunt's brew, gave him the impression the mist originated somewhere in the yard itself. As the cold vapor wafted about him, he realized that the unpleasant odor was quickly becoming a palatable stench.

He dipped his nose down into the mist, took a small sniff, and then exhaled in a rush, nearly gagging. The obnoxious vapor was itself the source of the odor, the air lying just above its surface smelled almost sweet in comparison. Suddenly Dan placed the familiar scent and turned back to a night several years before when he and his partner were disposing of a victim's corpse, dumping it into an old well on an abandoned farm. They had used the well for the same purpose several months previous and before leaving their victim to rot in peace, the two had placed a sheet of plywood to cover the opening. On this second occasion, removing the plywood from the well resulted in each of them turning away and puking in the grass while the gaseous corruption escaped in a nauseating rush from the watery grave below.

Danny cocked his ears, what was that? He looked toward the center of the yard. His eyes paused briefly near the base of the old oak then followed the trunk's outline as it rose up and above the fog, its leaf bare branches towering above them like boney fingers in the night. Was it his imagination or was the thick fog actually spewing out from a large hole in the tree just below the point where the trunk forked?

Hearing a harsh "psst," he turned his head away from the tree and toward his partner who stood some thirty paces or so ahead of him. The man turned toward him and growled, "Danny! For Christ Sakes move your bloody ass." The next instant, the man gave out a surprised grunt then disappeared, having either fallen or having been pulled downward into the deep bank of fog. At first, Danny figured his partner had simply tripped over something so he waited a moment, then several more, but the other man never reappeared.

The long seconds ticked by, then Danny heard what he thought to be a childlike whimper followed by a definite wet gurgling sound. There was a silent pause followed by muffled cracks of rending bone and cartilage. The sound was reminiscent of his mother stripping a turkey for soup the day after Christmas; ripping the meaty legs and wings away from the carcass.

A chill went up his spine. Incredibly, he knew with a clear certainty that his partner was dead. He stared wide-eyed into the misty gloom for a full minute, willing his eyes to focus on anything that might appear near the point the man went down below the fog but nothing disturbed the calm undulating surface.

Sudden movement! He saw the surface of the fog waiver and eddy, something was clearly moving beneath, and that something had eyes. Two large cold green orbs were obviously looking in his direction. In his mind's eye, Danny could see his partner's twisted broken body on the wet earth where it lay in bloody ruin. The green-eyed thing that had killed the man still slithered nearby and now became aware of new prey within the shadows.

His feet made the unconscious decision to run the thirty odd feet back toward the back fence, away from the gliding nightmare that slid so silently toward him beneath the fog. Somehow, he reached the fence without tripping over unseen obstacles or vegetation; he was going to make it! The biker hit the fence in a dead run slapping his hands down upon the top of the fence. Using the structure as one might a pommel horse; he flung himself upward, throwing one leg over the top, straddling the fence.

Danny paused and glanced back into the yard. For a second, he imaged he saw a narrow undulating tail writhe above the fog's surface, just like the dorsal fin of a shark breaking above the waves before it strikes. He started to swing his other leg over the fence but something bit downward into his thigh, he could feel its long teeth scraping along the bone. The pain was overwhelming and he began a squeal that ended a moment later in a high-pitched scream. As he cried out, his hand dropped to his injured leg, the palm of his hand now rested upon cold wart scaled skin, looking down he saw two glowing eyes staring back into his. Two viciously clawed hands shot up through the mist and stabbed deeply in his torso, the shock ended his shriek almost as soon as it began. Immensely powerful limbs plucked him from the fence dragging him back into the fog-shrouded yard where Danny managed to get out final muffled cry before vanishing into the mist that now suddenly turned a light shade of crimson.

Jim awoke to find himself lying on the cool basement floor. He sat up and looked about. Still working, the pen light lay nearby casting its thin oval beam across the surface of the dark floor. He picked up the small flashlight with one hand while his other strayed to the back of his aching head. He felt the large goose egg and a warm wetness where his scalp had split open upon meeting the cement floor.

He continued to check himself over and found that aside from the bump on the back of his head and a mild headache he was ok. He played the flashlight over the floor locating his gun that had slid from his hand and lay partially hidden beneath a nearby shelf. Retrieving the gun, he set about finding the shotgun shells and opened the cupboard door where he stored his hunting gear. If he remembered correctly, the box should be on the lowest shelf beneath the plastic decoys. He thought with dismay that the shells contained only light birdshot.

As Jim stood before the open cupboard, a loud bang and crash sounded from the main floor. Hyrum had shouldered his way through the front door sending splinters and shards of the wooden doorframe scattering before him. Startled, Jim twisted about with a start dropping the small flashlight. He watched it spin across the hard floor and disappear beneath the freezer. Jim ran over to the appliance and got down on his hands and knees peering along the floor beneath the freezer. The flashlights beam betrayed its location but it was jammed tight, Jim could only just touch the flashlight with a single finger.

He heard heavy footsteps taking the stairs to the second floor two at a time then move back and forth in the hallway as someone ran from bedroom to bedroom. There was a pause before he heard the footsteps pounding back down the stairs toward the main floor. Jim couldn't afford to spend any more time retrieving the light; he needed those shells! He crabbed his way back to the cupboard on his hands and knees carelessly brushing aside the decoys, desperately feeling for the box of shells. The hollow plastic decoys scattered out of the cupboard clattering loudly onto the cement floor. Jim heard the footsteps on the main floor stop abruptly. Whoever had been making them now knew he was in the basement.

"What's keeping those assholes?" Hyrum muttered to himself. He had been standing motionless on the front steps for over five minutes and he could feel the damp air begin to penetrate his clothing. Hyrum's ears picked up a commotion in the backyard when the creature snatched Danny Groves off the fence and ripped him to pieces. Hyrum mistakenly assumed that the men forgetting to signal, had simply broken their way through the back door, and were now inside.

"About frigging time!" Hyrum muttered and taking out a heavy steel flashlight from his back pocket flicked it on. The light was bright and steady. Firmly planting his feet, Hyrum thrust his full weight against the door. As expected, the door gave easily enough but the noise that accompanied its opening sounded like a howitzer going off in the otherwise tranquil night.

He moved quickly into the dark hallway, he didn't see or hear the other two men yet but true to his plan he set off up the stairs as fast as he could move knowing that surprise was everything in these situations. Reaching the top of the stairs he rushed down the hallway shining the flashlight into each bedroom and finally the bathroom, all were empty. He walked back into the master bedroom a second time checking the closet and under the bed. Satisfied the old man wasn't upstairs Hyrum headed back to the main floor and walked into the kitchen.

Hyrum saw the back door had somehow remained closed but upon hearing the tumultuous racket rising up from the basement, he discarded the thought, assuming that his boys had found the old man. He ran down the hallway standing in the doorway that lead down to the basement and shone the flashlight's beam onto the dark stairway. It illuminated the grey basement floor below but no one came into view, the earlier racket had ceased, now all he heard was a faint shuffling sound. Hyrum took several steps down the stairs then called out; "Jason, Danny, it's me, I'm coming down guys." All noise abruptly stopped as he continued his descent into the basement.

Jim had found not one but two partial boxes of shells on the cupboard's bottom shelf. He shook open one of the boxes spilling its' contents out on the cement floor, some rolling this way, others that, but managing to snatch up several, rose to his feet. He reached over and grabbed the shotgun he had propped up in a nearby corner. As he cracked the breech he heard Hyrum's voice calling down the stairs, the man obviously figured that some friends of his were already down here with him. Jim slid a shell into the open barrel of the gun completely aware that unless the light birdshot hit the man in the face it wouldn't do much to stop a determined man, but either way it would sure scare the hell out of him and that alone might be all Jim needed to survive.

Hyrum continued down the stairs and reaching the bottom quickly twisted the flashlight to his left, then his right where the beam came to rest on the old man. Jim's face was gaunt and haggard but Hyrum could see the man's eyes retained the steely glint of defiance, something was very wrong. The bikers' concern was confirmed as Jim closed the gun and cocked it, that sound caused Hyrum's flashlight beam to drop from the old man's face and play across the long barrel of a shotgun pointed right at his chest.

"Jees-sus!" Hyrum yelled as he spun about and took a step up the stairs. A bright yellow-white flash accompanied the tremendous blast that shook the room with its violence. The impact of the birdshot rained against Hyrum's side and back, it felt as though a giant had struck him with a baseball bat. The biker's heavy leather jacket absorbed or at least slowed most of the light birdshot but many of the pellets still managed to lodge themselves beneath the skin of his side and back.

Hyrum dropped the flashlight as he almost flew up the steps to the main level. Stumbling several times on the steep stairs, he used his hands and feet to regain his balance. Reaching the top of the stairs, he ran toward the back door.

Finding the door closed and locked he blindly fumbled with the thumb latch until he felt the mechanism turn in his fingers and the door swing outward. Staggering, Hyrum fell onto the porch then rose to his feet, his hands clutching the deck's railing. He stood motionless, staring down into the dense roiling fog that shrouded the back yard. Hyrum's eyes roved through the dark gloom. He could just make out the faint outline of the back fence, the tool shed and just to its right, the top of the back gate. Out beyond the gate, through the mist-veiled alley, stood the clubhouse and with it, the promise of refuge.

Hyrum stepped down the porch steps into the fog nearly retching as a terrible stench crept into his nostrils. The concrete sidewalk lay beneath his feet and he began to walk in rapid steps toward the back fence and safety. The sting of the BBs was constant. He could feel the blood running down his back and side, soaking into his sweatshirt and the belt line of his pants. Although the night air was icy cold, his face flushed hotly, rivulets of sweat ran down from his hairline into his eyes. He wiped his brow and looked about the yard, things had gone very wrong tonight, and Hyrum worried that worse was yet to come. The odious mist in the backyard was creeping him out. He was approaching the point where he actually considered going back into the house and leaving through the front door. The old man and his shotgun be damned.

Hyrum increased his pace to a trot. He had made it more than halfway across the yard when his boot unexpectedly struck something soft and yielding in his path. Losing his balance, he tripped over whatever lay beneath and unseen below the noxious fog. His hands slapped the sidewalk in front of him partially breaking his fall and saving his nose and face from the impact. Overtop the putrid stench of the fog; Hyrum could almost taste the coppery smell of fresh blood. Rising to his hands and knees, he saw what was left of the body lying close by. The disemboweled corpse gaped open, its glistening coils of intestine reached out into the gloom like an obscene garden hose.

Picking himself off the ground, Hyrum felt his gorge rise then spewed out the contents of his stomach covering himself in vomit. He wiped his mouth as he continued his staggered run toward the back fence that now lay only a few yards distant. Just a few more steps and he'd reach the gate, but something was approaching from behind, and whatever it was it was, it coming up fast; Hyrum knew he wouldn't make it.

Jim had been listening as Hyrum unlocked the back door and heard it slam shut behind the man as he departed. He waited another minute or so, and then satisfied that the house was empty he cautiously climbed the stairs, holding the reloaded shotgun pointing up and ahead of him just in case.

Only a matter of seconds after Hyrum disappeared into the fog for the second and final time, Jim arrived at the back door, closed, and relocked it. Setting aside the shotgun, he walked up the hallway toward his shattered front door. A powerful beam of light struck his eyes while a deep authoritative voice tersely instructed him to put up his hands.

An electrical repair crew came by to restore the power while an ambulance crew attending the scene patched up Jim's head and checked him out. He'd be ok but they advised him to visit his doctor in a few days time. When he exited the back of the ambulance Grant Higgins was waiting to speak to him. He and the officer walked back into his house where Jim gave a detailed statement about what had taken place. He showed Higgins and another officer the basement stairs where he had shot Hyrum. Half way up the basement steps a light blood trail began, it carried on through the hallway, the kitchen, and then out the back door onto the porch but ended abruptly on the sidewalk near the halfway point to the back fence.

Jim looked into his back yard, the mist had disappeared completely, the darkness dispelled by the brilliance of his yard light, and the floodlights of the adjacent compound. Everything appeared as it should. Looking over to the biker's compound, he noticed a buzz of activity taking place. Standing quietly for five or more minutes, he watched members of the local and state police walking in and out of the clubhouse carrying various items and placing them in the back of a large van.

Higgins saw Jim observing the goings on at the compound, "Search warrant.," he stated in monotone, "you wouldn't believe the stuff we're coming up with over there."

"I bet. What about the bikers?" he asked.

"No sign of them, the clubhouse was empty when we got there. We have an all points out for Hyrum, I'd appreciate you coming down to the station tomorrow and look over some photos, maybe we can identify the other guys you saw yesterday morning?" Higgins asked.

"Like I said earlier, it was pretty dark and I didn't get a good look at them but I'd be happy to help if I can." Jim suddenly felt a thousand years old. Seeing the man was in no shape to continue the debriefing, Higgins took his leave of the old man after helping temporarily secure the front door.

Jim looked at the calendar; 21 June, midsummer's eve, at least this year; the date tended to jump around a bit. Walking over to the kitchen window, he looked out admiring his fine yard and garden. The old biddy who wrote the Homes and Gardens column for the Chase Chronicle had described Jim's yard as a "lovely and many splendored thing"; he supposed it was a play on the title of an old movie but in this case he felt she could be forgiven. It was certainly splendid.

He took his mug of coffee and walked out into the back yard where the aroma of late spring and summer flowers filled his nostrils. Standing on his deck, he looked about, and felt a surge of pride in what both he and the little elf had accomplished together. The sunlight, filtered through the leaves and limbs of the ancient oak and dappled the lawn below while in its upper most branches a mating pair of bright yellow American Finches were perched watching him below.

He stepped down onto the sidewalk and began to slowly walk toward the shed. A gathering of Cardinals and Orioles were busily eating at several of the birdfeeders and as usual were spilling more on the ground than they actually ate.

As he passed by the huge oak tree, a voice with a Celtic lilt called out to him. "Now how would you be doin' this fine morn?"

"I wondered when you'd show up. The place looks even better than last year. Thanks." Jim took in the little man's unusual appearance. "After last summer, I thought I wouldn't see you again."

"Well, I don't much care for the younger set, they remind me of myself when I was..." the elf paused.

"A boy?" Jim filled in.

"No... just younger." the elf said, and then looked thoughtfully before continuing. "I understand you had some excitement around here after I left."

"You might say that. Someone tried to kill me! It had to do that bunch of bikers that lived across the way, just over there..." Jim said, pointing across the alley to a vacant lot. The town had bulldozed the old house to the ground a month earlier. You should have seen the commotion that took place here last Halloween.

The elf could tell the old man was winding up ready to retell the entire story as he had on many recent occasions to any and all that would stop to listen. "Hold up there lad, I've already heard all 'bout it?"
"Ugh?" Jim wore a puzzled expression. "How would you know?"

The little man smiled slyly. "We have ways of knowing lots of things."

Jim hesitated for a moment then trying not to sound like too much of an idiot asked in a low voice..."Magical ways?"

"Oh no lad, the wee lass to whom I sublet your apartment for the winter; she told me all about it she did." The elf grinned. "Aye, a fine time she had, said she'd never eaten any better in her life!"

And Midnight Came to Call

The Madison

Having run the last couple of blocks under the sweltering heat of the noonday sun, Tim pushed open one of two heavy glass doors. A welcome blast of air-conditioned comfort swept over his body from head to foot as he stepped through a second set of doors and entered the theater's lobby. The door's glass was heavily tinted, so that in comparison to the bright outside street just yards away, the dimly lit lobby appeared as dark as night, forcing the boy to give his eyes several moments to adjust to the change.

Tim glanced down at his wristwatch and saw that he had just made it under the wire. A good thing too as his manager stood by the food concession watching him hustle toward the staff's change room. The manager checked his own watch, looked up, and gave Tim a curt nod before returning his attention back to a technician who was busy installing a new popcorn machine behind the snack bar. Red-faced and still sweating profusely, Tim mopped his brow with the back of his hand blinking hard against the salty rivulets that ran down into and stung his eyes.

Inside the change room, Tim stood before his locker fighting with the troublesome combination lock while he thought about his conversation with the manager just the day before. Mr. Wallace had placed him on notice after he'd arrived ten minutes late for his shift. It wasn't as if Tim could blame the man, the manager had the patience of Job, a very useful trait when having to employ and work with teenagers. Thinking back, that had been the fourth time in the last several weeks Tim had arrived late, failing to greet the public as they arrived for the afternoon matinee.

He dialed in the combination for the third time and pulled down on the lock, this time he heard a sharp click and felt the shackle release. Pulling open the door, Tim reached in, grabbed his comb from the upper shelf, and ran it through his sweat-damped hair. A uniform jacket bearing the Madison Theater logo hung on the back hook of the locker. He pulled out the thread worn garment, taking a quick sniff near the armpit of the badly fitting maroon sports jacket before slipping it on. He made a mental note to take it home after shift and ask his mom to wash it, before it decided to leave the theater and walk off on its own. Adjusting his nametag and checking the batteries in his flashlight, he figured he was ready to go. "Ok folks, it's show time." Slamming the locker shut, he clicked the lock closed and headed out to a small podium in the lobby where he'd check and rip ticket stubs for the next hour or so.

Tim Walker had been working at the Madison since his sixteenth birthday, the day when Darnel Louis, his step dad had proclaimed it was high time the little bastard "got off his ass and made his own God damn money." The next day he began his search, it had taken him just one afternoon to land his job. Jimmy Worthington, aka "Jinxy," had been working at the Madison since the year before. Knowing one another since the second grade, his best friend had put in a good word on his behalf with Mr. Wallace.

Working at the Madison wasn't a bad job for kids his age. He'd run admittance before each show, then walk the side aisles with his flashlight. "Showing the flag," as the staff called it, took place once for adult audiences just after the show began but regularly at the top and bottom of each hour during a kid's matinee.

When you made your rounds through the darkened theater, you always made sure you held your flashlight tight to your hip and pointed down and slightly ahead of you. Doing so, gave the young couples in the back rows of "lover's lane" time to straighten up and pretend they were watching the movie before you actually walked by their seats. Considered both a matter of simple courtesy, it also served to ensure one's survival. This wasn't usually a big problem; for the most part these kids were about his own age and attended his school. The ones you had to watch out for were the guys belonging to the senior football team. Never considered a good idea; embarrassing a two hundred and fifty pound lineman and his date tended to bring about rather unfortunate consequences.

Keeping your attention level high and your flashlight low was even more important during the Saturday afternoon matinees when the bubble gummers packed in to see the buck-fifty horror marathons. The little creeps would throw crap at you as you passed their row or have their legs stuck out into the aisles at weird angles, tripping you intentionally or otherwise. Either way, if you weren't paying attention, sooner or later you'd regret it.

After the theater emptied, you flipped coins with your counterpart to decide who would work the garbage detail and who would run the vacuum. Running the vacuum was always preferable especially following the last show of the night. You never knew what you were going to find on the floors or stuffed between the seats. After the first couple of times collecting the trash, Tim came to learn just how piggish people could be as they sat in the dark and thought no one could see them. Marijuana roaches were pretty much a given but on occasion, he'd find used condoms up in lover's lane. A couple of months ago he even found a hypodermic needle.

That said, like every job, working in a movie theater had its perks too, but it certainly wasn't the pay; minimum wage if you were over eighteen, and a buck and a half less than that per hour if you weren't. Obviously, you got free admission to the theater but that was no big deal. After all, having seen glimpses of all the new movies while you were working, when you finally saw the movie on a day off, you already knew all the best parts, and how it would turn out in the end.

You could grab a small popcorn and a coke; they were free if the manager wasn't around, fifty cents for both if he was. The only problem was that you couldn't eat in public; you had to scarf it all down sitting in the staffroom by yourself, not much fun.

When you had a spare minute, and there were more than a few to fill between showings, you could hang out around the concession talking with the other staff and pretty much get paid for doing nothing, but after a while, the boredom got to all of them. He and the other kids would try to keep themselves busy in any way they could, always looking for ways to make the hours fly. Retrospectively, many years from now Tim would look back on his time spent at the Madison and realize that's where he learned to enjoy work.

The only job that Tim (or any of the other kids) didn't volunteer for were those thankfully infrequent times you'd have to venture down into the old theater's basement and bring up some additional popcorn bags or drink cups. He recalled his first trip down to the "dungeon" when Mr. Wallace had asked him to bring up a spare canister of cola syrup.

Opening the faded white door leading to the basement, he stood at the top of several long staircases, peering down into the inky blackness. The instant that door opened, the familiar warm smells of buttered popcorn and day old hotdogs vanished, replaced by the dank decades old odors that drifted up from the depths of the century-old foundation. The kids all agreed that it "wasn't as if it was a really disgusting smell, not something rotten, just something very old that hadn't seen the light of day"... in a very long time.

Unable to locate the basement's light switch, Tim had walked around the theater until he found Jinxy. As it turned out, you had to step down the first six stairs onto a small wooden landing where the cracked alabaster switch sat nailed into a thick wooden beam some five feet off the landing floor. Jinxy didn't bother going down to show him, he just grinned at his friend and shone his flashlight down into the abyss letting the beam play over the toggle switch.

Starting down the stairs Tim stepped onto the landing, reached up and hit the switch. Nothing happened... at least not at first. The lights didn't go on all at once but the individual bulbs each sort of flickered for several moments before glowing sullenly, emitting a pale sickly light that ever so slowly grew brighter. A little creeped out, the teen started downward along a long flight of wooden stairs that ran toward the basement floor some twenty-five feet or more below the landing. Tim glanced up toward Jinxy intending to ask him to come down with him but his friend had already turned away muttering something about having to go for his break.

The basement of the theater was without a doubt, the deepest of any you'd find in Chase. The Madison, built before the advent of moving pictures, existed in a time when theaters ran live performances. At the time of its building, the theater was the toast of the state and it, like all the best theaters of the day, would often have motorized lifts and trap doors incorporated below the main stage. During intermissions, these lifts could bring an entirely different set up to stage level quickly and with little effort. The Madison's overly large basement, designed to accommodate these anticipated upgrades awaited a day that would never arrive. When the surrounding coalmines played out near the turn of the century, the town's principal employer pulled up stakes taking three-quarters of the town's population with it. Seventy-five years later, the town was still pretty much the same size as it had been at the end of the First World War.

Tim stepped down the first few stairs then stopped, taking a hard look at the open door behind him. For some reason he couldn't quite grasp, the hair on the back of his neck bristled and a chill ran up his spine. Not being the nervous, overly imaginative type, he just attributed the unease to having to navigate his way down the steep, somewhat rickety stairs. That together with the flickering of the already ineffectual lighting produced all manner of odd shadows that wavered and played along the walls and across the dark dingy floor that still lay a good distance below.

Given the apparent age of the wiring that ran out from the light switch, he guessed the electric lights probably dated back to the 20's. Tim didn't know it but the system first installed at the turn of the century received its last upgrade in the 40's. Two decades ago, an electrician replaced several breakers and installed several additional light receptacles in the basement but only on the condition that the management promise never to use anything stronger than 40-watt bulbs. The tradesman who did the work told the previous manager that if he hadn't been such a close friend of the owner he would've insisted they rip out and replace the whole system or he would have reported them to the inspector.

As he moved down the stairs, Tim felt the chill in the air grow with his descent. He stepped onto a wooden planked floor and felt it give slightly beneath his weight; he'd expected solid concrete. Pausing, he took a good long look around. The basement, divided into several large open areas stored numerous boxes and wooden crates, each piled one on top of the other. The lack of adequate lighting gave the whole place an ambiance that reminded Tim of paging through an age-yellowed newspaper. Anyone gazing about the basement would invariably have his or her eyes drawn to a natural focal point; a large unlit opening placed in the center of the farthest wall where presumably a large sliding cargo door had once hung. The opening seemed to command attention; its black gaping maw rebuffing the feeble attempts of the cellar lights that failed to penetrate its depths any further than several feet. There and then Tim decided he didn't like the place and the sooner he left the better he'd like it.

It took him almost five minutes to locate the cola syrup; stashed along with a dozen other canisters of various flavors, they lay on their sides, stacked beneath the darkened stairwell. He had to use his flashlight to read the small printed labels while all the while checking his six every few seconds. Something had certainly given him a nasty case of the heebie-jeebies. His subconscious whispered that whatever it was, lay watching and waiting in the jet-black gap just beyond that stark empty doorway.

He finally located the cola syrup; shit could they make the writing any smaller on the freaking labels? Without further ado, he grabbed the thirty-pound canister as if it were a small can of chicken soup and scooted up the steep stairs in what had to be some kind of record. Tim didn't bother stopping on the small landing to flick off the basement light switch but continued to take the stairs two at a time until he reached the top and stepped onto the main floor of the theatre. Somewhat winded after his climb, he set the canister on the floor and bent over as he peered back into the cavernous basement. For a second, Tim considered going back down to the landing and turning off the lights, but instead simply muttered, "Screw that noise," then closed the door tight.

Tim watched Janice Pullman as she sashayed into Bernstein's café with a small group of other girls. Janice stood out in a crowd. A pretty little blonde with a great figure, Janice liked Tim for some reason he never quite figured out, she could probably have any guy she wanted in school. Tim thought himself an average Joe in nearly all respects; medium height, medium weight, medium brown hair of medium length; neither blue nor brown even his hazel eyes took the middle road. Most of his grades in school were above average, but not by much, even though he was quite aware that if he bothered to apply himself he could be near the top of his class.

She was about to sit down at a table with her friends until she spied him sitting on one of the bar stools at the lunch counter. Janice twittered something to the other girls at the table then walked toward him while the other girls watched and giggled among themselves.

"Hey you." Smiling, she slid onto the stool beside him. "Buy me a coke?" Her light blue cotton dress matched her flashing eyes while her long blonde platinum hair trailed down her back falling nearly to her waist. As average as Tim was, Janice was exceptional.

"Not a chance, it's your turn isn't it?" Tim grinned even as he reached for the wallet in his back pants pocket. "Wasn't sure you'd show up valley girl. How was cheerleader practice?"

"Computer club was very interesting today thank you!" Janice was about as atypical as anyone could get. Beauty and brains wrapped up in a nice little package. She and Tim had known each other since first grade and seemed to have taken an instant liking for one another.

Tim waved and caught a young waitress's attention behind the counter then ordered Janice's drink.

"You working tonight?" she asked. It was already Thursday and they still hadn't made plans for the weekend. She knew Tim, familiar with the way her mind worked, realized she was asking if they could go out Friday or Saturday night. She hated to press him, Tim's butt head stepdad had been on his case more often lately. Darnel would usually focus on Tim needing to put in more hours at the theater, reminding him that when he was Tim's age, he'd already quit school having gone to work and helping support his family.

The lay-about would go on to anyone who would listen when how at the tender age of only sixteen he had signed up with the B&L Railroad to pound spikes eighteen hours a day. He'd recite that, or some other bullshit story, depending upon what he was drinking that day. Of course, he didn't add that he hadn't held a steady job since. Janice wondered why his mother put up with the man; she was so nice.

He answered the girl, "Yeah, but only until eight. Short shift though, just covering for Jinxy." He paused and looked into her eyes, "wanna do something later?"

She bit the side of her lip and looked past him, through the café window and out into the street. Tim knew the look. A blatant over achiever, Janice took her grades seriously. If she didn't ace a test, he wouldn't see much of her until she corrected the situation. "Take me for a walk, but I can't be out later than ten, big test tomorrow... I'll study 'til I see you."

"No problem, be at your place around eight-thirty. By the way, Mr. Wallace asked if I'd work the matinee on Saturday, that'll leave me free after five. Think about what you'd like to do."

Bill Sheridan was a small man with a big thirst. A recovering alcoholic for the last twenty years, Bill would fall off the wagon then a few weeks or months later, climb back on. Ed, his sponsor at AA would frequently point out to Bill he was just one of those guys who'd climb the twelve steps then tumble back down just as he was reaching the top. The old dig didn't bother Bill in the least seeing as how Ed was the one person in his life that had never given up on him over the years.

A plumber by trade, Bill was a good one when he wasn't on the sauce, but his problem would inevitably become his employer's either sooner or later. When that happened, he'd find himself out of a job and justified to run off the rails entirely. Hitting bottom yet again Bill would slowly pick himself back up. The last time that happened was four months ago.

Ed phoned him the other day saying that he might have found a job Bill could tackle. It wasn't full time, not even part time, but it would last a couple of days and slide a few bucks his way. The job was located in Chase, a small town about an hour's drive from the city. The town's old theater was having water troubles and would probably need replacement of its aging pipes. Bill assured Ed he could handle the job and wouldn't let him down. Ed wasn't too worried, if Bill was anything it was predictable, his friend wasn't scheduled for another meltdown for at least another couple of months.

Next morning Bill arrived at the rear of the Madison, reversing the old Ford Econovan up to the maintenance doors. The manager of the theater walked out to meet the vehicle, the faded green lettering on the back and sides of the white rusted van proudly announced the arrival of the "Super Plumber" whose motto read, "Never pay until we make your day!" Stopping the van, Bill got out and greeted the manager who stood near the back doors.

Slamming the van door, Bill turned and approached the manager wiping his brow with a handkerchief while proclaiming, "Man! She'll be a hot one today!" Wallace looked up thinking the comment appropriate, the temperature was already eighty-five, there wasn't a cloud in the sky, and it was only ten in the morning.

Wallace examined the haggard features of the forty-something year old fellow who walked toward him. Not more than five feet high, Wallace figured his twelve-year-old son had more meat on his bones than did the plumber, whose appearance suggested that if a stiff wind came up, the man would simply blow away. Still, having a small stature could be handy if you had to crawl into tight narrow spaces, something men in the trade were expected to do. Something within the man bespoke of unusual strength in proportion to his size, that strength confirmed as Bill took Wallace's outstretched hand and shook it firmly.

"Appreciate you coming out so quickly, as you can imagine, a business like ours can hardly open its doors if we can't even offer our guests a glass of water." Wallace went on to explain the problem that had come to his attention just a day earlier as both the men walked into the Madison and made their way into the basement.

After the brilliant sunlight of the parking lot, the men found the basement's dim lighting to be a bit of a challenge, both Wallace and Bill gripped the stair's railings tightly while cautiously feeling their way down the steps with their feet. By the time they reached the floor, their eyes were pretty much accustomed to the low light. Bill watched as Wallace reached over to the wall and pulled off a large flashlight from its recharging station.

"Bit dark where we'll be going." Wallace led the way toward a large opening in the far wall of the basement.

The men passed through the doorway and into an area that Bill figured measured twenty by twenty feet at the outset. Christ, but it was dark in here, he'd have to bring down the twin-halogen work lights before he even began to examine the rats nest of pipes that ran along the walls and floor. As Wallace's light played deeper into the room, Bill recognized the old style well head and pump assembly that sat near the back of the room, the damn thing should be in a museum, it was a wonder to think it had lasted anywhere near this long.

"I'll bet you haven't seen too many of these, we get our water from a well instead of the town's water mains." Wallace was pleased to see this was the case from the rather surprised expression on the tradesman's face.

"How is the water? You get it tested regularly, right?" Bill asked. Wells were finicky and the water quality could change in a matter of months.

"Send it off to the lab every six months. Water's sweet as can be... I even take the stuff home with me. No chemicals you know, none of that fluoride, chlorine, and stuff." Wallace continued to watch the man's face that was now unreadable. Bill was recalling a distant memory.

"My grandparents had a well. My grandfather drilled it himself." Bill paused and looked back to Wallace who now wore a questioning look. Bill continued, "They lived near the river, the ground water levels were pretty high.

Granddad only had to drill down twenty-five feet 'til he hit good water. Put in what's called a sand point."

"Oh yes… a sand point." Wallace nodded.

Bill could tell the man hadn't the faintest idea what he was talking about, not that it was important. What was important was what had happened when he was twelve years old.

"Yup, good water until the river rose up one year and flooded a bit, not to the point where it hit their home or anything, just up a bit more than usual. Problem was the well got contaminated; they got sick. Both of them passed on within a week." Bill shook his head. "Never trusted well water since… won't drink the stuff."

They were both quiet for several moments. Bill broke the silence, "I should start by getting my stuff down here. You know Mr. Wallace; I can tell you right now that the building inspector is going to insist you replace the well water with treated water from the town's mains. This just isn't done anymore… that said, this shouldn't be a problem." Bill pointed upward, "see that big copper pipe there, 'bout half way up and runnin' along the far wall? That's the town supply. I can tap into that pretty quick, won't cost you much. But I'll still have to tear out the well head and seal'er up, won't be up to code if I don't."

"Well do what you have too I suppose, don't have much choice." The men turned and walked back into the main basement. "Will you need a hand carrying anything downstairs? I can have a couple of my young fellows help you if you do." Wallace replaced the flashlight into the charger near the bottom of the stairs.

"Thanks Mr. Wallace but no. If I run into something I can't handle I'll let you know." He smiled at the manager then the two men began the long climb up the stairs, heading back into the land of light.

Tim made it over to Janice's house just a few minutes before the bottom of the hour and was just about to ring the bell when she opened the door. "See ya mom I'm going now," She called out. Tim heard her mother call out to him, "Hi Tim, have my girl home by ten now. It's a school night."

"No problem Mrs. P." He smiled at the girl who tossed her head and rolled her eyes while closing the front door behind her.

The night was warm and pleasant, a soft breeze played in their hair bringing with it the aroma of summer flowers and green foliage. Ten minutes later, they were talking and holding hands, slowly walking along Main Street where the shops were readying to close their doors for the night. The kids watched as their employees hurried through their aisles with push brooms or wheeled their outdoor displays back inside the stores for the night.

"The water's still out at the theater, we're giving bottled water to customers if they ask for it. Of course, everyone does, people take anything that's free." He paused, "At the staff meeting, Mr. Wallace was telling us the theater is going to start showing classic horror films each weekend of summer starting the first week of July. They'll have two showings, one at seven the other at nine fifteen. I just know I'm going to be stuck doing both shows. A lot of the guys are going to be leaving on holiday with their parents. What a drag." They walked along for another moment or two when he realized that Janice had stopped walking. He looked back at her; she had a funny look on her face.

"Tim, that might not be a bad thing, it might keep you busy and out of trouble." She could see he was puzzled, "my parents, my parents told me we'll be going up to the lake for six weeks. Can you believe it, six freaking weeks! We leave July fourth." She wore a sad expression and watched his face as he became sullen.

"Six weeks? Oh Jan." he turned away and stared through the picture window of the bakery. The main lights were already off; the interior was only dimly lit. "Sure won't be much of a summer without you. When will you be back?"

"August 22; your birthday!" she tried to lighten the mood, "I'll find something extra nice for your present this year?" then gave his arm a squeeze and kissed his cheek. "I know it seems forever, I'll miss you too..."

Turning back to her, he gave her a long hug, burying his nose into her silky hair. Her perfume wafted in the air, God but he was going to miss the girl.

"Ok, turn on the ladies bathroom sink faucets now," Bill yelled up to a girl that stood at the top of the stairs. In turn, the girl called out to another who stood near the bathroom doors, "ok, turn it on." The teenage boy inside cranked each of the three faucet handles to the "on" position. The air-water combination spat and hissed into the basins with amazing force, splashing up and outward so that the bottom front of the boy's shirt and pants were soaked within seconds. "Oh shit..." Tim could already hear the others laughing and joking at his expense. A moment later, the water ran smoothly into the bowls.

Upon hearing the odd spats, gurgles and burps, the girl nearest to the bathroom door stuck her head in to see what was happening. Tim was standing near the paper hand-towel dispenser, a small bundle in his hand desperately rubbing his clothing. She smiled broadly, "Need some diapers in there do we Timmy?" she turned with a giggle and yelled to the others the water was on.

A half hour later the Madison's toilets, sinks, and soft drink dispensers were all up and back in action. Bill Sheridan had gotten the most important job completed in a fraction of the time he had first estimated. The theater's secondary pipes leading up from the well were in terrific condition, he couldn't believe they had been installed at the time of the original construction. All he had to do was reconnect and redirect the water from the town's mains into the original pipes. He wound up having spent more of his time inspecting all the piping in the old place than he did in the actual reconnection. In the end, only the boiler, periodically replaced since the building of the theater, looked as if it were on its last legs, but that wasn't his problem, he'd just make Wallace aware of the situation.

The floor of the pump room was concrete rather than wood, a necessity since wet wood eventually rotted. Bill sat on a large toolbox in the center of the room holding a smoke in one hand and a coffee in the other. The tradesman looked across the room at the corroded well seal that rose up several inches above the hundred-year-old concrete. The large pump connected to the wellhead by a short length of large diameter piping ran off to a storage tank sitting a few feet further away. It wouldn't take much to remove the storage tank, a newer aluminum model; it was probably installed a decade ago and when empty was probably lightweight. It was the pump and the well seal that gave him the most concern.

Like most repairs or renovations undertaken, any real difficulties the recent contractor might encounter were more often than not directly associated with the incompetence or error of the previous builder or installer. They may have cut corners in their work, installed cheap or even used components. In the case of the well seal and pump, the crew that poured the concrete floor in the pump room hadn't bothered to remove the apparatus first but simply poured the cement around and atop the footings. This meant that Bill would have to remove a good chunk of the concrete floor before he could release the equipment. He just hoped the bastards hadn't poured the floor any thicker than they had too.

The plumber rapped the floor using a small two-pound sledge. Not intended to break up the floor it would simply tell Bill where the ground below the concrete had slumped down and away from the floor itself, perhaps creating a hollow. This would be a good place to start the actual excavation. After ten minutes of poking around, he couldn't find a single weak point on the floor near the equipment. He scratched his head and cursed aloud, this was going to be a ball buster!

He started out using a ten-pound sledge gouging out a shallow ring in the concrete around the equipment footings. An electric jackhammer would accomplish the actual cutting; it would be noisy, dusty work. Bill inserted his earplugs, positioned the filter mask over his nose and mouth, and then pulled down a clear polycarbonate face shield that would protect him from the sharp chips of concrete and stone that would soon start flying about.

It was heavy work; the type that Bill used to do when he was much younger, the kind usually assigned to a helper or apprentice. He'd only been at it for fifteen minutes or so and hadn't made as much progress as he would have liked. The concrete was thick and very hard. He had to battle for every inch he removed. His chest and arms were already feeling it, they'd be aching when he got home tonight, he'd have a long soak in the tub and take a couple of Tylenol before he hit the hay.

He was about to stop for a well-deserved break when the blade suddenly broke through into a hollow sending the entire jackhammer plunging downward stopping only when the hilt of the machine met the concrete surface. Bill released the trigger and pulled the blade from the hole. If the concrete was thinner here, maybe he'd get lucky after all and things would go a bit easier. He positioned the blade near the latest hole and pulled the trigger a second time. The hammer rattled and clanked, sending up the occasional bright spark as the steel blade met stone, chiseling its way deeper into the hard gray surface. Once again, the blade punched through the concrete and into a hollow, only this time when the hilt of the heavy tool struck the floor surrounding the blade, a large chunk of the floor broke and fell away down into a black crevasse. If Bill hadn't kept a tight grip on the hammer, it too would have joined the chunk of cement floor that fell into the hole.

He placed the electric hammer against the far wall and walked out of the pump room into the larger basement before removing his safety equipment. Back in the pump room, the dust was still chokingly thick in the air, Bill would have to wait a few minutes and let it settle out before returning. Then he'd have a good look at whatever it was he had just broken into. Already, even through the cloud of dust, Bill could tell it was deep.

That small hollow might be a sinkhole. Only last week, he watched with incredulity when the evening news cameras had caught the scene of an entire house disappearing in slow motion, collapsing into a huge crevasse. Luckily, the homeowner had noticed a large hole in their backyard earlier in the day and called the city. The men who came out to investigate knew exactly what they might have on their hands and evacuated the entire neighborhood straight way. Otherwise, the owner and his family might have been in the house when the earth swallowed it up. All said, Bill figured the odds of something like that to be pretty remote, but you never could tell.

Bill considered going upstairs for a breath of fresh air but his overalls were already full of dust and he didn't feel like stripping down before he finished the job for the day. Instead, he lit up a smoke and walked about the perimeter of the dim basement to kill a few minutes. Halfway around the large room he paused looking into a dark corner beside a couple of wooden crates. An all too familiar shape had grabbed his attention. Stooping down, he reached into the corner, grasped a glass bottle, and held it up into the light.

A fifth of Scotch whiskey. Bill held it up to the light, a nearly full bottle at that! He turned it so he could read the label; the brand was one of his favorites. He wiped a finger over the glass, there was damn little dust on it… couldn't have been down here for too long. In all probability, one of the kids upstairs had hidden it, intending to bring it to a party after shift. He removed the cap and took a sniff, God but didn't it smell great. He quickly replaced the cap knowing he shouldn't tempt himself, Christ he was already thinking about taking a snort. Bill bent down, about to return the bottle to where he had found it but knew he couldn't. Instead, he'd stash it in his toolbox and bring it home with him. He'd save wrestling with his conscience for later that evening.

She had been sleeping in the dark for a long, long time. So long, she couldn't remember the light of day, the moon, the stars in the sky or even the warmth of the sun upon her face. What wasn't forgotten nor forgiven, was the day her supposed friends and kin had walled her up, sealing her within a small cave and burying her alive beneath the earth. They had placed the required talismans and charms about her living tomb to ensure against any escape while a shaman from a neighboring tribal village had uttered the words that began her long dream.

A rumble in the earth about her had disrupted her slumber and she had stirred in her crypt sensing that something had somehow changed. Quickly awakening, her mind traced and probed the walls of her tomb until she discovered what had disturbed her dark dream. A thin crack in the structure's ceiling had formed, fresh air accompanied by a fine stream of dust showered down upon her withered flesh and arid bones. The bonds of the old religion had loosened somewhat and while the tiny breach wouldn't yet allow her to fully escape her prison it would permit her to reach out beyond it and that would be enough for now.

Allowing her mind's essence to slip up through the nearly hairline fracture in the rock ceiling, it wound slowly upwards, moving within the narrow but ever-widening space toward what it perceived to be an incredible brilliance after so dark a night. She paused, unsure of what lay above her in the open air. She detected the familiar sounds but it was so long ago; she struggled to remember what made them... then suddenly she knew she was no longer alone. Someone approached.

Upstairs, Wallace sat in his office with the door closed. Several large accounting ledgers were sprawled across his desk. Realizing the cacophony that had been assaulting his ears for the last half hour seemed to have abated, at least temporarily; he removed his reading glasses and rubbed his eyes. His vision was getting steadily worse lately, he was spending too much time on the books. Why didn't the owners break down and get him a decent accounting program? Because old man Graham was about a hundred and ninety years old and didn't know how to work one, that's why! Time for a stretch, he'd fetch a coffee from the concession and drop down and see how Bill was making out.

Meanwhile down in the basement, Bill had walked back into the pump room and was about to place the liquor into his tool box but stopped when he saw a faint glow coming from the hole in the concrete. Damned odd he thought as he approached the break in the floor. Drawing closer, the dim light shimmered slightly. Unable to decide on its color, the light suddenly glittered then began to fade. He bent low staring down into the small but deep abyss. Blinking his eyes and shaking his head, he wondered what was he seeing? There was something else mixed within the light, something utterly dark that made the surrounding shadows in the hole almost bright by comparison.

A decrepit odor reached his nostrils, the powerful smell of old death. Seeking to filter the stench, he automatically brought his free arm up to his face pressing the sleeve against his nose. His eyes opened wide as whatever had lain hidden just beneath the lip of the broken concrete suddenly leaped upward, the blackness flung itself toward him, grabbing him by his head and shoulders. The liquor bottle fell from his hands breaking in two on the edge of the floor before the pieces of glass fell into the hole.

Bill tried to scream but the sound died in his throat, just as he did moments later when she dragged him headfirst down into the chasm. Crushed and deformed, the bones of his arms, legs, and skull cracked in a morbid requiem as she worked his corpse ever deeper, sliding it between the broken slabs of concrete, rocks, stones, and earth. Approaching Bill's unintentional breech within the crypt's ceiling, the now unrecognizable mass of reddish goo seeped and ran across the inner surface before dripping and dribbling onto the parched arid remains that lay below. Wherever the droplets made contact with her skin, the flesh bubbled up and swelled unnaturally, greedily consuming its feast of bloody tissue. Ever so slowly, her body began to reshape itself, assuming a barely recognizable human form, or as much as she ever had truly been.

Wallace thanked the girl at the concession for the coffee and walked to the door leading to the basement stairs. His hand gripping the doorknob, he paused for a moment thinking that he heard an oddly muted sound coming from behind the basement door. Whatever it might have been it was gone, if he even heard it at all. The manager turned the knob. Opening the door, he looked down the long flight of stairs that led into the dim cellar and began his cautious descent. Upon stepping down onto the wooden floor, he called out Bill's name. Receiving no response he did so a second time before crossing the floor and entering the pump room.

The twin floodlights illuminated the room, their bright halogen beams casting overly dark shadows among the piping and other equipment. The stark contrasts between light and dark were eerily familiar, reminding him of a movie scene where a group of astronauts stood in silent awe before a rectangular monolith recently unearthed within a lunar crater. He walked over to a jagged break in the floor and leaned over. Standing above, Wallace peered down into the pitch-black abyss, how deep did that go he wondered? Suddenly he caught a strong smell of scotch whiskey but only for a moment, then it was gone.

Wallace looked about the rest of the basement, pausing for a moment before beginning the steep climb up the stairway. He walked out to the parking lot at the back of the theater, the van was still there but hadn't turned a wheel; the man was nowhere to be found. Maybe he had left to grab a bite to eat or something. A few hours later, around dinnertime, Wallace checked the basement, once again calling out several times. Unable to locate the plumber, Wallace figured Bill must have gone home for the night. He switched off the basement lights and went back to check on his staff, the theater would be opening for the evening show in a few minutes time.

Not long after the last showing, the audience and staff had already left the building. It was just after eleven when Wallace checked and locked all the doors. Leaving the theater through the back doors, he noticed the plumbing van had remained unmoved from its original position. It stood parked on the dark, nearly vacant lot. Checking the vehicle and finding it unlocked and unoccupied, the manager felt honor bound to ensure the contractor wasn't still somehow in the theater. Although highly unlikely, Wallace considered the man might have injured himself and could even now be lying down in the dark basement, unable to move or even call out for help.

The manager reentered the theater, walked down the back hallway, and opened the basement door. Stepping down onto the first landing, his hand moved atop a thick wooden timber until he felt the familiar shape of the light switch beneath his fingers and flicked it upward. Standing on the landing, Wallace called down to Bill several times, waiting a minute or so for the lights to brighten fully before stepping downward and into the silent gloom. Wallace had descended these same steps a thousand times over the years, and unlike some of the kids, the basement held no trepidation for him. At least not until tonight, tonight something was amiss. His heart was starting to pound while his stomach tightened up then began doing flip-flops. Reaching the basement floor, he reached out and took the powerful flashlight from the recharger on the side of the wall. Quickly and in near panic he flicked it on, sweeping its bright beam across the floors and walls. The brilliant light instantly dispelled any menace within the shadows and banished the dark silly notions that had threaded their way through his thoughts only moments earlier. He felt his confidence rise.

Wallace carefully walked the entire basement, starting with the pump room then made his way upstairs where he searched the whole theater until he had satisfied himself that Bill was nowhere in the theater. Annoyed with the man's irresponsibility, he locked up and drove home. He'd have words with the fellow the next day.

Somewhat later, in the lonely hours before dawn, she explored her new surroundings, beginning in the basement's century old, but to her reckoning, still absurdly young foundations. She released her mind's essence. Moving in the deep silence, she swept up through the abyss feeling her way through the dark, sullen basement before discovering the stairway leading toward the main floor. If anyone was there to watch, she may have appeared as a semi-transparent specter, truly ghost-like as she floated up then above the wooden steps but suddenly, she felt her strength fail and depart. Too soon, it was too soon. Retracing her way to the pump room, she hovered shortly then slid vapor like, vanishing into the black pit and returning to her tomb. She must rest... yes, she would rest, and here she would wait until she once more grew strong.

Tim stood near the theater's front entrance watching the people leave and thanking them for their patronage. The last of them, a middle-aged man and woman smiled and nodded his way as they walked through the door and out onto the quiet streets. He checked his watch, ten forty-five, time to get the vacuum going.

Tim looked back toward the concession stand where Andrea had already cleaned the popcorn maker and was starting to Windex the candy display glass below the serving counter. Farther away near the auditorium doors, he saw Mr. Wallace speaking to Jason. The young staff member held a large garbage bag in one hand and a pair of rubber gloves in the other. Jason would be informing the manager that his parents had suddenly decided to take the family on vacation next week and that he wouldn't be able to work his shifts. Jason had already warned Tim before hand and apologized, knowing that Tim would likely be stuck covering for him.

Sure enough, as Tim walked to the cleaning room, Mr. Wallace came up and asked if he'd mind covering a couple of Jason's weekend late shifts. Tim smiled accommodatingly and agreed. It was no big deal. After all, Janice had left with her family just that morning and wouldn't be back until mid-August, he might as well make a few extra bucks. Tim asked the manager if the police had located the plumber who had gone missing the previous day, Mr. Wallace told him they hadn't as far as he was aware.

Earlier in the afternoon, Bill's employer drove out with another employee and picked up the van. The owner of the company apologized for Bill's absence adding it might be a couple of weeks until the company could complete the repairs downstairs. Since the water was already running, Wallace said the delay shouldn't be a problem.

During his conversation with Tim, Mr. Wallace didn't mention that Bill's employer told him the man had a serious drinking problem and that it wasn't the first time he had done something like this. That was when Wallace remembered the smell of scotch whiskey in the basement. After the plumbers left, he had called the police, saying that he suspected the tradesman may have started drinking in the basement, and then simply left the theater in the afternoon to go on a bender. He hoped it would help if they were still searching for the man.

Tim found the vacuuming went quickly that night. The Meryl Streep movie had ensured the Friday night audience would be an older crowd that translated into a lot less work cleaning up. Besides, Tim didn't have to vacuum between the seat rows, just concentrate on the main aisles. Mr. Wallace had told him the Saturday morning shift would take care of that job before the Madison opened.

Tugging on one of two large double doors that opened next to lover's lane, Tim stepped into the auditorium struggling with the vacuum's hose and canister, each insisted bouncing off or catching on the edge of the doorframes. After several attempts, he finally succeeded in dragging the awkward bulk into the room. The theater sat in total darkness with the exception of the two exit signs positioned above the back doors that opened on either side of the big screen, their dim orange glow provided the only illumination. Jason must have turned off the main lights out after garbage detail. No big deal, Tim leaned the long pipe and sweeper head against a seat and began to walk through the narrow back row of seats toward the other side of the theater where the room's light switches were located.

Tonight the large room was silent. Mr. Wallace hadn't bothered piping in the usual elevator music, something for which Tim and the other kids were only too thankful. As Tim reached the halfway point between the seats, he thought he caught something out of the corner of his eye, down near the "neck breakers," the seats nearest to the screen. It wasn't unheard of that someone either had fallen asleep during the movie or had intentionally hidden among the vacant rows waiting for the theater to close so they could rob the place, but nothing like that had ever happened since he had been there.

Still he stood in place watching the seats, nothing moved. Tim walked on but kept an eye fixed in the general area. There! He knew he saw something this time but now it had moved further over toward the left of the screen and away from where he stood. Whoever it was had dressed in dark clothing. Picking up speed Tim ran toward a bank of light switches mounted on the wall closest to the entrance doors. He had almost arrived when a sudden motion off to his right nearly caused him to jump out of his skin.

Jason stood next to the door he had just pushed open, "Well, I'm done. See you in a couple of weeks." Then seeing the startled look on Tim's face, Jason couldn't help but laugh.

Tim told him to shut up and hit the light switches, using his palm and lifting the six toggles together as a single group, turning all the lights on at once. "There's somebody still here! Down there in the neck breakers... saw 'em just before you came in!" Jason quit laughing; his face grew serious.

The boys stared down toward the front rows of seats sitting nearest to the screen. Nothing moved. After a few minutes, Tim looked to his co-worker who was looking at him with a smirk. "Oh yeah, right."

Tim countered, "No man, I'm telling you I saw someone!" He started walking down the carpeted aisle towards the screen. Jason followed him a few feet behind.

"I already did the garbage, walked through all the rows, there was no one here," Jason stated matter of factly then as they neared the seating area he followed up with far less certainty. "I'm sure I'd have seen someone, wouldn't I?"

Tim didn't answer but quickly walked to the far left side of the theater leaving Jason on the right. Then both the boys moved down together on each side, both looking across each of the six front rows of seating. Nothing. "I was sure I saw something."

Tim's vacuuming went quickly since Jason stuck around talking to him about the girls on staff and how he thought it funny how Andrea's tits seemed to get just a little bigger every week. Andrea was one of those late bloomers whose breast size simply refused to keep up with her age group. The boys correctly suspected she was wearing falsies or stuffing Kleenex into her bra. Jason held the door for Tim as he dragged the vacuum canister out the door. Jason shut off the lights and let the door close softly behind them.

Between the first and second rows of seats nearest the screen, a dark shadow rose over the seat backs, hovered shortly, and then floated over the rows of empty seats, moving toward the back of the darkened theater. Every so often, the jet-black shadow was replaced by a flickering gray cloud, almost as if a television set had been tuned to a vacant channel for several seconds, before growing dark once more.

She had been tempted to hunt within the darkened theater; she was still so very hungry. Bill Sheridan had made a nice appetizer but she much desired a full course meal. Still, one didn't hunt in one's own backyard. She had learned and paid for that mistake so long ago. This time, she would be patient, she still didn't know enough about the strange new world in which she had awoken, but she found the movie to be quite informative even if not quite to her own taste.

Saturday afternoon, Tim arrived at work a little earlier than usual. Mr. Wallace had asked Jinxy to teach him and Rory, another of the newer guys, how to change the sign on the front marquee. It was another hot one but at least the front of the theater faced north and the boys could work on the sign in the building's shade. There was nothing to it; the boys changed the sign's lettering quickly and without difficulty. Afterward, Tim joked, saying that maybe the manager would have to have Jinxy teach Rory how to wipe his ass after taking a crap. While Jinxy and Rory put away the ladder, Tim remained out front of the theater for another minute enjoying the fresh summer air before going back inside to his duties. He looked up at the marquee sign, black letters on the white background it read,

Summer Horror Spectacular
DRACULA LIVES!
A New Terrifying Classic Each Saturday!

They used bright red letters to spell Dracula Lives! The manager thought it would give the sign a little more "Pizzazz," looking at the sign a second time Tim thought Mr. Wallace might be right.

The horror flick ended around eleven thirty and only ten minutes after that the place was empty of people. Rather than have the kids stay and clean up until well after midnight, the manager kicked them out with the suggestion they go straight home. The next shift would take care of the clean up before the doors opened Sunday evening.

Tim left the theater walking out the back doors with Mr. Wallace and the other staff. A couple of parents waited in cars, waiting to give their girls a ride home. Tim and Jinxy said their good nights to the others then walked over to the rack and unlocked their bikes. Rory strolled up beside them.

Seeing only his and Tim's bike in the rack, Jinxy piped up, "where's your ride man?"

"Got a flat. I should have fixed it this morning." Rory passed the rack and began walking across the parking lot. As an afterthought, he raised a hand in the air without looking behind him, "See you guys tomorrow," and then kept walking.

Tim and Jinxy watched Rory leave, the other boy turned onto the next street then walked from their sight. The two boys mounted their bikes and rode off the lot. Half way to Tim's house, their paths parted, and each of the boys finished his journey home alone.

Rory walked along the sidewalk. It was a hot muggy night, the day had been a scorcher, and as he crossed Main Street, he could still feel the heat rising up from the sun-warmed asphalt. The streets were pretty much deserted except for the odd car. The shops along the street had all closed except for Bernstein's café, and it would close in another hour or so. A police car sat on the curb out front and two cops faced one another in a window booth, each sipping coffee, and chatting with the owner who stood next to the table. As Rory passed the window, one of the cops inside gave him a hard look before recognizing the boy, and then giving him a friendly nod.

The boy left Main Street and turned onto the side street that ran north toward his house, now only about a half mile distant. Rory looked behind him as he made the turn. Ever since he left the parking lot behind the theater he couldn't shake the feeling he was being followed. At first, he thought maybe Tim and Jinxy were trying to pull one on him, but they lived in the opposite direction and he'd been walking for almost fifteen minutes. The sensation left him briefly when he had passed the café but returned only a block later.

He chided himself for feeling this way but then remembered he'd watched pretty much near half the horror movie as he made his rounds or stood quietly in the back of the auditorium killing time. Simply put, the movie must have had some merit. It had obviously given him a good case of the creeps. Adults referred to it as being able to rationalize your emotions but having just turned fifteen, Rory had only recently discovered that simply knowing why he felt scared was often enough to break its hold on him. Tonight that wasn't the case.

Walking down the poorly lit street, overgrown hedges crowding the narrow sidewalk and the tall dark trees on either side spreading their upper branches arch like above the street drew the night even closer about him. Rory started to walk faster moving out into the center of the roadway just in case something thought about jumping out at him from the shadows. The night had been still and quiet but suddenly a cool wind picked up blowing through the leaves and branches. Though not a cold wind, it still chilled him to the bone and he realized he was shaking from fear. Something was coming for him, he just knew it.

He picked up the pace, walking faster now his head swiveling about as he glanced beside and behind him while moving down the street. Whatever it was, it was coming ever closer. He started into a slow run. The additional speed began to make him feel a little better and calmed his nerves a little. Only a few days earlier, Rory's mom had bought him a popular brand of sneakers, and as advertised, the Runner's Mate footwear was living up to its claims, they actually made him feel as though he was running on air. Rory increased his jog to a dead run suddenly feeling exhilaration as the wind rushed through his hair and clothes. He was making good time. Rory could even make out the porch light burning at the front door of his house. It wouldn't be long until he was in the kitchen eating a peanut butter sandwich and drinking a tall glass of chocolate milk... just a few more minutes away...

It was just before nine in the morning when the local Crime Scene Investigator's camera whirred and clicked several times before the policewoman picked up a single Runner's Mate shoe, carefully placing it in a plastic bag and attaching a label. She moved on to the corpse that lay face down on the dewy lawn. Collecting a rat-tailed comb and a thin worn black wallet from the back pocket of the dead boy's jeans, she photographed each article placing each in a separate bag. Slowly and methodically, the woman documented her activities, penning her detailed observations into an unused notebook that would hold the evidence leading to the identity and subsequent prosecution of Rory Jackman's murderer.

The CSI member waved to the two men who waited several yards away. Ron Charles, the uniformed cop that had nodded to Rory when the boy passed the café window the night before had been first on the scene earlier that morning. Now he and a grim-faced detective approached the body. Bending low, they carefully turned the boy over. Fixed and staring, Rory's death-shrouded eyes met the saddened eyes of each officer. His last expression was an unnatural rictus of fear and terror, his mouth gaped wide allowing the protruding tongue to loll out limply to one side. Rory's skin resembled a pasty white parchment that stood out in stark contrast to the pleasant sky blue shade of his torn short sleeve shirt. A single dribble of congealed blood ran down to his collar, just several inches below one of two deep puncture wounds inflicted in the side of his neck.

While the CSI's camera whirred and clicked, Deputy Ron Charles brushed several hot tears from his eyes wondering just what he was going to say to Rory's mom whom he saw had just arrived at the scene.

Rory's funeral took place Tuesday morning. All the theater staff and any of his schoolmates who were still in town showed up. After the police found Rory's body, Mr. Wallace had called the parents of the kids who worked for the theater the next day, the theater's closing would return to regular times and only those kids seventeen or older would work the evenings from now on.

The Madison had remained closed until the following Wednesday afternoon. Tim and Jinxy found it hard to believe Rory was gone. He had been several years younger, but the kid had been a hard worker and had gotten along well with everyone. The two boys hung out with Andrea at the concession stand while inside the auditorium, the Madison's mostly female audience sniveled and sobbed while watching some sappy tearjerker. As he was ripping the ticket stubs, Tim observed the few men who were being dragged along by their wives or girlfriends, most of them looked none too happy, the few that did were probably counting on getting lucky later that evening.

Officially, nothing much of Rory's death appeared in the papers or on the news. The cops weren't releasing any details until their investigation concluded, and maybe not even then. Unofficially, Andrea told them one of the waitresses at Bernstein's café had overheard a couple of deputies talking about the murder when they stopped in for coffee. One of them mentioned that the kid's blood had been drained from his body and there were some weird claw marks on his shoulders and arms as well.

That Saturday Mr. Wallace assigned Tim to Marquee duty. He spent the first couple of hours of his shift climbing up and down the shaky aluminum ladder updating the movie information.

Summer Horror Spectacular
The Wolf Man!
A New Terrifying Classic Each Saturday!

The evening went by quickly and uneventfully. When Mr. Wallace locked the doors at eleven most of the young staff members climbed into their parent's cars that waited for them in the parking lot. Tim's watched for his step dad's car but it wasn't waiting among the others. Instead, Mr. Wallace insisted on driving him home, that was just fine since he hadn't brought his bike to work that afternoon. His mom had given him a ride to work on her way to spend the rest of the weekend in the city visiting her sister. Tim thanked the man as he closed the car door then waved goodbye to his boss as he walked up the front walk to the front door of his home. All the lights were out, not even the porch light had been left on for him; thanks for nothing Darnel.

Throughout tonight's show, she had sat in her favorite seat in the vacant neck breaker row. Following her killing the young teen a week earlier, this audience had been older. In fact, there hadn't been a single child among them, the only age group that would have considered occupying the front several rows. No matter, she could visibly appear or remain invisible at will. During the movie, she found herself closely relating to the wolf-like creature that was quite literally on a tear, running amuck and rampaging among the townsfolk. A shapeshifter herself, she had spent many moon-filled nights prowling about in the darkness posing as a large bear, a wolf, or something else, much darker and far more dangerous.

Having dined upon the plumber and the young man, much of her strength had returned. During the hours of darkness, her essence could now range far and wide, her mind reaching the furthest limits of the town. This was quite unlike her body that still lay trapped and encased within her rocky tomb, restrained by the amulets and spells of the old ones. Perhaps she could find a way to break free and once again walk in the sun as she had before when she was a young, beautiful, and very powerful shaman. Those wonderful days before her people discovered the dark evil she had hidden so carefully within herself, but to do so, the witch would require many more lives, adding their life force to her own. Healing her body completely would be the first step of many that would eventually allow her to work, pry and widen the small opening of her crypt allowing her physical rise into the world of light.

Now in a park, near the rock quarry at the edge of town, something unworldly howled excitedly beneath the waxing moon.

CHASE TRIBUNE

YOUR NEWS - YOUR WAY - EVERY DAY

Sunday Morning Edition

....

Young Couple Brutally Slain in Lover's Lane Attack

Chase Police ask for State Assistance Puzzling Case

Chase Police responded to the scene of a double homicide early this morning where an unidentified couple, a man, and a woman believed to be in their early twenties, lay near their car in a secluded area of Quarry Park. The location, described as remote and ...

Passerby, Garry MacDonald told this reporter that he came across the bodies while walking his dog around six this morning. "Our dog, Bowser, was barking and carrying on something awful. He pulled on his leash so hard I just had to follow him. Well, it took me a while to figure out what I was seeing; I just couldn't believe it at first. Like I told you before, I was with recon in Vietnam and I saw my fair share of dead bodies over there but never figured I'd see anything like this. You couldn't tell where one ended and the other began... their parts were kind ah, well mixed up together! Ain't never seen so much blood..."

Chief of Police, Mark Robinson told the Tribune that he had placed a call to the State Authorities asking for their assistance in the matter. At the time of this report, the Chief was unwilling to provide any further information regarding the case saying they will release a statement when they know more.

The entire town was abuzz with the news. Even the major camera news teams were wandering throughout the downtown and locations where the murders occurred. Mothers were keeping a close eye on their kids, the hardnosed gun toting NRA types were publicizing their law and order agenda, the police agencies were pleading for calm while the town's politicians seized the opportunity to ask the State for a grant that would enable them to increase the number of deputies patrolling the streets.

When Tim's mom returned from her sister's and found Darnel hadn't bothered picking up her kid after the Madison closed, she went wild and sent his drunken bum of a stepfather packing. Tim had even helped Darnel load his suitcases and a few other miscellaneous items into the trunk and back seat of his dilapidated Buick, then smiled and waved as the man drove off down the street. Maybe some good had come from Rory's death after all.

That same morning Tim's mom called Mr. Wallace first thanking him for driving her son home but telling him that as of right now her son could no long work at the Madison. Tim wondered what he'd do for pocket money in the fall but for now, he had more than enough. Having done nothing but work at the theater, he'd managed to save nearly all his dough for the last three weeks. Sensing a unique opportunity, the following Saturday morning Tim asked his mom if he could have their car for the day, driving out and spending the afternoon and evening with Janice and her family. His mom figured that seeing as how the cops hadn't found the killer, getting her son out of town was probably a blessing. She gave Tim the ok and he was on the phone in a flash.

Saturday afternoon. It took him an hour and a half to drive out to the lake where Janice was staying with her parents. Of course, he first had to fill the family in on the latest he heard about the murders, which wasn't much more than they already knew. He and Janice spent the rest of the afternoon at the beach soaking up the sun and catching up. Following dinner, the two went for a long walk, holding hands and talking about friends, school and of course who might be responsible for the murders. Just after ten, he called his mom to tell her he was leaving for home then said his goodbyes to Janice and her family. He'd arrive home around twelve thirty.

He could tell something was amiss as soon as he turned off the interstate and entered the town limits. Hearing sirens and seeing emergency lights, Tim pulled over to the curb and watched no fewer than three fire trucks, two cop cars, and four ambulances race past him, heading towards the center of town. After they passed, he pulled his car in behind them. The speeding emergency vehicles quickly left him far behind. A few minutes later, Tim turned the car onto Main Street intending to take his usual route through downtown and then south on 2nd.

Approaching the small downtown core, Tim began to notice a pall of smoke that grew heavier the further into town he drove. Up the street, a block or so away, he saw a deputy standing in front of his police vehicle, its overhead emergency lights were flashing. The cop was waving traffic down and directing them either left or right down streets heading away from the center of town. Tim figured he'd go left and continue to follow the detour toward the south side of town where he lived, but once he'd gotten a block or so beyond the roadblock, curiosity got the better of him. Parking the car at the curb, Tim locked its doors and left on foot to have a look at what was happening.

It took him nearly ten minutes to walk the last couple of blocks and Tim had to watch where he stepped along the rubble choked sidewalk. On either side of the street, numerous stores and shops had already collapsed or leaning ominously, threatened to soon do so. Several water mains had broken sending rivers of grey debris-choked water streaming down into the streets and gutters while any number of fires still went unchecked. Flames and smoke billowed up forming crimson towers that rose above the fully engulfed structures below.

Tim made his way a little further up the street until he saw the Madison Theater. The old building looked as though it was pretty much in ruins. One side of the buildings brick façade was completely missing, the walls broken red bricks lay scattered in the streets. Wait, not missing, Tim thought, the wall appeared to have been blown from the inside out.

Only the front of the building remained intact, its marquee remained untouched, while its backdrop lights still randomly blinked on and off proclaiming the latest feature film.

Summer Horror Spectacular

Godzilla!

A New Terrifying Classic Each Saturday

Dog Days of Summer

Jilin watched the golden retriever running here and there, sniffing about for rabbits, squirrels and the occasional partridge it sometimes flushed up as it worked the roadside ditches. "At least someone didn't seem to mind the odd weather," she thought. The cobalt blue skies dominating this particular summer were almost completely unheard of since the season was normally quite wet and gray. As mid-summer approached, the unrelenting sunshine and drought refused to relinquish their hold on the countryside, leaving the normally lush green meadows a dull scrubby brown.

The dog was nearly three years old and had been a very special gift from her father upon her coming of age. Calling out to Henry, she saw the dog immediately abandon its hunt and run to her side. She crouched low, running her hands over the animal's scruff and scratching behind its ears. Jilin was pleased seeing how the dog tilted his head, first this way and then that, thoroughly enjoying his owner's attention. She felt the familiar gratification and pride that came with possessing such an animal, especially one as rare as a dog. It was her father who had suggested his name; a name he said harkened back to the kings who once ruled the island so very long ago.

Jilin gave Henry's head a final pat then turned and started walking back toward their ancestral farm situated on the outskirts of Lundane, the island's provincial capital. As she strolled along the abandoned roadway, she tried to visualize the odd wheeled vehicles she had seen in the historical repository, then imagined them rolling along the dark gray asphalt.

Without warning, something very large passed above her, eclipsing the sun and rousing her from her pleasant daydream. With the sun's reappearance, the earth vibrated beneath her feet. Moments later a thunderous roar echoed throughout the valley and Jilin glimpsed a large dark shadow sweeping out along the broad expanse of the valley before rapidly climbing the distant hills and disappearing. Her eyes darted skyward searching for the shadow's source. Finding it, she watched the silver warship race above the horizon then suddenly arc upward leaving a trail of white vapor in its wake before she lost sight of it in the brilliance of the noon sun. The appearance of one of the planetary defense force's few remaining ships brought home the worries she had been able to lay aside during their walk.

The warnings of an imminent invasion now came all too frequently. Jilin tried to remember a more normal time, before the war began, now well over a year ago. The first word of trouble came after several capital ships came under ambush near the Abakan quarter, only twelve light years distant. When the bulk of the fleet had responded to the area all they found was floating debris, the attacking spacecraft having disappeared after the hit and run strike. Jilin remembered the popular opinion that centered on the cowardice displayed by the enemy forces, obviously routing in the face of technological superiority.

The battle of Delmar only three months earlier had invalidated that point of view, the Hegemony having lost the bulk of the home fleet during the engagement. The utter destruction of no fewer than thirty-two of their first line ships meant that the security of the planet was uncertain. That balance had further swung in favor of the invaders only a short time ago when the system's outer perimeter defenses were tested and then breached.

Now as word came that the Hegemony was abandoning the planet, invasion was imminent; a fact demonstrated by the departure of the quadrants last remaining capital warships only the day before. Any who remained would fight at close quarters in a no doubt futile attempt to defend their cities and homes in the face of a vastly superior enemy. The primary defensive lines, manned by the District Militia were located several miles away, toward the provincial capital. If those defenses collapsed, whatever was left of the militia would retreat to her family's farm, originally constructed to serve as a fortified barracks. Jilin and Henry arrived home to find her mother and father worried and waiting for her return within the farm's large walled compound.

Looking around as she walked toward her parents, Jilin noted her brothers had already reinforced the makeshift barricades positioned at the front and back entrances to the small aging fortress. She watched a number of her neighbors as they strategically placed heavy farming implements and vehicles about the compound, with the objective of obstructing the enemy should they attempt to land troops by air. Others mounted small caliber energy cannon atop the wall turrets. All this activity took place as Henry went about the important business of being a dog.

Her father appeared apprehensive, "Daughter, while you and Henry were walking, the final warning sounded. We must be prepared to defend our home." The old man waved and pointed to the east side of the farmyard where a small concrete dome rose up from the ground. "Quickly now, the invaders have landed and even now they assault the outskirts of Lundane." Her mother stood beside her father holding his other hand. She wore a weary harried look; her voice wavered as she said, "people evacuating the small coastal towns of Yelink and Ginva say the aliens spare no one"! Jilin nodded her head then gave each of her parents a quick hug. Desperately wishing she had words or time to console the old couple, she ran toward the small bunker joining her brothers, sisters, and several neighbors who waited inside.

Constructed centuries earlier, at a time when the Hegemony was still actively expanding its sphere of influence, bunkers similar to theirs dotted the pastoral landscape. There were several in nearly every small town and many hundreds more in Lundane. Even though the Hegemony had not known war for hundreds of years, mandatory military service was still required. Its' youth could serve at home within the citizen's militia or join the regular forces off world, but they would serve. All the Hegemony's citizens were required to ensure the bunkers were properly equipped and maintained at all times.

Passing through the open blast door, Jilin entered the bunker and ran down the concrete steps welcoming the cool air that wafted about her body. The others inside the bunker stopped what they were doing and nodded to her as she entered. Jilin put on a brave smile attempting to exude a sense of confidence she did not feel. The others present returned similar expressions.

Some people donned antiquated body armor while still others stripped and cleaned small arms and several heavier weapons that someone had discovered within the bunker's armory. A short time later they filed out, grim-faced and prepared to defend their homes and family to the death if need be.

Walking quickly, the small group reached the militias muster point several miles away where they joined other members of the force who had already arrived and were milling about. The District Militia's defense perimeter had been hurriedly but effectively established in only a matter of a few days. The people who manned it were both able bodied and fully trained, and their combat skills were highly formidable. Steeped in militaristic tradition, Jilin's civilization and its members prided themselves in knowing that if need be each individual would trade his or her life at great expense to any enemy that might come against them.

Their group quickly disseminated, joining their respective units. Her brothers along with most of the other men would operate the heavy weapons stations while Jilin and her sisters, being elite skirmishers, would man the front lines and barricades. Even if the militia had not carried the archaic yet effective energy weapons into the fray, the close order defense they planned to mount would be extremely ferocious and deadly.

There was no explaining the reasoning and methodology guiding the invaders actions. Jilin and the others speculated as to why the invaders had resisted the use of powerful space-based weapons to obliterate the planet's defenses and populations before pressing their advance toward the bulk of the Hegemony's interstellar empire. To attack her people in this backwater, en mass and in open battle was an action that was certain to result in massive losses and casualties within the enemy's ranks. Her heart jumped as the action station alarms suddenly sounded from several strong points positioned along the far edge of the perimeter. Punctuated by the sounds of small arms blaster fire, the high-pitched wails of the sirens and the occasional discharge of a high-energy weapon signalled the enemy's approach.

Less than eighteen hours later, it was over. Overrun during the night, Jilin, her entire family, and all their neighbors had died. Their bodies lay strewn about the ground where they fell. The dawn's early light revealed that the members of Jilin's valiant militia had not died alone. Just as the defenders predicted, the number of enemy dead easily outnumbered that of the defenders by a margin of at least three to one. The alien victors moved across the field of battle, taking grim stock of their losses, the remaining soldiers seeing to their wounded and collecting the dead.

It had been a long sad day. Dusk was setting in when a group of invaders set up camp in the farm's compound. Across the farmyard, small camp lights started to appear. Soldiers gathered about small cooking stoves and camp fires interspersed among a squadron of armored vehicles bivouacked for the night. Throughout the island, similar scenes were unfolding; the strongholds of the defenders had fallen. The next morning would bring a mop up of any remaining militia before the victors continued their assault on the mainland.

Some of the invaders went about preparing their meal while others watched televised entertainment, caught up with off world news, or spoke with family members. On a nearby comwav, an announcer stated the taking of the Province of Isle and its provincial capital Lundane held particular meaning. Closer to the edge of the compound, a young infantry soldier listened to the same broadcast while heating her stew and biscuits on a small stove. The escaping steam suggested the meal had warmed sufficiently and she gave the contents a final stir with her spoon then removed it from the heat.

It had been a hellish day. She sighed and leaned back on her stool trying to relax and release some of the day's tension. Suddenly she heard a small twig crack nearby. Sitting up, she reached for her weapon straining her eyes as she peered into the gloom. Hearing the dry vegetation rustle again, this time much closer, she leveled the weapon in the direction of the sound and waited. The soldier lifted the weapon to her shoulder preparing to fire on any danger. She flicked on the rifles small but powerful torch sending a penetrating beam out into the darkness. She played the light back and forth across a nearby hedge, something was moving on the other side of the foliage. The soldier heard a snuffling, sniffing sound and her finger tightened on the trigger.

That's when Henry wandered into the light wagging his tail and panting, the soldier sighed audibly as she immediately relaxed once again.

Lowered her weapon and propping it up along the side of the armored vehicle next to her, she extended her hand toward the dog. Henry was a little wary and did not immediately approach but hearing her gentle words and tasting the small tidbits of food she tossed in his direction, he decided to venture a little closer. A half hour later, Henry had decided he liked the girl and lay nearby while the soldier finished her meal and listened absentmindedly to the broadcast.

Throughout the collection of tents and vehicles, she and her companions heard a gruff voice speak out across the land. The voice spoke an ancient version of their language, in a dialect not heard for many centuries past. The historical broadcast began softly then quickly gained volume as additional soldiers throughout the compound tuned in or turned up the volumes on their personal comwavs.

"We have victory - a remarkable and definite victory. I have never promised anything but blood, tears, toil, and sweat. Now however, the bright gleam has caught the helmets of our soldiers, and warmed and cheered all our hearts." The young woman reached down to the dog, gently petting his head. The girl's touch brought with it a strong racial memory, something very old, a primeval stirring; the retriever tilted his head and leaned into the soldier caress, allowing her to rub his ears with her hands. The voice continued to speak, booming loudly and echoing throughout the compound.

"Now this is not the end. It is not even the beginning of the end. But it is perhaps, the end of the beginning." The powerful voice of Winston Churchill droned on in old English as Henry enjoyed the slender hand that massaged his ears and scruff, a touch Henry found to be oddly satisfying, even if it had but four stubby fingers and a single opposing thumb.

A Dark Voyage

A concerned Thomas Jakes stood on the Amity's bridge watching as the white billowing tops of cloud breached then quickly climbed above the eastern horizon. Jakes instructed his first officer to send an experienced man aloft with a glass for a better look. His hat off and head back, Jakes watched the old seaman as he slowly climbed the heavy hemp rigging carefully making his way toward the crow's nest. The lookout was perched high atop the towering center mast which swayed precariously in the growing ocean swells. Having reached his lofty vantage, the seaman removed a small spyglass from his belt training it on the far horizon. As the old man had been at sea since he was a boy of twelve and considered most capable in such matters, Captain Jakes simply nodded and issued instructions that the old man receive an extra ration of rum that evening. Informed the storm would reach them in less than three hours, Jakes issued the appropriate orders knowing the time was more than adequate to ensure the ship would be prepared for the heavy weather.

The Amity was a three masted slaver and boasted a crew of thirty-two men and three officers who routinely sailed her about the points of the "Black Triangle," a reference to the familiar route known to those who traded in the lucrative commodity of human bondage. Typically, such a voyage could commence from any one of a dozen European ports. The holds of the ships would contain manufactured goods that would be unloaded at various African ports in exchange for human cargo. With the slaves stowed aboard like so much cordwood, the ships would begin their long westward Atlantic crossings. These voyages easily stretched a month or more in duration and if the sailors themselves found the trips difficult and onerous, the slaves below decks, chained and lying on stacked wooden racks would have endured a living hell while being transported to multiple destinations dotting the eastern Caribbean and Americas. Upon reaching port, the unfortunates disembarked and sold like cattle at auction. Torn apart, families would see husbands separated from their wives, and children taken from their mother's arms;

in many cases, these people would never see their loved ones again, at least not in this lifetime. Meanwhile, the emptied ships refitted and loaded with burgeoning cargos of raw commodities, began their return voyages toward their homeports in Europe. So too, had the Amity found herself on the return voyage sailing home from New Orleans where they had delivered the last of her slaves to market.

As he stood at the prow watching the cold grey seas vanish below the hull, Jakes had plenty of time to contemplate the morality of his command. He recalled the first occasion when approached with the offer of such a command. At that time, he flatly declined to enter the despicable business, considering it an evil affair in every sense of the word, even if both legal and highly profitable. Several years later, following Jakes investment in several failed business ventures, his bankers finally persuaded him he could ill afford to set aside any further moral concerns he held regarding the slave trade. Now, as captain of the ship and a junior partner in the firm that owned the Amity, his fortunes had reversed quickly and now rose into the black. This latest voyage should prove to be the most lucrative yet.

With her cargo of manufactured goods, the Amity had sailed out of Bristol arriving at Dakhla three weeks later where the captain had her refitted to accommodate the slaves bound for the American colonies. Cruising along the east coast, the Amity visited six ports of call. At each port, a number of the slaves would be unloaded and the empty cargo space reloaded with molasses, tobacco, and a wide variety of other raw materials for their return trip to England. The slaves themselves travelled in a manner that was termed as either a "loose" or "tight" pack, depending upon the ratio of slaves loaded in relation to the cargo space. The tighter the pack, the greater the misery and hardship suffered among the blacks who were as a rule laid flat and chained to wooden slats below decks. These harsh conditions increased the rate of mortality but while tight packed ships suffered more losses, they were often favored since they could bring more slaves to market in a single voyage thus lowering the freight costs to the company.

The torment suffered by these people during transportation was unimaginable. Poor food and inhumane treatment were the norm over a voyage that could last anywhere from six weeks to several months over which time the women aboard the vessel could look forward to servicing the carnal needs of the crew. Those slaves that attempted suicide by refusing to eat were often force fed, dunked, flogged, or tortured in some other fashion until their appetite returned. As such, it was common for both male and female slaves to jump from the ship's decks when taken above for fresh air and exercise, suicide being preferable to the life of pain and servitude that awaited them at their final destination.

Sailors serving aboard these ships would often tell of the sharks that constantly followed many of the older ships, the creatures dining on any who entered the water; living or dead. Many captains forbade dunking slaves as punishment for refusal to eat since the moment a person entered the water the sharks would immediately attack. Of course there were other commanders would make use of the practice to discourage other slaves from jumping overboard.

James Dowry, the Amity's first officer, had sailed with Jakes over the last four years and both he and Dowry had cut their teeth coming up the ranks in the English navy. The man was highly thought of by his captain. Dowry was good with the men, a firm, but fair officer able to keep the riff raff in line without the need to resort to floggings. Together Jakes and Dowry enjoyed a reputation for their timely Atlantic crossings and the additional profits resulting from a higher than average survival rate among the slaves they carried.

His junior officer, Lieutenant Henry Snow, was a lad of only seventeen years but came from good stock. His father and an uncle who were owners in the firm insisted on Henry's assignment aboard the Amity, and while at first take, Jakes took the boy to be a spoiled dandy, he quickly found he could not have been more wrong. Young Snow proved his worth during his first crossing only three months earlier, now Jakes figured the boy could have a command of his own in as little as five years time.

The wind had come up quickly; growing rapidly in strength it carried with it the promise of a full gale. Jakes thought it fortuitous that his crew had completed their heavy weather preparations within only an hour's time. All their previous estimates of the storms arrival had been very much in error, it was now evident to all the storm would break upon the vessel within a matter of minutes.

Jakes and his first officer stood on the bridge looking at the approaching storm clouds. The Amity's bow was already cutting through the heavy swells that had risen an additional four feet in height within the last twenty minutes. "Everything prepared as ordered Sir," Dowry stated factually.

"Very well Mr. Dowry, we could be in for a pounding." Jakes held a small spyglass to his right eye and swept the horizon pausing at a point ten degrees to port. "What do you make of that?" Jakes indicated the position with his left arm while handing the glass to his First.

The first officer took the small telescope and observed a definite break in the towering clouds that swept rapidly toward the ship. "Appears to be a rift of sorts doesn't it. Are you thinking we might escape the worst by making for it Sir?" he handed the glass back to the captain.

Before answering Jakes looked up, noting the position of the small pennants flying atop the masts. "Let's have another look shall we Mr. Dowry." He scoped the cloud formations once more. "Appears to me that we may be dealing with two separate squall lines, did you notice the turquoise colors near the tops of the clouds?"

Dowry nodded, "Tempests," the blue-green colors often seen in the sky both before and during extremely severe weather.

"Indeed. It appears we have a choice, turn into the heavy weather to starboard or port, or make for the calmer waters between the two." He rubbed his chin then continued, "Of course we run the risk of being trapped between the fronts, but still," he paused, "still an acceptable risk I should think Mr. Dowry."

The first officer coincided and the captain instructed the helmsman to make west-south-west, a course that would take the ship between the squall lines. "James; please go below and ensure the cargo is properly secured." The first officer left the bridge.

The captain called to his second, "Mister Snow, have lifelines rigged fore to aft." The young officer acknowledged the order directing several of the crew to place ropes along the sides of the ship. The ropes could be grasped by a crewmember should a large wave break atop the railings helping prevent the man being swept overboard.

The Captain and his officers assumed their action stations along Amity's decks as the ship began to slip through the narrow gap that slowly widened between the soaring walls of clouds to either side of her passage. The waves within the gap were still rough but easily managed. The sturdy little ship's sails caught the stiff breeze that drove her forward at a favorable clip. A half hour later, the Amity had succeeded in avoiding the squall lines of the violent storm. Jakes and Dowry watched the narrow rift they had navigated only minutes earlier disappear as the weather fronts shut tight behind their ship like a sprung trap. The captain had a sudden thought, wondering if he had avoided one snare only to sail into another.

The watch sounded eight bells; reminding Jakes that daylight would be gone in less than half an hour. Jakes waved Dowry and Snow to the bridge. "Damned odd wouldn't you say?" saying to no one in particular, his eyes concentrating on a high ring of cloud that completely encircled the ship. In the last few minutes, the previously stiff wind had dropped to a gentle breeze slowing the Amity's speed accordingly.

"Mr. Snow, double the last dog watch if you would. Instruct the cook to arrange a hot meal for the men while the calm holds." Snow slipped away to attend his duty. "James, following supper, I'd like you on the bridge. I'll relieve you toward morning watch." Captain Jakes looked to the dark horizons once more. "I don't trust this weather. We mustn't be caught unaware." The first officer nodded to Captain Jakes who left the bridge with the intention of addressing the ships log in his cabin.

At four-thirty the next morning, the captain relieved his first officer who reported that the night had proved uneventful; if anything the wind and seas had becalmed even further. Jakes looked up at the sky. "Stars Mr. Dowry?" Jakes recognized the shapes of a number of familiar constellations tracing them from the zenith downward to perhaps thirty-five degrees off the horizon, beneath that the stars vanished.

"It's my belief the storm still surrounds us Sir, although I think we'll see our way clear come dawn." The man yawned and covered his mouth. "If I may be excused Sir, it's been a long day."

"Yes of course Mr. Dowry, I think we're in good shape." The captain watched his second take his leave of the bridge and go below as he bid a good morning to Jenkins, the helmsman who currently manned the ship's wheel. Concluding the brief conversation, the captain walked to Amity's bow where he stood quietly. Jakes lit his pipe and watched the smoke swirl in the air while enjoying the familiar feel of the sea rising and falling beneath his feet in the now gentle swells.

Out at sea the dawn broke with surprising rapidity. Dark crimson laced the edges of the cloudbanks that still lay unbroken in every direction, while higher in the dawn sky; pink wisps of light cloud formed a light veil above the ship that steadily thickened. Young Snow joined his captain on the bridge where Jakes predicted the day would be a gray one. Taking his spyglass from a vest pocket Jakes swept the horizon in every direction, so far he had not seen a single break in the wall of high cloud surrounding his ship. "Just a moment," he said to himself. A set of sails he had not noticed earlier, had suddenly appeared two points off starboard. The ship was of similar design to the Amity and flew a small British Ensign. He raised his right arm at once catching the attention of his helmsman then instructed the crew to begin making way for the other ship's position some ten miles distant.

As the Amity approached the second ship, the captain noted she was riding low in the water and listing somewhat to port. Jakes scanned the decks with his glass then passed the telescope to Lt. Snow. "Opinion Mr. Snow?"

"No one appears on board sir, could be an abandoned derelict," the young officer offered.

"Look at her sails lieutenant, neatly furled as if she was in a Portsmouth berth. No something else is at work here." He adjusted his hat.

"Aye Sir." The young man handed his captain the glass.

"Do you recognize her Mr. Snow?" the captain asked.

"No sir?" Unsure of his answer the lieutenant decided he had better take a closer look at the ship.

"You should, your family owns her. She's our sister ship, the Ipswich." The man held out his arm for the spyglass that the lieutenant quickly returned to his outstretched hand.

"Be a good fellow and rouse Mr. Dowry... with apology. Have him report to me at once." The captain's eyes had never left the other ship. The captain scanned the waters surrounding the Ipswich for any long boats launched in anticipation of the ships demise, but found none.

The ships were within a quarter mile range when Captain Jakes ordered the Amity to hold her position. Having instructed his lookout to hail the Ipswich, and receiving no answer in return, Jakes had instructed Snow to have the gunnery crew run out the Amity's cannon training them upon the other ship. He had heard of pirates using a similar ruse to capture merchant ships that had stopped to help or salvage such vessels. He determined to send a small boat over to the ship before approaching any closer.

The ship's name gracing her stern, the captain watched through his glass as one of the Amity's long boats cautiously approached the Ipswich off her aft side. Mr. Dowry was in charge of the boat, he and his six men were well armed, four of them with long and short barrel muskets. Dowry and four of his men climbed aboard the vessel then walked about her decks. The ship was now riding somewhat lower in the water than she had only an hour before when Jakes had first spied her.

The captain recognized his first officers' voice as Dowry shouted a challenge to anyone aboard the ship. Hearing a muted reply

Jakes waited several long minutes before one of his crew came to the ships nearest railing shouting that everything was under control. Jakes gave the order to have the Amity pull alongside the Ipswich.

Two people came aboard the Amity that morning, a man of advancing years and a black child, a boy perhaps ten years of age. The older man informed Captain Jakes not to expect any others to arrive from the Ipswich. For his part, Jakes immediately recognized the older man to be the master of the Ipswich, Captain Tyler McCrery.

From the start, McCrery noticed Jakes' questioning glances toward the young black boy at his side. The Ipswich's captain explained that "Toby" was his cabin boy and a deaf mute. McCrery told Jakes the Ipswich encountered a privateer. His ship's hull sustained damage below the waterline during the ensuing battle causing his ship to take on water. The pirate gave chase but McCrery dodged into a storm front to escape.

Some hours later, McCrery, believing that his ship had only minutes left to live gave the order to abandon ship. As the captain, he remained on deck and was about to board the last long boat tied to the side of his ship when a series of huge waves swamped two of the three small boats drowning all those aboard. The third boat, caught in the ravages of the storm and quickly swept out of sight, left McCrery to wonder what had become of it and his men. He asked Jakes when a search might begin for the missing long boat, but Jakes remained mute while watching his first officer return from the Ipswich.

Minutes later, Mr. Dowry informed Jakes and McCrery of his assessment of the damage he found on the Ipswich. It was his opinion that the ship could be seaworthy within less than a day. Sending men over to the ship to man the pumps below decks was the first order of business; the second would involve the immediate repairs to her hull. The overriding concern was whether they would have the time necessary to repair the vessel, given that every man aboard believed the storm's full fury would return well before nightfall.

Captain Jakes gave the order to do so and asked Captain McCrery if he wished to supervise the repairs. Jakes saw the captain look toward the cabin boy who almost imperceptibly shook his head from side to side. McCrery declined the invitation, professing his full confidence in Dowry and the Amity's crew to do whatever they could to save the Ipswich. Jakes was more than a little taken back by the captain's reaction but reconsidered, remembering the man had just lost his entire command to the sea.

Like Thomas Jakes' vessel, the Ipswich pursued a brisk and lucrative trade engaging in the trafficking in human misery, but unlike the Amity, McCrery believed in and practiced the "tight pack" method of transport aboard his ship. Slaves were plentiful and cheap when acquired in the many African ports; the cost of their ocean voyage to the markets that lay thousands of miles to the west accounted for the lion's share of the slaver's costs. By overcrowding the poor souls within the hold like so much stacked cordwood, a higher death rate among the slaves during the crossing would be a given. McCrery and other practitioners of the method gambled that even considering the higher number of fatalities, an even larger number of people would eventually survive and sold at market at the completion of the voyage. Jakes himself had prior experience serving aboard a tight pack vessel as a junior officer and resolved never to follow the practice should he ever discover himself holding a similar command.

It is not to be assumed that Captain Thomas Jakes was a man who gave a Christians' damn about a slave's situation in any regard whatsoever. Instead, Jakes was a shrewd businessman concerned with the health of his crew. Debilitating illnesses often arose given the filthy conditions found within the crowded slave holds and these afflictions inevitably spread among his crew. If fortunate, the illness would appear in the form of dysentery or "flux," although other more serious maladies including cholera, malaria and a variety of exotic fevers might appear. Given an opportunity, such an illness could overtake the entire ship adding precious time to the crossing, sometimes by as much as several weeks. Taking into account the additional time spent in transit, the reduction of delivered cargo, and the legal obligation of the ship's owners to compensate a deceased crewmember's family for his loss quickly tilted the balance sheet in favor of a loose pack vessel.

The Ipswich's owners and any subsequent board of inquiry required that Jakes obtain a factual and truthful account as to what happened to the Ipswich while under McCrery's command. Accordingly, Captain Jakes invited McCrery to his cabin to discuss the matter. As they entered his cabin, Jakes noticed the cabin boy had followed them. Jakes walked to the cabin door calling out to a passing crewmember instructing that the man take the boy topside, but McCrery politely requested, and when pressed, vehemently insisted that the boy remain with him; the Ipswich's captain offered no further explanation. Jakes acquiesced in light of recent events; taking into account the child was a deaf mute and wholly unlikely to influence the proceedings in any event.

McCrery began by requesting the transfer of his personal belongings, including his ship's log and charts to the Amity. Jakes assured the captain that Lieutenant Snow was already in the process of doing just that. Reassured, McCrery outlined his voyage and ports of call, stressing to Jakes that he had not lost a single slave during the voyage and that all had arrived in good health. Jakes did not believe this particular claim for a second but allowed the man to continue without rebuttal.

McCrery rubbed his scalp and glanced quickly over to the cabin boy for an instant before looking down and away, he continued, "We were only a week out of Jamaica when the lookout saw a sail to the stern; it was too far to make out her class or nationality. After a day and a night, the other vessel neither had gained nor fallen behind. After the second day I gave her no further thought" he paused and took a deep breath before continuing, "Which in the end turned out to be a mistake. I made the course change that would take us home. When the dawn broke the following day, we found the ship had intercepted us during the night. I made her out to be the Black Prince and she challenged the Ipswich sending a shot across our bow."

Jakes broke in. "The Prince was Ephraim Adams' ship wasn't it?" The ship had reported to have been taken by pirates eighteen months previous and it was rumoured she was very heavily armed.

"Yes. Rather than fight we decided to run. Ipswich is reasonably quick when well handled and we gave the bastards a good run leaving them in our wake until we ran into this damn weather." He waved a hand about in no particular direction. "I know it sounds absurd but the winds came at us from various directions. The swells grew rapidly, pitching and rolling us about, I wanted to run before the wind but to be honest for some time didn't know in which direction to head."

Jakes nodded. So far, the account made sense to him, especially given the two unusual squall lines he and his first officer had seen forming the previous afternoon. He himself had expressed the concern that the Amity might find herself pinned between the opposing fronts.

McCrery continued. "The weather shook the privateer off our backs but the Prince got off a single barrage at distance before breaking off. An eight pound ball struck us amidships below the waterline as our hull rose in a swell." Jakes saw the captain lick his lips nervously and glance toward the cabin boy in a distinctly odd manner that left Jakes with the impression the man was somehow seeking the boy's approval.

The captain continued, telling Jakes that he eventually ran with the wind but the heavy seas were preventing the crew from adequately repairing the ship's hull. He had four men on the pumps but the water was coming in above and below faster than they could pump it out. Several hours later McCrery believing his ship was in imminent danger of sinking, ordered his crew to quickly provision the long boats and prepare to abandon the ship. Following tradition, the captain was the last to remain aboard and would soon depart on the final boat that lay tied alongside the Ipswich. Suddenly, a series of huge rogue waves struck the vessel. The waves engulfed and swamped the smaller boat tied alongside and swept the men down into the sea where they quickly drowned. The same fate befell another of the two boats previously launched and waiting short distances out from the Ipswich. Alone and unable to do anything to help, McCrery had watched the members of his crew perish in the cold gray waters. The single remaining boat quickly vanished from his sight, caught up within the heavy swells and hidden behind the driving torrential rains.

Remaining aboard, McCrery watched in wretched silence as the heavy weather subsided and the seas quickly becalmed leaving the Ipswich listing, adrift and gently rocking on the now peaceful waters. Only this morning the captain realized he was not alone aboard ship when the cabin boy who had hidden below decks reappeared. It was less than an hour after that when he heard Dowry's voice calling out topside.

Jakes listened to the account in silence, which if true, was a tragic turn of luck for the ship's compliment, whose lives would have been spared, if they had only remained aboard the ship. It now appeared likely they would have been able to make repair at sea and journey safely home. It bothered Jakes that the obvious question remained unanswered; at what distant port did McCrery expect the small flotilla to arrive before their water and provisions were utterly exhausted? McCrery would be obliged to explain his actions before a court of inquiry, but in the meantime, Jakes believed he would extend to the man the benefit of doubt.

On several instances while McCrery spoke, Captain Jakes had observed Toby the cabin boy watching McCrery intently. Jakes got the distinct impression that the child heard and understood their discussion. On several occasions, Jakes saw the boy avert his gaze when he noticed Jakes watching him. When the boy flinched at a sudden loud bang echoing down from the upper decks, Jakes ascertained the boy had at least a limited sense of hearing. Something was definitely amiss here.

Jakes thanked the captain for their conversation and asked the man to attend to his vessel topside while he made the required entries into his log. He watched McCrery leave the cabin with the boy in tow. Just prior to leaving the room, the boy paused and looked back towards Jakes. For but a split second, the boy's meek appearance abruptly vanished. His gentle, dark brown eyes became a pair of black dead orbs while his mouth parted wide to reveal a glistening array of jagged teeth. The thing's features assumed a terrible grimace that quickly assembled itself into an evil smirking grin.

Time stopped for Thomas Jakes as his mind reeled, refusing to believe the implacable horror before his eyes. His heart became a trip hammer that pounded in his ears while his blood raced through his veins running as cold as the sea upon which he sailed. It had begun and ended in but an instant. The living terror that had stood before him had resumed the common and acquiescent demeanor of the young slave boy. The cabin boy tilted his head shooting Jakes a questioning glance before turning and following McCrery through the door, leaving Jakes to mull over what he had ... or more probably had not seen.

A half hour later, there was a knock on the captain's door. Bid entry, Lieutenant Snow entered informing Jakes that the repairs would likely succeed. Dowry and Captain McCrery believed the Ipswich would be seaworthy in a day or so. The captain thanked the young officer and told him he would come topside shortly after completing his log entry. Jakes looked to the small chest containing McCrery's personal items his lieutenant had brought to Jakes' cabin an hour earlier. Presumably the trunk contained the log of the Ipswich, it might make informative reading but Jakes was not about to violate another captain's privacy on mere whim.

Jakes had just finished placing the Amity's logbook in his desk when he heard a loud commotion taking place topside. Hurrying to the bridge, he met his first officer who informed him that McCrery had jumped from the rail, throwing himself into the sea. The captain of the Ipswich had been lost.

Inquiring if anyone had witnessed the event first hand, Mr. Dowry quickly summoned two sailors, Jenkins and Savoy who were already standing nearby. According to the men, they had been working near the bridge when they saw Captain McCrery and the boy speaking together near the stern of the ship.

Jakes interrupted the men, asking if they were sure that the captain and the boy had been talking. The crewmen looked at each other, then Savoy said there was no question about it. A moment later, they saw the captain raise his hands up to his head and cover his ears, as if he did not want to hear what was said to him. Suddenly, McCrery screamed out something that neither Jenkins nor he could make out. That was when the captain ran to the port railing, climbed over and threw himself overboard without hesitation. Both crewmen yelled "man overboard" and Lieutenant Snow ran to the rail ordering the two to go into the water after him and fish him out. The seamen made ready to do so but Snow grabbed their arms, stopping them when he saw the sharks arrive. Snow and the other two watched the poor man as the fish ripped and shredded him to pieces before their very eyes.

"Sharks...?" Jakes questioned looking at Snow for clarification. The likelihood that sharks would instantly fall on a man who had jumped from the ship just moments earlier seemed remote.

The junior officer verified the men's account. "Yes Captain, sharks. It was almost as if they were waiting for the moment, the captain didn't have a chance." Snow wrung his hands. "Thank God our men didn't enter the water after him."

One of the crewmen spoke up. "Begging the Captain's pardon Sir?"

"Yes, Jenkins isn't it?" Jakes said.

The crewman cap in hand stood facing his captain. "Yes sir. Captain, I have worked on slavers for seven years before signing aboard the Amity sir. As you know we'd toss slaves that died overboard; the sharks were always there waiting, just like today."

"I'm aware of the practice seaman. It only makes sense that the fish would follow the vessel if they're being regularly fed." He was ready to dismiss the man before Jenkins added.

"Yes, but the sharks followed our ship even when we were on our way home without a single slave aboard. One day I asked one of the officers why that was so? He said the sharks could smell the stink of the blood through an old slaver's hull. The blood soaks into the wood, you see? All slavers have the touch of blood, it never leaves the ship, it never leaves the men who sail them." The sailor's eyes held fast to Jakes own for several long seconds, then wavered as the crewman remembered his place and quickly lowered his gaze toward the deck.

"Hmm. Very well Jenkins, Savoy. Well, at any rate, the fish seem to have made short work of Captain Tyler McCrery," Jakes added. "An extra ration of grog for these two men." Both the seamen's eyes grew wide with gratitude and they thanked their captain profusely then left re-attending themselves to their duties.

Dowry turned and faced his captain. Jakes felt the time had arrived to acquaint the officer with a brief summary of McCrery's account of Ipswich's battle with the Black Prince. Once finished he noticed Dowry's face bore a queer expression.

"Took a ball below decks sir?" Dowry asked and Jakes nodded. "Captain, I judged from the damage that someone had tried to scuttle her. There were several other charges set along her hull." The two men looked at one another in silence for several moments. Jakes turned his gaze toward the Ipswich, still tied to the Amity, then forward where his gaze came to rest on the small black cabin boy. The child sat quietly perched upon a water barrel lashed fast to the bow rail; the expression on his face fathomless.

The rest of the day remained cool and dull. Looking out from the ship in every direction, one could see distant high walls of cloud boiling up from the ocean's surface in unmistakable violence. Despite the severe weather surrounding them, the Amity and the Ipswich continued to drift lightly upon the calm water with only a gentle waft of air occasionally gracing the sails, but stubbornly refusing to fill them. Every once in a while, crewmen working top side would stop to watch and comment on the many varied and unusually large sharks that swam leisurely about in the waters surrounding the two ships.

That evening, the weather was the main topic of conversation at the dinner table. Captain Jakes commented to his fellow officers, that while he had heard the term "of being in the eye of the storm," and its description provided by other mariners, he himself had never before seen such a thing. Dowry speculated that it appeared that the ships sat dead center of the calm but felt they would eventually re-enter the storm fronts from one direction or another. The captain agreed saying that they would have to be prepared for some very heavy weather when that occurred. Lieutenant Snow asked how soon this might happen as there had not been a breath of wind in the sails for a full day now. An answer was not readily forth coming from any seated at the table.

"So now it falls to us as to what to do with the Ipswich." Jakes looked in the direction of his junior officer. "Mr. Snow, your opinion on the matter?"

"Might the ship be considered abandoned?" Snow said in askance as he looked at his seniors for an indication that he was on the right track, but their faces remained stoic. The young man continued, "As such wouldn't the vessel fall under the laws of salvage?" The officer referred to the law that stated that anyone who recovered another's ship or cargo after hazard or loss at sea was entitled to a reward commensurate to the value of the property saved and returned to the owner.

Jakes looked at Dowry then both men smiled. "Quite so and well done Mr. Snow! You have been studying I see." Jakes was pleased and smiled broadly, Snow continued to display intelligence and common sense in his duties. He would be an asset to any ship on which he served in the future. "This said you forget that the Amity and Ipswich are together owned by your employers; full compensation wouldn't apply in this case." He saw the lads face fall somewhat. "However, a very handsome reward for returning the ship intact may still be expected."

Remembering the weather, Jakes smile faded. "A handsome reward indeed Mr. Snow, provided we can get her back safely to a friendly port... and ourselves as well." The men went on to discuss the logistics of manning both vessels for the trip, the captain asking Dowry if he thought the repairs to the Ipswich's hull would hold in heavy weather. The first officer believed that the hull remained reasonably sound; adding they were fortunate that only one of the charges McCrery had set in the hold had detonated. This kept the damage to a minimum; if all had exploded, Dowry held little doubt the ship would have dropped to the bottom of the ocean long before their arrival at her location.

Jakes wondered why a captain would scuttle his ship. The undeniably odd connection between McCrery and the slave boy flashed into his mind, as did the terrifying image he might have witnessed earlier in the day. He urgently hoped that whatever madness took McCrery was not catchy. Jakes determined not to give the matter further credence and dismissed the thought from his mind, at least for the moment but as the dinner ended Jakes casually asked his two officers if they had noticed anything odd about the cabin boy since he had come aboard.

The two officers told the captain that they had not, Dowry adding he noticed the boy kept to himself spending much of his time sitting alone above the prow of the ship simply gazing out at the horizon. Dowry stated this did not strike him as being particularly odd since after all he was quite young, new to the ship and perhaps most importantly a black slave. The officer added he had not yet assigned any duties to the boy but considered having him assist the cook.

Jakes agreed with Dowry but asked that the men keep an eye on him musing aloud that the boy was perhaps neither deaf nor mute. That being the case, why then would McCrery state that he was? Lieutenant Snow commented that just that afternoon he had approached the boy from the rear asking if he would help the men swab the deck, the boy did not respond until Snow had laid a hand on the boy's shoulder and in so doing appeared to have startled the lad. Jakes considered the statement then did not press the matter further.

Later that night Snow walked the decks of both ships. The hours passed quietly for the young lieutenant who commanded the night's watch on both the Amity as well as the Ipswich. A plan formed during dinner; Mr. Dowry would take command of the Ipswich taking with him half of the Amity's crew. When the weather eventually broke, both ships would then make sail for Bristol.

Captain Jakes retired to his cabin for the evening entering the day's final entry into the log before turning in. Lying in his bunk, he waited for the sleep that continued to elude him. He could not clear his head, his mind insisting that he continue to mull over the details of the voyage awaiting the two ships. Jakes finally relinquished all thought of sleep as he arose from his bed and relit the cabin's lanterns. He sat in his heavy desk chair, stoking his pipe and studying the chart that lay open on its surface. Remaining confident he had not overlooked anything, he considered taking a short stroll on deck before his eyes glanced toward McCrery's personal locker lying in a nearby corner and set atop a steamer trunk that contained his clothing.

Curiosity and boredom getting the best of him, he retrieved the chest and placed it atop the desk. Opening it, he found the sailing charts, personal letters, and the Ipswich's official logbook. Jakes quickly skimmed over the log entries that began with the ship leaving Bristol. The entries traced the ship's journey's to the Africas and later the Americas and concluded with details presumably written the evening before the ship had the supposed encounter with the privateer, the day before the ship made contact with the Amity. As Jakes presumed, nothing appeared out of place in the log entry, no sign that anything unusual had occurred aboard the vessel, at least officially, but many captains keep one log for the company and a second more personal diary for their own thoughts.

Jakes located McCrery's private log beneath a small painting of an elegantly dressed woman he presumed was McCrery's wife. Jakes laid the picture carefully aside then reached for the diary. Sheathed in soft brown leather and bound with gold stitching, he opened the book to the middle, then noting the empty pages flipped back toward the front of the journal until he located McCrery's recent entries. The first entry date of May 1, 1789 was the day the Ipswich had departed Bristol.

The first pages were of little interest, the entries covering his expectation of the voyage profits, assessments of his officers, and little else. The vessel continued to travel along "the black triangle" stopping at numerous ports of call. Evidently, McCrery was quite pleased. He had filled his ship in only a single month, buying the majority of the cargo at a discount. He also made note of several shore side landings where the local chiefs presented him with captured slaves and tribal members who had fallen into disfavor.

It was during the last of these impromptu landings where McCrery noted the captain had taken aboard four slaves, two men, a woman, and a young boy, all who were offered at no cost to the ship whatsoever. According to the chief, the boy was the son of a shaman, taken captive with the others during a local raid. Local custom and superstition dictated that the boy could not die at his hand nor could the chief profit in any way from his disposal. In fact, the chief seemed very anxious to rid himself of the boy, so much so the others were thrown in for good measure. The group being in good health boarded without question and McCrery noted the new additions to Ipswich's cargo would fetch a very good price at market.

As Jakes continued to read the entries, he became aware that McCrery had a definite dark side to his personality. It was common practice for the officers and crew to take sport with the women or men during the voyage just so long as they did not damage the cargo. Jakes himself had taken numerous "bed warmers" to his cabin to pass the lonely nights. McCrery however, had an appetite for young boys and girls and according to several entries obviously enjoyed inflicting pain on the innocents. Since young children did not fetch a high price at market, the slaver had not bothered concerning himself with the overly gentle treatment of his victims. Over the six-week voyage to the Americas, he abused and murdered four of them, three girls, and one boy disposing of them in his usual manner, by throwing their bodies to the sharks.

Filled with disgust, Jakes read the horrific entries describing McCrery's sadism and found he utterly reviled the man. He had it in his mind to let the diary remain in the chest, leaving it delivered to his widow and family as a final testament to their "loving husband and father" but later reconsidered, determining instead to burn the book when he had finished its reading. According to several entries, the sick bastard was looking forward to entertaining the shaman's son on the final night of their voyage before they entered port the next day. The diary's entry dated and written the day before the Ipswich docked in

Kingston was McCrery's last; following that, there were no further personal entries whatsoever. Jakes fed the pages of the odious journal into his small stove one by one, committing them to the flames while hoping its author was experiencing a similar fate. The reason behind the cabin boys presence aboard the Ipswich was abundantly clear.

The next morning found the ocean in a rough chop; a blustery wind had picked up following the dawn. Still, the officers and crew of the ship were surprised and grateful to see that the horizons had cleared. The towering walls of unusual cloud that had held them surrounded over the last several days had dissipated into common fair weather cumulous. Jakes had bid Dowry and fifteen of the Amity's compliment to board the Ipswich and begin preparations to get underway.

By noon, both ships were under sail once again and continuing on an easterly heading that would take them toward their homeport. Standing on the bridge in the stiffening breeze, Jakes reflected it now appeared their odyssey might be coming to an end. Barring terribly inclement weather, the journey to port should prove uneventful while their recovery of the Ipswich should bring about a highly profitable conclusion to the voyage.

Captain Jakes glassed the horizon as the ship's bells sounded the passing of the hour first on the Amity, then several moments later echoed aboard the Ipswich. Their sister ship ran a parallel course with the Amity a half leagues distance. As the last chime of the bells died away, so too did the breeze that up to now had filled and billowed the Amity's canvass. Jakes felt his ship slow noticeably and looked upward into the masts and rigging then glanced over to the Ipswich, whose sails still strained, catching the wind and propelling the ship forward at speed.

Several minutes later the Amity was almost motionless, her sails slack in the dead calm, mast flags drooped with only an occasional flutter. Jakes took out his small telescope training it on the other ship noting the Ipswich too had appeared to have lost her wind, He estimated the other ship now lay a little more than a mile distant.

The captain looked toward the bow of his ship and saw the cabin boy sitting quietly on the oaken water cask watching the crewmembers working along Amity's deck. As Jakes continued to watch the boy, the young man's face turned toward him and the boy's eyes locked and bored into his. The slave's eyes were hard and flinty, experienced eyes that bespoke of an age well beyond that of the boy, or perhaps even the eldest man aboard the Amity. Jakes imagined he felt the young slave's mind reaching toward him, attempting to delve into his mind and uncover his very thoughts until his rational mind rebelled and shelved aside such a ludicrous idea. Even so, as Jakes struggled to break away from the icy stare he found it nearly impossible to do so until a loud voice originating somewhere high above the deck shouted out a warning breaking the spell of the moment. Having succeeded in pulling himself away, Jakes found himself frozen in place for several long minutes. He came to his senses suddenly realizing he was shaking and that his young lieutenant was staring at him uncomfortably; Jakes strove to calm himself.

"Weather coming in Sir," The lookout sitting atop the forward mast repeated his call out to the captain. "Out of the west."

Sufficiently recovered, Jakes looked forward to see a dense white mist gliding quickly across the water approaching the ships from east to west; it would reach the Ipswich first. He felt the warmth of the sunlight cool then vanish as thick clouds flooded into the previously clear sky from every direction. Casting a quick glance toward the boy, he saw the child's mouth work into a thin smile then a cruel sneer; the boy's eyes betrayed a hatred and disdain that Jakes felt extended toward every soul aboard his ship. The captain's gaze fell back to the Ipswich then quickly returned to the slave boy still seated on the cask. The lad's face had become a blank, if anything it now wore an innocence that bore no sign of the animosity and rage that the Captain believed he had experienced only moments before. Jakes mind wrestled with the obvious conundrum; were these flashes of insight based in reality, or that of insanity?

The entire crew of the Amity were now up on deck. They stood along the starboard rail watching the heavy fog swirl about the Ipswich's hull then rise to cloak the ship completely from their view. Several members of Amity's crew yelled out "ahoy Ipswich", "ahoy mates", as similar replies were shouted back to the Amity from men aboard the distant ship. The feeling of all aboard the ship was one of anxiety and apprehension, Jakes thought the underlying fear nearly palpable. He would have to dispel the atmosphere and did so by quickly ordering his crewmembers back to their original duties. To those previously idle Jakes assigned new tasks.

Captain Jakes and Lieutenant Snow now stood together on the bridge. The two men watched as the heavy mist met the bow of their ship then climbed up over the railings spreading out across Amity's decks. The crewmen crooked their necks downward looking toward the deck as the flat white haze obscured their legs and feet. That was when Jakes noticed that the fog had not enveloped the cabin boy but had instead parted before him, slipping by the boy to either side. The child continued to sit upon the cask while his head slowly began to swivel over his left shoulder toward the location of the Ipswich. The boy's head continued to rotate to such an unnatural degree it appeared more akin to that belonging to an owl or some predatory bird rather than a boy. This was not lost on the other members of the crew who stood nearby. Taking notice of this peculiarity they cautiously backed away, muttering and occasionally glancing at one another and then toward their officers.

Jakes looked at Lieutenant Snow considering the officer who stood beside him. He suddenly recognized his officer for who he was, a young and very inexperienced man. Jakes realized he must act to buffer the officer from the weight of command that would test the lad's metal much sooner rather than later. Somewhere deep inside himself, the captain feared a series of exceptional circumstances were to befall his ship and crew. The next few minutes confirmed his worst fears.

The mist thickened and pooled near the base of each of the Amity's three masts. The flat white mist turned to a dull grey and then darkened further to the color of gunmetal while at the same time each of the now substantial mists began to swirl counter clock wise about the base of each mast. The crewmen fell away from the structures, their backs pressed hard against the ships side rails, others had fallen to their knees in fear.

Having prudently joined their men at the rails, Jakes and Snow watched each of the gray whirlpools of fog whip ever faster about the base of the masts. As the motion quickened the fog's shade darkened noticeably. The color was approaching that of midnight black when several of the crew yelled and pointed upward toward the top of the center mast. Daemon fire had appeared in its high rigging then jumped from the center mast to those both forward and aft. The spinning black fog now began to climb each mast rapidly, rising ever upward until it reached a point just below the points where the eerie blue-green light gleamed and fluttered. This frightening apparition lingered for several long minutes, bringing to Jakes mind black candles spouting an iridescent ghostly flame. Not a sound came forth from any man aboard the ship... the silence seemed complete.

A sudden, thunderous clap caused the entire ship to shudder and quake, any man that had not taken hold of the rail fell to the deck. The flame tipped blackness that coated each mast had morphed into three thick tentacles that flung themselves outward from the Amity and toward the last position of the Ipswich. Through the thick fog came faint voices crying out from the Ipswich in horror and despair. The thick black tentacles that clung to each of the Amity's three masts undulated and twisted about in a macabre dance. Jakes heard the distant sounds of canvass tearing, wood straining, groaning, and then cracking as it ripped asunder. How long the terrible ordeal lasted was impossible to calculate. Seconds or perhaps even minutes passed by, all the while the impossible and terrifying din continued without respite. Then suddenly, it was over as quickly as it began.

The thick black tendrils and daemon fire vanished in an instant, the last echoes of the thunderous tumult resounded across the waters, the silence left in their wake was equally deafening. The thick fog about the Amity's decks quickly dissipated, fleeing the decks back into the sea, then racing further outward from the ship in every direction until reaching a point perhaps a mile or more distant. The Ipswich however, was nowhere to be seen.

Later that afternoon all that remained of their sister ship floated slowly past the Amity. Snow commented to Jakes that it appeared to him that the ship had been crumbled into ruin as easily and thoroughly as one might crush a stale day old bun. Jakes could not make a better comparison himself.

Suddenly a sailor shouted out and pointed into the sea. Jakes and several other men who stood nearby stared down into the calm light grey water. The body of Jakes first officer floated face up, it drifted only inches below the ocean's surface. Dowry's eyes and mouth gaped widely, his death mask testifying to the undeniable horror of his passing. The body slowly settled more deeply into the cold waters, mercifully disappearing from their sight.

Captain Jakes ordered Snow to assemble all the men on deck at once, no matter where they were or what they were doing. Visiting his cabin Jakes retrieved his copy of the King James Bible. He could hear the Lieutenant above decks ordering the men about while he paused for several minutes considering what he would say to calm the crew... what he might say to calm himself before heading topside.

"Seventeen men now stand on the decks of the good ship Amity; seventeen men have borne witness to the evil that befell the Ipswich, our crewmates, and our friends. They are taken from us and we are poorer for their loss." Jakes remembered their lost comrades speaking each name aloud before turning to a marked page in his bible. "What then shall we say to these things? If God is for us, who can be against us; he who did not spare his own Son but gave him up for the sake of each and all of us." Jakes closed the book, searching first the frightened eyes of his crewmen, then his young lieutenant. Did his own eyes betray the mantle of dread weighing on his every thought as it strove to steal the very heart of him?

He summoned his courage, drew his wind, and then shouted out "God Bless the Amity and all who sail her!" He repeated it; the crew taking up the chant and repeating it several times. Each word they uttered summoned forth renewed strength in their voices. The service ended and the captain dismissed the men who resumed their duties; the evil mood of the day had lightened considerably. Snow approached his captain complimenting Jakes on the heartfelt words he had offered to the crew adding that they provided great comfort to him as well. The Lieutenant took his leave of the captain, leaving the bridge to the solitary figure that stood gazing out across the ocean. At this moment, Jakes acutely appreciated the crushing weight of command he had previously only taken for granted.

Captain Thomas Jakes contemplated his next move for some time. His eyes expertly moved about his ship, surveying her masts, rigging and sails, seeking any sign of damage. Finding none, he gave silent thanks and sent several of his more seasoned men aloft to confirm his estimation. His eyes wandered about the deck where they came to rest on the oaken cask where the cabin boy had sat, the spot was vacant. Several hours had passed since the disaster that befell the Ipswich; the Captain marveled that up until only several seconds ago he had completely forgotten about the young slave.

His eyes scanned the deck for the child but the boy was not among those above deck. He summoned Mr. Snow issuing instructions that the boy was to be located immediately and brought before him, the captain adding that the boy might be hiding. Snow affirmed the captain's order without comment and set about organizing a search party. After a half hour of fruitless searching with Snow's five men, the captain ordered all aboard to scour every nook and cranny of the vessel. A full hour quickly passed without results; the boy had vanished.

Hours later, alone in his cabin, the captain updated his log. "... and following the destruction of the Ipswich and our inability to locate the young slave that came aboard with Captain McCrery, we have given him up for lost, perhaps during the events that I have herein documented." Jakes didn't share his personal suspicion that the boy may have been the shaman's son mentioned in McCrery's diary, in fact he shuddered to even consider the possibility; it tied in all too well with the events of late.

Setting aside further thought of the boy he continued to write. "The afternoon has passed into early evening and the winds have not returned. The fog bank that surrounds our ship remains stationary, holding its position about a mile off each compass heading. I remain hopeful that a change in weather shall allow us to continue to our destination tomorrow." The captain closed the logbook and headed to dinner.

"If, Mr. Snow, our search determined the boy could not be aboard this ship, then it must be assumed that he has left it, in some fashion... I for one will not mourn his departure. I sensed something foul in his countenance or perhaps beneath it." The captain took a sip of wine from the goblet then returned to his roast beef.

Snow agreed with Jakes adding that the men considered the boy a Jonah of some sort. "Did you know that not one sailor saw the boy take a sip of water or eat so much as a crust of bread while he was aboard? I for one cannot remember a time I did not see him sitting or standing near the bow of the ship, he never left. There are even some aboard that think he was responsible for what happened to the Ipswich."

Jakes saw the cook out of the corner of his eye fussing with a small platter of food nearby pretending inattention to the conversation, just as he should. However, as a seaman, the captain also knew there were no secrets aboard a ship, at least none that remained secret for long. He would have to put an end to this type of rumor immediately.

"Nonsense Mr. Snow!" Jakes exclaimed loudly. Rejecting the lieutenants' conjecture in such a forthright manner immediately lent him a feeling of confidence even as the phrase left his lips. "I won't permit such drivel to be spoken aboard my ship. Won't hear of it, am I understood Lieutenant?"

"Yes, yes of course, Sir." Snow replied meekly and concentrated on finishing his dinner.

The following morning the captain and Snow found themselves alone on the bridge. Jakes explained his blustery words spoken during their last meal. Mr. Snow thanked Jakes for his explanation then stated his belief that his captain's performance had indeed produced the intended result. Not another word about a Jonah had reached his ears since the meal. Jakes smiled and replied, "A good captain must occasionally become an actor as well. Keep this in mind when you have a command of your own." The two men fell silent and searched the sky and horizon for any indication that the dead calm might soon break but found none.

A full week passed by, the Amity's sails remained slack and empty, the ship besieged by an interminable dead calm. Motionless, the ship drifted atop a grey sunless sea, surrounded by an impenetrable wall of fog that neither approached nor retreated. The concern among Amity's officers and crew had become conspicuous as of late and Jakes worried that a general panic would set in if things did not improve. He had to act, not withstanding result or consequence.

Having had the crew rig towropes from the Amity's bow to several long boats, the captain instructed the men to row forward taking the ship toward the nearest fog bank. After rowing for more than an hour, there was no sign that the ship had made any headway toward the distant cloudbank whatsoever. The fog continued to surround the ship at an unvarying and even distance. The only things moving relative to the ship were the huge sharks that maintained a tireless vigil swimming about the ship in endless circles.

During the day the pervasive dark grey skies continued to prevent the captain from ascertaining their position with respect to the sun, but oddly the night sky would clear somewhat, allowing some of the brighter stars to appear. At such times, Jakes was able to take a number of readings; after doing so, he called Snow to his cabin.

"According to my readings taken over the last three nights we are drifting on a heading SSE..." The captain looked at his officer then continued, "And at a speed of 15 knots." Snow's face expressed his disbelief. "I know what you're thinking Mr. Snow, the speed is quite impossible but ... but true. I've tracked our progress on the chart, see here." He pointed out to Snow the ship's course. "Just as interesting is the fact that there is not a hair variance in our course direction, we are certainly not simply drifting with the currents. We have travelled over two thousand miles from our original position where we first encountered the Ipswich."

"What are we to do captain?" Snow's anxiety was clearly present in his voice.

"Frankly I don't know lad..." Jakes replied. "I just don't know."

The real troubles began the following morning.

The cook's assistant found the porridge unattended on the boil. Fearing that it might "brown bottom" before the cook returned, he removed it from the fire and set about making the officer's morning's tea. After serving the tea, the assistant noted that the cook had still not returned to the galley. When the officers noticed the meals delay, the captain ordered the assistant to begin serving the crew. The man doled out the thick paste into the wooden bowls presented to him by each of the crewmen in turn.

One of the crewmembers piped up asking the assistant since when had cookie begun to add meat in the porridge? Then another added, "Pigs knuckles for breakfast, not a bad choice." The rest of the crew mumbled in agreement, anything new to the bland menu was always welcome.

That would all change a minute later. With breakfast at an end, the cook had still not returned to the galley. His assistant was scraping the last of the porridge from the cauldron with a wooden spoon when he noticed there was something silvery dangling from the ladle. He brought the spoon up closer to his face for inspection when suddenly one of the men cursed and shouted an obscenity pointing into his half empty bowl before throwing it in the direction of the assistant. The bowl hit the floor in front of the startled man spilling its contents onto the galley's dirty wooden floor.

Among the gray brown cereal, several pieces of meat rolled along the floor stopping at the assistant's shoes. He bent low using the spoon to nudge the pieces that he first took to be small sausages before recognizing them for what they were. With an oath he jumped away from the gruesome discovery and stood ramrod straight then slowly brought the ladle up before his face. There, dangling from the spoon was the cook's St. Christopher's medal; where the remainder of the man's body lay would forever remain a mystery.

Over the next night, one of the two men assigned to the night watch went missing. A thorough search of the ship was mounted for the missing crewman. The effort ended without success while Savoy, the second man on night watch was found still standing his post at helm; but being quite dead the man did little to resolve the mystery, much rather the opposite.

The cause of Savoy's demise was both apparent and ghastly, the man having been first disembowelled and then presumably strangled with his own intestines. Several moist coils still drooped down about his chest while yet another strand protruded from his mouth. The rest of his innards lashed the body to the wheel, preventing it from dropping to the deck that was awash in dark jelled blood. Even several of the Amity's most battle hardened seamen blanched at the sight. It was Jenkins, Savoy's best friend that pointed out the small bloody footprints that led away from the corpse, heading forward along the deck and ending where the small oaken water cask sat near the ship's bow. The footprints disturbed Jakes immensely and he gave orders to have the mess upon the deck scrubbed clean immediately. Savoy's funeral began and ended within a matter of minutes. Following a few phrases from the bible, the captain had his corpse unceremoniously thrown overboard where it disappeared among the sharks.

Another day and night passed without further evil levied upon ship or crew. The Amity continued to drift in the grip of the unnatural current. Heading south by east, the vessel found itself constantly surrounded by the unabating curtains of fogs and mists, her masts at times gleaming with St. Elmo's fire. While her sails remained empty, the ship itself was fully ripe with fear and apprehension.

In the dead watches of the night, the crew, including both Jakes and Snow, sometimes recognized the familiar voices of their missing friends and shipmates they had sailed with only days before. Those lost souls hailed the Amity and her remaining crew by name; faint cries, sometimes-urgent shouts, but most often their soft muffled pleas for help reached out through the dark and lonely mists, seemingly breaching death itself.

It had been exactly a fortnight since the Amity's encounter with the Ipswich. As of only this morning, the members of the Amity's crew had numbered fourteen. Fourteen men from a crew of over thirty able bodied seamen. Now on the evening of the same day, Captain Jakes found himself writing yet another sad entry into the ship's log; common seaman John Edwards in an attempt to commit suicide had tied a rope to the stern railing, placing it over his head he had flung himself into the sea.

In his urgent desperation, the man had miscalculated the length of the rope. Rather than his body being suspended in midair and breaking his neck; the man simply splashed into the water to be slowly dragged behind the ship like so much bait behind a trolling rod.

Several of his mates who witnessed his jump rushed the rail watching the half choking, half-drowning seaman's hands grasp and clutch at the hemp that encircled his neck and darkened his face. The men at the rail took the rope in hand and began pulling on the line causing the man at the far end to thrash about violently as their actions only caused the rope's pressure about his neck to increase by several fold. His mates aboard ship now realizing their initial efforts to save the man were not helping in the least, untied the rope from the rail and let it play out into the water hoping the man might loosen the coil about his neck, free himself and swim back toward the ship.

Somehow the tactic worked and the seaman now having freed his neck from the rope's noose grabbed the end of the rope hoarsely croaking out a call to his mates to drag him in. The arms of four strong sailors seized the hemp rope; their muscles strained and bulged as they strove to retrieve their comrade as soon as possible.

A sharp shout from the lookout gave the sailors cause to realize things were not apt to end well. The sharks appeared as if by magic, their familiar sharp triangular dorsal fins broke the water's surface some thirty yards to every side of the floundering seaman. The new urgency of the situation had not been lost on Edwards. His pleading eyes bulged from their sockets, his head tossed first left, and then right as he frantically searched the waters for the gray lethality that lurked and glided only a matter of yards distant.

The first shark to reach Edwards took his right foot off at the ankle, the pain causing Edwards to lose his grip on the rope. The hapless seaman screamed and flailed in the water, his position now utterly hopeless. A second shark swum lazily toward the man removing a hand while a third grey shape took another nibble severing Edwards remaining foot... and so it went for several long minutes. It seemed to some who watched, that the sharks intention was not to kill the man outright, an observation later shared among the crew.

Incredibly their shipmate somehow remained afloat; those men aboard ship who had not turned aside from the terrible scene clearly read every expression, emotion and nuance that swept across the man's face... pain, surprise, fear, anger, and finally deep sadness and acceptance. It was only then that a shark of immense proportion arose from the depths, swimming directly up below the man. The beast's maw gaped open taking the man's lower extremities deeply into its throat, its massive jaws engulfed Edwards torso to a point just below his shoulders before slowly, almost delicately, the jaws closed tight. In those final seconds, Edwards's friends watched his face in a silent grimace of pain and horror before his mouth and nose gushed forth his life's blood into the foaming crimson sea.

The night was still and soundless as Jakes slowly closed the logbook before him, his fingers resting briefly upon the pen that he had returned to the inkwell. The captain sat motionless at his desk staring at the far wall of the cabin where his cutlass hung in its scabbard, the silver hand guard caught and glittered with the light of a single flame that alternately guttered and gleamed outward from a small lantern suspended from one of the thick wooded rafters. The lamp swayed gently back and forth with the action of the waves, the motion setting dim shadows dancing upon the wall.

As the captain continued to stare, he slowly became aware that the shadows seemed to be taking on peculiar and definite shapes. The silhouettes evolved before his widening eyes into the forms of men, women, and children, Jakes recognized them for who they were; black slaves. The lantern's reflection glittered along the silvered hilt of his sword splashing their pitiful ragged outlines upon the cabin's walls. Jakes watched the eerie shadow dance taking place before him, the arms of the figures seemingly rising and falling in unison as if moving to a yet unheard cadence.

Then, through the deep silence within his cabin, Jakes believed his ears caught the faint sound of drums and tribal chanting. In the center of the circle the scattered candle light grew to become a brilliant bonfire, the fire's light illuminated the outlines of the people who now became three-dimensional; he could see their faces and expressions, even the whites of their eyes and teeth. Their chanting grew in strength and power coaxing forth and summoning a small dark figure that squatted within the flames and embers of the central bonfire.

The creature rose up from deep within the flames themselves. Ever so slowly, the form grew and expanded, at first obscuring the blaze, then cloaking and consuming all remaining flame and light within the blackened folds of its shadow as it drew itself erect. The slaves dancing and chanting had fallen suddenly silent; all that remained was the slow rhythmic boom of a heavy drum and the growing darkness of the figure that continued to expand before him. The black outline assumed huge dimensions, completely occupying the entire far wall of Jake's cabin and swallowing up any remaining light in the cabin.

The slow drumming stopped abruptly. Jakes sat on his chair staring forward into the silent darkness, his heart beating wildly in his chest, his brow covered in a cold sweat. The absolute blackness of the form was changing now, the dark outline grudgingly giving leeway, brightening ever so gradually, until Jakes could just detect dim facial features taking shape on the apparitions face. As he continued to stare, he began to realize the face bore a certain familiarity that congealed within into his mind then snapped to crystal clarity as he recognized the face before him to be that of Toby, the cabin boy. The cabin boy's eyes slowly opened, a pair of fierce fire-laced black eyes glared toward Jakes who felt his own eyes instantly held and transfixed upon its menacing features. Jakes watched the boy's mouth sneer and contort into a familiar hate filled grimace. Slowly the boy's mouth parted and continued to open until it reached impossibly wide proportions revealing a maw of razor sharp teeth, the teeth Jakes now recognized as being those of a shark.

Jakes mouth opened to scream but found his breath caught in his throat. The horrible countenance wavered before him driving all reason from his mind and replacing it in turn with abject fear. Then in an instant, the images were gone and the room was as before. The orange candlelight flickered lightly upon the walls and floor, the logbook still sat closed upon the desk, the pen in the inkwell. He sat quietly for several minutes, looking about and listening to the familiar and comforting sounds of the ship. The rhythm of his heart slowed and his shallow breathing deepened. Jakes stood, taking up his cloak and hat then as an afterthought picked up his favorite pipe from the desk before going topside allowing the sea air to clear his thoughts and mind.

The next morning Jakes was speaking with Snow on the bridge when a delegation of crewmen approached the officers. The men hesitantly informed their superiors that they could no longer serve aboard the ship and pleaded with the captain to allow them to provision several of the long boats and leave the vessel to whatever hell awaited it. The crewmen need not have pleaded whatsoever, as Jakes and his junior officer had already decided it necessary to abandon the ship if anyone was to survive the evil that they had inadvertently taken onboard.

The preparations filled the morning and half the afternoon. Two of Amity's four long boats would carry the crew and as such were equipped with small sails and oars. Each of these would tow a second boat heavily provisioned with sufficient food and water to give the crew a fighting chance of reaching another port or perhaps coming across another ship. It was agreed that Lieutenant Snow would take half the men aboard his two craft while the captain would lead the remaining two boats and generally command the small flotilla.

Before leaving the ship, the Captain and his lieutenant spoke in his cabin out of sight and hearing of the crew. It was important that what the Captain planned for the Amity never reach the ears of the ship's owners or initiate a general board of inquiry. As for the details regarding the abandonment of the ship, he and his lieutenant figured they had at least a month to concoct whatever need be said about the matter. Although most seamen were superstitious at heart, it would hardly do for any captain to admit abandoning or worse, scuttling his vessel because of a haunting.

Late that afternoon, Jakes ordered the crew into the long boats that waited alongside the ship with the explanation that the Amity's captain and lieutenant would need additional time to inspect the ship. In doing so, the officers hoped to improve the odds of the ships remaining afloat thus providing at least some chance of salvage in the future. This was of course completely at odds with what the officers truly planned to accomplish.

Working together, the officers carefully set two heavy charges of black powder against the port sides of the hull, one forward and the other aft and both positioned well below the waterline. Long coils of slow burning fuse would ensure detonation some hours after departing the ship. With any luck, the small boats would be over the horizon and out of site when the Amity met her end.

All preparations made and standing topside, Jakes ordered Lieutenant Snow aboard the first two boats instructing him to have his men row out and hold position a hundred yards from the ship. Jakes planned to return to his cabin, collect the log, charts and navigational instruments then return to the remaining boats. Retrieving what he required, the captain left his cabin, then turned one last time, reflected upon what he was doing then slowly closed the door. Before going above decks he lit the two fuses, one would burn its way forward, the other aft.

Captain Jakes began his assent topside when he heard confused shouting and the occasional scream coming from the side of the ship where the long boats waited. Upon reaching the upper decks, he ran along the wooden planks toward the railing attempting to see the cause of the commotion. In his haste and scarcely believing his eyes, he dropped and scattered the instruments and charts along the deck.

Several large schools of sharks were circling and bumping up against the sides of each long boat. Watching in amazement and horror, Jakes saw several sharks swim toward the nearest boat still tied fast to the ship. He gasped aloud seeing the creatures heave themselves up and onto the narrow gunwales, their jaws snapping at the terrified seamen who scrambled further into the boat in a vain attempt to avoid being bitten. Several of the men struck and prodded at the huge fish with their oars. Just when it appeared that the tactic was working an evil transformation took place before the astonished eyes of the crew and the captain alike.

The upper body and fins of the sharks in the boats began to elongate and change. Their sleek grey forms began to metamorphosize into the more familiar shapes, of heads, torsos and arms of black men and women. Their hands grabbed and held the crewmembers fast before dragging them back into the sea where savage teeth and jaws waited to mangle flesh and bone to the tune of the high-pitched screams coaxed from the throats of their hapless victims.

The captain continued to watch, completely powerless to assist his dead and dying men as one by one, they were pulled into the sea from the boat still held fast to the side of his ship. Looking further outward toward Snow's boats, he saw that only the young officer and two of his men now remained aboard, the rest had disappeared, no doubt dragged into the sea by the monsters. Snow's two crew men could be seen sobbing, their heads in their hands while the young officer much to his credit, stood oar in hand; still prepared to defend his command to the end.

Ten minutes had passed since the attack. Snow directed his remaining two men to row towards the ship where they would pick up their captain. Snow's boats arrived minutes later and his men held the boats to the side of the ship while the lieutenant hastily climbed to the deck where the captain waited. Jakes handed his junior officer the logs of the Amity and Ipswich as well as the charts and instruments saying that Snow would require them for the voyage. Snow looked questioningly at his captain.

Jakes face was ashen, his own expression quite blank while he spoke. "Mr. Snow, you will leave the area immediately and take yourself and crew to safe port. I intend to stay aboard the Amity." The young man began to blither and plead with his captain asking the man to join them but Jakes cut him short. "You have your orders Mr. Snow! I expect you to obey them." the captain spoke firmly then followed more gently, "Good luck son and God Speed you now." Snow's face was wet and his cheeks inflamed with color as he turned from his captain and set about climbing down the netted rigging and into the long boat where the last two remaining crewmen waited.

Jakes watched the two small boats grow ever smaller in the distance until they finally disappeared over the horizon. If possible, the constant grey cloud above the ship grew darker and more brooding; any hint of sunlight now banished from the sky. He stared silently a few minutes longer and then spoke. "There, it is done. Do I have your promise?"

"My good captain," the very words dripped with distain, "I have given you no promise to keep." The captain turned about coming face to face with the black shadowed monstrosity that stood before him. The body of the creature was nondescript, ever changing within an irregular ebony outline. Its only consistent features were the unblinking, staring eyes that gleamed malevolently at Jakes. The creature continued to converse in a manner that continued to amaze the captain who could only guess that its thoughts were somehow projected into his mind. The strangest part was that the words, clearly articulated, were his own; it was as if he were speaking to himself.

Suddenly a thin, clawed appendage stretched out beyond the creatures black outline as it glided noiselessly toward Jakes, it held two long coils of fuse. "Something else I learned from McCrery," Its eyes narrowing to the sharpest slits before continuing. "Other than torture, perversion, malice, and self-interest. I couldn't have you sink our ship just yet could I?" The coiled fuse dropped upon the deck in front of the captain.

"No I suppose not." Jakes spoke without emotion realizing that his plan had failed then pressed his previous question, "My crewmen in the boat, are they safe?"

The creature hissed, "Unlike you I do not persecute or profit from the agony of the innocent... I avenge them. Your

Lieutenant Snow and the others took their leave with hearts were not yet utterly blackened and corrupt." It paused and then continued. "A stark contrast to you captain. One who profits through the sale of his fellow man. Know now you have only succeeded in wholesaling your own immortal soul."

The captain shivered in fear and apprehension as he attempted to state his case to the blackness that now began to shrink before his eyes into something more familiar. "I simp, simply conducted my lawful business and duties as captain." A sudden evil hiss unnerved Jakes and he stuttered out. "I ne, never intentionally mistreated my carg ... oh". Jakes paused then added, "... my legal charges..." His head dropped "... those people."

In an instant, the sun flashed forth into an unusually blue clear sky. The small cabin boy once again sat before the captain, as he had before, atop the small oaken cask. Toby's face grinned happily, as he pointed down into the waters below the ship's starboard rail. Jakes could make out the sounds of something thrashing in the water and drew closer to the ship's edge allowing his eyes to follow the boys lead. Below him, the water teemed and boiled with sleek gray bodies of all sizes.

The boy spoke into Jakes mind yet again. "It won't be long now my captain; it seems that my friends smell fresh blood in the water." The cabin boy arose from the cask and stood motionless looking far out to sea.

Adrift somewhere within the Dark Triangle, the Amity's captain slowly lifted his head and using his hands, shaded his eyes from the brilliant sunlight. Searching the cold waters - leagues beyond where the sharks still circled endlessly - Jakes could just make out a familiar shape.

A small white sail had just breached the distant horizon.

Reap the Whirlwind

Following his summons, the pleasant young woman arrived at the reception desk outside the office of the Director of the North Korean Meteorological Institute. Located in Pyongyang, the Institute had recently found itself in a state of upheaval ever since their glorious leader had panned the Institute's inaccurate weather forecasts. Apparently, an elaborate picnic for his favorite general's daughter had been ruined by a light but an unforeseen sprinkling of rain that had fallen in one of the country's poorest, drought ravaged provinces. Now it appeared that heads might roll and the institute's Director was quite certain that one of those heads would be his.

Yi Min-ji had worked her way up the bureaucratic rungs within the forecast center where she had shown an amazing aptitude in divining accurate forecasts, even when the most unusual and perplexing weather patterns presented themselves. Then without warning, her position within the institute was re-evaluated. China had provided the Korean institute with a sophisticated meteorological program it had recently procured. Considered as no longer essential, Min-ji's position of principal analyst went to the Director's nephew, a captain in the People's Army. She in turn, returned to the administration pool.

Upon seeing the young woman approach her desk, the receptionist, a young army corporal, buzzed the Director then waved Min-ji through the ornately carved mahogany door and into a large corner office. The Director's nephew brushed past Min-ji as she entered, throwing her a scowl as he walked from the office. The Director stood beside his desk and pointed to a hard wooden chair centered before his huge walnut desk then sat behind it in a well-appointed leather chair. The unsmiling uniformed officer wore the rank of light colonel and struck a distinctly pissed off expression as he shuffled through the papers on his desk. Colonel Kim was used to having things his own way but the Supreme Leader made it abundantly clear that either he would improve the track record of the institute or he'd be out, all the way out!

"Tongmu Min-ji Yi is it?" the director addressed her as if he had just laid eyes on her for the first time in his life. Tongmu or comrade was used to address people of common status, but the DPRK also ensured that superiors were paid the proper respect and so invented another version of "comrade" that would signify a higher status, that of Tongji.

"Tongji Colonel, what may I do to serve the People?" The petite woman was quite sincere in both her address and desire to do all she could to forward the agenda of their Supreme Leader, who after all was only concerned with what was best for his people. Min-ji was pleased and well aware as to why she was sitting in the Director's office although it would not do for her to show it. To do so would rob Tongji Colonel of whatever face remained to him, following the Supreme Leaders recent and most uncomfortable visit.

"You may be quiet Tongmu." The man stared hard at the woman through the small round lenses of his glasses. While not a member of the military, she sat at attention, patiently and politely awaiting his response. Reassured that he had saved face he could now proceed to save his ass. "Your superiors have determined that you deserve to be immediately reinstated to your former position. I trust that your performance will continue to improve in the future." He studied her face waiting to see if she would request further details regarding her reinstatement. Questions, even those that were pertinent, were generally viewed in a negative light. When the question failed to arrive the Director's expression and tone softened. "You may go Tongmu."

"Thank you Tongji Colonel." The woman rose from her chair and bowed to the man who had once again returned to his pretense of paper shuffling. As she turned and walked toward the door, she could feel his cold eyes on her back.

Several months later Min-ji Yi sat at her desk staring out into the courtyard from her second floor cubical. She had done well, well enough for the director to single her out for high praise at the institute's last general meeting and provide her a "cubical with a view". Min-ji had bravely gone out on a limb, presenting the director with a forecast that directly countered that of the institute's meteorological computer program.

That program had forecast that a weak cold front would sweep across the northern part of the country bringing with it only a smattering of light snow. On the other hand, Min-ji insisted the front would strengthen, growing into a monstrous blizzard that would paralyze half the country for nearly a week, that same week the DPRK would be conducting some of its largest war game exercises. To make matters worse the Chinese would be taking part in the exercise, four armored divisions worth to be exact.

This placed the Tongji Colonel in a tight spot. Stay the course and support a computer forecast that to date had shown itself to be reasonably accurate, often agreeing with the girl's own independent forecast or, choose to support Min-ji's severe winter weather advisory that if followed would postpone the war games. Colonel Kim was also very much aware that the Chinese' weather forecasters having fed the same raw meteorological information into their program, would no doubt arrive at the same conclusion as did the Korean model. To make matters worse, state institutions such as his could not exchange information with those of any other country, to do so would be considered an admission of the North's inferiority. It was time for Kim to go big or go home. For once, he went big.

The Koreans postponed the exercise and while the Chinese generals first complained bitterly, they were deeply grateful when the full fury of the winter storm broke upon the borderlands between the two countries. The growing extremes in the weather caused by global warming had created yet another dangerous situation that may have cost hundreds of lives. The Supreme Leader took the opportunity afforded by his institute's success to rub the noses of the Chinese in the apparent lack in their own. Tongji Colonel Kim was once again in favor with the Party and far more importantly, enjoyed the high personal regard of the leader himself.

The girl sat at her desk and watched the people as they went about their business in the oppressive summer heat. Far from being a light blue, the hot cloudless sky above the city choked in a brown haze, the result of the coal-fired electrical generation stations located near the capital. It had not rained in nearly a month, and then the shower had lasted less than an hour. The leaves on the trees and bushes in the city were wizened and brown, while the grass lawns surrounding the government buildings were almost none existent, except for a small well-watered patch directly outside the beloved Supreme Leader's office.

Min-ji Yi suddenly felt an incredibly deep and urgent desire for rain. She glanced at the computer monitor on her desk providing the latest forecast model for Pyongyang. The forecast, continually updated by the minute, still predicted the high-pressure system would remain stationary and unchanging over the capital. Min-ji closed her eyes and leaned back in her chair.

She thought back to one of her favorite memories. Min-ji imagined herself back at her family's small country farm when she was but seven years old, so many miles and years distant from the huge capital. It was mid-morning on a fine spring day. Min-ji stood together with her parents and brother on the porch of their small house overlooking the garden. They had just finished seeding and now watched the rising columns of cumulus clouds boiling up along the horizon. Even back then, this was one of her favorite pass times; watching the ever changing weather. The billowing towers of brilliant white cloud having climbed high into the stratosphere now met with resistance from the layers of warmer air that lay above. Unable to continue their rise, they swept outward, assuming classic anvil shapes that sailed atop their darkened bases.

Min-ji imagined she could see the line of thunderstorms approaching the farm. The shadows of the giant clouds moved slowly over the low hills lying to the west, until the leading edge of the front finally obscured the noon sun. Solitary random peals of thunder rang out and echoed as the dark clouds swept across the valley floor. The intense flashes of lightning and booming roars grew in frequency and volume as the storm continued its approach. Min-ji could smell the rain in the air and began to hear the first oversized droplets of water falling on the tin roof of their little home. As the first drops rapidly became a deluge, Min-ji felt the welcome drop in air temperature accompanied by an increase in humidity. A huge flash of light instantaneously followed by a tremendous report sounded directly above her cubical, the force of the supersonic blast rattling the office windows within their frames and shaking the building to its foundations.

Her eyes popped wide as she stared with incredulity at the downpour taking place outside her office window. Booms of thunder immediately answered the lightning that flashed in brilliant sheets. The rain beat and pelted against the windows, at times slowing somewhat until again renewed by alternating waves of lightning and thunder. Min-ji watched the raindrops striking the surface of the small puddles that had formed in the courtyard. A few minutes later, the puddles had joined becoming small rivers that headed off in a mad rush, coursing atop the asphalt and streaming toward the curbs and sewer gratings.

A half hour later, as Min-ji watched the dark clouds fleeing to the east, and the sun emerging to shine anew in the refreshed, clear cobalt skies above the capital, she realized her gift. Not only could she predict the weather; she could make it!

The girl was young, impressionable, and naive. A forgivable and predictable result of the party doctrine she and her generation had been spoon-fed. The oppression to freethinking, the discouraged individuality, and the unbroken wall of isolation the regime built and maintained around the country saw to that. The Supreme Leader and his cronies also realized the benefits of ruling over an impoverished people. When the vast majority of your citizens were unsure of just when and where their next meal was coming from, the people tended to tow the party line more fervently and ask fewer questions.

All regimes, no matter their economic or political philosophy worked on some variation of the "carrot and the stick" principle. People had to understand that working together with the status quo was preferable to working against it. This said, a simple and basic problem plagued all governments to some degree; the people at the top too often wielded the stick but frequently forgot to supply the carrot. This failure to understand this fundamental rule bore consequences. In democracies, the results were elections that swept the governing party from office while in dictatorships the consequences wore the face of revolution.

Over the next six months, Min-ji practiced, tested and documented her efforts quietly and with great care. So far, she had manipulated weather patterns to provide the drought-stricken provinces with more frequent rains while reducing the climactic extremes that had recently become the norm rather than the exception. All in all, things were going very well, so well in fact that she decided she would soon reveal her secret to the institute's director. She harbored no doubt whatsoever that her newly discovered abilities would result in recognition, a promotion of sorts and possibly even an increase in salary; a substantial part of which she could send back to her parents and family.

Min-ji had correctly predicted the "blizzard of the century" saving the lives of soldiers and quite possibly that of the Tongji Colonel the year before. Since that time, the Director saw to it that Min-ji enjoyed immediate access to his office. Like the weather, circumstances had improved for the institute and especially its director. The Minister to whom the Director reported made it clear that the Colonel was once again in favor and could expect advancement. If what Min-ji had been telling him were true, his future would be promising indeed.

The colonel sat behind his desk, his face blank and unreadable as he listened to the nervous girl spin an incredible story about her ability to control the weather. Six months earlier, he would have considered her mentally incapable and had her sent off to an asylum, one of the brutal and ill-managed Number 49 Hospitals situated far off in the northern mountains; but that was six months ago. Ever since Min-ji began to exert control over the weather, Kim and his staff had been working to understand the unusual improvements of the local climate. Together with the unprecedented inclusion of their counterparts in China, the Institute, and all its resources had sought to determine just how it was that North Korea's climate had suddenly taken an incredible upturn, while just across the border in China and

South Korea, the situation continued to remain abysmally poor. Up until this minute, neither team had been able to furnish any explanation whatsoever.

Min-ji left the Director's office smiling and considering the bright future the director had outlined for her and her family. The minute he was alone he placed a call to his superior then had his driver take him to the government offices. The minister looked at Kim as if he were quite mad but after the colonel had laid out the extraordinary evidence gathered over the past six months, Kim found himself standing in the presence of none other than the Vice Premier of the Workers Party of Korea. Had the colonel had known or even suspected what would happen in the coming days, Min-ji would have been dead and buried five minutes after speaking with him in his office.

As it was, Yi Min-ji met with the Vice Premier to display her abilities. She did so by creating a rather small thundershower from an otherwise blue clear sky and having it end and disappear completely within the space of fewer than ten minutes. The next morning she bowed deeply before the beloved Supreme Leader who politely requested she create a much larger storm, once again from a cloudless sky. Halfway through her performance, the Vice Premier leaned over and whispered in her ear. Min-ji nodded obediently and moments later the group witnessed several tornadic funnel clouds make their way to the earth then scour their way along the ground, taking out some small, unoccupied buildings in the process. That evening Tongji Min-ji dined with the Supreme Leader and his closest and most trusted ministers; Tongmu Colonel Kim was conspicuously absent.

Several days later, the newspapers reported that the esteemed Director of the North Korean Meteorological Institute had taken his own life. Shortly after, a purge of the Institute concluded several section heads to be insurrectionist. Without trial or hearing, they were imprisoned and shortly thereafter hung themselves from the bars of their cells.

The government was quick to tell Min-ji they wished to reward her and her family, as she was now a hero of the nation. The Supreme Leader himself asked her to provide a list of her family members. The following week Yi Min-ji had an opportunity to meet with each of her relatives during a large and well-attended gathering. The Vice Premier himself bestowed his august presence to the group just as lunch was served. After the meal, Min-ji said her farewells to her parents, brother, and the others before being whisked away to her new office located at a top-secret base near the Yongbyon Nuclear Scientific Research station. Confident that she was improving the lives of those closest to her she completely threw herself into her work.

The secret base was a division of the Ministry of State Security or the MSS. Min-ji's handlers were careful not to broadcast that fact. Having created an ambiance of fear that had crept into every facet of life; the North Korean secret police became utterly despised. To avoid any association with the MSS, the newly founded Ministry of Social Welfare would administer the project. Min-ji found herself in the company of scientists who seemingly shared her heartfelt resolve to improve the lives of their people.

To determine just how Min-ji did what she did, the girl was studied and put through physical and mental testing much the same as a lab rat; a very precious lab rat. Failing to determine any hard or fast answers to their many questions, one of the project's team leaders felt compelled to subject Min-ji to a powerful combination of psychotic drugs without seeking proper approval. The result was nearly a disaster.

The MSS facility and the nearby nuclear research station responsible for the development of the country's atomic weapons soon found themselves surrounded in a terrifying storm. The immense electrical tempest, complete with tornados and downdrafts of various intensities struck the mainly underground facility. Even so protected, the storm still managed to cause extensive damage; damage that had to await repair for nearly a full week until the heavy July snowfall sufficiently melted. Whatever happened to that particular team leader was sufficiently unpleasant to ensure any further independent and unauthorized testing would never again take place.

When Min-ji received the injection, its combination of hallucinogens and stimulants caused something to stir deeply within her mind. The effects of the drugs were terrifying; in other words, they functioned exactly as intended. According to previous "volunteers," the exotic cocktail caused all those under its influence to experience deep feelings of extreme isolation and solitude. These emotions forced the person to consider anyone they reacted with as their best friend, possibly even their savior given the drug made them feel they were physically dying of loneliness. In this way, information of a highly confidential nature was readily disclosed.

The drugs had a similar effect on Min-ji as they raced through her veins. In the short minutes before losing consciousness she found her mind reaching out, desperately seeking other people, some within her building and then others within the nearby nuclear research facility. Min-ji subconsciously expected to discover other minds containing thoughts and feelings like her own, minds that were warm, generous, and compassionate but instead, she found individuals whose characters were based on deceit, cruelty, and self-interest. Just before passing out, Min-ji had directed her anger upward, into the skies above the MSS facility and the nuclear weapons research station.

Following the unauthorized test, Min-ji stayed in hospital for nearly a week before returning to the hurriedly repaired MSS base. The girl had become morose and withdrawn, so much so her physicians feared she may have experienced some degree of brain damage, but their prognosis could not have been more wrong, brain augmentation would be a more suitable term.

That said, for now the girls mind was a flutter of confusion. She found herself unable to establish any consistent train of thought. Min-ji felt as if she was in a whirling room full of screaming maniacs, each vying for her attention. The flood of totally random and unrelated snippets of ideas and emotions invaded and disrupted her entire being. As those first difficult days passed, Min-ji slowly discovered that she could block most of the thoughts except those who were physically closest to her.

During that week, Min-ji remained in bed, unresponsive to the comings and goings of the doctors and project directors. Recovering, Min-ji received a bedside visit from the Vice Premier. The politician spoke in warm fuzzy terms telling the girl how important she was to her country, to her many good friends here at the project and of course, her family. When the Vice Premier mentioned her mother and father, Min-ji found she could bring his thoughts and memories into tight focus. The girl probed deeper into the man's mind and was shocked and dismayed at what she discovered.

Moments after Min-ji left her joyful family reunion; everyone who had remained at the party were crowded into three large olive green trucks and driven to a specially constructed camp. Upon arrival, scientists probed, tested, and studied her relatives in an effort to determine if any of them possessed similar forecasting abilities. The one person they identified as possessing a mild predilection for meteorological matters was her brother. He could accurately forecast the next day's weather but only in the local vicinity. The other members of her family had no such ability at all and as such did not rejoin their communities. There was too great a risk of them disclosing what they may or may not have heard regarding their talented relative; instead, they were shot in the back of the head.

Her brother continued to endure the intense physiological and psychological investigations. Once every method and effort had failed to produce tangible results, in desperation he underwent vivisection over a number of days. The study into the phenomenon finally concluding, her brother's body joined those of her parents and the rest of Min-ji's family in an unmarked mass grave located beyond the camp fence.

It had been over a month; Min-ji had now recovered fully and was eager to continue her work. She would make use of her abilities to defend her fellow workers from imperialist aggression. Truthfully, Min-ji told her handlers that she was not able to create and project violent weather conditions any further than perhaps ten to fifteen miles distant but felt confident she could expand the scope of her abilities with time. The MSS team were already well satisfied with the results of her efforts; Min-ji didn't mention her ability to read thoughts.

As the months passed, the girl's powers grew quickly and Min-ji found she was able to project atmospheric control several hundred miles distant. Moreover, the level and duration of the incidents had greatly heightened; her handlers determined it was time to turn her abilities toward the enemy. When asked, Min-ji stretched her consciousness toward the South Korean border, and while doing so, probed the minds of the soldiers who manned the fortifications. The intentions of the South Korean soldiers were definitely hostile; truly hating the North's regime, they would gladly destroy it if it were possible. Min-ji could not allow them to harm her people, even if some of the men and women in their government were lacking what her father would have termed good character.

Min-ji launched her first attack in the form of a severe electrical storm that took out the many radar and communications stations near the border. Her second attack, less than an hour later was a tremendous squall that overtook a small flotilla of South Korean patrol vessels near one of the disputed islands in the West Sea. The massive waterspouts Min-ji conjured within the storm picked up several of the vessels and brought them crashing down on one of the enemy's artillery garrisons located on the nearest island. Other ships were simply swamped, and disappeared beneath the huge waves that relentlessly assaulted the small vessels.

The next afternoon the beloved Supreme Leader personally took the time to visit the MSS center. Meeting with Min-ji, he extended the country's gratitude while saying on a personal level he was extremely pleased with her efforts. The girl softly probed his mind but was unable to focus on any part of it that thought of her family. His only interest centered about the destruction of the American and South Korean forces massed on their country's borders. It was time to get him on track.

Smiling sweetly Min-ji asked quietly, "Supreme Leader, might I see my family, I do so miss my brother, my father, and my mother. Do you know how they are doing?" She deliberately paused as she mentioned each person letting the suggestion coax any memory of her family to the forefront of his mind. It worked.

His face was blank of expression and completely unreadable as the man lied to her. "Yes, we shall have a visit arranged as soon as possible." He continued, "Your family is doing well! I myself issued special instructions ensuring they have everything they require." He smiled sweetly at her. "Your brother and parents even have a new home, far out in the hills, out to the west of the farm where you grew up." Even as the words left his lips, she could clearly see the camp within his mind, the barbed wire, and the mass grave just beyond. The cruel bastard had even visited the camp personally to ensure the soldiers and staff followed his instructions to the letter. Without pause and hiding any emotion other than what she wanted to show, the girl smiled and expressed her gratitude for the leader's thoughtfulness.

The Supreme Leader blustered, "It's time to make the South pay for their crimes against our people. A huge typhoon lies several hundred miles off the coast of the Yellow Sea. I would like you to take control of it and guide it toward our enemies in Seoul." The man looked into her eyes, seeking any sign that she might resist the suggestion. To his own surprise, he saw an expression of distress cross the girl's face; she announced it verbally a second later.

"Beloved Leader, the storm is unusually violent; bringing it to shore and placing it atop a city will kill thousands of innocent people!" Her eyes did not lie; there was no need to do so.

He expected as much, although he had hoped the girl would be more fervent in her nationalism. It was time for him to get tough. "Yi Min-ji, you will do as you are told. The nation asks much of us all. Remember, your actions reflect upon you and your family as well! Consider their welfare." He and the party often used thinly veiled threats toward family members, as a means to further their aims, this time would be no different.

She pretended to capitulate immediately, "Of course, I will do as you ask Beloved Supreme Leader. I am yours to command!" She allowed her eyes to fall subserviently to the floor.

"Of course you will... but of course you will." The short moonfaced dictator smiled coldly, then turned and waddled out of the room followed by his regular entourage of personal assistants and bodyguards. An hour later, his helicopter landed in the courtyard of his favorite residence, the fortress of Ryongsong Palace.

As Min-ji worked to strengthen her now very considerable control over the weather, she equally strove to develop her mental abilities to focus or "listen" as she coined it, to other people's thoughts at great distance. With practice, she found she could probe other's thoughts at will. If her beloved leader had any inkling of her true power, she would have been dead before he left her room that first afternoon.

Min-ji focused her mind, allowing herself to sweep out and range to the south, far beyond the barbed wire, landmines and heavy fortifications that separated her country from South Korea. Doing so, the thoughts of the ordinary people in the countryside reached her mind. Min-ji was not surprised to find that nearly all of those her mind touched wished only to live their lives in peace. The same had been true of her people in the north. Reaching the enemy's capital city of Seoul, she prodded and probed random individuals within the city seeking to locate the minds of those within government. Quickly finding what she sought, those minds guided her toward her ultimate goal, the South Korean President.

Min-ji found the man sitting alone on a sunlit balcony quietly watching the bustling city before him. As guarded as was her beloved Supreme Leader, the man whose mind she now touched was instead an open book! She "listened" to the man's thoughts and found him thinking of his aunt and uncle who had remained in the North; her country, he was wondering if they were still alive. She actively probed his mind and was amazed to find he actually cared about her people. The president looked forward to the time when they could again be a single country, a unified nation at peace. She pressed harder, deeper; her efforts revealing the South Korean leader had been very concerned with the reports of widespread starvation in the north. He and his government had even made quiet offers of assistance... all had been refused. As circumstances improved in the north, the man had been truly grateful for the end of the drought and the starvation that had accompanied it.

Yi Min-ji continued to "listen" to the Tongji President Park Seo-jun for some time. Having learned what she sought, Min-ji withdrew her mind from the South's capital then reached to the west. Somewhere offshore, her awareness touched and interacted with the warm waters of the Yellow Sea and the fierce winds that swirled above the waves. After a time, Min-ji became aware that she was losing her own individuality, joining and becoming one with the colossal storm. Slowly, ever so slowly, she bent her will and that of the storm's path northward, towards Ryongsong Palace.

The storm's powerful outer winds would soon buffet the fortress and minutes after its arrival, Min-ji would bring the fortified compound down about the dictator's ears before seeking out the other criminals within his government. Eventually a handler's bullet would end her life but it would arrive far too late to prevent Min-ji from saving her people.

An Angry Dragon

Jiang Wang aka "Jimmy" and his wife, Lei Wang aka "Will ya clear the tables for Christ's sake!" ran a small eight-table restaurant just off Edmonton Trail, a thoroughfare that bordered Calgary's China town. Coming to Canada over twenty years before, Jimmy and his wife Lei had opened the Angry Dragon in the late nineties. Over the first fifteen years, the now middle-aged couple just managed to keep the doors open trying to compete with the much larger and more established restaurants. Then suddenly five years ago, the popularity of the restaurant took off, and since that time, the little eatery had become a fixture in the Asian community.

If you were to walk in for a bite before the noon or evening rush, Jimmy might spend five or ten minutes at your table. He would beam with pride as he directed your attention to the far wall. The one nearest the takeout counter, the one plastered with the testimonials and reviews of the city's papers, travel magazines, and numerous local and even international celebrities. Carefully arranged across the top of the wall were no fewer than, count 'em now; nine 8x10 glossies of visiting movie stars who having heard of the restaurant, just had to pop in for a nosh of Jimmy's signature dish, the Angry Dragon. Below each grinning face was a hastily scribbled "thank you Jimmy" or "best Chinese food I've ever eaten!" followed by an incomprehensible signature that would feel right at home below an MD's drug prescription.

This hadn't always the case. Not that long ago Lei actually worried they would have to close the Angry Dragon's doors. None of her hard work had brought in many repeat customers, and what little money the diner brought in Jimmy would gamble or drink away. Coming and going as he wished, or out tomcatting about, her husband would leave Lei and her sister to run the cafe. Aside from his other failings, Jimmy had a mean streak in him a mile wide. Every so often, Lei would bear the brunt of the man's failings, sporting a black eye or a fat lip; frankly, back then he was not much of a catch.

One could say Jimmy didn't see eye to eye with many people. The man had a huge chip on his shoulder but who could blame him... after all the whole world had it in for him. These were the same people that took his money each week at the poker or Mahjong tables. They were the do-gooders, churchgoers, or anyone else who occupied a higher station in life or enjoyed better fortune, earned or otherwise. The list was extensive and unlikely to end anytime soon.

Then in 1999, just before the Chinese New Year's celebration on February 16th; an old Chinese gentleman walked into the Angry Dragon dragging a large heavy suitcase. The old boy had his choice of tables, as was usual back then since the place was usually deserted. He paused and looked around, then chose a small booth for himself near the window. Easing himself into the booth, his pants slid atop the shabby, cracked red vinyl that covered the bench seat. He pressed his body deeper into the booth until he found himself sitting comfortably behind a worn and chipped Formica tabletop. He removed his hat, placing the black bowler on the vacant seat beside him while propping an ornate ivory handled cane up against the bench.

In the back room, Jimmy heard the bell that had tinkled softly as the front door opened and gruffly told his wife to see to the customer while he sat at a table in the back room finishing off his third rye and coke of the day. It was just after one in the afternoon and Jimmy was planning to close early before walking, or more correctly, staggering over to the Chinese Community center where he planned to attend the New Year's Eve party.

Lei walked from the kitchen toward the diner's sole customer who quietly observed the world through the window glass as it went about its business. Considering his dress and deportment, Lei could immediately see he was a newcomer to the country. She greeted him speaking Mandarin, "Good afternoon grandfather, welcome to our restaurant." Lei smiled kindly at the old gent.

The man returned her smile, gave his head a slight nod, and then in turn greeted her in Cantonese. Lei was pleasantly surprised to hear the far less common Chinese dialect, the language of her birthplace. Mandarin had recently become the official language

172

of China and Taiwan, and most commonly spoken by the majority of Chinese who had immigrated from the old country.

"I'm very sorry sir, my husband and I will soon be closing to attend the New Year's celebration." She shrugged her shoulders and frowned in apology.

"Ah, I see." The elderly man reached for his hat. "Is there another restaurant close by, I'm hungry and very tired from my walk. I only arrived in your city an hour ago by bus." Suddenly the old fellow looked positively ancient and bone tired. Noticing the cane leaned on the bench seat beside him Lei concluded he probably had difficulty getting around, even without having to lug the rather hefty looking suitcase about.

She reconsidered. "Please wait. If you don't mind I'm sure we have something we can serve you, something left over from lunch perhaps." That didn't come out quite right she thought, and then added. "You needn't pay; it would be our pleasure... a New Year's gift?

The man reset his black bowler on the seat then looked up at the woman and smiled. "That's very kind of you. I haven't much money. You see my great grandchildren were supposed to meet me at the station and take me home with them... but they seem to have forgotten." Looking a little sad, he shook his head from side to side. "I have a phone number but I couldn't find a payphone anywhere." With the advent of cell phones, these days the old phone booths were as rare as hen's teeth.

"Now you just sit grandfather, I'll get you a pot of tea to start." Lei felt genuine pity for the man and not more than a little contempt for the thoughtless relatives who had stood him up. She retrieved her cell phone, bringing it to the table and handing it to the old gent before returning into the backroom. A short while later she returned with a pot of tea. The old man thanked her then handed back her phone saying he had left a message for his great grandson to pick him up at the restaurant.

A little later, Lei brought him a plate of food and asked if he would like some company. Lei hadn't enjoyed a conversation in Cantonese for quite some time. Besides, just before she came out she noticed Jimmy had mixed yet another drink and stood outside in the alley smoking and bullshitting with the fellow that ran the second-hand shop next door. She needn't worry rushing to close up.

Although they spoke for more than an hour and a half, Lei thought it felt like only minutes. She had learned the man's name was Song Fui Song and that he had been born over one hundred years ago, back in 1895, in the year of the Wooden Rooster. He was a magician by trade, spending decades entertaining in the finest Asian theaters and even having performed before royalty. Lei smiled at the thought. If he was as old as he said he was, he'd have to be a regular David Copperfield, as he certainly hid his age up his sleeve, and while the man professed to be aged he still looked no more than eighty at the most. While the food quickly vanished on his plate, the magician provided her an interesting summary of his life story.

Before the Japanese arrived in 1938, he had been living in Nanking for nearly a decade performing regularly at one of the city's largest theaters and receiving top billing. Song's eyes flashed with an unusual combination of anger and sadness as he told Lei of Biyu, a pretty actress with whom he had fallen in love. The couple lived together in a small room above the theater where they had performed for nearly a year, making plans to marry and eventually raise a family. That all ended with the Japanese invasion of China, the war effectively ending their careers and changing the outcome of their lives in the process. Rather than leaving the city, Song and Biyu decided they should stay thinking life would continue more or less normally. The couple would ride out the war; in hindsight, it was a decision he regretted.

Lei sat spellbound as the old man relayed the atrocities he had witnessed occurring during the occupation of the city. Now labeled the "Rape of Nanking," the Japanese tortured, raped, and murdered no fewer than three hundred thousand people. The calloused soldiers had devised many different and novel ways to murder the city's residents. Death might find their victims through fire, live burial, mutilation, or even the use of starving packs of nearly feral dogs. The men took part in contests to see who could kill their victims the quickest or the messiest.

Following their military duties, the conquering invaders would strut about the streets searching for women to rape and degrade, young, old or pregnant it wouldn't matter.

Song had kept Biyu hidden in the basement of the theater along with several other young girls bringing them food, water and anything else he could scrounge from the ruined city. Then a week or so later, he returned from one of his forays to find that three Japanese soldiers had discovered the women. Several of the men were in the process of ravaging two of the girls while a third stood holding a long blood-stained bayonet. The soldier stood over top of his beloved Biyu who face up and motionless, lay still in a growing pool of dark blood.

Song stood in the doorway to the cellar holding a bottle of water in one hand and a small bag of rice in the other, his eyes staring down into Biyu's unseeing eyes. The glass water bottle fell from his hands and shattered on the concrete floor. Suddenly aware of his presence, one of the soldiers quickly pointed his rifle at Song while the other two left the women, ran to where he stood then restrained him. After tying him to a post, the three men took turns beating him while continuing their abuse and abasement of the two remaining girls. A half hour later, one of the soldiers slammed the side of his head with the butt of his rifle. Song's knees buckled as the blow rendered him unconscious. Hours later, he came to and looking about found the soldiers had murdered the other two women as well, their bodies lying beside his beloved Biyu. Song spent the long dark night tied to the wooden pillar passing in and out of consciousness, listening as the rats fought, squealed and scuttled about the earthen cellar floor.

When Song came to again it was midmorning. A narrow sliver of sunlight found its way through a hole in the foundation, the result of a small caliber artillery shell. Song saw just what the rats had been busying themselves with the night before. His head swam and he vomited what little food remained in his stomach before gagging once again, this time bringing up only sour bile before dry heaving a few minutes later. His head aching and his mouth parched with thirst, the magician remained tightly bound to the post, forced to endure yet a second terrible night in the cellar. It was only when an old woman who was rummaging about for food discovered him in the cellar the next afternoon and set him free.

Desperately thirsty and weak from hunger, Song staggered back to the small apartment he and Biyu had shared. Finding the two small rooms completely ransacked by marauding troops, Song somehow managed to recover several photographs and the small china doll he had given to Biyu early in their relationship. He sat staring at a picture of the two of them taken in much happier times and felt a surge of anger growing in his chest, a powerful urge to avenge his love and visit wrath and ruin on the men who did this terrible thing, yet he knew he was powerless to do so. He had no weapons, he was small in stature; he had never even thrown a single punch in anger. Frustrated and sobbing he closed his eyes and laid his head in his hands.

Later that day, Song walked the ruined streets of the city, passing by burned-out shops and homes. A pall of smoke and fume filled the air above the city and the smell of death and decay was everywhere. As he moved through the rubble, he and everyone else on the streets was constantly on the lookout for danger. Sometimes the Chinese found themselves dodging enemy jeeps and trucks that occasionally attempted to run pedestrians down as they drove passed. They avoided the military patrols whenever they could and anyone else among them that might harm or rob them of the meager food they managed to find in the ruins.

He wandered through the broken city. Song was not going anywhere in particular but still somehow found his way to a familiar street where he had visited an old friend many times before. Looking down the street he expected to see the man's house demolished or at least badly damaged but instead found it fully upright, and apparently unscathed by the shelling. Perhaps more exceptionally, the home had been untouched by the Japanese troops, some who even now marched past its intact front door.

Moments later, Song stood before a large ornately carved door marveling at a stained glass oval window positioned in its center. Within the multicolored glass, an artisan of the highest order had created and set in place an incredibly detailed image of a Chinese dragon. The visitor grasped a small porcelain button attached to the end of a slender cord running out from of a small hole in the wall. Pulling it, he heard the delicate tinkle of the small bell sound within the home.

Song had met Chung Ling Foo several years before the invasion. The older magician was highly gifted in his craft and was frequently sought out and welcomed at any of the city's very best theaters and clubs. He and Song had struck up a professional friendship, discussing the ins and outs of their art over tea or beer. The performer, now quite elderly, had obviously seen something special in the younger man and had taken Song under his tutelage, passing on several amazing tricks that brought Song considerable prestige among his peers.

As he waited by the door, Song looked back up and down the destroyed neighborhood. He had the sudden thought that perhaps his friend was a collaborator having somehow curried favor with the enemy, but when the door opened and the magician's face appeared he put those ridiculous thoughts aside and smiled expectantly.

"My dear old friend!" the magician exclaimed happily. "I feared you were dead, like so many others in our poor city. Come in, come in." The man opened the heavy door and with a flair for the dramatic, gave a grand sweep of his arm as he bid Song entry.

The men walked through the magician's home. Aside from needing a good dusting, no doubt the result of the shelling, fires and the like, the interior was exactly as Song remembered. Chung led him down a long hall on the main floor toward the back of the house where a large kitchen was located. A petite middle-aged woman bowed low as the two men entered. Chung clapped his hands together and the woman ran about preparing tea and putting together an assortment of food on a large silver tray. They left the kitchen where Song followed the old man who led the way down the hall and into his study where they sat and talked as they had so many times before.

In time, the servant arrived bringing the tea and cakes into the study placing it atop a leather-covered table that sat between the two men. Thanking his friend and taking a small bite of a sweet cake, Song realized just how famished he truly was and how much he relished the taste of the fine tea from a proper porcelain China cup. Chung said nothing, pretending instead to feign interest in something he saw while gazing out the nearby window that overlooked the street.

Song had nearly finished all the cakes on the tray before he noticed his host hadn't eaten a single bite. Rather sheepishly, Song looked up toward the older man who simply smiled and tilted his head slightly to one side. "You have had several very hard weeks I fear. Now I hesitate to ask, what of Biyu?"

Song hung his head breaking down as he told his friend the whole story. When he was finished, he dried his face with a sleeve then looked back to his friend. The old man shook his head sadly; Song noticed a single tear that lay on the man's cheek. Each man collected themselves in their own way for several quiet moments. Song was the first to break the silence, "So Ling Foo, I have to ask, how is it that your house has not been blown apart?"

Sensing Song was going to follow with a barrage of additional questions his friend held up his hand, "Let me explain everything... but tomorrow, after you've had a good sleep." Song considered resisting his host's suggestion but found he was simply too tired. He gratefully accepted the man's hospitality acceding to Chung's request that he remain at least a few days in his home.

The next morning after breakfast, the two again retired to the study where the old magician told Song that he was a practitioner of Gong Tau, the dark arts. Chung had practiced the rites since his youth, taught to him by his father and grandfather, both of whom were very powerful sorcerers. The very morning when war broke out, Chung placed an incantation of protection about his house and explained that he would have done so for the homes of his neighbors as well but the dark arts' powers founded and based in self-purpose and individual gratification, would not permit him to help others. In addition to simply protecting his home, Chung had used the magic to gain influence over the Japanese captain responsible for the troops in his neighborhood. The captain's soldiers supplied Chung with whatever he needed including food, water, and even a few delicacies now and again. Once more, the older man explained to Song that the principals of Gong Tau forbade charity toward his neighbors.

Song asked the magician why he treated him with such kindness. The old man's reply was quite simple as it was startling; Song was to be Chung's understudy. The old man would pass along the secrets of his art but only if that was what Song wished. The sorcerer could see that the younger man was hesitant in his reply, clearly thinking before he answered. Chung took this to be a sign that he had made a good choice for his protégé and waited patiently for the answer he knew would be forthcoming.

From the moment Chung Ling Foo learned of Biyu's death, he had sensed the rage within his friend and the growing desire for retribution. Using his mind's third eye, Chung looked deep within his friend and saw there a small dark seed of hatred that would soon ripen and blossom. Song's black rage when properly groomed and channeled would form the basis of his becoming a very powerful practitioner of Gong Tau. Chung also believed his friend possessed the strength of will required to control the awesome power, bending it to his service yet avoiding the trap of becoming enslaved by the very evil of the magic he sought to wield.

As expected, several hours later Song told the magician that if becoming his student would allow him to avenge Biyu he would happily become his understudy. The next morning Song set about beginning the study of the craft's basic tenets. Several weeks later Chung came to him saying that the Japanese Captain had informed him that the men who had murdered Biyu were moving to a new garrison in only several days time. It was time for Song to take action; and Chung would provide him the means to do so... tonight.

The magic itself was surprisingly simple and something that Song could accomplish on his own even at this early stage of his training, but then again it wasn't necessary that the subject of the enchantment possess any skill at all, only the desire to seek reprisal for some wrong done to him or herself; imagined, real or otherwise. Chung cautioned the man that the results of this spell were quite disturbing. If desired, the conjurer could work the magic to entrap a soul in hell forever, but to do so would require using a portion of flesh from the very victim whom he wished to avenge. If such eternal finality was not required, his nemesis would still meet a particularly nasty demise that usually precluded an open casket ceremony. Occasionally the enemy might simply disappear, or perhaps be delivered back to the conjurer for use in some still darker design.

As an apprentice, Song learned the intricacies and nuances of the spell that Chung would work that evening. Song asked if he would remember his transformation in every detail. Chung stated that he would. Song might even exercise a small degree of control although the actual command of the beast's actions would lie in the hands of something else, from somewhere else. Even Chung had no firm idea as to just what it or they might be, or could even guess at their origin.

Back in the Angry Dragon restaurant, Song told Lei of Chungs' conjuring and the way the man prepared the unusual meal Song was to eat before retiring to bed but in doing so, Song left out several important details. First, that the complex recipe required a portion of flesh from a recent corpse and secondly, that a small amount of the conjurer's blood must be added at the proper moment. From the start, Song had already determined to condemn the soldiers for eternity. Toward this end, Song left the magician's home making his way to the theater basement where Biyu still lay among her two friends and the ever-present rats who kept watch over the dead.

At one point, Lei tearfully stopped Song, inquiring where and how the poor man managed to bury his Biyu. Song explained to Lei that had it been possible, he would have properly cared for Biyu's body, but at the time, there were more of the dead in the city than the living. Song and the city's remaining residents had grown accustomed to seeing the bodies of the dead and dying that lay strewn in the streets and rubble. The smells of putrefaction and decay no longer registered in their nostrils while their eyes blindly refused to take notice of the swarms of insects, birds, rats, or even the once beloved but now starving pets that tore into and fed upon bloated corpses. Every horror that walked hand in hand with the specter of mass murder had become commonplace, the people had grown immune from its dread and yet it took all of Song's strength of will to cross the threshold and enter the subterranean gloom where his Biyu still lay.

Song ate the food Chung had prepared along with some steamed rice and green tea. He had prepared himself for the disgust he no doubt would experience as he ate the grisly meal but was surprised to discover after his first mouthful that would not be the case. As much as he tried to find dissatisfaction with the meal's taste, the more he came to enjoy and even savor its subtle flavors. He finished dinner and went directly to his room. He was not tired in the least and wondered if he would be able to sleep. Song's head swam with anticipation but as soon as he laid his head on the pillow he felt immensely weary and immediately fell asleep. As Chung foretold, Song could expect to dream. Not the types of dreams that everyone regularly experiences then immediately forgets upon awakening but the oddly vivid and very rare sort that mirrors real life and stays with a person forever.

Caught up in the throes of vivid illusion Song found himself walking upon a dirt road that ran through a dense forest of immense trees with thick brush lining each side of the path. It was twilight but he was unable to tell if it were dawn or dusk. Song walked on until he came to a tall archway. Two massive trees on either side formed its sides while thick vines grew about their trunks covering them completely before rising and bridging the distance between the trunks then arching overtops the roadway below. He considered stopping but Song found his feet refused to obey his will and he continued to walk on beneath the archway.

Song quickly passed to the other side finding he was alone in a stark forbidding nightscape. Looking upward, he saw bright stars studding unfamiliar constellations that slowly wheeled about the jet-black sky. Below his feet, the road on which he stood gleamed with a pale silvery light. Some motion in the distant caught his eye. Whatever it was, it flew above the road, an

181

expanding patch of blackness on the skyline, blotting out the stars as it approached. He waited and felt his heart quail. Song found himself wanting to turn and run but remembered he was already bound to his fate. He had fully accepted all of the spells conditions and consequences once he had placed that first morsel between his teeth.

Quickly approaching, the shadow rode atop the cool night air. Much closer now, Song thought he could make out a dark winged shape. He cringed slightly expecting to feel an impact of some sort as it reached him but it simply vanished. Song looked about for the shadowy figure but could not see it, nor could he any longer see the stars, they had vanished...as had the road beneath him. He stood alone, encompassed within a deep blackness... but no wait, he was not alone, slowly, he perceived another presence but whether it was beside him, within him or perhaps him within it, Song couldn't guess.

Slowly Song sensed a change was occurring. A light appeared from nowhere and everywhere at the same time. The skin on his entire body tingled then stung painfully, he dropped to his knees and cried aloud as he felt his very bones bent and twisted like a pretzel, but then remembered Chung explaining that he was to be re-made in the image of the beast. Song brought a hand up to his eyes and saw it was no longer human but instead a scaled twisted claw. He shut his eyes seeking a reprieve from the incredible assault that swept up his senses but rather than a comforting darkness, he continued to see himself undergoing his transformation. He was trading his human shape for that of a dragon, not the huge beasts that St. George and his steed were depicted battling valiantly, but a smallish version of the Chinese dragon, the long thin centipede types carried about by the street dancers on important festivals.

As his body painfully contorted and rearranged itself into its new form he also became aware of another mind merging with his, an alter ego that spoke and elicited ancient racial memories of itself and its kin. Somehow, he found himself remembering the shared history of the Yinglong dragons. These vengeful serpents were both the oldest and most terrible of the eastern dragons, being the only ones who actually flew or breathed fire. Song recalled that like all dragons of legend, they had at one time shared the earth with humankind but vanished with the coming of the new age many thousands of years before. Since that time, they had endured but only as creatures of magic resurrected by Chung and a select few who still delved in the ancient mystical arts.

At the restaurant table, Lei listened intently as Song described how wonderful it felt to shed his physical constraints and frailties, replacing the constant fear that had shadowed his every thought since the Japanese invasion. What the old man held back in his story was just how rapidly the last shred of his humanity departed, fleeing his innermost being, leaving his soul an empty vessel to be refilled by the nameless dread that seeped ever deeper into his heart and mind.

Lei heard the old man describe how his absurdly small wings somehow defied gravity and carried him aloft and soaring across the dark night sky high above the rooftops and blackened streets below and how upon landing the wings had folded out of sight, tightly held to either side of his sleek armor scaled body. Song told Lei as how he somehow knew exactly where to find the murderous soldiers. He smelled their guilt, felt their callous disregard for the lives of their victims and perhaps even their own distasteful existence. Song, who was now the dragon, felt his way toward them using his incredibly long and sensitive whiskers that protruded and squirmed out from two orifices located just below his gleaming ruby eyes. Even in the black of night his vision was still bright and clear enabling him to see every detail that surrounded him. Since returning to earth, Song glided silently among the broken ground and ruins. Criss-crossing and occasionally hiding, he would coil within dark corners, his whiskers writhing and alert continued their animated search. Picking up the nearby scent, he wriggled and weaved across open ground on his four stubby feet, the scales of his stomach held only inches above the earth.

The dragon approached the bombed out building where he sensed the men had bivouacked for the night. Song felt his long tongue run across and then between each of his sharp yellowed fangs before rising up, coiling as a snake poised to strike, and resting his eel-like body on the base of his long muscular tail. His sensitive ears picked up the soft clicking of his taloned claws, their long razor honed tips opening and closing as the beast within Song's body anticipated the imminent excitement and bloodlust that would soon follow.

Where Song had consciously directed his flight and approach while hunting and stalking his prey he now found himself removed to the sidelines. He watched from a unique perspective as he assumed might a rampaging mad man, who unable or unwilling to stop himself in the partaking of slaughter suddenly grasped the realization of what was taking place with horrid stark clarity. Remaining completely aware and conscious of his surroundings, the magician found himself captive within the mind of the raging beast. A scrap of his humanity remained though powerless and detached, now completely relegated to the position of a mere spectator. Just as well, in retrospect Song wondered if he could have lived with the terrible memories if he had actually authored each detail of the carnage that would take place only a few moments later.

From within a deeply shadowed corner, crouched behind a wall of rubble, the creature watched the three soldiers who sat around a large round table. They joked and laughed as they smoked and drank their rice wine. Atop the marred surface of the table sat several large wine bottles, a lantern, and three stubby candles that provided a dim illumination. A young Chinese girl sat, head bowed and trembling on a wooden chair beside the soldier who had killed Biyu. The girl was naked and sobbing quietly, apparently the soldiers had decided to save her for later. One of the men laughed nastily and threw a small crust of bread that bounced off the girl's forehead and tumbled down into the dirt. "Payment for your services bitch!" The other men joined in with the first, discussing the manner in which the poor wretch would shortly repay their kindness.

Song felt the dragon's lungs fill and then with a light hiss, exhale in the direction of the small group. Only a shallow puff of air escaped its mouth yet from a distance of at least twenty feet away an icy blast struck the candles set upon the table causing their flames to gutter. One after another, the small lights dimmed and then went out as the stinking draft crossed the table. Only the lantern remained lit before an even louder hiss sounded back among the shadows, a second and much stronger gust arrived in the form of a noxious evil smelling cloud that upset the lantern, glasses, and bottles alike sending them all crashing to the floor.

The room fell utterly silent. The soldiers were plunged into a darkness that was no longer simply the absence of light but a black velvet cloak that draped itself about the men, stifling their lungs and stinging their eyes causing the men to squint painfully as though having to peer through dense smoke. This was not the case for the girl who watched in awe as the room was awash with a rainbow of crimson, blues, greens and brilliant yellows that gleamed forth from the scales of the dragon's body as it rose from its hiding spot and glided silently into the dingy room. With a shrill scream, the terrified girl leapt up, running from the room and fleeing into the night. The soldiers jumped to their feet taken completely by surprise. The three now stood beside their chairs, alert and watchful yet completely unaware of the girl's recent departure and most certainly the eerie glittering arcs of light that now enveloped the room. But, what the soldiers could sense with great clarity, was the hatred and purpose behind the slow slithering evil that approached.

The dragon had allowed Song the honor of selecting his first victim. Without hesitation, the beast slithered toward the man who had murdered Biyu. The soldier stood beside the table, shuffling and twisting, first in one direction and then another, his hand waving a long bayonet before him as he did his best to peer into the shadowy gloom.

The dragon crept slowly closer then allowed itself to become visible, but only by its immediate victim; the other two men remained enshrouded in the utter darkness but clearly heard all too well what was happening around them. As soon as the first soldier saw what drew near, he froze in place, raving incomprehensively. The other men listened as their companion screamed out something about ghosts or demons but very soon these rants changed to urgent pleas for help and shortly thereafter, pitiful begs for mercy. The dragon wound slowly up and about the man as it climbed him like the red stripe on a barber's pole binding the soldier's arms tightly within its powerful coils. Drawing level with the man's face, it looked the soldier squarely in the eye, allowing its victim to view the means of his imminent destruction, much as a rat caught in the clutches of a constrictor just moments before its death. The dragon paused in all of his terrifying magnificence. Then, ever so slowly, it sank its needle sharp talons into the quivering flesh of the man's thighs, midsection, and chest, savoring the agony it inflicted with each delicate incision.

The dragon watched and studied the man's tortured eyes, appreciating the unique quality of the shrill screams and howls that rose and fell in his throat. Waiting until the moment the soldier had finally expelled all the air from his lungs and longed to gasp and refill his aching lungs, the dragon relaxed his grip slightly and breathed forth a long slender flame towards the man's face. The sulfuric thread briefly encircled the soldier's head before being drawn into the man's nostrils and yawning mouth. As the soldier took the sordid breath deeply within his lungs, his features contorted in agony and grew ruddy with the dark coursing blood that gorged the veins of his face. The creature opened its massive jaws then slowly slid them over the man's still astonished face. The soldier's head, now completely engulfed within the creature's maw, the dragon slowly, almost tenderly bit down, its sharp teeth piercing the scalp then scraping against the hard bone of his victim's skull. As the pressure increased and finally became insurmountable, Song felt the bone depress, heard it crunch then explode between the powerful fangs. Hot blood gushed across their tongue, spilled down their throat or spewed out between their razor-sharp fangs splashing and gouting across the table and floor in brilliant crimson-laced shards.

Each of the other two soldiers met with a similar fate. When Song and the dragon finally withdrew from the gory scene, the mess they left behind would suggest that a powerful bomb must have dismembered and torn the men apart.

Back in the restaurant, Jimmy staggered slightly as he walked through the back room door and into the cafe arriving just as the old man was finishing his story. Upon seeing Lei's blanched face Jimmy slurred out, "what's wrong with you woman, your own cooking finally disagreeing with you?" Lei swiveled in her chair turning her back toward her husband. He scowled and laughed unpleasantly adding, "Stay home if you like but I'm going out, it's New Years Eve for Christ sake." Waving his hand in dismissal Jimmy began walking toward the back room.

As Jimmy departed, Lei shook her head in embarrassment then smiled kindly at the old man. She placed a hand to her cheek and was surprised when it returned wet with tears. Evidently, the old man's crazy story had touched her on a deeper level. As her face cooled and she regained her composure, she made light of the matter introducing her now quite drunk and departing husband to the magician. Without saying anything more, Jimmy disappeared into the kitchen.

Moments later, the old man's grandson rushed through the front door apologizing profusely for the mix-up and the delay of their meeting. As his grandson carried the old man's suitcase out the front door to the waiting car, Song expressed his gratitude to Lei asking if he could come by again for tea sometime in the future. Lei readily agreed and over the coming years, Lei would find herself sitting spellbound listening to the magician's incredible tales while they smoked their strong Chinese cigarettes and drank green tea from her favorite porcelain cups.

Up in the two-room suite above the restaurant the door buzzer rang angrily and continued uninterrupted until Lei finally shook herself awake. She searched in the dark room for her slippers, finding them she walked stiffly from the bedroom and navigated her way down the steep stairway where a back door opened into an alley. Turning on a kitchen light she glanced at the nearby clock, it was just after three in the morning. She leaned into the door and peered through the peephole. A small light illuminated the outer doorway's alcove where two police officers were waiting impatiently. An unexpected chill ran through her as she unlocked the door.

The older police officer spoke up asking if she was Lei Wang. Saying she was, he asked if he and his partner to come inside and speak with her. She nodded quickly and threw the door aside, waving a hand toward the kitchen just as Jimmy walked into the kitchen still in his shorts, yawning, and scratching his ass. He approached the kitchen countertop where he picked up a deck of cigarettes. Shaking free an unfiltered Camel from the nearly empty pack, he shoved it into the corner of his mouth then bringing the match up to light it he mumbled, "how's it goin' tonight boys?" while giving a quick nod to the cops. The younger officer, recognizing Jimmy as a participant in a small brawl he broke up the week before threw him a stern look. The other officer ignored Jimmy as he removed his forge cap and prepared to address Lei. The woman's eyes betrayed her fear and dismay as to what she imagined might follow.

"Please sit down ma'am. We have some bad news." The cop waited for the woman to sit then pulled out a chair beside her and sat down. His partner remained standing, his eyes slowly moving from Lei to her husband Jimmy and then back to her again. The seated officer watched Lei's face as he took out a small blue notebook from his chest pocket with practiced ease. Flicking open the book to a page marked and held in place with an elastic band, he swiftly reviewed his notes before continuing. The cop glanced up at Lei, "you have a niece, Julie Chan?" Lei nodded and the cop's eyes dropped again to his notebook before he continued, "… at 3725 25 Street SW?" Looking back at Lei, he saw that her eyes had already begun to tear. "I'm so very sorry to tell you that she is dead." Lei's hands flew to cover her mouth as if she were trying to shush herself.

This was not the first time the officer had to provide a death notification to a loved one. Breaking this type of news was one of the worst parts of the job but the man broached the task with professionalism and compassion. The officer told Lei that Julie had been to a movie with several girlfriends earlier that evening. On the way back home, she had separated from her friends choosing to walk the remaining few blocks on her own. It was still reasonably early when she entered a short walkway beneath a bridge that ran across the Elbow River near her apartment. Someone had been waiting close by. That someone had grabbed Julie and dragged her off into the bushes near the riverbank.

The police officer spared Lei the worst of it, she would learn the rest when she and the rest of the family met with the coroner and received his report. The poor girl had been savagely beaten and brutally raped. Once the scum had finished with her, he had picked up a fist-sized rock striking her atop the head numerous times until he finally succeeded caving in her skull.

"Do you know how I can get in touch with Julie's mother and father?" asked the cop.

"You can't, her mother is dead, and we haven't heard from her father since she was very young. She lived with my sister when she was a teenager until she moved out on her own." Lei saw the man preparing to write in his notebook then added, "Oh, my sister died last year, Julie had no other family but me... oh, and Jimmy. Are you in charge of the case?" Lei asked.

"No, my partner and I work in your neighborhood. The CID investigates these types of serious cases, detectives in our Criminal Investigation Division. Sergeant Stacy is the man in charge. He will be in touch with you very soon. Stacy instructed me to give you his name and phone number, it's written on the back of my card." The officer stood up, placed his cap on his head moving toward where the other officer stood waiting, "If my partner and I can do anything for you, please call. Again, we're so very sorry." They let themselves out the back door.

Song walked up to the front door of the Angry Dragon shortly before 9am giving a soft pull on the door, it was still locked. Using the bottom of his cane, Song rapped on the bottom of the door then waited patiently. Presently, he heard footsteps approach. Jimmy opened the door, scowled at the old man, and then cocked his thumb toward the kitchen, motioning the man to enter. Walking inside, the man waited for Jimmy to close the door and lead him back into the narrow kitchen where Lei sat at the small table smoking a cigarette, a cup of cold tea sitting before her. She watched the old man approach the table and butted out her cigarette in an ashtray while waving a hand in the air attempting to clear away a small cloud of smoke drifting above the tabletop.

The magician stood at the table noticing the woman's eyes were red and sore, Lei had been crying for some time. Song looked over at Jimmy who simply stood by silently wearing a bored expression. Evidently, the man had done little if nothing to console his wife. Lei had telephoned Song several hours ago, in a broken and weak voice she had asked Song to come by the restaurant before they opened. Knowing something was seriously wrong; he did not require any further explanation. Dressing quickly he walked to the transit stop and rode the #8 bus that took him down into China town.

Without asking, Song pulled out a chair opposite his friend and sat down. Lei looked up at him and thanked him for coming then asked her husband if he would make them some tea. Jimmy nodded sharply, then huffed noisily as he turned away, making sure that Lei and her guest knew just what an imposition was being asked of him. Song said nothing but waited patiently for Lei to begin the conversation. She attempted to begin speaking on several occasions but on each attempt her voice broke, the strong emotions welling up within her chest and choking off her words. At last, she had calmed sufficiently to find her voice and begin.

"Thank you for coming Grandfather." She always referred to Song in that manner; it always had seemed so natural to her. As she looked into the man's kindly face she was suddenly struck by the fact that in the fifteen or so years since their meeting, the man hadn't seemed to have aged a day. According to her own reckoning, that would make him over one hundred and twenty years old. She resolved to ask him about that in the future but now was not the time, and she continued to speak as her husband approached the table.

"Here..." Jimmy growled. He placed a small pot of tea on the table and slid a second cup in front of the magician saying, "I've got to clean up out front" as he left the room.

Lei spoke up. "I met with the police yesterday afternoon. Sgt. Stacy, the man who has been investigating Julie's murder? They had arrested Cameron Ray back in May? Well, they had to let him go... something the judge called insufficient evidence. Do you remember I told you that Sgt. Stacy said they found a pack of cigarettes and a lighter near Julie's body. His fingerprints were found on the lighter... and his DNA was found on the cigarettes and on, and in Julie." She broke down for several minutes before she could continue. The old man reached over and touched her hand.

"All of the evidence is gone... vanished. Someone went into the room where they keep these things and removed it all!" Sgt. Stacy says it has never happened before. They still have the lab reports but the Judge refused to allow them to be entered into evidence. Stacy said the Judge's decision was very unusual, but Ray's lawyer is apparently one of the best, he convinced the judge that allowing the reports to be used would prejudice his client's rights." She spat out the last words. "Cameron's family has money, lots of it. Sgt. Stacy didn't come right out and say it but he didn't have to. Someone paid someone else a lot of money to make this happen."

Lei took a final drag on her cigarette and butted it out in the ashtray then looked up at Song. "Now there will be no justice for Julie, her murderer will go free, unless..." Her voice trailed off as she searched the magician's eyes.

"Lei, surely... surely you do not want this." The old man stammered, his face froze in an expression of surprise and dismay.

The magician tried to persuade Lei against using the magic, but in the end, Song had little choice. The rules of Gong Tau forbade him from refusing a request to use the dark arts for the purposes of vengeance and retribution. Song instructed Lei how to prepare the meal then double-checked the lengthy list of the required ingredients he had written down. "My girl, you will need all of these, you may find them at the Chinese herb shops nearby." Lei nodded somberly. Song apologized "If it were only in my power to do so" he stammered, "I fear I am far too old to safely transform myself." He went on to describe the details and procedures that underlay the spell.

Song continued, hesitantly asking Lei if she might have kept a lock of Julie's hair. Once added to the stew this might allow the dragon to seek out Julie's murderer, like a hound dog presented with a piece of clothing to get the scent of his quarry. Lei considered for a moment then remembered she had kept Julie's antique hairbrush upstairs. Perhaps it may have some of Julie's hair caught in its bristles. The old man told her this would do nicely but there was still a final ingredient. She must acquire flesh obtained from a recent corpse.

Leaving this matter aside for the moment, he continued. "Lei, this is very important. You must allow the stew to simmer for several hours then just before you eat the meal you will add several drops of your living blood to the mixture, this will guide the demonic spirits to your soul allowing you to transform yourself and ride upon his wings." Half an hour later, a saddened old man looking exhausted and weary, walked slowly away from the restaurant.

Having bid the old man goodbye Lei retrieved the hair brush managing to pick off nearly a dozen long hairs she was sure had belonged to her niece, the strands were easily recognizable as the girl had been a dyed blonde. Lei made a cup of tea then sat at the kitchen table wondering where or how she could possibly obtain the last crucial ingredient before becoming suddenly inspired. She walked to the front of the restaurant retrieving the morning paper. Scanning the paper's index, she opened the edition to page 32, "Births and Deaths." She was in luck, there was a funeral viewing taking place that very afternoon. She left the cafe taking a small pair of wire cutters with her in her purse; surely, no one would notice a missing pinkie?

The next morning Lei left the restaurant visiting the herb shops and stores in Chinatown seeking the other ingredients required for the spell before returning to the restaurant and preparing the stew. By mid-afternoon, she had finished its complex preparation. All that was required now were a few drops of her blood, she would add these several hours later when the stew was fully cooked. Lei left the kitchen to sit at one of the restaurant's tables nearest a window. It was a bright lazy sunny afternoon. She picked up a magazine casually thumbing through its pages but not absorbing any of it. Wrestling with her conscience, she contemplated the dark course she had set in motion.

Several hours later she finally stirred, she had fallen asleep at the table! She glanced up at the clock and saw it was nearly five and the stew should be nearly ready. Just before she fell asleep, she had made her decision. She would pour out the evil brew leaving justice to the courts or revenge to the gods. Rising from the table, she heard the light clatter of plates coming from the kitchen and hurried through the door into the back.

What she saw horrified her. Coming home half-drunk and hungry, Jimmy had helped himself to the stew. Sick to her stomach Lei watched Jimmy finished off the last several bites from the pot.

Finally noticing the woman who stood off to his side, Jimmy shot one of his shitty looks her way, "Finally some decent food! Woman! Why can't you cook like this for our customers? We might actually make some money for a change." He backed away from the table. "I'm going to have a nap... I have a big game tonight... one of us has to make a living." She watched as her husband walked out of the kitchen and made his way up the stairway to their suite.

Five minutes later, as soon as she was sure Jimmy would not be disturbed or overhear, she was on the phone to the magician blurting out what had happened. "He ate the whole thing; Jimmy ate all the stew... what am I going to do?"

"Settle down Lei, settle down." An old frail voice spoke slowly from the phones' earpiece, "without adding his blood to the stew it's simply that, stew. Nothing can, or will happen."

Less flustered now, Lei confided in Song that she had changed her mind and would not be seeking revenge on Julie's murderer. The old magician said how relieved he was to hear her decision; such experiences could change people, most often for the worse. Lei hung up the phone feeling very much relieved and checked the time on the kitchen clock. It was still early; she felt like going out; she had not gone out on her own for so long.

The next morning, Lei was cleaning up the previous night's dishes and pots when Jimmy ambled down from the upstairs suite looking quite refreshed. "I had a very interesting night and I feel great!"

"I take it you won at the games," Lei said hopefully; his losses had been more substantial lately. Jimmy ignored her and continued.

"By the way, where'd you learn that recipe, the one I ate last night? We should be serving that to our customers... there would be standing room only... we'd make a fortune!" He had an odd look on his face, one she had seen before, the one that cautioned her to be careful.

"Oh that, it was something I came across in an old cookbook... but I misplaced it." She kicked herself mentally; no one would buy that excuse. She waited for one of Jimmy's inevitable berating comments that never came. Instead, he simply stood beside her and slid a long piece of paper with the magicians scribble along the counter in front of her.

"Maybe this would help?" Jimmy smiled thinly.

"I don't have all the ingredients, some are very... very hard to get!" She stammered unconvincingly as she continued to fuss with the dishes. She picked up a band-aid wrapper that lay near the sink and was about to throw it into the trash can when she looked at the countertop beside her. A sudden sinking thought swept across her mind. Without saying another word, she began to wipe up small droplets of blood that lay dried and spattered across the counter top. The dribble continued crossing the top of the stove, directly in line with the very burner where the pot of stew had sat simmering yesterday afternoon.

She could feel her husband's eyes on her back and knew he was smirking as he spoke, "cut my finger, but it's just fine now." She spun about looking to her husband.

Jimmy stood near the kitchen's walk-in cooler and slowly opened the heavy insulated door to reveal Cameron Ray's body hanging from a meat hook; directly beneath the corpse a pool of blood had spread and congealed forming a large dark stain on the cold concrete floor. "I think our customers will appreciate our new signature dish."

Jimmy sniggered nastily; "Yes wife, I think business will take a turn for the better from now on. Don't you agree?" Lei simply shuddered, wiping away a small tear that had crept down her cheek before she continued to wash the dishes.

The Angry Dragon's menu would see its menu grow substantially longer in the near future. There would be little problem in obtaining all the necessary ingredients. You see, Jimmy had a huge chip on his shoulder but who could blame him... after all, the whole world had it in for him. These same people were the ones who took his money each week at the poker or Mahjong tables. They were the do-gooders, churchgoers, or anyone else who occupied a higher station in life or enjoyed better fortune... earned, or otherwise.

Kindred

Sitting in a plush leather chair behind an ornate mahogany desk, the Malaysian Sessions Court judge glanced at his watch and took a final sip of the strong Arabian coffee from a small cup before setting it back on its saucer. It was almost time to return to court and set this matter to rest. Without warning the pictures on the wall trembled and the china cup and saucer began to clatter atop his desk. The small quake rattled the windows in their frames while the drapes at either side swayed slightly for perhaps thirty seconds before the tremor died away. The judge stood up and made his way from chambers.

Ten minutes earlier, the public prosecutor, and Paithoon Deep's defense counsel had joined the judge in his chambers. The three men concluded that it would not serve the public interest sentencing the well-known gangster to a prison term any longer than two years. On the other hand, even considering the generous nature of Deep's bribe, his Honor could not afford to bring the administration of justice into disrepute by handing the criminal a sentence of any less duration. The agreed upon terms included the judge sweetening the deal by allowing Deep to serve his time in a minimum-security prison, a country club atmosphere in comparison to the rock hard time he would do in a maximum-security facility.

The judge walked into the courtroom taking his seat upon the high bench. As he flipped through some loose pages on his desk the judge off headedly addressed Deep's lawyer asking if he and his client wished to make an application. The smiling defense counsel addressed the court, "Thank you my Lord. Mr. Deep wishes to vacate his plea of not guilty, and enter a new plea of guilty as charged." The judge turned his chair toward the prosecutor who needing no prodding quickly followed up, "Crown has no objection my Lord."

The judge sat and stared out at those seated in the courtroom then asked the prosecutor, "please read the facts of the matter before us today." The prosecutor cleared his voice then proceeded to speak. "My Lord, between the twenty-sixth day of

April and the seventeenth day of May 2013, the accused, Paithoon Deep, to wit; did unlawfully and willfully conspire with person or persons unknown to commit assault occasioning bodily harm to the personage of one Damia Ong in violation of section"... Following the formal reading of the legal charge, the prosecutor summarized the offense continuing for several minutes using a combination of legal jargon and fifty-cent words sufficiently obfuscating the truly base nature of the crime.

In a nutshell, Damia Ong was witness to a shooting between two mid-level drug dealers and was to have given evidence with respect to what she saw. The gang leader, wishing to make sure she did not testify, instructed another of his gang to run her down in a car as she crossed a street. While the young woman did not die, she suffered significant brain damage ensuring she would no longer pose a threat to the original gang member awaiting trial. The prosecutor advised the judge that the crown now believed the accused's statement that it was never his intention that the woman be actually hurt, but only frightened and that in fact, the whole affair had been a tragic accident for all concerned. The court now adjourned, the judge nodded in the direction of each lawyer taking his leave of the room leaving the gangster and his counsel to chat cordially with the crown prosecutor who leaned with his back against his desk.

Frowning and shaking his head, the victim's father stood up then moved into the center aisle where he stood watching Deep while mouthing a silent curse. Noticing the man's stare, the criminal nudged the elbow of his defense counsel giving a quick nod in the father's direction. All three men shared a knowing smile while Deep smirked, throwing an offhand salute toward the girl's father. In return, the man angrily flipped the three men the finger, spun on his heel and stormed down the aisle. A small group of Deep's men chuckled and berated the father a he strode past slamming the heavy door shut while making his exit from the room.

The tiny island of Palau Kona is an emerald green speck in the Gulf of Thailand lying but twenty-three miles off the Malaysian peninsula. The rounded tip of the dormant undersea volcano had only recently become an island, at least in geological terms.

Thrust upward into the light from the dark depths of the sea, it was evidence of the ever-present, slow-motion collision between the Australian and Asian tectonic plates.

By all accounts, the island must be considered primitive and remote by western standards. Palau Kona's close proximity to the mainland failed to guarantee its few visitors access to even a modicum of civilized comforts. Depending upon the season, the mainland ferry would typically arrive at the docks every third day while stopping in turn at each of the other four islands in the chain. The ferry was the island's lifeline, supplying the village, the medical clinic, and the research and weather stations with whatever was required. While the island had no airfield per sec, air transportation via seaplane or helicopter was available privately.

Until just recently, nearly thirty farmers and their families had called the one time deserted island home. The villagers raised domestic pigs and fowl while also harvesting the many varied fruits and vegetables that grew in abundance within the tropical setting. Known as the "boat people," they arrived on the island in the thousands, the wayward refugees having fled South Vietnam in the regime's final days as the United States military pulled out and abandoned the country to its fate. Over the next decade, the vast majority of the refugees found themselves forcibly repatriated to the newly unified Socialist Republic of Vietnam. By the turn of the new century, those a few that remained on the island were told they must leave as well.

The climate change movement had gained traction during the last decade. Nearly every country on earth had now agreed to take the necessary steps to rein in their carbon footprint and contribute to the scientific studies looking for ways to reverse the damage already done to the environment. The mainland government had seized on an idea that proposed to eliminate human habitation from a contained locality then study the time required for the original environment to recover fully. It was determined that the small isle of Palau Kona would be the perfect spot.

The ferry had taken the last of the farmers and their stock from the island several weeks ago, now the only people that remained in the village were the few workers who took care of the docks, the staff working at the research facility, and the small garrison of prison guards and their work crews. The prisoners were primarily responsible for clearing the brush and vegetation from the island's only road. The route whipsawed its way up the steep hillside from the village to the island's summit where a small weather station and automated air radar terminal were located. Lately, additional prison labor arrived from several mainland prisons helping to dismantle the recently abandoned farm buildings.

Near the midpoint on Weather Point road, Kenny Sukarno flailed his machete cutting back the dense wall of brush that crept within several feet of the road's graveled surface. He stopped for a moment looking up and then down the two hundred yard length of gravelled road that was visible along its steep meandering path, no one was in sight. Not that he expected to see anyone; this was hot solitary work. The guard truck had dropped him and three other prisoners off along the road at half-mile intervals earlier that morning. The truck would not be due until lunchtime, some two hours away. Propping the machete against the side of his leg, he took his water bottle from his belt and drank several mouthfuls before pouring a small amount into his palm and spreading it across his face washing away some of the dusty grit and sweat that covered his forehead. Checking the sun's position in the sky he figured it was time for him to leave for the boat.

Only thirty yards or so from where he stood, was the start of a steep game trail that led down from the highlands falling away toward the east shore of the island. The plan was simple and straightforward. Kenny was to leave the main road near mid-morning following the path down to one of the few points on the far side of the island where a small boat could reach shore after negotiating the treacherous rocks and reefs that surrounded its perimeter. With any luck, his brother-in-law would be waiting there to pick him up and take him back to the mainland and freedom.

After ten exhausting minutes, Kenny had only managed to travel several hundred yards from the main road. The jungle trail had been beaten into existence by the domestic hogs that escaped the confines of the farmer's pens. Their once frequent forays along these forest trails ended as the last escapee was shot or trapped more than half a year before. Left undisturbed, the jungle rushed back with a vengeance leaving the narrow pathways overgrown with brambles, vines, and dense brush. Kenny's machete rose and fell in a slow steady rhythm as he cut his way along the trail, if things didn't improve in the next several minutes he'd have to turn back, rejoin the work crew and rethink his escape route.

As it happened, he soon made much better time where the vegetation thinned somewhat as the pathway wound about a wooded ridge. An hour later, Kenny was nearing the halfway point where the path ran dangerously close to the rim of a towering cliff. Seeing a break in the jungle growth near the cliff's edge, Kenny stopped and making sure his feet were securely grounded, cautiously parted the leaves of a low palm. The view was magnificent in scope. The earth fell away in a near vertical sweep for at least five hundred feet before gently sloping outward where it reached the rocky shoreline a half mile distant. Kenny's eyes scanned the light green waters of the coves and small bays searching for any sign of his brother-in-law's small cabin cruiser. Sukarno was just about to give up and continue onward when he noticed a small boat bobbing in the gentle surf. Smiling broadly, he backed away from the edge of the precipice and started back down the trail.

The scout first noticed Kenny's approach while the man was still several hundred yards out from its position. Conversing in a rapid series of high-pitched clicks, clacks, ticks and pops, the dark green sentry sounded its alert. It was but part of an advance force regularly stationed along a three-dimensional skirmish line that began at ground level then extended upward into the highest branches of the jungle canopy. Kenny's ears caught nothing of their nearly inaudible exchange, barely perceptible within the background sounds of the jungle. Now alerted, the sentries stationed closer to base reported the violation of their territory and awaited orders. Moments later, the coded instructions from base flashed out to the sentries; intercept and identify the interloper. Several more scouts fanned out towards Sukarno's position.

Reaching a fork in the path Kenny stopped to consider his options. The main trail ran off to the east and away from the coast while the secondary path continued to wind down and shoreward, but was choked with dense brush. He would have to use his machete and cut his way through, but at least he would continue moving in the right direction. He started hacking at the growth and after several yards was grateful to see that the brush obstructing the trail was again thinning out. At this rate, Kenny calculated he would arrive at the boat in another half hour.

The lead scout watched as Kenny walked into view then sent a clipped message back to the others. It had been weeks since anything larger than a rat had ventured into their territory. The word had obviously gotten out. Lately even the fruit bats and birds had avoided trespassing, and for good reason; yet here came this ungainly human, blundering and crashing through the bush as if he owned it. The sentries arranged themselves in attack position concealing themselves on each side of the trail watching patiently as the man passed by and continued further into their territory where the main force would be waiting, if needed, their job would be to ensure that retreat was impossible.

Kenny stopped in a small clearing, set down his machete against a tree stump enjoying a long slow drink from his water bottle. Taking the bottle from his lips, he came to realize the jungle had fallen strangely quiet. The chirps and cries of the rain forest's many songbirds, the occasional rustle of small animals in the ground cover, and even the constant drone of insects now seemed muted. In this new silence, his ears picked up a growing series of crackles, snaps and pops coming from somewhere in the path ahead.

The attack was organized and precise. The first assault approached from the rear. Half a dozen attackers simultaneously alighted on the middle of the man's back, landing just between his shoulder blades. As soon as they touched down the insects thrust their quarter inch long stingers through the fabric of the light cotton shirt penetrating deeply into his flesh. Sensing contact of their small abdominal hairs with the surface of the man's back, small sacs automatically activated forcing a potent brew of poison through the hollow shafts of their stingers to enter and swell within Kenny's subcutaneous tissues.

Their chemical ordinance delivered, the first of his attackers immediately withdrew leaving Kenny to scream and flail about while reaching toward the small punctures in his back whose pain grew more intense by the second. For over thirty seconds, the man pitched and wheeled within the small clearing, shouting and crying out until realizing the attack had ceased, at least for the moment. Kenny moaned in pain standing still and took stock of his situation.

This was precisely when the second much larger wave dove down upon him. No fewer than forty of the giant insects, each the length and width of Kenny's index finger swarmed about his back, legs, and upper body. Every individual sting felt like a red-hot nail as it entered his flesh. He spun and danced about in agonized panic, his body feeling as though it had been set afire, his eyes frantically darted about the foliage looking for any avenue of escape. Instinctively he began retracing his steps back up the trail from where he came but instead of salvation now came face to face with the dozen or so sentinels that awaited and blocked his retreat. Now they flew into action.

Landing several well placed stings in his forehead and cheeks, the hornets again withdrew, hovering just out of Kenny's reach but close enough to give the impression they were about to attack once more. The wounded man wailed as he spun about and began to run the opposite way, crashing through the brush and once again moving ever deeper into their territory. Another minute later, knowing they had inflicted sufficient damage the hornets halted their assault and waited for the poison to take effect. There was no sense in taking any needless chances by exposing any of their members to further risk.

Kenny staggered further down the path; his running had slowed appreciably. The stings on his face had swelled his eyes nearly shut while the venom circulating within his bloodstream busily destroyed everything it met. In the immediate location of each sting, the man's flesh dissolved about the entry point leaving a gaping wound while the virulent chemical cocktail continued to overwhelm his senses. The potent venom triggered an almost immediate and highly intense allergic reaction within his body. Kenny's blood vessels dilated en masse causing his blood pressure to fall precipitously while his lungs wheezed and gasped as he tried to catch his fleeting breath with ever diminishing returns.

What remained of the man's vision quickly left him and Kenny's surroundings drifted dizzily in a haze of greens and browns. Feeling himself trip over his own feet, he instinctively thrust his hands out before him intending to break the fall but instead spun head over heels as he vaulted off the nearby cliff. Plummeting some forty feet down in free fall, Kenny felt and heard the air surge past his face and ears just before he crashed into a small clearing below the cliff face. Grasping the soft earth and ground cover in his fingers, he tried to drag his broken body upward in a final half-hearted attempt to rise before passing out and falling face first into the ground.

The main body of insects resumed their duties at the nest while the scouts and sentries returned to their original stations. Having sustained the loss of only a single individual, a member crushed as it stung Kenny's face; the hunt had been an overwhelming success. Now all they had to do was wait several days leaving the body to corrupt within the jungle's heat and humidity... that, and for the flies to arrive.

By most standards the research facility on Palau Kona was rather small, although compared to the cramped offices Harvey Jacobs had occupied back in Cambridge England, the place was nothing short of a palace. The latest equipment his team brought with them was truly state of the art, and donated through the generosity of an undisclosed and very wealthy Pakistani benefactor who for whatever reason had taken an interest in Jacob's works. The professor's team and not a small number of his rather jealous colleagues back home would have been flabbergasted to learn his benefactor's interest came by way of a very personal nature. Harvey had been and was very careful never to let his previous relationship with the lovely princess pass into general knowledge.

This sunny morning found Jacobs and one of his graduate students waiting on a long wooden dock jutting out into the blue-green waters of what the team referred to as Banana Bay, a nickname coined due to its general appearance from the air. Peering into the sky beneath a wide brimmed Panamanian straw hat, the professor stared into the azure blue expanse while worrying the end of his favorite brand of cigar held firmly clenched between his teeth. The pretty young woman at his side would occasionally shift about the rotund middle-aged man, moving from his left side then over to his right, doing her best to dodge the aromatic clouds of gray cigar smoke the wind constantly shifted in her direction.

The pair had been watching for a plane to appear in the western sky, somewhere beyond Banana Bay toward the mainland some twenty miles distant. Both jumped with surprise when the loud drone of the single engine seaplane suddenly roared in behind them, its pilot having flown around the island's summit in order to give the planes passenger a better look at his new home. The scientists watched the small seaplane touch down and kiss the calm surface of the bay with its twin pontoons sending up white rooster tails of spray and foam.

A few minutes later, the plane pulled up dockside. Several of the local workers rushed forward, grabbing the mooring lines they quickly secured the ropes to the rusting metal cleats embedded atop the weathered wood. A tall thirtysomething man exited the plane carrying a small satchel. Nimbly stepping off a pontoon onto the dock, the young woman found herself taken aback by the man's rather obvious good looks and was suddenly dismayed at the prospect of having to leave the facility for the next several weeks. During the rushed introductions, the dockworkers retrieved the passenger's bags then set about loading the girl's luggage onto the plane. Waving at the two men, the woman smiled then blew her balding professor a kiss as she stepped up into the plane's cabin. Once seated, the pilot started the noisy engine for the return journey; effectively drowning out any hope the men might have had continuing their animated conversation.

The professor tossed what was left of his cigar into the bay before picking up the smaller of the man's two luggage bags and walking his guest down the wooden platform toward a small jeep that sat waiting on shore. Their conversation continued as Harvey drove the vehicle through the deserted main street of the village, across several untended rice paddies then turned up a small hill toward the facility's compound.

"Nice digs Harvey!" the darkly handsome man in the passenger seat smiled as they pulled up and stopped in front of the brilliant white stucco two-story building. "Please explain again how you managed to pull this off?" The man laughed heartily as he climbed from the cab. Several young men who also worked for the professor immediately greeted him.

The professor took advantage of the momentary distraction to parry his colleague's good-natured teasing and introduced Dr. Alex Henry to the others. With pleasantries and introductions completed, the younger men insisted upon taking the doctor's bags to his room leaving Harvey to give Alex a brief tour of the facility. The compound's residence could house a maximum of eighteen staff although there were only seven permanent members at present, including Alex.

The professor led Doctor Henry through a series of biology labs and a medical clinic that also served the sixty or so islanders that called Palau Kona home. One of their last stops was the computer and electrical equipment workshop. A middle-aged man hunched over top an electronics bench peering intently through a large desk-mounted magnifying glass. Holding a pair of long tweezers in one hand, and suspending a soldering gun in the other, he carefully positioned each both above a small green transistor board that lay below. A small puff of white smoke blossomed atop the board. Harvey waited for several seconds until it became apparent the man had completed the rather tricky operation. He apologized for the interruption then introduced Alex to Jimmy Harding.

"Jimmy is our token Aussie and resident electronic magician; he can and has, built nearly all of the specialized equipment we use here." Alex looked at Harvey and realized the man was not simply mincing words. The boss apparently held a healthy respect for the man's abilities.

"Everything he says about me is gospel!" Jimmy quipped then extended a friendly hand out to Alex. "Unless he tells you that I like the bugs."

"Not fond of our subjects?" Alex smiled and was surprised how quickly Jimmy's face screwed up as a look of absolute disgust crossed his face.

"Doctor, I can't stand the little blighters, they bite like the dickens and truth be known they scare the hell outa' me." Jimmy watched the surprise on Alex's face then softened his tone and smiled, "Just don't care for 'em much I guess, not enough personality for my liking." He turned back to his bench, "nice meeting you Alex, anything you need just ask mate."

The scientists left the man to his work and climbed the stairway entering the second-floor office area where several people sat in a series of small cubicles busily working at their computers. A short middle-aged Asian man approached and looked at each man in turn, "a moment of your time Harvey? And you must be our newest addition... Alex Henry?"

"And you must be Lucas; Harvey has sung your praises throughout my tour." The men shook hands then Lucas turned back toward the professor.

"Sorry to disturb you but I thought you should know another of the prison workers has gone missing this morning, probably another escape. One of the supply boats reported they saw a small craft near the far end of the island earlier." Lucas frowned.

Harvey asked, "How many does that make so far this year, six?"

"Seven." Lucas answered adding, "Well, I'd best be getting on the blower and call for a replacement. Nice meeting you Alex." Giving the men a small wave the man walked off.

"Escaped prison workers?" Alex queried.

"Yes, nothing to worry about, they're from the minimum security prison on the mainland, completely harmless bunch but every once in a while one of them decides to bolt. They take care of our roads and the like." Harvey continued the tour.

Following a series of final introductions, Harvey directed Alex toward a large corner office saying "this is mine." then stopped and pointed a finger at a similarly large office that lay across a considerable expanse of carpeted floor, "and that's yours."

"Whoa, what did I do to deserve that?" Alex grinned and followed Harvey into his office, at the same time he took note of the rather important sounding sign painted on the glass door, "Office of the Director."

"You know exactly what you did and why you're here. By the way, I for one am grateful you took me up on my offer. I'm hoping you'll soon feel the same way." Harvey walked toward a bar fridge and laid a hand on the door. "Beer... Whiskey? It's after five somewhere out there in the world." The other man shook his head.

Harvey stretched a hand out toward a small table and several comfortable chairs that sat in the corner of the office surrounded by wall to ceiling windows. A cool breeze entered the room through an open shutter. Now seated, Alex admired the multicolored slate patio and the many varied flowering plants and vines that hemmed the courtyard walls. A velvet quiet descended upon the courtyard as the birds and even the insects fell silent.

A distant, almost imperceptible rumble began somewhere in the unfathomable depths of the earth. The rumble became an audible din that rapidly increased in volume as the tremors rose upwards; penetrating the miles thick layers of rock below the island. The walls and floor now visibly shaking, Alex heard the buildings foundations groan beneath the strain. Shooting up from his seat, his face bore an expression of alarm as he looked about the room first at Harvey and then out of his office and into the larger workplace area. A puzzled look replaced that of alarm as Alex realized that everyone in sight, including Harvey, continued to sit at his or her desk sporting "business as usual" airs. Seconds later as the tremors abruptly ceased, Alex noted that several staffers were observing him with mild amusement while the others, simply ignoring the situation had continued working at their computers. It was over as soon as it began. The faint echoes of momentary chaos had died away completely and now in their absence, the birds and insects resumed their calls.

"I've never been in an earthquake before..." Alex started to reseat himself nervously.

"And you still haven't." Harvey smiled, "That was just a small tremor, most of the islands get them, a lot of people scarcely notice them after they've been here a while although I must say we've been getting more than our fair share lately."

"Did you report them?" asked Alex.

"Well, the island is an extinct volcano so I made an inquiry with the USGS several weeks ago, the agency assured me there was nothing to be concerned about." The professor paused then sitting forward in his chair then continued speaking. "Let me bring you up to speed. Over the past year, we've been studying various species of giant Asian hornets living here and on several other islands in the local chain. Originally the bulk of the research budget was provided by Draphus Pharmaceuticals who were interested in the viability of using sting venom as the basis for relieving symptoms of various neurological and autoimmune diseases, we completed our research in that regard."

Alex broke in, "Apitherapy, certainly nothing new, Aristoteles was investigating the medicinal properties of bee stings back in 300 BC. Why was Draphus interested?"

"As you know the venom of bees, wasps and hornets differ significantly in composition as do the reaction of those who are stung." Harvey adjusted a window shade to block a shaft of sunlight that fell into Alex's eyes.

"You refer to the sometimes severe allergic reactions of a person to a single bee sting rather than a reaction slowly brought on by multiple stings over time, the type more often seen in beekeepers and their families?" Alex queried.

"Yes. People who are allergic to bee venom are seldom allergic to that of wasps. What we discovered was that the venom of a select few species of Asian hornet had similar chemical characteristics to that of bees." Harvey watched Alex's reaction knowing the man was incredibly intuitive.

"Interesting, giant hornets feeding on bees, their grubs, and even honey might over time; might I say, possibly have some effect on the composition of the venom produced. I suppose that Draphus is thinking that a more potent but less allergic venom might be better suited for a new version of Apitherapy?" Alex scratched his chin.

Harvey smiled; the man sitting across from him was still as sharp as he remembered. "Precisely. We have examined the venom from numerous species and they showed excellent promise. Then about four months ago, one of the farmers on the island brought one of our graduate students a wasp of a species we hadn't seen before. Said he found it on the ground near the base of a hollow tree that had housed a beehive where he used to collect honey. Of course, the hive had been recently destroyed by the hornets."

Harvey got up and walked to a display bureau on the opposite side of the room. Opening the glass door, he removed a square six-inch transparent case that he brought over and presented to Alex. A large winged insect hung mounted at its center, suspended by slender strands of fishing line attached to the inside of the case. "Alex, meet Vespa Mandarinia Kona." Harvey set the case down on the table before the doctor. Mounted with its wings extended as if in flight, the insect measured four and a half inches long and nearly a full inch in width while its quarter inch long stinger could be seen protruding from the base of its abdomen.

"Dark green?" Alex picked up the case and examined the insect inside. "Dark green...and not a spot of bright color anywhere!"

To date, all of the giant hornet species known exhibited bands of orange or yellow splashed across their bodies or heads. In fact, most insects and poisonous animals displayed brilliant colors as a way of informing potential predators that they should not be messed with. Harvey continued, "And that's not all..." watching as Alex brought the case within several inches of his face for a closer examination he added. " Look at the sides of the thorax." Harvey referred to the middle section of the insect.

"What's this then?" Studying the area, Alex could make out small ovals of light brown on either side of the insect.

"They're vocalization centers." Harvey watched the man's reaction. Alex peered at him above the top of the case with a frown while Harvey continued. "No, I'm quite serious. The ovals you see aren't simply different colourations, but a thin, fibrous membrane separate from the thick chitin making up the surrounding exoskeleton."

"Let me get this straight. You think that the insects are communicating by vibrating these membranes? Like a cicada or cricket calling by rubbing its legs together... what would be the point? Tactile, visual, and chemical communications are commonplace in these insects. " Alex looked back into the case.

"We think they communicate on a much deeper level than just telling each other where a food source is located or raising an alarm." Harvey waited for Alex to mull over the implications. "We've been studying them in the wild for the last six weeks. Harding built some rather sensitive directional microphones and a unique filter system allowing us to isolate the sounds they make while we remain a safe distance from the nest." The man seated at the table stared hard in the professor's direction; Harvey saw he had Alex's full attention. "Doctor Henry, the hornets show definite signs of sentience, possibly self-awareness perhaps even sapience.

The gang member had waited outside the library where Damia Ong worked. When she appeared making her way across the street and into a parking lot, the man slowly brought the heavy car up behind librarian waiting for an opportunity to strike. Just as she crossed a series of vacant stalls, the man gunned the car's engine, speeding up, and running the woman down just as she turned toward the noise of the spinning tires. The car's grill caught the petite woman at her waist but instead of pitching her up and over the car's hood, instead threw her down to the pavement where her head bounced off the concrete fracturing her skull in three places. The vehicle continued forward, its frame and suspension grinding across her body, shattering bones and damaging internal organs. Dragged and mangled beneath the vehicle for nearly a hundred feet the car finally jumped a curb, releasing her broken body and leaving the woman to whatever fate awaited her.

As it was, Damia exceeded the expectations of the trauma team that first treated her in the emergency ward by continuing to live at all. Six weeks following the attack, her other wounds were healing nicely but her brain had received significant damage that promised little sign of improvement being eventually transferred to the long-term care ward.

Her father pushed through the set of double doors walking down the wide aisle on his way to his daughter's room where she was being treated, or as he thought dismally, simply warehoused. He recalled bitterly that at first, the doctors were hopeful that she might recover much of her cognitive functionality although they stressed Damia would never again walk on her own. But now, six months later, spoon-fed by the nursing staff, she was still barely able to chew her food never mind being able to speak or communicate in even the simplest of terms. It was time he faced the reality of the situation and began arranging the transfer of his daughter to another hospital, exploring new avenues of treatment.

Unlike other giant hornets that typically construct their nests beneath the earth, the nest of this new species had built their home within the hollowed out crux of a dead tree, its opening sitting a full five feet above the ground. Wearing a specially designed suit that offered the minimal acceptable degree of full body protection, Alex Henry stepped quietly into the large well-sealed blind. The small shack ensured that the myriad of giant hornets that came and went about their routine some hundred and twenty yards distant would not find entry. Closing and securing the blind's door, Alex first ensured none of the insects had followed him inside before he removed the bulky gear. Since employing the use of the small structure, none of the insects had bothered any of the staff who came or went, nor had they attempted to enter the blind although the researchers realized the insects were well aware of their presence.

The blind's distance of one hundred and twenty yards from the nest was found to be the minimum tolerated by the hornets, any closer and the researchers would be relentlessly attacked, the special suits they wore prevented the staff from being badly stung but could not provide full protection from the insect's vicious onslaught. Safely within the blind, staff could visually observe the insect's behaviour employing the use of a selection of small but powerful spotting scopes. Supplementary video feeds were captured using a battery of automated instruments, and had been set up seventy-five yards closer, and in the dead of night.

As with the automated video cameras, a series of directional two-way microphones had also been set in even closer proximity to the nest, once again at night, but on this occasion costing Jimmy Harding a good number of nasty stings. Apparently, the occupants of the nest never really slept or perhaps posted nocturnal sentries that seemed to have no trouble seeing or navigating in the dark.

As was his routine, Alex would bring with him a small bucket of honey hanging it from one of the numerous short poles visible from the blind's large observation window that looked out toward the nest. Setting each pole at a specific distance and direction out from the nest, the staff would detail the hornet's behavior and communications while the insects discovered and harvested the food. Similar motivational techniques included the recent introduction of ground crawling and flying drones that had so far proved highly effective. The drones stimulated the insects within much closer proximity to the nest allowing the recording of their language, behaviour and responses accordingly.

Completing any work that might be required outside the blind, the staff members would enter the enclosure, adjust information feeds, and check on the monitoring equipment. Less frequently, they might make specific observations before heading back to the primary biology lab located at the main facility. Any onsite staff maintained a constant connection with the main lab for safety considerations. The dangers posed by this particular species demanded a significant degree of respect.

The team had already determined that individual insects communicated at slightly different sound frequencies, allowing one insect's call to be differentiated from other members within the community. The scientists believed that they had identified the "voice" of the queen although they had never actually seen her, presumably, she seldom if ever left the nest. The drones, similar in size and appearance to the workers also possessed unique calls but unlike the males of other social species, these possessed potent stingers. Another peculiarity to this hornet species were the wide variations of size within the worker cast that strongly suggested specialization. One of Harvey's grad students had postulated those differences in size could have evolved as a result of their function, similar to that of the ants and termites whose species had also developed specialized members such as soldiers, gatherers, nursemaids etc. As the weeks went by, the team's observations continued to support this theory.

Jim Harding's specialized microphones picked up the insect's communications then relayed them back to the lab. The selected snippets of recorded insect dialog, transmitted via satellite back to England then fed into one of the latest supercomputers, would undergo intense analysis. So far, they had obtained over one hundred hours of specific insect communication.

The software chosen for the project was very similar to that used by the military intelligence community in the decryption of highly complex codes. To date the program had encountered little difficulty working out the basic syntax of the hornet's language correlating the data with individual insect vocalization and activity, the local atmospheric conditions, time of day, sun, shade, lunar phase, then combined with any artificial stimuli. The results so far had been nothing short of astonishing.

Having succeeded in identifying a little over one thousand separate and unique vocalizations, Harvey and Alex engaged one of the university's top linguistics experts who rendered her opinion that the language was the insect equivalent of American Sign Language! The next step would be to transmit selected portions of the insect language back to the nest. If true communication were possible... who might then answer?

The day was sunny and hot as Paithoon Deep stepped off the prison cutter wearing a baseball cap, an orange jumper and carrying a large blue duffle. He shuffled down the wooden dock beside his single guard to where a large open boxed truck sat parked on the small patch of sweltering asphalt. He and the guard approached two young and rather bored-looking men dressed in light green uniforms and standing near the truck's tailgate smoking cigarettes. Deep's escort handed one of the men a clipboard and pen. The guard signed the attached form handing the item back to the escort who casually ripped off the bottom of the signed form thrusting it back into the others extended hand. Without having uttered a single word the man turned and walked back down the dock toward the boat leaving Deep with his new escorts.

"Okay," The guard looked down at the transfer form. "Deep is it... as in deep in shit?" The guard grinned at his companion then turned back to Paithoon who just smiled sourly, "Ok asshole, jump in the back." The prisoner climbed into the box and took a seat on a wheel well. Moments later the truck's motor revved into life and Paithoon Deep took a short drive into the village towards the prisoner's barracks.

As far as prison sentences went, Deep figured this one would be quick and easy, and he should know, having spent much of his early life either on the streets or in jail in Thailand. The hardest time he had ever done was the three-year stint in the infamous Bang Quang or Bangkok Hilton prison when he was still just a kid of eighteen. Deep had been born Farizul Deep but while he spent time in prison he changed his name to Paithoon or "Cats Eye."

Farizul started his criminal career as a teen, working as a local runner for a drug dealer until he was ripped off by a rival gang on his way to make a delivery. During the robbery, the boy had been badly beaten and hospitalized. In retrospect, Farizul figured the beating might just have saved his life. His boss was one cruel dude and would have had no qualms about killing him if he suspected the boy had double-crossed him.

When a still recovering Farizul left out of hospital, several of his gang drove him to a warehouse where the two rival gangsters who had robbed him each sat, hands and legs bound to arm chairs. Asked to identify them, the boy readily did so; that is when the boss handed him an electric drill. Farizul looked down at the drill in his hands and then at his boss seeking direction. The older man just sneered pointing to the knees of one of the bound men. Realizing the drill might be turned on him if he refused, Farizul knelt before the closer of the two men, placed the six-inch drill bit to one side of the man's kneecap, pulled the trigger and pushed hard.

The screams and blood each flowed liberally and in equal measure from his victim. After Paithoon had made several well-placed quarter inch holes in the now ruined knee, he became physically ill and puked up his breakfast across the man's sandals. The boss laughed uproariously. Obviously satisfied and amused with Farizul's performance the leader had several of his men prop the boy up in a chair across from the two very frightened looking men. Wide-eyed with puke and mucous dribbling down his chin, the boy watched as several of the more experienced thugs set upon the poor bastards, drilling out their knees and thighs then using a heavy ball peen hammer to flatten and smash their fingers and toes into mush. Himself, still weakened from his ordeal, Paithoon passed out amid the tortured screams and unheeded pleas for mercy.

Minutes later the police raided the warehouse. Unable to run with the others Farizul was left at the scene with the two victims, one who was killed as the last blow of the hammer fell against his forehead, punching out a dangling eyeball that now jiggled spasmodically above his cheek as death rattled dully in his chest. The other gangster was also nearing death's door but was not quite ready to push it open just yet. Slowly bleeding out from a jagged gash in the side of his throat, a detective quickly asked the man who was responsible. The man waved a bloody ruined hand in Farizul's direction just as he died. Given Deep's obvious weakened condition, the court questioned the degree of his participation in the actual murders, but harboured no doubt whatsoever that he had somehow been involved in the affair.

The judge handed him five years. The first three years were to be served in a federal penitentiary; the remainder split between halfway houses and parole.

The Bangkok Hilton enjoyed a bad reputation but one that was truly deserved. Overcrowded and understaffed, the conditions were horrific by any measure; filth, rats, and lice were ever present. Like all who arrived at the prison, Farizul was fitted with a set of heavy welded leg irons he would wear for the first three months of his term. The rasping welded joints of the shackles rubbed the skin of his calves and ankles raw and bloody before he thought to tear his shirt apart and wrap the scraps of cloth about the rough iron to shield his flesh. The padding went a good way to relieve the pain in his lower limbs but did little to ease the agony he suffered from the guard's brutal caning; punishment meted out on account of the damage to his prison uniform.

Degrading conditions, the brutal treatment received from the guards, the near daily occurrences of rape and abuse at the hands of other inmates drove some foreign prisoners, and others not affiliated with a larger group to despair, ultimately taking their own lives. Suicides were commonplace among prisoners, often taking place during the lonely desperate hours of early morning before dawn could offer some small measure of hope to the hopeless. Slitting wrists, ingesting rat poison, shards of glass or even gagging down drain cleaner, they would flee the hell of Bang Quang prison with full acceptance of whatever judgment might await them in death. The overworked prison staff evidently did not view frequent bed checks as a priority, more often than not, discovery of a corpse waited until mid-morning or even early afternoon.

This was not true of the scavenging hordes of rats who regularly wandered in and out of the cells of the living and the dead alike. Often feeling more like live bait than men, Farizul, and the others slept fitfully within the confines of their dark, dank concrete bunkers. The inmates soon learned to cram their clothing into the cracks of the cells attempting to prevent the sharp-toothed vermin from squeezing and squirming their way inside. Every third night or so, Farizul would wake to hear another man cry out screaming in the darkness having awoken to discover he had lost a finger or a toe to a nocturnal visitor.

Following Farizul Deep's release from prison, he was not the handsome, naive young boy he had been when he walked in. Farizul's gang was one of the smaller groups in the prison and as such, they were constantly alert and watching their backs. One morning, while he was in the showers, one of the guards had his friends escorted out and back to their cells leaving him separated and alone. A few minutes later, the leader of a larger rival gang walked in accompanied by two of his henchmen. The sadistic jail guard watched and masturbated excitedly while he watched the other men beat, rape and degrade the young man for well over an hour before dragging the unconscious Farizul back to his cell.

Unable to walk for several days and occasionally bleeding from his groin and anus, he sat motionless in a corner of the cell while the mind of the young man cocooned within itself and slowly metamorphosed into something cold, terrible, and vengeful. Two weeks later, they found the sadistic guard propped up near an overflowing toilet with a long shiv protruding from one of his ears. It took somewhat longer for death to find the leader of the other gang, the staff discovering the man in the showers, his cock and balls crammed down in the back of his throat, his body stiffened and soaking in a dark bloody pool.

Three years had passed when a smart, stone cold killer walked out of the prison rejoining his gang on the outside. The hardened gangster quickly rose in the ranks of the organization until the "Cats Eye" finally replaced his boss through a not so subtle assassination.

Alex Henry and Jimmy Harding sat in the blind overlooking the nest and readied themselves to observe the occasion first hand. The rest of Harvey's team busied themselves back at the facility's main lab, several sitting behind a long countertop while others had filed in behind the first; their eyes glued to several big screen monitors displaying the real-time activities taking place near the hornet nest. Harvey operated the lab to blind communications with Alex and Jimmy while the team's linguist, Wanda Reynolds and another female staffer monitored the linguistic program running on the supercomputer back in Cambridge. Suddenly Jimmy Harding's two-way microphones crackled into life at the site.

Before attempting first contact, Alex, Harvey, and Wanda had given some thought as to how to begin striking up a conversation with the hornets. While the two men were pondering over just how to initialize the conversation, their linguist suggested they would first need to determine what call frequency to use while saying whatever it was they intended to say. Up to that point, the two men had not given the call frequency any thought at all, simply intending to replay the language phrases back in the same frequencies in which they received them. They quickly understood that in doing so, they would probably sow confusion among the insects and thwart their efforts.

Wanda further added that it appeared to her that the insects conversed in a manner more consistent with individuals rather than that of a shared hive mind. In a word, she explained to the men that she did not believe their first phrase would be something like "we are the Borg... resistance is futile" a reference to a re-run of a popular Star Trek series.

Neither of the two men had been thinking along these lines and realizing their error had postponed first contact, preferring to study the matter further. In hindsight, the two entomologists concluded that they had continued to harbor the precept that the insects were merely small robots that in going about their day-to-day business remained completely oblivious to the larger world around them. In an effort to get their head around the question of sentience, they elected to consult several leading neurologists specializing in the study of zoological brain function.

Alex and Harvey were surprised to discover that having a large brain size was no longer an indicator or prerequisite of intelligence. Instead, the number of neurons within a brain seemed to have little bearing on the matter. Recent speculation had it, that within larger brains, the additional neuron patterns were no more complex than those in smaller brains but were simply an endless repetition of the same neural circuits. Several of the specialists consulted, suggested that as an animal's body became larger, its brain size was required to increase as well, but simply because there were more nerve connections required in controlling a body of a larger size. It was their shared opinion that quite advanced thinking could be possible even with a brain having relatively few neurons in comparison to our own.

With the new input, the team had decided to modify their approach, instead adopting a unique call frequency, one within the normal range of the hive's members but also one that suggested the speaker was a male drone. Using a masculine "voice" might preclude an immediately aggressive response from the solitary and presumably jealous queen. Secondly, they would follow the linguist's suggestion that they make use of an echelon specific syntax, signally the communication originated from a hornet holding significant rank within its own community.

The team would soon discover neither approach would have been necessary, the bugs knew exactly to what and to whom they were speaking.

As soon as the microphone positioned closest to the nest began to replay the team's carefully chosen words and phrases, the entire insect community fell silent. The near constant drone of their wings ceased as each individual hornet alighted on nearby earth or vegetation and then remained motionless. The video footage of the nest indicated that something unusual was stirring and taking place deep within its catacombs. Suddenly, a handful of oversized insects appeared at the nest opening, obviously guards who took up what the staff recognized as defensive positions about the main entrance way. Several moments later, a single very large, multicolored hornet emerged from the interior of the nest and stood in the entrance surrounded by her bodyguard.

There was no doubt in the minds of the team that the insect before them was the queen, and like any queen, she was resplendent. The colors of her body shimmered with her every movement. Harvey quickly speculated that her exoskeleton possessed parallel microscopic ridges that acted in a similar fashion to the grating of a spectroscope, and like the grating or a prism, broke up, and scattering the light, presented the observer with rainbows of color.

In the forward blind, Alex suggested they replay the original greeting; Harvey gave a quick nod to Wanda who reactivated the phrase within the translation program. The language that the staff commonly referred to as "insectese" was hardly flowing or eloquent but instead halting, redundant, and extraordinarily simplistic. Wanda had explained earlier that the usual connective words and phrases used in normal language were completely missing in this limited edition, frankly she speculated there was a good chance they might not exist at all. Language was both a function and reflection of thought and at this early stage, the team had no notion as to how or what the hornets might think about anything.

The microphone crackled and popped, repeating the previous basic greeting; ***"Attention... no threat...drone alpha..., attention... no threat...drone alpha."*** The first phrase was a simple introduction that roughly translated said, "Hello... I'm friendly...and an important guy."

After several long seconds, a reply crackled from the microphone positioned closest to the nest.

"Untrue... aware... enemy... aware... destroyer... nest ... aware... destroyer... all," the translator working quickly in the background immediately displayed the queen's reply on the screen; to the ears of the staff it sounded like someone crushing rice paper in their palms. The young female graduate student at the terminal next to Wanda muttered; "sounds like they got our number doesn't it."

Harvey cranked his head back toward the girl at the desk behind him and frowned. "Cheryl, why don't you activate "text to speech"... give it a female voice if you will?" The girl nodded and smiled somewhat sheepishly while silently mouthing "sorry."

The queen's voice over came over the terminal speaker, this time in English. ***"Sentry unknown designation... fly...enemy...origin...co-ordinate {option specify 3D Cartesian units}...identify."***

Beside the queen, a large hornet immediately lifted off the nest flying rapidly toward the blind while ignoring the closest two-way microphone that broadcast the initial greeting. Instead, it flew in a beeline, only stopping when it reached the blind's large observation window. The huge insect hovered, buzzing slowly from side to side for nearly a minute, coming face to face with Alex and Jimmy. The two men stood frozen in place as they watched the hornet closely inspect each of them in turn from the other side of the window. Suddenly, a new hornet voice chirped out a reply picked up by one of the microphones positioned closest to the blind.

"Enemy unknown designation... enemy unknown designation not repeated...." the hornet turned and flew back to the queen.

Harvey spoke slowly and deliberately from the lab, "My God. Alex they know that the microphone is only a tool, I'd say they've also guessed where we might be speaking from."

Alex replied, "... and I believe they also know us to be specific individuals. That bit about enemy unknown designation, and unknown designation not repeated. It would seem to refer that it views Jimmy and I as both separate and identifiable."

"Bullshit!" Harding spat out and pounded the observation windows glass with his palm. "No way does a bunch of fucking bugs have a complex three-dimensional coordinate system, never mind the ability to differentiate one human from another."

Beside Jimmy, Alex spoke up, "Well, we know that honey bees do a little dance to let other bees in their hive know where the best pollen can be found. Those bees, in turn, have been shown to fly directly to the spot without following the bee that originally communicated the location." Alex explained. "While I doubt these insects have developed a complex spatial coordinate system, why couldn't a similar species vocalize the information rather than act it out?

Harvey spoke up. "As far as recognizing individuals, we've suspected for quite some time that some insects can differentiate between various humans although we assumed they used smell, not vision. Guess we learned something new today."

"Enemy unknown designation... enemy unknown designation not repeated...not... come...nest...sentry attack." The female voice of the queen spoke out once again from the master terminal. The video camera showed the queen re-entering the nest and move out of sight while the larger hornets remained to guard the entrance.

Harvey spoke to no one in particular. "Well, I suppose we've been told. Not exactly the way I thought this would go but then again how could anyone even guess how something like this might turn out."

Wanda spoke up. "People, this has been an incredible breakthrough, not just for us but for mankind. Don't you realize we have just communicated with a completely alien race, even if it is one that might have been living on earth since before the age of the dinosaurs?"

The terminal speakers clicked suddenly coming back to life, the queen's synthesized voice spoke once more, *"enemy unknown designation... enemy unknown designation not repeated...speak...again ...astronomical designation syntax error..."* Nothing further came from the speakers.

"I think she just said we just might talk again sometime later?" Harvey's face beamed.

That night everyone got rather drunk.

Over the next several weeks, members of the team regularly conversed with a few select representatives of the nest but the queen herself remained silent. During that time, Wanda proved invaluable to the project as she went about designing an automated dialog program between the Cambridge decoding program and the hornets. In a nutshell, Wanda had set up a "Rosetta stone" language course for each race.

In a progress meeting, a month later Wanda announced their mutual understanding of the other's language was as complete as it was ever likely to get. Talks could begin whenever Harvey gave the ok... they would start first thing next morning.

As for Paithoon Deep, things pretty much unfolded the same way for him every day. Wake up at seven, take a cold shower, eat a cold breakfast, then spend the rest of the day sweating his shorts off in the sweltering jungle heat while constantly beating back the encroaching vegetation. He spent half his time slashing and clearing brush in the village or along the fences of the research compound with the remainder taken up working the ditches of Weather Point Road and its summit.

Last night just before going to sleep Deep had finished off the last of his cocaine. Every second week a cook who worked in the small barracks would receive a phone call from the mainland specifying when and where one of Deep's men would meet him. The cook told Paithoon his next care package would arrive the day after tomorrow, timed to coincide with Deep's clearing duties along the road. One of his men would watch for him, staying just inside the brush until it was safe to approach then pass along the small package to the boss before hiking back to a solitary beach where his comrade remained by the boat. God but Deep was looking forward to the delivery.

Of all the work assignments, by far Deep's favorite was working near the island's automated radar and weather stations. At the higher elevations, the jungle was less intrusive, meaning that he did not have to work nearly as hard. This provided time to sit in the cool gentle breeze while enjoying the stunning view of the island below and the surrounding ocean. Today was just such a day. He thought the island would make a nice getaway, if it were not for the damn quakes. They were regular enough on the mainland but lately these were starting to freak him out. The tremors had increased in number, strength, and duration over these last several weeks.

Paithoon stood at the highest point of the summit, atop the radar stations catwalk. His unbuttoned, light cotton shirt billowed in the cooling breeze while the photo identification card he wore about his neck twisted and fluttered about like an errant kite. He looked down at his cheap government issued watch; the truck would arrive to pick him up in another hour.

Only sixty wonderfully cool minutes before he would be heading back down the mountain with the rest of his sweaty stinking work crew, back to that oven they called the prisoners barracks. He cursed loudly into the wind as he calculated he still had nearly another three months to go before his parole came up for review. Suddenly, Deep's ears caught a familiar sound coming from the direction of the road. The guard truck approached, engine revving, its tires spinning in the pea gravel, the vehicle mounted the last leg of Weather Point Road then stopped. The driver of the truck leaned into the horn as he waved him over.

"Dirty Bastards!" he spat, Paithoon's ride back down the hill had arrived.

Professor Jacob's team had been regularly conversing with the "Kindred," as the hornets referred to themselves, for just over a month. The team was justifiably pleased when the Kindred no longer referred to the humans as the "great destroyers" settling instead for a phrase that loosely translated into "the curious ones."

The researchers quickly discovered that while the members of the Kindred were capable of individual thought, they were also thoroughly devoid of emotion, highly logical and utterly subservient to any member of higher station within the rigid echelons of the community. The vital need for this type of society was clear to the staff given the fierce competition in which the insects had evolved throughout the millennia. Notwithstanding the dangers posed by individual predators such as scorpions and spiders, the hornets found themselves in a constant state of war participating in an evolutionary arms race with the other social insects. So far, the Kindred found themselves near the top of the heap along with their eternal enemy, the ants.

The team was fascinated to learn that the Kindred considered the larger animals in the world as simply natural phenomena, similar to how humans viewed extremes of weather, earthquakes, or volcanoes, occasional inconveniences to be tolerated or avoided if at all possible.

On the other hand, hornets viewed humans and their machines as a thoroughly destructive menace. For millennia, the hornets had relied upon the island's many bee colonies. Surviving by raiding the hives and taking honey, bee larva and even the bodies of the adult bees back to their nests as food for themselves and their young. Unfortunately, this activity destroyed the hive in the process. The island's farmers who tended and harvested the beehives for honey would defend the hives when possible. For their part, the Kindred could do little matched against the awesome might of humanity. Massive resistance and retaliation usually met with the utter destruction of the hornet's nest and their entire community. In most cases, discretion continued to prove the better part of valor.

As the exchange of information proceeded, the insects were very troubled to learn that not all the humans on the island were aware of their "non-aggression" pact with the research team. In order to placate the Kindred, they posted photographs of the facility's staff near the entrance to the blind. Now readily identified by the Kindred, the staffers could approach the nest allowing them to adjust and clean the microphones and video cameras without being stung although the sentries still swarmed uncomfortably close and only a matter of yards away. Anyone else approaching the nest would be fair game.

The Kindred had a collective hive memory that extended well over a hundred generations into the past. Using this racial memory and their own highly developed instincts, the Kindred could predict storms, monsoons, typhoons, and dry spells. According to the insect's history, a mass migration involving multiple colonies occurred just prior to the eruption of Krakatau in 1883. Harvey and Alex almost drooled over the prospect that the Kindred might even be able to detect and predict significant geological events before they happened, but for now, if that ability existed, the Kindred were playing things close to their chest.

Even given their obvious talents and resourcefulness, the numbers of Kindred colonies had gone into steep decline over the latter part of the twentieth century due to habitat destruction and human encroachment; an all too familiar situation. Now the honeybee populations across the globe and most lately on the island itself were collapsing. Referred to as the Honeybee Colony Collapse Disorder or CCD, the phenomena was linked with the wide use of pesticides and new bee viruses, but perhaps the biggest cause was a parasitic mite called the Varroa Destructor. Either way, the bees that the hornets relied upon as an essential food source had been disappearing. In some way, the Kindred were aware that the vast majority of their colonies on the mainland had already disappeared.

When the beehives on their island began to thin out, the resourceful hornets had yet another trick up their sleeves. The swine the Vietnamese refugees brought to the island in the seventies often escaped their pens wandering about the island eventually creating a considerable feral population. Every so often the hornets would ambush one of the pigs as they ran along the numerous trails that spider webbed the mountain slopes. Although the Kindred were not interested in eating the flesh of the pigs themselves, they were quite happy to feed on the fly maggots, worms and other larva that riddled the corpses as they decomposed in the jungle underbrush. This new food source had supplemented their diet until the recent removal of the swine had taken place.

The Kindred had found themselves in a tough spot. Another readily available food source would be required if they were to survive. To the hornets, whether prey had four legs or only two it wasn't about to make much of a difference.

The three men met in Lucas' office. The deputy warden of the mainland prison wore an expensive looking suit and sat on a chair before the facility manager's desk. The ranking guard, responsible for the island's work detail, stood cap in hand appearing exceedingly uncomfortable at the side of his superior. Together, with his duties at the research facility, Lucas was also responsible for supplying the jail and guard barracks and assigning the prisoners their work schedules. Now moments earlier, Lucas had made it crystal clear to the visiting deputy warden that ensuring the prisoners remain on the island were not included in any of those responsibilities.

The deputy's face flushed as he raised his voice. "Well, I'm not sure we can continue to provide inmates to the island detail, there are simply too many of them going missing. What's more, no one on the mainland has heard from any of the prisoners since their escape."

"And just why would that be a surprise? Just how many escaped criminals make their location known to the authorities when they're on the run?" Lucas faced the angry official with a smirk. "Has anyone attempted to catch them?"

"You know as well as I do we don't have the resources to arrest these men. We're talking about minimum-security prisoners, men who hardly represent any real danger to society. Quite frankly our police have more important things to."

"Once again" asked the manager, "why would any of this be my concern?"

"It's your concern if the men never left the island. Maybe it's a safety issue of some kind or maybe they've established some half-assed colony somewhere. Either way, I've arranged for a search of the island to be conducted ten days from now using federal troops, choppers, dogs you name it." The warden blustered and stood up from his chair preparing to leave. "This meeting's over!"

"Commence your search Commandant, I look forward to it." Lucas watched the warden storm out of the office. Reaching for the office door the uniformed guard turned towards Lucas frowned and shrugged his shoulders as he left.

Lucas thought to himself, "Not so much of a mystery as you might think warden."

While it was true that Lucas was not responsible for the security of the prison's work detail, he was ultimately responsible to the Ministry of the Environment to ensure the island was purged of its collection of farms and shanties found throughout the island. He and the uniformed officer who had just left his office a moment before had met on many occasions to discuss the ongoing problem of missing prisoners. There was little to go on aside from the guard's suspicion that one of the cooks was somehow involved with their newest arrival, Mr. Deep. Lucas determined to take steps to discover what escape routes the prisoners might take as they fled the island.

At forty-eight years of age, the facility manager was remarkably fit, spending much of his free time running along the numerous forest trails for exercise. On yesterday's run, Lucas had discovered the skeletonized remains of one of the first escapees along a well-used hog trail that branched off Weather Point Road. He made a mental note of the body's location intending to report the situation upon his arrival back at the facility, but that intention evaporated completely when he discovered no few than three additional bodies in various states of decomposition further down along adjoining trails.

The latest missing prisoner came into view as Lucas rounded a sharp bend in the trail and came across the body of Kenny Sukarno. He had gone missing only days before, but already was only barely recognizable. The man's blackened corpse, swarmed noisily being covered head to foot with maggots, flies and at least thirty large green hornets, some that had just alighted while others were in the process of returning to the nest, their jaws full of wriggling fly larva. The pungent smell of corruption caused him to gag and he had brought his arm up to his face burying his nose in the shirtsleeve. Surprised by the manager's sudden appearance the hornets had flown up in a single mass, swarming, and circling above Kenny's body but had not appeared intent on attacking or even approaching Lucas; and the manager suspected that he knew why.

Invited to sit in on the scientist's weekly research briefings, Lucas was quite aware of the latest updates regarding the project. After all, he was required to requisition any equipment the group might require carrying on their research studies. Lucas was well aware that his photograph, like those of the other research staff, had been posted at the blind site and as such, he was considered persona gratissima and "off the menu" as far as the Kindred was concerned.

Immediately upon arriving back at the facility last evening, Lucas had called the cook into his office and questioned the man at length regarding his association with Paithoon Deep. He finished proposing a generous offer the cook quickly jumped at. By the time the shaken cook departed his office, Lucas had all the information he required. The cook would pass along his private message to a certain prisoner before he left the island for the mainland the next morning.

Lucas Ong walked over to a large corkboard affixed to the office wall. Taking down the clipboard that held the current prison work schedule, he carried it back with him dropping it on the desktop. Sitting in his plush leather chair, he smiled thinly as he ran a finger down the schedule's list until it came to rest next to a single name; Paithoon Deep. Pushing back in his chair, he stared at the ceiling for several minutes lost in thought, then returning to the present, leaned forward and picked up the telephone receiver. He dialed the phone number of the mainland hospital by memory; it was time he checked on his daughter, Damia.

The following day dawned later than usual. A thick bank of high dark cloud lay far off to the east as the prisoners filed out, one behind the other, waiting their turn to climb into the back of the truck that would drop them at their various work sites for the day. The truck slowly rumbled up Weather Point Road until it stopped just a little more than halfway to the summit. Paithoon climbed down from the rear of the truck and stood to wait on the road for the guard in the truck box to toss down a long scythe and a machete. Together, they clattered onto the gravel a few feet away from the prisoner. The guard banged his fist on the back of the cab and the truck resumed its steep climb up the hill. The prisoner waited until the guards back was turned then flipped him the bird, he saw the other prisoners laughing among themselves then immediately clam up as the guard swung around to see what had amused them.

Paithoon picked up the scythe and looked at his watch. Eight thirty, he had an hour to kill until he had to walk down the path and meet his contact. Figuring he better get some work done in the meantime, he started swinging the wooden pole, working the sharp blade against the tall grass and weeds that lined the shallow ditch beside the road. Since he had arrived on the island, the hard work and long hours had hardened his muscles and reshaped his body. He laid a hand on his flat stomach and smiled as his hands moved over his smooth ridged abdominals, he felt like he was in his twenties again.

A faint rumble sounded somewhere deep in the earth, shook the foliage, and then quickly subsided. He was getting used to the tremors. He barely felt them anymore.

Harvey, Alex and several other members of the staff stared at the alert message flashing in red atop the news site displayed on the large television monitor sitting in the main lab. According to volcanologists, Anak Krakatoa, aka the "son of Krakatoa" was once again beginning to stir from several decades of dormancy. The massive 1883 eruption of the original volcano had left a large sea-filled caldera when the island blew itself to smithereens. Then in 1927, a new volcanic cone had slowly rebuilt itself, climbing above the surrounding waters in the strait between Java and Sumatra, the same location where the previous volcano had once stood.

Anak's volcanic dome was still comparatively small as measured against that of its predecessor. Many of the world's prominent geologists had expressed confidence that a large eruption of the volcano was not in the cards anytime soon, but now their opinions seemed to be wavering. Recently measured using the latest technology, the lava pool lying below the island while not having risen closer to the dome's surface, had instead expanded. The magma reservoir was much wider and deeper than previously thought and somewhat more worryingly, had extended its tendrils into the numerous geologic faults scattered throughout the region. The swarming tremors of late indicated that the entire area could be at risk, just as it had one hundred and thirty some years before with Krakatoa.

The television screen displayed an active video feed of the smoking island for several minutes before flashing to a time arranged series of images of the volcano taken over the last year. The group of staff members stared at the screen with increased concern.

"What do you think Harvey?" asked Alex while watching several of the female staff members as they twittered together excitedly; several others were talking in serious tones on their cell phones.

"I did some homework on the internet last night. During the last eruption, the positioning of our island chain spared it from all but the most massive tsunami waves that followed. The mainland took the brunt of the damage, that's where the greatest loss of life occurred." Harvey frowned. "This said, just how big the waves were that hit this island are anyone's guess."

Alex suggested, "Why don't we have Wanda ask someone who was here back then?"

"Wanda? Oh, the Kindred," Harvey answered his expression was deadpan. "I doubt we'll get anywhere but I suppose it couldn't hurt?"

The hundred or so virgin queens, together with multitudes of their drone suitors had flown off, leaving the hornet nest for the last time they climbed through the warm mists of early morning to circle high above the island and consummate their mating ritual. A single queen might join with many of her male pursuers before something within her said she had achieved the ability to found a clan of her own, in an area of her choosing. Some of the newly fertile queens would disperse across the chain of islands of which Palau Kona was a member while others would fly even further toward the distant mainland. While the female monarchs flew off to begin their reign, their brief consorts having given their all, now spiraled downward from the skies and having fallen to earth would never rise again.

Leaving the scythe at the roadside, he stuck the machete in his belt and following instructions relayed to him from the cook the night before, Paithoon Deep left the main road and walked into the forest. The cook had told Deep that his people on the mainland insisted the meet would take place four hundred yards down the path leading from Weather Point Road. This extra degree of caution was required since security patrols on the island had recently been stepped up, a fact not lost on Paithoon, who only this morning, had overheard several of the guards talking among themselves.

Within the few days that had passed since Kenny Sukarno had originally broken the trail, the jungle was already encroaching on the path. That portion of the path near the road's immediate proximity had already become overgrown. At any point where the undergrowth received full sunlight, the vegetation sprang up with amazing speed. Deep had to use the machete to clear his passage but once the path wound below the shading jungle canopy, the undergrowth, deprived of direct sunlight soon thinned out and Paithoon found he made good time. He checked his watch; it was nearly ten o'clock in the morning. He felt certain he had already walked nearly a half mile but still had not met his contact. Deep went over the instructions once again in his head, still confident he had gotten them right. That being the case, the guy that got it wrong would have some explaining to do when his boss returned to civilization.

Deep had reached the edge of a steep cliff that overlooked the far side of the island and a series of isolated beaches. Like Kenny had before him, Paithoon parted the underbrush and stood looking out across the island, scant feet from the cliff face. Searching the coastline below him, he was pleased to see a powerful cigar boat pulled up on a deserted beach. He himself had purchased the boat over a year ago. Using the speedy craft to run contraband back and forth along the coast, his men would meet at rendezvous locations and dead drops. Paithoon pulled back from the cliff's edge and backed onto the path.

Cupping his hands to his lips he called out several times then whistled loudly. The sound would not carry too far but now he was sure he was in the right area. His man should be along shortly. He sat down on a stump at the side of the trail and listened intently. A sudden noise drew his attention toward a bend in the trail just yards up ahead. Deep stood up and called out the names of several of the men who might be making today's delivery but there was no answer. Paithoon walked several more yards down the path. Still hearing the faint rustling noise as he approached a bend in the trail he suddenly realized the sounds originated off to the side of the path, somewhere deep in the dense brush.

Deep was a hard man, one not accustomed to feeling fear of any kind; he had left that fragile portion of his humanity in a prison cell a very long time ago. The odd sounds coming from the undergrowth were quite unlike anything he had ever heard before, yet he still somehow knew they represented a very real danger. That sudden realization sent chills running up and down his spine as he backed away from the growing volume of snaps, pops, and crackles that now filled his ears.

All of his senses alert and tingling Deep backed several steps away from the noises. As he did so, his foot stepped on a dry branch that lay in the pathway. As his full weight bore down on the wood it broke and splintered with such an unexpectedly loud report that Paithoon first thought that someone had fired a gun nearby and froze motionless trying to determine what had just happened.

The next instant a massive tornado of hornets spun up in an angry swirl, rising up from the surrounding grass, brush, and trees nearby. The insects were huge! Larger than any Deep had ever seen before or imagined were even possible. He stared, watching in horror as they formed a crude phalanx and flew directly toward him. He turned away screaming in terror as they raced toward him. Down at the beach, the gangster assigned to remain with Paithoon's boat thought he heard a shrill cry coming from somewhere deep within the forest, far above the shoreline.

"Well; still no answer, not a word." Wanda shrugged her shoulders as the two men beside her stared blankly at the inactive monitor.

Alex looked a little perplexed. "But I definitely hear something coming from the area of the nest."

Wanda explained, "The program we use to decode their language is designed to filter out sounds, or anything that is not recognized as belonging to the insects. The longer we communicated with the Kindred, the more efficient our filter became. That's why the monitor fails to report any activity."

Harvey walked over to another desk several feet away and typed briefly on the keyboard. A video appeared up on the lab's main screen. The image of the hornet's nest filled the screen, its surface teeming with insects crawling atop every nearby surface. "It looks like the entire colony has been mobilized!"

"But why?" Alex asked as he and Harvey looked questioningly to one another.

"They're swarming!" Wanda's shrill voice caused the men's heads to swivel back to the large screen. The entire group of hornets suddenly began flying from the nest, within only mere seconds they had left the viewing range of the video camera traveling off at high speed deeper into the forest.

Deep's initial scream trailed off to a muted whine as he dove forward into the trail's soft earth covering his head in his arms expecting the insects to attack in any second... an attack that never came. The loud drone of insect wings became deafening as the colony whirred above him crossing the trail where he lay and flying off from the cliff's edge, setting out above the island in a compact group. Their Queen and her bodyguard in the lead, the swarm set out in the general direction of the mainland.

Still lying motionless in the earth, Paithoon realized he could no longer hear the beating wings. After another couple of seconds, he found the courage to rise up to his hands and knees, then to his feet, all the while keeping his eyes fixed in the direction where the insects had flown off. Looking out to the sky above the island, all he could see of the swarm was a small black dot quickly receding into the distance. Giving quick thanks to whatever god might have saved him; he brushed the forest litter from his clothes and once again turned his attention to discovering what might have delayed his contact. He felt the earth heave slightly beneath his feet then groan deeply. "Not a big deal, just another tremor" he told himself but this time, the groan quickly grew in volume not stopping until it had become a full-throated roar.

Miles below the earth's crust, the semi-molten rock composing the upper mantle suddenly shifted with incredible speed. The violence of the movement forced huge sections of the bedrock that lay above to turn and twist in a sympathetic motion. The island of Kona Palau sat directly above this fault. The power of the thrust broke through and shattered the thick layers of rock above. Now fractured, each edge slipped against the other, one side of the island thrust upward while the other side dove downward virtually splitting the island apart top to bottom.

Paithoon once again found himself on his hands and knees groveling in the center of the trail beneath a constant shower of leaves, twigs, and branches that rained down from the forest canopy. He felt an intense pain in his ears and screaming aloud covered them with his palms but it did no good. Even after his eardrums broke and he lay bleeding from his nose, mouth and eyes he could still hear the angry roar of the earth as it penetrated the very bones of his skull. Seconds later, the cliff face lying only several yards away collapsed. The subsequent landslide of broken rock, earth, vegetation and what little was left of Paithoon Deep fell away in a crushing jumble toward the beaches far below.

Back at the facility, Lucas Ong stood at one of the main laboratory's picture windows that provided a beautiful view of the island's base through to its summit as it rose majestically from the ocean. From this vantage, Lucas could just make out the distant radar and weather stations; white pearls perched atop the deep emerald green of the mountain. He glanced down to his watch; Deep should reach his judgment soon if he hadn't already met it. Lucas smiled as he imagined the wholly suitable and terrible vengeance the hornets would met out to Deep on behalf of his daughter.

Harvey, Alex, and Wanda stood watching the now vacant nest on the big screen monitor when the entire building shook with primordial violence throwing everyone in the room to the floor. The thunderous growl became a throaty roar as the earth suddenly sprang to life. A second later, the overhead lights dimmed and faded while the computers fell silent as the building's power was abruptly cut.

As the magnitude 9.9 quake continued, Lucas looked up through the window toward the summit just as the frame of the facility twisted on its foundations. The glass in the windows cracked then exploded outward and inward at the same moment sending razor sharp shards of glass whistling through the air slicing and cutting down anything in their path. Just before the blood that filled his eyes and turned his vision to a fading scarlet, Lucas would have sworn he saw a huge crack appear, beginning at Banana Bay and running upward along Weather Point Road making toward its very summit.

Then as suddenly as it began everything became still and silent. Harvey and Alex helped Wanda to her feet then all three walked slowly to where Lucas had stood only moments ago. He now lay motionless in a widening pool of blood before an empty jagged and twisted window frame. There was nothing to be done for the man.

Wanda crossed herself and said a little prayer... it was never heard. The rumbling quickly renewed and within the space of several seconds, the radar and weather stations, the facility, the village, and barracks together with the entire side of the huge mountain simply slumped downward. Gaining nearly supersonic speed in a matter of a few seconds, billions of tons of earth and rock crashed into the ocean and slid beneath its surface.

The main swarm of the Kindred had already traveled far from the island when the tsunami first appeared below. Swiftly overtaking their progress, the waves below the swarm rushed on toward the mainland that lay only some twelve miles in the distance. A series of huge waves had already risen several hundred feet above sea level and would rise even higher as they made their way up the quickly shallowing continental shelf. When the waves struck the mainland, they would break over a thousand miles of coastline sweeping inland for a hundred miles or more, destroying everything and everyone in their path before its forward momentum stalled. At some point, the flood would then reverse itself, dragging debris, flotsam, and the lifeless remains of its many thousands of victims back with it, retracing its journey back toward the ocean.

For the Kindred's old queen this would be her swan song, she would live long enough to establish a final new colony among the thousands of square miles of destruction that would greet their arrival. There, they would have their choice of nesting sites; places where they wouldn't be disturbed, places where she would be free to give birth to yet another generation of drones and virgin queens before she died. While the old queen didn't possess emotions that you or I might recognize, it was sufficient to say her Majesty was quite satisfied in the knowledge that while the Kindred might not discover any additional beehives; the insects would find that their newest and frankly preferred food source wouldn't fall in short supply anytime in the foreseeable future.

The Rattle of Bones

The young girls sat cross-legged on the ground to either side of the old man. Necks bent low above their work, their hands moved busily over the low table before them. The long workbench, centered beneath a simple grass thatched roof, helped provide welcome relief from the noonday sun's powerful rays. The afternoon promised to remain hot in every aspect, the dead calm and high humidity combining to affect even those long accustomed to Cambodia's tropical summers. One of the girls at the table, head still lowered, allowed her eyes to carefully stray upward and to her right, her gaze falling upon a boy about her own age.

She watched her twin brother as he knelt before a large bloodstained wooden stump. The machete in his hand rose and fell in a slow, rhythmic tempo, arching downward to meet the surface of a large partially denuded bone grasped firmly in his other hand. Her brother's well-practiced aim directed the rust dulled blade toward the bone at an oblique angle where it sliced and tore away the raw flesh. In ragged tatters, the meat dropped into the dusty reddened earth below. Pausing briefly, the boy set down the machete and wiped his brow with his forearm, his face turning toward the shelter where his sister watched. The children's eyes met and locked before her brother quickly looked away shaking his head.

She watched her twin bend forward, reaching down, he snatched up a large chunk of raw meat throwing it toward a shallow pit several yards away. Slapping down atop the other grizzly remnants, the meat made a moist sloshing sound as it slid and came to rest at the far side of the hole. The boy's casual toss had disturbed the hundreds of flies that coated the gruesome mass. Arising in an angrily buzzing cloud, the insects swarmed about for several minutes but soon resettled, returning to their awful banquet. The girl felt a sharp elbow strike her ribs and heard a growled warning from the old man next to her; lowering her head once more, she resumed her work.

Satisfied with the girl's response, the old man carefully set a sharp cleaver upon a large piece of raw bone propped atop the table. Pausing for a moment, he positioned the blade exactly before tapping the top edge of the cleaver with a heavy wooden mallet. The measured blow sent its razor-sharp cutting edge slicing through the milk-white thighbone separating a narrow even strip from the original piece. When he had finished cutting perhaps half a dozen strips, the man tossed what remained of the original bone into a growing refuse pile nearby. Now taking each strip in turn, the old man used the cleaver to precisely cut and trim each length. Incredibly, given the crude means employed, the dimensions of each rectangle relative to those of the others were almost identical. Picking up the pieces, the man carefully set each within the jaws of a small wooden press; this would ensure that the edges of the work would not curl while drying. Filling the press, he closed it tightly and set it aside.

A second girl at the same table picked up a bone press from a group that had already been drying for several days then removed each of the thin wafers. Spreading a thin layer of glue across the surface of the bone, she pressed the small rectangle tightly against a thin piece of stained hardwood of the same dimension. Satisfied with the fit, she replaced the piece in the press together with the others she had already completed. Finishing the last rectangle, the girl reclosed the press to allow the glue to cure for several more days.

By the time the afternoon had arrived, the old man had finished the day's cutting. He reached for a press that held a dozen or so fully cured wood-bone wafers. Taking up the first of the small rectangles, he positioned it on the bench in front of him, then using a sharp bradawl; carefully bore into the bone's surface creating a series of small holes forming a precise grouping. Completing the task, he replaced the piece within a specific position along a small wooden rack lying nearby.

The young girl watched the man add to the rack's contents then reached over and selected one of the wafers. Holding it firmly in one hand, she dipped a thin brush into a small pot beside her. Removing the brush and taking great care not to smear the paint, she applied a single dot of the thick black gloss to each separate indentation. Satisfied, the girl replaced the rectangle into its corresponding position along a long wooden rack before her. The girl, like the others who worked here, had to be very careful not to make mistakes; mistakes were not tolerated... mistakes were considered a crime against the regime.

The commotion began somewhere beyond the cluster of small village huts near the prisoner's compound. Selected and removed from the compound for questioning, the children heard the usual chorus of protests erupt from the prisoners. Their objections quickly escalated into yells of anger, but the thorough beatings and brutal treatment doled out by their captors inexorably resulted in their abject acquiescence. During their interrogations, each person would provide their inevitable confession. Once decided, the justice of the Khmer Rouge was as cruel as it was arbitrary; its victims would find themselves dispatched quickly, or perhaps slowly, but in a manner utterly dependent upon the whims of their executioner.

Choosing not to use bullets that might be better employed fighting external enemies of the state, the authorities preferred alternate methods of dispatching their victims. The executions were primitive and brutal by any standard. In the past, the duration of the high-pitched screams typically continued perhaps several minutes, but as of late, the terrifying vocalizations often continued much longer. The end would only arrive when the victim could manage no more than a low moan despite the evil perpetrated on their person.

Selected for questioning, a young married couple, both teachers within the village, found themselves dragged to a large hut that served as the regional headquarters of the Khmer Rouge. Two officers awaited the couple's arrival. For most of the morning, they had drunk Sraa Sor, strong Khmer rice liquor, anticipating what would soon take place with almost giddy excitement.

The senior officer held and maintained unquestioned authority within a score of surrounding villages. His real name had gone unused for some time, referred to now as "Chhaya Neak" that in Khmer roughly translated to the Shadow Dragon. Together with his sadistic lieutenant, they systematically terrorized and murdered anyone accused of being an intellectual, a previous figure in authority, or just an unfortunate soul who living nearby, had been randomly chosen to serve as the principal actor within their demented genre of entertainment.

Over the next several hours, the heads of the young worker's would occasionally lift from their work, their attention drawn by the cries and screams of their teachers that rose and fell with each new atrocity inflicted. Eventually, the screams subsided and the young painter set down her brush. Picking up each of the twenty-eight domino tiles, she slid them into their corresponding positions along the drying rack.

Meanwhile, beside the other hut where her brother waited, the teachers had just arrived.

On a lovely Saturday morning in June, Agnes Grayson slipped into her walking shoes, grabbed her purse, and slipped out the door of her small townhouse. Smiling and squinting in the bright sunlight, she was amazed that even after seventy-two years, the natural beauty of these early summer days still filled her with the same delight they had in her youth. The aroma of her prize roses merged with the myriad of other blossoms gracing her flowerbeds, their muddled perfumes wafted upon the gentle breeze as she walked the curved flagstone path that led to the street.

This morning Agnes was a woman on a mission. Walking briskly and with a sense of purpose, she covered the six blocks leading to the corner of Railway Street and 7th Avenue in the short span of only twenty minutes. Rounding the last corner, she spied her objective that spread itself out across a large vacant lot. A host of haphazardly arranged sun tents, plywood kiosks, and open air tables spilled out across the emerald green lawn; each connected to the other by brown foot-worn paths that weaved among the small booths. Brownville's summer flea market was an institution that dated back to the early sixties.

Agnes checked her Timex and smiled to herself, her early arrival would allow her to browse the marketplace at her leisure, before the inevitable crowd of weekenders arrived. Driving in from the big city, they would transplant their own little traffic jams and choke the market's narrow pathways. She bypassed a few of the larger, more polished looking booths knowing that she wouldn't locate her quarry amid the recycled fare of department store junk or among the displays of poor quality homemade jellies and preserves. Instead, she made her way to the more obscure tables that sat along the less traveled paths; this is where she might find a real treasure!

A half hour later and somewhat disappointed she was ready to leave for home. Sure, there were some interesting pieces but they were overpriced or her collection already contained something similar. Consisting of small unusual antique ornaments, figurines, music boxes and the like, her menagerie harkened back to her youth or better still, to that of her mother and fathers. Many years ago, Agnes found that she had a tendency to buy collectibles that were simply too large. The limited and precious space in her curio cabinets and on her display shelves led her to adopt a simple rule. The rule demanded that the item be sufficiently small, so that it fit into the compact brown leather purse she carried upon her shoulder during these outings.

Not having found anything that piqued her interest, she began to make her way along one of the pathways leading homeward when she spied someone she had not seen in some time. The man who walked in her direction was only some thirty feet distant. Shooting a quick glance up the narrow pathway, she looked to her left and right seeking a quick detour amongst the small tables that crowded either side of the route. Finding none, she quickly spun toward the nearest table where she feigned interest in the goods, appearing preoccupied, busily picking up and inspecting the numerous items that sat upon it.

Normally a friendly easygoing person, she was unused to the uncomfortable sensation that suddenly welled up within her. An odd sense of embarrassment, responsibility, and fault swirled among distant memories lifting and flinging them into the present as so much scrap paper caught up within a whirling dust devil. She stole a sideways glance toward the man and saw that he too had paused and stood browsing at the next table up and to her rear. He remained there for a minute or so conversing with the vendor before turning and walking back in the direction from which he came, turning right he disappeared from view.

She let out an almost audible sigh; Matthew Holder. Agnes had not laid eyes on the man for what, she quickly calculated, at least several years, but they had not spoken for several decades before that. She had a sudden flash of insight. Brownsville was a small town; the odds would favor a casual meeting of two longtime residents. Perhaps Matt had seen her this morning as well but decided not to approach her, perhaps he even held feelings similar to hers.

She considered their shared past. Elementary, middle school and into their final year at Harrison High, they had remained nearly inseparable. The movies, dances, and shared lunches in the school's cafeteria had given rise to dreams and plans for a future that would never come to fruition. Agnes was an honor student and her parents were people of means. They insisted their girl attend a good school out of state whereas Matt's talents clearly lay in working with his hands. On the night of their High School Prom, he had proposed to Agnes, but she refused to give him an answer that night. The following afternoon was dull and rainy. The young couple sat on a hard wooden bench in Founder's Park where she informed him of her decision to leave for college in the coming fall.

Crushed, Matt smiled through his tears saying he understood, although she knew he couldn't possibly. He had kissed her cheek then left her sitting on the bench. Watching Matt sadly walk away, she suddenly wondered if she understood it herself. They did not see each other the rest of the summer; he had taken a job in his uncle's lumber mill several towns over and she had left for school by the time he returned. Ten years would pass until their paths crossed once again on the streets of Brownsville.

That first meeting was cordial but estranged. Whatever fondness each still felt for the other had grown disguised by time and life's burdens. Agnes had returned to her hometown a somewhat embittered woman following her failed marriage to a philandering investment banker while Matt's detached demeanor was a result of his simply never having found anyone else that truly mattered. Either way, it appeared that their once shared feelings were captives of the past and there they would remain.

Watching him leave, Agnes became aware of the item in her hands that she had unconsciously reached for when Matt approached. Her fingers ran across the top of the smooth hardwood box and her eyes appreciated the fine mother of pearl inlay on the cover. She turned the box over in her hands examining it closely, and then opened its small brass latch to reveal the contents.

"Dominoes." The old oriental woman croaked out through a cloud of cigarette smoke.

"Oh yes." Agnes briefly glanced up at the woman before again lowering her gaze and inspecting its contents more closely. The rectangular playing pieces measured a half inch by an inch. Agnes plucked several tiles from the box and noticed that each dice-like face had uniformly yellowed with age. Turning them about in her hand, she appreciated that the wooden backing of each piece precisely matched the same dark brown hardwood used in the container's construction. She replaced the tiles then closed the lid, considering the delicate pink Jasmine blossoms and vines that adorned the case.

"You like?" A dull cough followed the seller's question. Agnes looked up and studied the woman standing across from her. About her own age, the years had not favored the woman's personal appearance or likely her financial standing. The seller's leathery face resembled a withered prune. Her thin smile revealed a mouth of chipped, missing teeth and any that remained were brown, and tobacco stained. The woman wore a faded, overly large, print dress that hung loosely about her scrawny frame while a kerchief of the same material covered her graying head. "You like?" the woman repeated.

Agnes did not answer immediately, but looked back down onto the tabletop where she saw a second box similar to the one that she held. Setting the first case on the table, she picked up the second noticing that it too displayed a similar floral pattern, although the flowers on this box were soft white in color and the wood backing of the domino tiles were a light birch. Something about this particular case and its contents piqued her interest. She plucked up one of the dominoes turning it over in her hand.

As her fingertips caressed its smooth face, she found herself enjoying the comfortable sensation, one of peace and well-being.

The seller spoke again; obviously annoyed her words were clipped and sharp. "Lady... you like? You buy?"

"Why... yes I do." Agnes replied, and then added, "How much?" already knowing that she must have the little box even if the deal was too rich.

Agnes left the flea market with the little case tucked away in her purse knowing she had overpaid for the set. She shook her head, how unlike herself, she had not even bartered with the woman, just paid the asking price. Half an hour later, she carefully positioned the box upon the upper shelf of her favorite curio cabinet. Closing the glass door, she detected a hint of Jasmine in the air, but the faint aroma vanished just as quickly as she had dismissed the thought with a smile.

The old Asian woman walked directly to the cash register then paused, allowing her eyes to scan the restaurant. There were but a few customers sitting at a table near the entrance, she opened the till and quickly slid three twenty dollar bills beneath the cash drawer. She couldn't believe her luck on finding not one, but two gullible round eyes who each bought one of the two dominoes sets at prices she considered far too high, but who can tell with white folks, she thought to herself. She counted the rest of the money she got for the two sets, an even hundred; a price that she thought Sok would accept without too much question. She had to be careful of this old man. Sok Charya had a hard face, steely cold eyes, and a ruthless reputation. She had heard other disturbing rumors, some going back to the old country many years before he came to America. She had no interest in discovering whether these reports were true.

The cook came up from behind her as quietly as a ghost, then laying his hand on her shoulder growled in Khmer "You got my money old woman?" He smiled as she jumped in surprise, her face betraying a fleeting glimpse of fear before she regained her stoic composure. Without saying a word, she fanned out the bills and thrust the money toward him holding it in front of his face. Sok waited for a moment and searched her face and eyes before reaching his hand toward the cash. "Good," he said curtly, and then plucking a single ten from the cash held up before him stuffed the bill into his shirt pocket beside his cigarettes. It had the desired effect, her surprise immediately turned to suspicion, but none the less, the old woman tightened her grip on the cash just in case Sok changed his mind. She nodded as Sok turned away, the trace of a thin smile on his lips as he walked back into the kitchen.

Sok stirred a large pot of noodles thinking of just how startled and off balance the bitter old woman appeared when he had not taken the cash. It brought him little satisfaction knowing he had surrendered what amounted to nearly a full day's pay and irked him further to know that had he wished to, he could have pushed the old bitch to cough up the rest of the money she no doubt had held back from the sale. Still he was only too happy to rid himself of the two items and the frightening memories they embodied; but it had not always been that way.

He had carried the small wooden boxes along with other important papers, photographs, and personal items on his person when immigrating to America some thirty-five years before taking only items that could pass any amount of scrutiny shown by an overly zealous customs officer. A month later, Sok took delivery of a second box containing all of what remained of his old life in Cambodia. Placing the unopened crate in the center room of the small flat he occupied, he had waited nearly a full month before unsealing its contents.

If he was anything, it was a patient man who had gone to great lengths to conceal any trace of his past. If an investigator or government agent were to conduct a search of his premise, the odds of finding anything incriminating would be slim. True, he could have consigned Chhaya Neak's cherished photos to a burning barrel in Phnom Penh. Instead, he carefully concealed them between two cardboard sheets in the bottom of a crate containing several blankets, some clothes wrapped about a small lamp and its unique custom made shade. Before packing the lampshade, Sok had attached a small tag. The tag proudly proclaimed the shade to be a "Product of China," although the Peoples Republic was hardly in the business of manufacturing light shades constructed using human skin. Hidden deep within the wide body of the lamp's hollow porcelain base, he had secured a miniature audio tape. The recording held his favorite and most particularly pleasing interrogation, that of a pretty young woman and her intellectual husband.

The old man smiled as he considered the irony that lay in his taking the name Sok Charya, a name that roughly translated from Khmer meant "good character, without worry." How very different from his old nickname, Chhaya Neak or Shadow Dragon, the fitting nickname he was pleased to assume as a captain within the brutal regime of the Khmer Rouge. He and his men had killed thousands of their fellow citizens and would have killed thousands more if the stinking Vietnamese had not invaded and put an end to their ruthless subjugation. Forced to flee to Thailand, he waited in hiding until the newly formed Cambodian government eventually tired of their search for he and other war criminals. Together with money, gold and other valuables looted from his victims, Sok had brought along his cherished souvenirs, but living in Thailand, he quickly found that silence cost money, lots of it. Nearly five years later, he entered the United States flat broke, just another poor Asian immigrant who would support himself waiting tables, and cooking in various noodle houses.

After arriving in the States, Sok had married but the union had no time to produce children. A cruel and domineering husband, Sok was surprised to find that unlike women who had been raised in Asia, his American wife was not about to put up with his antics and left him. He had been alone now for over twenty years. Sok would entertain himself playing dominoes and card games with the other men in the small Asian community, but lately had discovered he preferred his own company. Finishing his shift at the noodle house, he would arrive home in the late evening and rarely venture out afterward. Sok was a loner and to those few that knew him or cared to, he was considered decidedly odd and somewhat of a recluse.

Night after night, Sok sat at his kitchen table drinking his Sraa Sor, smoking the strong unfiltered Cambodian cigarettes, once again imagining himself as Chhaya Neak; the ruthless tyrant who had held lives within his grasp, a man whose very name elicited fear from those who dared speak it. The dragon reminisced about those uniquely satisfying occasions when he and his lieutenant carried out the slow torture of men, women, and even children. If a woman caught his interest they would have sport with her often making her husband or children watch their perversions before killing her ever so slowly, sometimes using the sharp edges of a palm leaf to slice strips of skin away from the underlying flesh or by simply garroting her with a silk scarf. This pleasurable pastime came to an abrupt end the very evening before he gave the domino sets to the old woman to sell at the flea market.

On that particular evening, Sok found himself in a dark funk, sitting morosely at his kitchen table. Unexpectedly, he had gotten home from work much earlier, just after six. The domino tiles lay spread out before him; each tile set face down on the table. As was his custom, he selected several of the tiles from the boneyard caressing each of the smooth yellow surfaces with his thumb. He anticipated the sensual pleasures that would soon arrive, and was disappointed and surprised when they eluded him. Minutes later, the sun fell beneath the kitchen windowsill bringing with it the gloom of twilight. Sok set down his glass and reached over the table, turning on his special lamp. He let the tips of his fingers caress the shade's satin surface before returning his attentions to the tiles lying beneath its soft yellow glow. It was of no use, the old excitement refused to return. Then he remembered the audio tape contained within the base of the lamp, the cassette had remained concealed there since the day he hid it.

He retrieved the small tape player from the bedroom then reached up and into the lamp's hollow base. Using his fingers, he probed the interior but was having trouble locating the cassette. His heart leapt with worry, where was it! Sok forced his arm and hand ever deeper within the porcelain recesses until he rediscovered the cassette, finding it still taped securely to its side, he felt himself flush with relief. As his fingers brushed against the plastic case, they tingled with an electrifying sensation.

Peeling away the plastic tape, he removed the cassette from the lamp.

He held the black plastic cartridge before him for several moments then smiled while placing the cassette into the machine. Butterflies arose and stirred within his stomach; this would be a good night. Refilling his drink, he leaned back in his chair and lit another smoke taking several long drags before setting the cigarette down into a dark brown ashtray on the table. He studied the tiles lying still and face down in the bone yard. Was it just his imagination, or did even they long for his personal attentions. Soft voices in his mind spoke in agreement; did he detect a slight touch of angst within their answer? Sok pressed down on the play button and expelled his breath in a ragged cough only now realizing that he had been holding his breath in anticipation.

The dragon sat back in his chair adjusting the volume of the tape deck so that the voices became little more than a whisper in the room, after all, the apartment walls were paper-thin. Not that the low volume mattered, the whispered conversations virtually shouted into his ears. He listened with relish as his lieutenant began the typical one-sided conversation with the young couple beginning with their identification, occupations and of course, the serious charges each faced. There were the usually excited denials of wrongdoing but since each had been teachers in the village the couple knew their guilt had already been precluded making any additional confessions quite unnecessary. The kangaroo court could now move to sentencing, a simple matter since all offenses were punishable by death, and the punishment would begin at once.

The screams of the woman began soon enough, eliciting begs and pleas of mercy from her husband. Sok felt his member stir and harden between his legs as he listened, vividly recalling the young wife's violation taking place before her husband's eyes. The dragon's breath became rapid and shallow, his pulse a pounding backdrop as he relived the slow torturous murder of the girl's husband. The man's shrieks and bawls drove his sexual intensity ever higher, the fingers of his hands that up until this moment had gently caressed the tiles suddenly pressed down hard onto the smooth bone surfaces. The couple's desperate squeals and screams rose to an overwhelming crescendo the very moment he reached climax, mere seconds before the recording ended.

When the tape had run its length, a sudden mechanical thunk boomed out from the machine, the noise echoing off the walls until the room once again became silent. Sok's racing heart slowed and his breathing deepened. A cruel satisfied smile replaced the sardonic mask he had worn while in the throes of his perversion.

The bulb of the table lamp to his left dimmed and flickered, the action drawing his eyes to the shade where he began to glimpse movements taking on vague shapes and silhouettes that sharpened into stark clarity. Sok stared unbelieving at the ghastly images that had come to life on its surface. Reminiscent of the silent movies from the nineteen twenties, the figures engaged in a macabre dance, moving slowly across the tanned velvet surface of human skin. Somehow snatched from his own mind, the fragments of distant memory once again played out before his astonished eyes. The Dragon and his soldiers, were once again clubbing, stabbing, or in some other manner, murdering anyone not in uniform. Some of their victims cowered, others knelt, but far more simply lay prostrate on the ground, a few of these held their arms weakly upraised, a vain attempt to shield themselves from the savage blows that rained down upon them. The hellish flickering vision ended abruptly as the light bulb burst apart with a soft pop, and thrusting the room into sudden darkness.

Sok sat motionless, allowing his eyes to adapt in the decrepit light that seeped past the yellowed lace curtains covering the tiny kitchen window. Slowly the familiar shapes of his table and the chairs emerged from the gloom, faint outlines etched within the room's dark shadows. Out of this emptiness, an infinitesimally small but brilliant white light sparked into existence. Expanding rapidly it grew to become an edge blurred, ever-shifting shape. Its previous brilliance fading in proportion to its increased size, its white-hot luminance blushed into the dull rose of hot iron. A profile, somehow vaguely familiar to Sok, flickered briefly then set itself into razor sharp focus. His former Khmer lieutenant,

Kiri Leng, now sat in the chair directly opposite to his own and stared back at him across the small table. The feeble glow accompanying the Khmoc or spirit presence illuminated the small room, as would the light from a single candle.

The Vietnamese army had killed his long dead officer nearly forty years ago when the foreign troops arrived at what was left of their compound. He and his lieutenant had planned to leave together having just stowed their things in the only running vehicle in the village, a rather dilapidated jeep. Just as they prepared to leave, several advance scouts entered the compound surprising the two officers. Sok leapt into the jeep fleeing the compound in a cloud of dust and leaving his young lieutenant to face a firing squad several hours later.

His kitchen basked in the dim radiance emanating from the creature while Sok recalled his cowardly departure from the camp so many years before. The familiar apparition said nothing but glared across the table for several moments then shifted its glance down to the scratched arborite surface of the table. Sneering, the ghost picked up a random selection of tiles from the boneyard then slowly lay each of the tiles down on the table before him, just as he had done a thousand times before in the Cambodian camp. Quite shaken at first, Sok soon understood the ghost's intent and the two struck up the first in a long series of silent games that would carry on for many hours.

Numerous times throughout the evening, the ghost and Sok would select and set down tiles from the bone yard, a term for the collection of downward facing tiles randomly spread out upon the kitchen table. The most recent game was ending when Sok noticed that the numbers of each newly laid tile and the one previously played, were producing sums that invariably added up to ten, a number considered by the Khmer to be quite unlucky. Nor was this coincidence lost on the ghost whose eyes now carefully followed the order of the tiles in play. As the game drew out, the sums of the laid tiles changed once more, now consistently coming in a series of fours, a much unluckier number since the number four when said in Khmer sounded very much like death.

Sok laid his final tile; the face displayed a four with a blank partner; he blanched. When shaman chose to use dominoes to divine the future, it was given that such tiles represented impending death. Hesitating for a moment, the ghost laid his final tile precisely as the clock struck the hour of 10 pm; both sides of the tile were blank.

As the bell rang out from the wall clock in the next room, each subsequent chime that followed sounded increasingly hollow and distant. Sitting motionless, the ghost's glowing eyes darted left, then right before settling on Sok whose own face betrayed his obvious fear. The perpetual sneer worn by the creature throughout the evening had vanished, replaced by a look of distinct apprehension. Sok suddenly realized the significance of the unlucky hour just as the tenth and final chime rang out faintly. Turning his head slowly from side to side, he cast his eyes about the room, something was changing; something was coming.

The air in the kitchen was hot and close. Choked with cigarette smoke, the liquor staled atmosphere in the kitchen suddenly cleared as a light breeze swept about the room bringing with it the overpowering fragrance of Jasmine. The cool air caused Sok to shiver where he sat. Looking toward the ghost, he watched the creature's glowing outline fade noticeably returning the kitchen to its original gloom.

A faint glow appeared above the domino tiles, then seconds later, a thin mist casually swirled and brightened ever so slowly. Sok and the lieutenant's shade stared, watching the vapors thicken and twist into two separate glowing filaments, one pink, and the other a soft white. The colored strands danced and weaved in unison, the end of each strand encased within a thick gray fog that swiftly obscured the entire surface of the table. Sok could not move, neither apparently could his officer's ghost, it remained motionless across the table. The lieutenant's face betrayed the beings abject fear forcing Sok to consider what could possibly frighten a man already long dead and rotted away somewhere in a lonely unmarked grave.

Sok blinked and rubbed his eyes. When they reopened, two colorful serpents, one a brilliant white, the other a shocking pink had replaced the fog and mists. Heads bobbing and weaving before the lieutenant, their long fangs gleamed within their gaping mouths and their forked tongues flicked in and out, nearly caressing the shades' horrified face. The vipers drew back, collecting themselves within their coils then launching themselves forward, embedded their sharp fangs in either side of the lieutenant's neck where they writhed and worked their fangs ever deeper into his throat. With a loud shriek, the wounded specter jumped from its chair, flinging itself back and away from the table. The ghost shook and swayed in obvious agony, the serpents refusing to unclench their jaws, while the officer's mouth worked up into a silent scream.

Unable to move a muscle, Sok watched as his lieutenant's eyeballs slid back in their sockets. Quickly transformed, they evolved into mere blobs of greenish phlegm drifting upon the watery yellow pools within their orbs. The being that only moments ago resembled a young officer in the full bloom of youth now stood before Sok in a form that was at once, both hideous and pitiful to behold. The serpents, now seemingly content with the damage they had inflicted, released their fangs and pulled back. Their long bodies continued to writhe atop the kitchen table for several moments before losing form and cohesion, once again becoming a hovering vaporous cloud that sank, then seeped and disappeared within the tiles. Throughout the entire affair, the yellowed bone dominoes had somehow remained in their places, undisturbed throughout the mayhem. Sok's eyes darted back to the macabre scene that continued to play out on the other side of the room.

Sok stared in horror while his lieutenant's face contorted into an obscene grimace as its skin, now as thin as rice paper, tightened about the contours of his skull. Moments later the nose followed the creatures' eyes, falling back into a black hollow of putrid rot while its luxurious black hair fell out in irregular patches. It appeared to Sok that he was watching the natural decomposition of a corpse in time-lapse photography, but in this case, the corpse itself was still alive. The shrieks, groans, and guttural cries rose in volume until they reached an impossible climax forcing Sok to cover both his ears with his palms in a futile attempt to block the raging discord. At last, the corruption that wavered before him bore only a passing resemblance to a human figure; it quivered slightly then collapsed and fell toward the floor in a rush of black dust. The unholy chorus fell silent with the specters departure.

Sok's eyes scanned about the room trying to locate the source of a single lingering scream that wound down ever more slowly. The fading cry ended in a whisper and he became aware it had originated within his own throat. Gasping, Sok discovered that his airway had slammed shut; he could not draw a single breath! His hands flew to his throat and for several long seconds he fought unsuccessfully to inhale. Feeling he would black out any moment, he concentrated... using his mind to force the muscles in his chest and throat to relax and loosen. Doing so, a narrow stream of air slowly penetrated his oxygen-starved lungs. For what felt like an eternity, each passing second brought only the slightest promise of relief. Suddenly, a torrent of air gushed and flooded into his chest. Sok sputtered and coughed between his frantic gasps.

Recovering sufficiently, Sok lurched to his feet leaving his chair to fall and tumble to the floor in his haste to flee the dreadful scene. Stumbling into the dark living room he felt his shin glance off a sharp corner of the coffee table, the pain caused him to gasp and utter a curse but failed to deter or hinder his hurried departure for even a second, carelessly slamming shut the door of his suite behind him. Sok hobbled through the poorly lit hallway and rushed down the concrete stairwell. Reaching the main floor, he quickly crossed the dingy lobby, bolted through the set of double entrance doors, and found himself standing in the middle of a deserted street.

Sok spent the rest of the long night in an illegal "after-hours" bar. Hidden away in the worst end of town, he only left when the bar keeper kicked him out at 6 am. Still limping, he walked to a nearby coffee shop where he sat for the next several hours nursing several cups of coffee, a splitting headache, and a dismal hangover before setting out once more to wander the town. Reluctantly he found himself moving among the streets and roadways in a lazy spiral, one that slowly and inevitably led him back toward his apartment.

Arriving home in late morning, Sok slowly pushed open his apartment door. Sunlight streamed in from a single uncurtained window and spilt out across the living room's dark hardwood floor. A slender shaft of brilliant daylight spiked into the grungy kitchen. Ensuring the apartment door remained open to the hallway; Sok cautiously entered the living room. Moving in several feet, he paused, first looking this way, and then that, carefully checking all the room's nooks and corners. He stole second then third glances behind the couch, the easy chair, and the old broken television propped atop a small end table near the center of the opposite wall.

Convinced there was no immediate danger, Sok took slow deliberate steps stopping when he reached the kitchen entrance. His eyes reconnoitered every corner as he bent low scanning beneath the dining table and chairs before straightening up. The cheery sunlight acted to dispel the previous night's horrific events. The black memory faded and became distant, its power diminished within the confident rationality of day.

He picked the chair from where it fell the night before and set it beside the table. Taking another quick glance about the room, he walked to the fridge, opened the door, and leaned in. Selecting a small cardboard milk container, he closed the door taking a long slow drink. He felt the cool milk running the length of his throat flowing into his acidic stomach in a rush of welcome relief. Taking the milk container from his lips and setting it atop the table, he stopped in startled surprise.

Each set of domino tiles sat replaced in their respective polished teak boxes. The inlaid mother of pearl Jasmine flowers on each of their hinged covers sparkled and gleamed in the sunbeams that played across the table. He felt the milk sour in his gut as he walked out of the apartment, closed, and then securely locked the door.

Sok sat at a table in the back of the noodle house awaiting his shift that would start in just another half hour. Having gulped down no fewer than eight Tums and three Excedrin tablets he figured he'd manage to get through the evening. He sipped a cup of green tea considering last evening's events in a detached and calculating manner. Sok strove to remember the details of the old ghost stories and spirit tales he had heard as a child growing up in Cambodia.

Slowly a degree of clarity emerged from those ancient memories buried so long ago in the past. Instinctively he knew the domino tiles were the receptacles that held two angry spirits that he unintentionally awoke when he played the tape recording. From what he recalled of the old legends, anyone so tormented must rid themselves of the accursed items but in a manner that would not destroy the items themselves. Doing so, would in all probability, release the vengeful ghosts who might then be free to torment their victim unceasingly and at will. Sok determined it was preferable that the domino sets should remain separated; keeping each set a healthy distance from the other might diminish the spirit's remembrance of their shared fate, and hopefully their powers as well.

The metallic chime of the cash register drew his attention as it opened. Sok stood up then approached the old cashier with a proposition that would begin with her stopping by his apartment after the noodle house closed for the evening.

It was late October, Halloween was only a week away, and soon the little goblins would be rapping at her door. Agnes donned a warm coat planning to venture out and resupply her candy stores after noting with some dismay she had finished off nearly all of the small chocolate bars she bought specifically for the occasion just days before. No wonder her diet wasn't going anywhere. With that thought, she placed her hand on the doorknob when the phone rang.

Agnes picked up the receiver and heard Hazel Murphy's voice at the other end. A good friend and self-styled spiritual medium, Hazel had reputedly assumed a mantle of authenticity, at least among many of the town's older crowd who continued to believe in such things. While Agnes had her own doubts as to Hazel's abilities, there was no question that her party readings were highly entertaining. Hazel explained that her apartment was undergoing a small renovation and asked if Agnes would be good enough to allow her home to host a small gathering next Friday. Seven people were expected to attend, including herself and Hazel. Agnes hummed and hawed shortly before Hazel pushed on informing Agnes that each guest would attend the gathering with food and or drink in hand. With that assurance, Agnes readily accepted.

Friday had arrived far more quickly than Agnes anticipated, once more confirming the old adage that time passed ever more quickly as one grew older. Hazel was the first to come through the door, a full half hour before the other guests were due to arrive, and true to her word she produced a small bottle of gin from her purse. She handed it to Agnes with a wink and a smile, "fix a small one for us dear?" Returning her infectious smile, Agnes headed off toward the kitchen to prepare two gin fizzes, their favorite party drink.

Hazel went about setting up her few props atop the crisp ironed linen spread across the top of Agnes's dining room table while prattling on about the latest bits of juicy gossip she picked up while conducting private readings about the town. Her task completed, Hazel seated herself on the living room couch just as Agnes arrived. Drinks in hand, Agnes sat down beside Hazel offering her a glass.

Agnes held up her tumbler, "Cheers, to the first one of the day..." she paused before both added in unison, "in this hand!" They each laughed and took a sip. Knowing one another since grade school, they took care to retain their close friendship throughout the passing years.

Hazel glanced down at the drink in her hand, "I invited a special guest today, and I'm hoping its ok?" She raised her eyes and studied her friends questioning face before continuing, "Matt Holder." She allowed the name to hang for a moment. "He has something I think everyone will be interested in."

Agnes's face fell. "Oh Hazel... you know how I feel about just seeing him, never mind having him here."

"I know, I know... he wasn't sure he wanted to come either, at least not at first." There was a long pause. "Then I told him how silly it was that two people that have known each other for over sixty years couldn't get together for a single evening. Ok so you used to date, so what?" Hazel pursed her lips.

"We didn't just date, we expected to marry; raise a family..., but things just didn't work out as we hoped." Agnes paused, "it was my fault. I still feel so guilty every time I see him. He must hate me." She set her drink on a coaster lying on the coffee table in front of them.

"Of course he doesn't hate you! I rather think he still has feelings for you. You know when I asked him to come to this reading he almost said the same thing to me, word for word?" Hazel thought she saw a dent in her friend's armor.

"Really?" Agnes asked, wearing a hopeful expression.

Hazel put her own drink down on the table and took up both of her friend's hands in her own. "Yes... really!" Hazel smiled sweetly at Agnes as the doorbell rang.

Flashing her friend a hesitant smile of her own Agnes rose from the couch "well I'd better get that." Noticing that October's early dusk had already arrived in the room she quickly added, "Turn on the lamps would you dear, it's rather gloomy in here."

An hour later, all the guests had finally arrived. Following a short meet and greet session they took their places about the large dining room table. While the first seconds of their meeting were rather tense, both Agnes and Matt quickly found their concerns unwarranted, discovering themselves directing somewhat long glances and exchanging smiles in the other's direction. Hazel stood up from her chair at the head of the table. Addressing the small gathering, she thanked Agnes for the use of her home and those present for their attendance then got down to the meat of the matter.

A large rather rotund woman, Hazel had clad herself in her usual gray and black pantsuit outfit. Aside from keeping with the somber tones of her readings, she had also been recently told that the colors tended to slim her appearance. Hazel remained quiet for nearly half a minute collecting her thoughts, then paused an additional ten seconds or so, further elevating the anticipation of the guests. After all, as she had explained to Agnes at one time, such drama was to be expected from the so very gifted.

At last Hazel began to speak. "As I'm sure you have all heard I conducted a private reading at Matt Holder's home last Saturday. Matt and I came away from that reading; both of us rather... well, breathless to say the least?" She looked to Matt raising her shoulders and nodding slightly, her face beamed expectantly.

Normally a very quiet and unassuming man, Matt was obviously startled. Despite his not having expected to contribute to the presentation, he gamely acceded to her request despite the heated blush he felt grow in his cheeks. Starting slowly, he began describing his previous reading with Hazel, but very soon, Matt's address quickly grew more animated. After another minute or so, it became clear his unbridled enthusiasm and recollections now threatened to go completely off track. Agnes chuckled to herself and smiled at Hazel who playfully rolled her eyes before interrupting Matt.

"Thank you Matt." Ignoring her prompt, Matt continued to speak rapidly over the next half-minute or so until Hazel once again injected, "Matt, thank you so much." He continued unabatedly until Hazel finally turned and faced him. Raising her voice slightly she addressed him. "Matt?" then quite loudly, "MATT?" Suddenly realizing he had overplayed his role, the man's face flushed an even deeper shade of scarlet as he quickly shrank in his chair.

Hazel continued, "All of you are familiar with the way I conduct my private readings. Matt and I were seated in his living room. I began in the usual manner, reciting a little prayer asking for protection and enlightenment. Our chairs faced one another and we held hands across a small table. I suppose we were about five minutes into the reading... I was truly amazed how easily the voice of the spirits flowed through me from the other side." Hazel looked about the room and took in the expectant faces of those seated at the table before continuing.

"Well, Matt's mother and sister came through just as clearly as if they were sitting right there. His sister, Sharon, actually told us what had become of her mother's antique ivory cameo and chain. It had been lost so many years ago and was something that Matt has never been able to find despite all his searching. Turns out Sharon told us it had slipped out the back of a drawer in the dining room buffet and fallen down into the heat register at the back. Matt actually retrieved it during the reading!" Hazel looked over to where Matt sat and gave a slight nod.

Matt reached a hand into his blazers inside chest pocket then removed it a moment later, an object dangling from his fingertips as he displayed the jewelry for all to see. "Absolutely true folks... completely true." he added.

Hazel gave a quick nod of approval, watching as those at the table passed around the cameo. Comments such as "amazing, incredible, or how very special" accompanied its examinations as if it were a holy artifact recovered from centuries past. Hazel waited patiently until the cameo finished making its rounds, finding its way back into Matt's jacket pocket.

"And that's when something truly wonderful happened!" she paused and looked each person in the face before going on. "Matt and I were holding the cameo when we heard a sort of thumping in his study. Now Matt doesn't have any pets, and there wasn't another soul in the house. Well, we walked into the den..." she looked directly at Matt, "Matt why don't you tell the folks here what we both saw with our own eyes."

Somewhat hesitantly, Matt nodded, then reached down to the side of his chair and came up with a light suede valise that he placed in his lap. Opening the top of the thin case, he reached in and removed a small rectangular wooden box that he placed on the tabletop before him. "This thing here was banging and thumping on the top of my desk" he held the little box in his hands and demonstrated what they saw. Matt moved the long ends of the box up and down against the table then gently replaced it on the surface. "Just like that folks... it stopped just a few moments after we walked in... Then suddenly there was the smell..."

Hazel interrupted; Matt had had his second brief moment of fame now she took back the attention of the small audience.

"After it stopped moving we caught a beautiful aroma on the air", Hazel turned her face upward and flung her arms out from her body in a wide dramatic arc, "it came on a breeze that filled the air with the wonderful fragrance of some kind of flower." Once again facing her audience, she noticed that Agnes had stood up and backed away from her chair. Her friend's face had become an incredulous mask as her eyes stared with wonder at the small wooden box that sat on the table in front of Matt.

"Agnes?" Hazel looked at her friend apprehensively. Agnes made no response; some of the other guests now began to focus their attention on their host's unusual behavior. Hazel asked again, "Agnes is there something wrong?"

Agnes shook her head then turned without speaking a word. Walking to her curio cabinet, she opened the glass door removing something before returning to stand in front of her chair. She placed the object gently upon the tabletop. There was a collective gasp from the group as they realized the close resemblance of each small box to the other. In fact, the only difference between the two was the color of the mother of pearl inlay in the top of each box... Matt's box was a soft light blush while Agnes' inlay was a warm off white. A long moment of silence followed as everyone's eyes darted from one container to the other.

Agnes barely whispered, "Domino tiles, I bought my set at the flea market months ago, I saw you there too Matt, but we never spoke." Matt frowned a little sadly, nodded and then added softly, "me too."

A slight but noticeable vibration began to stir in the room. Those guests that had been resting their hands or elbows on the dining table now removed them from the table's surface, all now aware the source of the tremor originated from within the two wooden boxes containing the domino sets. As the sensations slowly grew in force, a new sound came to their ears, the clicking and clacking of wood and bone as the domino tiles rattled about in each of their containers. A soft breath of air stirred about the room. The ladies seated at the table who had worn dresses were the first to feel the light breeze as it caressed their ankles then glided upward across their knees then rose above the table itself.

The unmistakably pleasant aroma of fresh Jasmine blossoms graced the nostrils of those present while the clamoring of the boxes and their contents continued to quicken and beat about their ears.

Then, as suddenly as it began, the clattering of the tiles ended and the room fell completely silent. The cessation of noise was probably lost on all present, their wrap attention directly focused on the strange sight taking place before them.

The little audience gasped in unison while Hazel uttered in astonishment, "Oh my dear God!" Both boxes had risen up from the table and gently floated nearly a foot above its surface. For several seconds nothing else happened, then, ever so slowly, the lid of each box cracked open allowing slim bands of multicolored light to flash outward from their interiors. As the cracks continued to widen, the tiles themselves slowly began to leave their containers and churn about above the table in a manner reminiscent of dry fallen leaves caught up in a stiff autumn wind.

As the last of the tiles freed themselves from their containers, the comfortable breeze vanished in an instant, replaced by a violent rush of cold air that forced the ladies to clasp their arms tightly about their bodies and the men to pull their jackets closed at their necks. Meanwhile, the tiles increased their frenzied dance above the table, now moving at speeds that prevented even the fastest eye from perceiving an individual domino among the whirling mass.

Glazed with their pupils dilated, Hazel's vacant eyes had slowly risen toward the ceiling where they remained affixed, unblinking and yet unseeing. In the same instant, her lips parted slightly to release an unearthly, wavering voice that boomed aloud... "Vengeance... to the dead, from the dead... and to the living, from those who yet live"...

Since ridding himself of those accursed dominos, Sok tried his best to become more sociable, venturing out in the late evenings to gamble and carouse. As of late, he found himself consistently winning at the Mahjong tables, tonight had been no different. Sok was in a fine mood, having crushed the other three players at his table, he left the games room stopping for a nightcap in a small bar not far from his apartment. Sitting on a stool in the near deserted dingy bar, he cast his eyes about his surroundings. Assuring himself that no one was paying him undue attention, he thumbed through the thick wad of cash he held in his hands, his winnings for the night. As he counted the money, Sok found himself continually glancing about the room. He could not shake the feeling that he was being watched, maybe even followed. Sok stashed the wad of cash in his windbreaker, threw a bill on the counter, and nodded to the bartender before rising from his chair, heading out the door and stepping onto the dimly lit street corner.

A matter of yards from the bar where Sok had emerged only moments before, a young Asian man stood motionless, hiding within the deep recesses of a doorway. While studying his quarry, the dark clad figure slowly ran his fingers over the hilt of the military killing knife that protruded from a sheath secured to his belt. The old man stood at the street corner pausing to light a cigarette, cupping his hands to protect the sputtering flame from the small breeze that arose unexpectedly. Sok took a heavy drag from the cigarette then slowly blew the smoke into the air where it briefly roiled then vanished. The old man took a long look up and down the empty street then spat into the gutter before beginning his walk homeward.

Within the space of only a block, the breeze had transformed itself into a cold sharp wind that cut into the folds of the old man's thin breaker chilling him to the bone. Sok ducked into an alleyway he hoped would shield him from the elements, the detour would only add several minutes to his journey but somehow the bluster had abruptly changed direction and ferocity. The weather's violence stirred up small bits of dirt and tiny pebbles sending them flying into his face, peppering his cheeks and narrowing his eyelids with their assault.

Sok never heard the footsteps of the stranger's approach, nor would he have even if there had been no wind or sound at all, the assassin's long practiced stealth assured this inevitable outcome. A vague outline within the alley's dim light, the man was but a shadow that rushed forward, swiftly crossing the dark gray asphalt of the alleyway. Having reached his quarry, the stranger's left hand quickly drew the long killing knife from its sheath, then wrapping the old man's neck within the crook of his right arm, he plunged the long blade into Sok's back with a well-practiced thrust. The knife bit deeply, entering just below Sok's ribs, then arched upward, the keen steel slicing through back muscle and rib bone as it penetrated ever more deeply into his chest cavity.

As intended, Sok discovered himself paralyzed by pain and shock, which was precisely the reason the technique was so popular among those trained in the use of such weapons. The last words the old man would hear were those spoken in Khmer. A venomous and breathless whisper hissed in his ear, "Dragon, your death will be scant payment for that of my mother, my father, and all those others." The Shadow Dragon gasped, struggling weakly as the figure behind him drove the knife in and up to its hilt. Having set the blade, his assailant gave it a vicious twist to the left, then the right. The action destroyed the dragon's lungs while the knifepoint penetrated and tore deeply into his heart. Sok moaned as his attacker slowly extracted the long blade from the wound then allowed his body to slip from his grasp and fall to the ground.

From his prostrate position in the alleyway, Sok watched the elusive figure dart back into the shadows. For several long bitter minutes he lay motionless, unable to move even while a terrible pain racked his body. Sok tasted the blood that frothed on his lips as he gasped in a painful spasm. He felt the cold spread with an agonizing apathy as it made its way up his arms and legs. His life ebbed, slowly distancing the Shadow Dragon from the rest of the world. Sok surrendered his tortured existence as a final shudder rattled in his chest.

In Agnes' dining room, no one had moved from his or her seat. Instead, the people quietly looked about at one another, each taking stock of their own rather shaky perceptions of reality. The debate as to the duration of the madness they had witnessed would carry on for years to come, but all agreed it ended with an incredible boom of thunder that seemed to shake the very foundations of the earth. No one could, or would ever claim to have seen so much as a single tile fall back to the table but somehow, the domino tiles lay positioned face down, within a bone yard, each set intermingled with the other and forming a neatly arranged figure eight. Only one among them immediately recognized the pattern, what it truly represented, the symbol of the infinite, but Hazel said nothing and nothing continued to happen for several long minutes; it seemed to all present as if the world had paused to catch its collective breath.

It was early evening, several days later when Agnes and Matt found themselves happily walking hand in hand along a narrow street that bordered the Asian section of town. As they passed a small Thai restaurant, an old woman in a faded floral dress swept the sidewalk near the restaurant entrance using a worn corn-straw broom. Noticing the couple was somehow familiar to her, the woman paused in her work to think where she may have seen the two before. Unable to recall, she shook her head turning toward the cafe door as the old couple continued their stroll.

A small bell jingled atop the doorframe as the old woman entered. Pausing briefly, she propped open the door with a hip, then reached over and into the front window where she straightened a small sign, "Cook Wanted." Stepping into the noodle house, the tiny bell gave a soft final tinkle while the door swung in, quietly shutting behind her.

Vagrant

In the fall of 2015, long-time New York City resident Jeremiah D. Jennings decided it was time for a move out to California. Stuffing everything he owned into a single dirty knapsack, he began train hopping his way toward the west coast. Now thirteen days later he found himself sitting on a deserted siding, stuck out in the middle of nowhere, spending his third night of what should have been the short final leg of his journey.

Jeremiah or JJ as his friends called him, remembered the final conversation he had with his old pal Jamie Nichols on the day he left. "JJ, you're one gutsy ol' fool leaving here for California. You'll be getting your sorry black ass back here ah for you know it... if you're smart that is. Think man, you can barely get yourself around the corner on those bad legs of yours." As he massaged his painful knees with the palms of his hands, JJ was thinking Jamie might have hit the nail squarely on the head. Sure, he suffered from advanced arthritis; all the guys in the old neighborhood knew that. What they did not know was he also had an arrhythmic heart condition. Given JJ's lifestyle, the doctor told him he would probably kick off in two to five years, if he were lucky. JJ figured he'd be damned if he were going to spend whatever time he had left living out of a cardboard box somewhere within the New York sewer system.

By the morning of the second day, his freight car and seven others continued to remain sidelined, hell, another train had not so much as passed by. Around noon, JJ drank what little was left of his water from a large plastic Coke bottle. An hour later, believing he faced the very real prospect of dying out here in the desert, he decided to walk.

He started out following a set of tracks running off to the west thinking they might lead to a nearby town or farmhouse. Now having walked several miles from the siding, the oppressive desert heat and the sharp pain in his knees dissuaded him from going any further. That afternoon, the temperature had nosed past one hundred ten degrees Fahrenheit, an exceptional occurrence, especially this late in September. Taking a moment to rest atop a small boulder, he gazed up into the hot cloudless sky. High above him, a half dozen or so dark specks wheeled and soared on the hot desert thermals. "What the hell...?" JJ shouldered his knapsack and began walking back to the boxcar; no damned vultures were going to enjoy a free lunch at his expense.

As night set in, he realized he had become severely dehydrated, he had not passed water since early that afternoon. The boxcar had provided some respite from the blazing late afternoon sun, although JJ had not sat in car's sun-baked interior, but had chosen instead to lie beneath it. There he waited the long hours until the arrival of sunset. His head upon his knapsack, he shifted and tossed about, attempting but failing to discover any comfort atop the cool but overly course gravel of the rail bed.

It was nearly midnight when something roused him from a fitful dream. Something or things moved near the boxcar next to his. In a sleepy daze, he wondered what they could be until a chorus of loud yowls and howls only a matter of feet away roused him into instant action. Uttering a string of curses, he forced himself to his feet, grabbed his knapsack, and leapt back into the relative safety of the boxcar. Lying motionless in the dark night, he listened to the animals prowling about but would have no idea how long the coyotes remained having eventually drifted off into a deep dreamless sleep. Sometime later, JJ abruptly awoke to a heavy metallic bang and thud. Bucking violently, his car along with the others on the siding had rejoined a late night train. Minutes later, gently rocked and hypnotized by its rumbling tempo, JJ dozed then nodded off to sleep within the walls of his iron cocoon that rolled ever westward atop its thin ribbon of iron and steel.

Someone was shaking his shoulder, hard. He awoke to find himself in the strong grip of a railway bull. When the cop first saw JJ, he figured him for dead. Tasked with making his rounds about the rail yard, the man would check the freight cars and mechanical shops on a regular basis; on this job, coming across the occasional corpse was pretty much a given.

At first badly startled and frightened, JJ slowly calmed down, then after a little while, he figured the rail cop wasn't a bad sort, not by a long shot. The bull dragged his sorry, thirsty butt off to the cop shop where he gratefully took a glass of water, a cup of coffee, and a few stale doughnuts while the officer checked on his background. Not that JJ worried, he wasn't a crook, he'd never hurt anyone, hell he'd never really stolen anything unless you counted the odd apple he pilfered from the grocery when he hadn't eaten for a day or two. He was just another old man who having frittered away the promise of youth now found himself utterly defeated by life and circumstance. All he wanted was a quiet place in the sun to rest his bones.

JJ crammed the last morsel of the doughnut into his mouth washing it down with the dregs of the lukewarm coffee as he thought about the past he left behind. He had descended from a long line of losers. Having grown up in the worst part of the Bronx, his father an abusive drunk, his mother a junkie, maybe he was lucky not to have ended up as something much worse than a simple bum. It had not been much of a life but at least back there it felt like home.

Summers in New York City had actually been pretty good; he would panhandle, squeegee windows, and pick bottles. JJ always stashed a few bucks away in his shoe for a few luxuries, a pack of smokes or the odd bottle, though he was always careful not to wind up a drunk like dear old dad. There was many a summer night he would sleep outdoors, finding it too hot and muggy to spend the night in the shelter. The good folks down at the center had never turned him away. Unlike many of their customers, JJ wasn't rowdy, never a thief or troublemaker, and very seldom drunk. They would let him in even when they were busting out full at the seams; they would always find old JJ a quiet corner somewhere.

That all changed when the new "by the book" bitch took over last December. For reasons he never could quite figure out, Ann DeLauro took an instant dislike to him. She would tell any who listened that he was a sneak thief or worse. Hell, a couple of the guys he had known for years kicked the shit out of him in Central Park then told him they had overheard DeLauro saying he was a bum blaster; a kiddie diddler on parole. The woman wouldn't let him stay at the shelter, even during the coldest night. Forced to move into the sewers, JJ figured it was either that or freeze to death, something he had come close to doing on several occasions. Yes, it was Ann DeLauro that finally provided the incentive for JJ's own little California dream.

The rail cop walked back to where JJ sat, returned his wallet and telling him he was not wanted by the authorities. The officer had a soft spot for fellows like JJ; his own dad had wound up an old man, half-crazy from the booze and the hard lifestyle. Then the winter before last, he had received a phone call from an officer working out of the Portland yards. The man had discovered his father's body during his patrol, according to the officer; it appeared he had frozen to death in a boxcar.

JJ asked where he was. The cop sat at his desk sipping a cup of coffee and smiled telling JJ that he had arrived in the world famous Palm Springs. He went on to tell JJ that the town had been home at various times to the likes of Bob Hope, Frank Sinatra, and George Hamilton. Hell even President Obama stopped in to play a game of golf every so often.

The officer filled him in on the best places to go, the shelters and the like, as well as what neighborhoods to avoid. The cop also warned him to stay well away from the local police who would like as not hand him a can of whoop ass whether he deserved it or not, adding that the Palm Springs and the Coachella Police Department shared an equally bad reputation. The younger man escorted him along the tracks leading out of the yard. JJ shook the man's hand and thanked the cop, throwing him a small wave as he headed towards the city.

JJ took his time but it was not as if he had much choice. His arthritis was bothering him more than usual but he put it down to the simple fact that his activity level had greatly increased as of late. Trying his best to avoid the main streets, JJ negotiated Palm Springs' network of back alleys and laneways.

Just after he entered the first alley, JJ had picked himself up a well used, but perfectly good cane from a trash can, so far it seemed to help his aching hips and knees. Besides the cane giving JJ some welcome support, it had plenty of other uses as well. It came in handy when rummaging through some interesting looking trash, fending off an unfriendly cur or another bum that might be interested in the same goodies he was picking through but more than that, it was the perfect sympathy prop for the old panhandler.

The elderly cripple routine had proved very effective when it came to prying donations from the wallets of middle-class rubes, and JJ had turned it into an art. He would start working the downtown office areas just before lunch hour then again mid-afternoon; those times people were not in a mad rush to arrive at work or board their homebound trains. JJ would slowly hobble along the sidewalk, going against the majority of foot traffic. That way people would have little choice but to slow a bit for the pathetic broken down old man in their path. Adopting his well practiced hang dog look he'd watch the eyes of the people as they approached, if nothing else, JJ was an expert when it came to picking up on folks who had compassion for those less fortunate.

He usually looked for smaller numbers of three or four, making sure there was always at least one woman in the group. When the marks were close enough, JJ would stammer out an apology for being in their way and quickly sidestep making sure to trip over his cane and tumble to the concrete; a small moan here was a nice touch. Now if JJ's intuition was right, and it usually was, at least one person would be helping him stand while the others were asking if he was all right. At this point JJ would shake his head sadly as if trying to make sense of life while saying to no one in particular, "sorry folks, guess I'm just a little weak, haven't had a bite since yesterday." Then, quicker than you can say Jackie Robinson, people would start pushing a few bills his way.

Over the next several weeks, JJ explored his new surroundings, walking through various neighborhoods. Some of these were pretty fancy while others in the north end were dangerous enough to remind him of the bad old haunts back east. He quickly learned to avoid the areas near Gateway Drive, especially at night when the Gateway Posse Crips and their rivals, the Barrio Dream Homes, battled it out. They were a nasty bunch and although they probably would not bother with the likes of

JJ, he still gave them a wide berth. No doubt about it, the Palm Springs gangs were tough customers, so JJ figured that the cops that held the lid on the garbage had to be even tougher.

It was several weeks later when he met a fellow outdoors enthusiast, Credence Miller. Credence was a reformed crack addict who had made his way to the Springs from Oregon in the late nineties. He filled JJ in on the finer points of where to go, what to do, and who to avoid while they did it all. Credence and JJ bummed around together for several weeks and JJ was glad of the company, so when Credence took up the pipe again for God knew what reason, the old man was disappointed and saddened. As they parted JJ waved goodbye, watching Credence head back towards his old hang out near the Royal Springs apartments, aka Crack Towers, a move that ensured access to an endless supply of what Credence had termed "good shit."

Once again on his own, JJ decided to leave the north side of town, feeling the area unsafe for someone like himself. True he blended in, but recently had a narrow escape when several whacked out stoners came across him while he slept in the small park off Gateway. Besides, he was sick of the persistent wind that blew into town from the nearby expanse of empty desert.

Built across the natural flats of the desert, the lie of the city snaked about the contours of the surrounding hills and mountains. The Coachella Valley wound its way out of the west and down to the south on its approach to the Salton Sea. The hills on either side of the upper valley acted to create a giant wind tunnel and since the north side of the Springs wasn't sheltered by the mountains, that part of town got a real pounding when the winds picked up.

JJ discovered a little distance could go a long way when it came to changing the character of the neighborhoods he passed through. Walking only six miles farther south and moving away from the rough and tumble of the north end of town, you couldn't ask for a nicer spot to put your feet up. Overall, the Palm Canyon area had a pleasant feel about it, and the pickings in the restaurant garbage bins in this end of town were first rate. They didn't even lock the dumpsters as they did further north. You just had to make sure you flew below the radar. That meant moving frequently and minding your manners while you worked the street.

JJ had propped himself up against the trunk of a large shade tree and sat on a cool patch of grass near the rear entrance to one of the Palm Canyon Resort's kitchens. The late afternoon sun beat down on the asphalt road and the empty undeveloped real estate lots that lined the avenue off to the east. JJ figured the temperature still had to be at least ninety in the shade. He checked his water bottle and figured he had better make another trip to the water fountain that sat near the second hole of the Indian Canyons golf course. Getting to his feet, JJ took a long stretch then bent low reaching for his backpack, when a man's voice spoke out nearby.

"Hey there." The voice was thick and gravelly.

JJ thought, "Ah shit, here we go." Assuming he may have overstayed his welcome in the small oasis, JJ simply gave a small wave of his hand without looking in the direction of the voice. Swinging his pack over his shoulder, he grabbed his cane from where it leaned against the tree.

"Hey you... yeah, I'm talking to you old man.", the voice continued; JJ paused. Deciding the voice likely belonged to that of a cop or private security guard, he turned to face the man.

"You thirsty?" The huge man cocked his head and smiled good-naturedly. "We don't get many of our older brothers out this way." The man's ebony skin bore a striking contrast to his apparel. The giant wore a large white apron embroidered with the resort's logo overtop a spotless short sleeved white shirt and long pants. Tucked under one arm was a tall chef's hat, a bulging green garbage bag hung from the hand of the other. With an effortless toss, he pitched the heavy bag into a nearby dumpster that JJ had inspected only twenty minutes earlier. "Where you from?" the man inquired pleasantly.

JJ smiled back at the man who he could see was not much younger than he was. "New York City." He scratched the back of his head, "Got here a couple of weeks ago." JJ searched for something to add to the conversation but as he had not spoken to anyone else in nearly a week, it was all he could do to come up with "Nice place you got here."

"Yeah, she's fine ain't she, even if the weather gets a little too warm for my likin' from time to time?" The man pointed to an entranceway that JJ assumed was probably the kitchen. "Care to come in fo' ah minute or two, we have air conditioning, and I can fix you up a plate of somethin' and a glass of lemonade if'n you like."

Immediately JJ flashed a brilliant smile, "What's not to like? It sure would make my day sir." He shuffled over toward the cook who waited at the doorway extending a huge mitt of a hand that JJ grasped; the hand very nearly enveloped his own. The cook was easily three hundred pounds and as close as JJ could estimate, at least six foot six high.

Noting JJ's obvious though polite interest in his size the large man chuckled deeply, "Arnie's the name, that or the Black Butcher as I was called on the wrestlin' circuit." He looked thoughtful, "but that was a long time back."

"Jeremiah Jennings sir, at your service." He gave a slight nod and a wink. "My friends call me JJ."

"Well come on in JJ, we'll see what we can rustle ya up." The big man filled the doorway as he turned and entered. JJ followed the cook into the back of a spotlessly clean kitchen. As he ate, each man gave what amounted to a friendly biography of his life. JJ learned that Arnie had been born and raised in Chicago spending his early life wrestling his way across the east coast and even down into Florida. A car accident ended his career when he was in his late twenties just about the time he started making some decent money. "And that's when I figured to become a cook!" the big man held his belly and patted it with both hands. "I came out here; let's see... damn near thirty-five years ago now. Lordy don't it fly though, time that is."

"Yeah, it does." JJ looked a little sheepish, "I never really did much with my time, not what I probably should have done with it anyway. You know I always thought I'd have more of it... then before I knew it, I look in the mirror and see an old man looking back." He shook his head, why was he bothering to tell his life story to a cook that he met only a few minutes ago but damn, didn't it feel good to do so. Gratefully JJ continued to bend the man's ear because he was old, played out, and lonely for some good company and a kind word.

"My old man was a lot like ya JJ. He had more hard times than soft... he jus' got knocked into the dirt once too often... finally, he didn't bother gettin' up again." Arnie looked at him and refilled JJ's glass from a large pitcher atop the table. "But you JJ. You gotten back up... back up and a 'come travelin' way out here. Maybe y'all can make a new start? I suppose yo' never really too old, jus' so long as yo' on the right side of the grass. Hey, if'n ya like, ah could line ya up a small job here, helping clean up the alley, the bin area 'n such. Only downside be'n ya have to put up with Wallace, the restaurant manager, a total waste of white."

"Thanks for the offer Arnie, really, but I'm not too sure about things yet." JJ looked up at the big man's face, "hope you don't mind."

Arnie tilted his head to one side, "Naw, offer still stands if you change yo' mind." The two men spoke for another couple of minutes then Arnie had to get back to work. JJ thanked his new friend and went on his way. As he strolled about the neighborhood, he remembered how Credence had once told him that if you weren't too pushy, folks near the golf resorts would throw a buck or two your way; over the next several days JJ found Credence was right.

That was especially true of the fat cats that parked their Bentleys, Porsches, and Jaguars in the golf and country club parking lots. JJ's favorite target was an older guy returning to his car with a young hottie on his arm after spending a few hours at the nineteenth hole. The couples were usually half drunk and when JJ approached them the old dude always felt pressured to look generous in the girl's eyes; even though if he were alone he'd probably rather run you over in his corvette than spit on you. JJ would give a courteous tip of his hat to the couple, smile, and say something completely sappy like, "what a lovely couple you young folks make" or some other bullshit comment. Sure enough, the girl would sweetly smile his way while the man would scowl and dig about in his golf pants looking for change. Of course, he wouldn't find a dime, after all, no one driving a "loaded to the nuts" ride would be caught dead carrying change in his pants, no; the dude would grab his ass for his wallet, which usually meant at least a fiver, maybe even a ten for good ol' JJ.

Yeah, life on the streets was good out here, but things were really cooling off in the late evenings, especially now that JJ acclimatized himself to the warmer weather. He was surprised to find just how cold the desert could get at night. He would have to find a spot to call home, besides, pickings being what they were; he had been able to afford a decent sleeping bag and some other camping gear that went a long way towards making life pretty comfortable. The problem was he had to have a safe place to stash it. While there weren't too many other bums working the neighborhood, the staff at the country clubs did not appreciate the local vagrants welcoming the first foursomes who began to arrive just after six am. Only one morning, just last week a pissed off greens keeper had come across the gear JJ had stashed in some bushes near the twelfth hole. If he hadn't come by in the nick of time he would have lost it all, the keeper was getting ready to load it up in that little trailer he always pulled behind the mower.

He would have to find a new spot, something close enough to his livelihood but far enough and out of the way so he wouldn't be bothered. He spent the next several days trying to find a good place. Making his way up the Garstin Trailhead, just a hop skip and a jump from the golf club, he left the road walking eastward, up and into the nearby hills.

It was by complete chance that he came across the cave's entrance that lay less than several hundred yards off the trail, just over a small hill and well hidden from any tourists or hikers. Actually, the entrance was well hidden from anyone at all; he had almost missed it himself. If it were not for his having to retrieve a frying pan that slipped out of his pack and had fallen into the thick brush concealing the cave entrance, he would have likely passed right by.

The cave's opening was only about four feet high and as many feet across. JJ had to stoop to look inside. As expected, the cave was cool and dark, but with the brilliant desert sunlight behind him, he couldn't see a blessed thing. Just how deep or how far back the cavern stretched was anyone's guess. Setting the pack and his other equipment down beside the entrance, he rummaged about for his flashlight. Finding it, he turned the small tube toward his face trying to tell if it worked. Being unable to detect the beam, he shielded the tiny bulb from the sunlight. Finally glimpsing the filament's tiny spark, he crouched low and cautiously entered the cave.

After moving only a matter of several feet into the caves interior, the light entering from the cave's opening fell off rapidly. Using the flashlight to guide his way in the dim light, JJ discovered that once he got past the initial narrow passageway the cave opened up into a sizable cavern. Moving in only several more feet, he found himself able to stand erect. His flashlight beam lit the way forward and he stepped deeper into the cave soon reaching the rear wall of the cavern.

Turning about he played the conical beam of the small flashlight about the rocky interior. JJ estimated the grotto measured perhaps thirty feet wide on average, fifty feet in length and anywhere from ten to fifteen feet in height. The floor of the cave was relatively smooth and with the exception of a large flat boulder lying near the center of the cavern, it was surprisingly free of any other large stones or debris. In places, the floor almost gave the appearance of having been swept clean. He heard the telltale gurgle of running water off to his left and shone the flashlight toward its source.

The small stream of water ran across the smooth stone following the edge of the cavern wall. JJ walked over to a point where he noticed the tiny stream had widened to form a shallow crystal pool perhaps three feet in diameter. Leaving the pool, the little stream continued across the entire length of the cave's floor before disappearing beneath a thin crevasse just feet from the entrance.

Supporting most of his weight with his hands, he slowly lowered himself down to kneel at the water's edge, wincing as his arthritic knees sang out their usual protest. He set the flashlight down then scooping up a single handful of water, raised the hand to his nose and took a sniff. Finding no discernible odor, he licked a finger; the water was sweet. JJ cupped his hands and dipped them into the shallow nearly ice-cold liquid. Bringing his hands to his lips, he took a first hesitant sip before enjoying a refreshing mouthful. That was when the flashlight batteries gave up the ghost.

If alone or within unfamiliar places, people suddenly thrust into darkness often discover the experience to be rather shocking. This is particularly true if that place happens to be of an odd and eerie sort, such as a cavern hidden deep beneath the earth. JJ was no different. His heart leaped into his mouth and he felt his body instinctively cringe and tighten in a motionless rigor. The old man knelt and held that position for ten very long seconds. Ears pricked and alert, except for the gurgle of the stream, JJ was unable to pick up any other sound whatsoever, with the notable exception of his rapid heartbeat and shallow breathing. He couldn't see a damned thing; the blackness being utter and complete. Then as the initial shock lifted, he realized he could not even make out the light at the cave's entrance. With a start, he realized he had his eyes tightly shut.

"Idiot!" he berated himself as he forced open his eyes and reached in the direction of the flashlight. "What?" surprisingly, the flashlight sat within arm's reach and in plain sight; JJ looked about the cavern realizing he no longer had any need of it. The walls and ceiling emitted a faint but definite blue-green glow that his eyes must not have been able to detect until they grew adapted to the dim light. Looking about at his surroundings, he noticed that with the exception of fine details he could easily see well enough to navigate his way about the cave without too much difficulty. He muttered to himself "This is too good to be true."

A half hour later, he had moved into his new home. Not yet having complete confidence in his choice of residence, and given the likely presence of bats and bugs, neither of which he had yet seen, JJ still decided not to take any chances. Erecting his little pup tent, he laid out his air mattress and sleeping bag inside, then tightly zipped closed its entrance then set about inspecting each square foot within the small cave.

At the back wall of the cave, he located a small niche in the rear rock wall where the small stream of water emerged. Unlike the rest of the wall, that portion was not solid and smooth but consisted of broken rock in various sizes. JJ reasoned a cave-in had occurred there sometime in the distant past. Perhaps the fallen rock obstructed what had been another passageway extending beyond the present confines of the cavern. Five minutes later he had finished exploring the remainder of the cave and still marveled at the fact that he hadn't found anything else alive, not so much as a beetle.

Several weeks had passed since JJ took up residence in the cave and the location was proving ideal. The cave provided shelter, security, and a mercifully short walk to the dumpster that sat at the rear of his favorite kitchen. His arthritis had not been acting up as much lately, perhaps an unexpected benefit of living in the dry desert air. JJ remained curiously surprised by the absence of any vermin living in the grotto and for the first time felt confident enough spend the night on the cave floor without benefit of his tent.

JJ lay atop his bedding on the cave floor listening to his small clock radio. He concluded that the air temperature in the cavern was even more comfortable than he had expected. An hour later, with the radio's volume fading as its batteries ran low, JJ reached over and switched it off. That night, sleep refused to come quickly. JJ gazed up into the intricate spider web of cracks, pits, and irregularities within the cave's walls and ceiling for nearly an hour before noticing the brightness within the cave began to vary, increasing ever so slowly. The blue-green color associated with the cavern's eerie glow had previously remained doggedly consistent, but now he watched with fascination as the colors shifted first into violets, then muted oranges and yellows. The erratic waves of light originating near the center of the ceiling fluttered and quivered, then expanding outward, moved gracefully in an unhurried dance toward the cave walls.

JJ thought it rather odd to discover that this new and somewhat weird light show did not bother him at all; in some way, he thought it quite tranquil. For nearly half an hour, he considered the source of the light until placid acceptance replaced any need of a rational explanation, and he drifted off into a deep sleep not stirring again until mid-morning.

JJ seldom slept in, and not having to get up and pee at least several times each night was something that had not happened within recent memory. He washed, dressed, and then filled his water bottle from the crystal pool before ducking low and sticking his head outside the cave entrance. Pausing for several moments, he listened carefully for the sound of anyone who might be walking nearby. Hearing nothing, he continued moving through the brush and then walked off onto the barren hillside.

October 1st was shaping up to be a fine day. He guessed that the air temperature had already risen to nearly seventy degrees. Glancing down at his watch, he saw it was nearly eleven in the morning. JJ did a quick calculation. By the time he reached the dumpster it would already be close to noon and the breakfast leftovers would have been sitting around too long for his liking; he would have to wait another hour or so before they dumped out lunch. "You're getting spoiled JJ," he said to himself. Grinning, he thought that not too long ago he would have gladly fought his way into a long line to get a mere taste of grub that was nowhere near that fresh. His stomach gurgled and churned reminding him of his hunger. No, he would walk over to the park, check out their garbage bin or maybe mooch some fries at the lunch stand. He reached a hand into his back pocket and pulled out a thin billfold. He still had almost twenty bucks from a couple of good scores he made at the country club a couple of days ago, maybe today he would even buy lunch.

He made the mile and a half distance in record time going cross-country over the series of small rolling hills that separated his valley from the park. He was pleasantly surprised to discover a bounce in his step that he had not felt for some time. Over the last year, it had become his habit to monitor his heart rate. Laying several fingers upon his jugular, he took a quick count of his heartbeats, comparing their frequency against the second hand of his Timex. He watched its movement as it twitched and edged across the faded roman numerals lying below the cracked crystalline face. Seventy-five beats per minute, nice and slow, hell he hadn't even broken a sweat this morning! Even more interesting was its regular tempo, for once his heart wasn't beating about like a syncopated bongo drum.

Arriving at the lunch stand, JJ figured he owed himself a treat. He bought himself a beer, a plate of French fries, and a side of gravy then sat at a small round table positioned beneath a bright striped umbrella. Glancing around at the other patrons, he began to feel himself fitting in with the lunch crowd, imagining himself as simply another of the people visiting the park that day. As he ate, JJ quickly skimmed over one of the park's brochures reading about the Murray Canyon's hiking trail and other nearby local attractions.

"The Cahuilla Indians and their decedents have been living in the Palm Springs area as far back as 3000 or even 5000 years ago... significant trading networks with other bands living in distant valleys as far as the coast. A peaceful agrarian society, their irrigation ditches could still be seen in yet undeveloped areas near the city... Palm Springs itself was named after the hot spring waters that provided a cultural focal point for the society, and a source of safe, clean water..."

JJ breezed through the usual tourist crap and ads until he came across a photograph of a grotto. The location was apparently the study of a team of archeologists from the University of Southern California. The dig focused on learning more of the Cahuilla people's supernatural beliefs, specifically the Nukatem, the ancient spirits that haunted the numerous springs and grottos in the area. A picture beside the column depicted one of the gods as he ate the soul of some poor bastard. In bold print just below the picture was a tacky warning; "Keep an eye out for Tahquitz!" He remembered a hotel, a diner, and even a roadway apparently named after the guy. As he finished off the last of his fries, he read on.

"Tahquitz apparently pronounced "Taw-kwish" in the old tongue was said to be the first and most powerful shaman made by the creator and one greatly respected and feared by all. A shapeshifter, at first he shared his knowledge with the tribe's medicine men through dreams or chance physical meetings, but then, became selfish and evil."

JJ took another sip of beer and took notice of a large group of tourists who were milling about in the parking lot looking like they were just about ready to line up and board a waiting bus. He would have to hurry if he was going to work the crowd and score a few bucks.

"Today Tahquitz is usually associated with malevolence and to this day he is often believed responsible for local disasters and accidents, even missing hikers. The demigod hunts for victims stealing their souls and trapping them for all time..." Blaa, blaa, blaa ... he glanced up seeing the bus driver walk up to the vehicle, open the door and step inside.

JJ gulped down the last of his beer, wiped his chin and headed off, sporting his well practiced "limp and wince" routine as he headed off toward the lineup. Having only crossed half way through the parking lot, JJ had already apprised the tourists and had his eye affixed upon a thirty-something, well-dressed black couple with a young child in tow. JJ figured at least a fiver from those folks was already a given. Once they donated to the cause, the others in the group would be easy pickings as they slowly filed by. God but life was good out west!

Nights came a little earlier and the days began a little later this time of year. This evening the desert sky blazed with the brilliant colors of the sunset. It had been a good day. JJ had taken in forty-six bucks from the tour group at the burger stand then later, enjoyed the remnants of a poorly attended buffet he retrieved from the dumpster at the rear of the Howard Johnsons on his way home. As he arrived near the cave entrance JJ realized that after such a long and busy day he hardly felt tired, "damned curious" he thought to himself. As was his practice, he stopped and took a long look around making sure the coast was clear before vanishing into the brush and entering the cave.

JJ lay on top of his sleeping bag taking a quick look at the radio he had propped up on a small rock chosen to serve as a night table. The glowing red numbers of the liquid crystal display changed rapidly while he played with the radio dial for several minutes. He could not bring in a station; getting good reception in the cave was always sort of hit or miss. Turning off the radio, he peered about the cavern. At least he still had his light show and tonight looked like it could be pretty good. The colors were far more vibrant and moving at a much faster rate than he had ever seen before. As they whirled and flashed about the cavern's ceiling, the old man felt caught up in their wild dance.

His body lost substance, suddenly weightless, he felt himself slowly rise from the cave floor. Somewhere in his head, he heard his mind complain this could not be right. An overpowering urge possessed him to look downward. In an instant, he was seeing the dark cave floor from ceiling height. Part of him marveled at the fact that he had not had to turn about, in fact, he found he could look in any direction without having to physically move at all. The illumination within the cave suddenly grew even more intense and JJ glanced back down toward the cavern floor. He could swear that he saw himself still lying peacefully upon his sleeping bag staring upward into the darkness...

...the blue-white after-image of a brilliant dawn blazed forth across the eastern valley and JJ physically reeled against the dazzling light. He stood erect, palms pressed tightly against his face for a long moment, warding off the painful assault to his senses. Dropping his hands, JJ squinted tightly as he urgently forced his eyes to open. Slowly, he began to trace the familiar skyline of ridges that surrounded the valley where his cave was located. He was standing on a small hill, a good mile or so from the cave entrance. Continuing to look about, he quickly took his bearings then realized that something was missing. From this vantage point, he should be able to see the entrance to the State Park, and over there, just a little further should be the lunch stand's parking lot where he had fleeced the tourist group yesterday afternoon. In their stead, nothing met his eyes other than acres of scrub, jumbled boulders, and several large flat sections of rock outcroppings.

He was about to take a step then stopped to take stock of his own condition. Inspecting his body, he felt his head and arms then continued the examination moving his hands along his chest and belly then finally bending at his waist to check out his legs and feet. From a personal viewpoint, everything looked as it should. JJ still wore the same old shirt, pants and runners he wore the day before. He chanced a few careful steps being careful to avoid a small cactus whose sharp spines thrust up in his direction. His balance felt a little off, it would not do for him to fall into that thing.

He waited a few more moments and took a series of deep breaths. The clean fresh morning air that filled his lungs and invigorated him caused him to realize something else. The light brown smog that normally drifted in the distance during the morning rush hour was nowhere in sight. Gone too was the constant drone of heavy traffic that should be cruising along the 111 highway. Looking up, he marveled at a sky that never seemed so blue...so clear. He considered his options and decided not to walk back to the cave just yet. He would carry on walking to the northeast and follow the dry wash that ran along the eastern ridge leading toward the golf courses and hotels; if they were still there. Intuition whispered in his ear not to expect to see them.

When he reached the edge of the wash, JJ was amazed to see a small river rushing along where only yesterday; there had been nothing but dry sand and rock. He made his way to the stream and crouched at its edge. Immersing his hands in the cool clear water, he splashed his face, wetting and ruffling his hair. It was only after he had stood up once again that he realized the complete absence of pain that should have accompanied his movement. How on earth was this happening?

"Hello?" You're new here aren't you?" a soft lilting feminine voice broke like a thunderclap above the rivers gentle murmur. Realizing he was no longer alone, JJ whirled about in the direction of the voice.

To say she was merely beautiful would have been a vast understatement. The young aboriginal woman was perhaps the most beautiful creature JJ had ever seen. Her brown skin was silken; her oval cherubic face became almost radiant as she flashed her warm smile. JJ noticed her forehead bore faint delicate bands of color that he assumed were tattoos of some sort. Her luxurious black hair was parted in the middle and fell flowing and tumbling about her bare shoulders and breasts before crossing her waist brushing about the only clothing she wore; a simple woven skirt that came down to her knees. JJ watched the long strands of colored beads about her neck swaying gently as she walked toward him in bare feet. She circled him, slowly looking him up and down, carefully assessing him.

Whether due to his being completely preoccupied with the beautiful girl or perhaps experiencing a light state of shock, JJ had just now taken notice of the other people milling about nearby. One at a time, they began appearing just moments after she began to speak. There was little question that these were her people. Clothed in similar style and dress, or more correctly, undress, the people ignored his presence as they went about the business of daily life. He listened to them casually speaking to one another in a language that upon reaching his ears sounded as different as it did oddly familiar. Closely observing the people, he allowed his eyes to wander further afield then felt them widen with renewed incredulity as an entire village began to appear before him. To him, it was as if a curtain of mist was being drawn back to slowly reveal one feature and then another.

A minute later, he stood in a village of perhaps twenty huts, a community of several hundred people all of whom speaking a language was definitely not English but a language that JJ somehow was clearly able to understand. He figured it was like reading the subtitles in a foreign film, at first you find it somewhat inconvenient, but after a while you accept it, a little later you hardly notice it at all.

He stood slack jawed and wide eyed while the young woman peppered him with questions. What was his name, where did he come from, and how long he'd be staying, asking each in turn before JJ was able to stammer out an answer. Seeing JJ's obviously confused state the girl must have decided it might be best if she gave the man some breathing room. Now quiet, she stood beside him waiting for him to speak. As the moments sped past, JJ observed that aside from the young woman, the other villagers continued to pay him little if any attention at all. A strange situation given the obvious and rather glaring physical differences, a tall Afro-American man fully dressed in modern garb, towering above the short and rather naked locals.

JJ looked back to the young woman who remained at his side smiling sweetly but expectantly. Pointing an index finger to his chest he croaked out his name, then realizing he was breathless, inhaled deeply before attempting to speak again. He frowned slightly then spoke, "JJ... my name's JJ," he said to the girl. She smiled and gently touched the hand at his side. "I'm Menily, welcome to our village."

"Thank you, I think?" JJ spoke slowly and deliberately, trying to comprehend just how it was that the girl understood his English. "What is this place?" JJ waved an arm about the village then looked back to Menily.

She looked at him questioningly, "this is our village, is this not where you chose to come?"

"I come from a far away land, a place called New York, many days travel to the east." He continued, "I didn't know your village was here until just this morning." He watched the girl as she nodded thoughtfully then turned away, walking slowly along the riverbank. "You are a stranger to our lands but a welcome stranger, we have long expected you."

"Expected me?" JJ asked he walked beside her.

"Yes for many years we have waited." The woman went on adding he was in the village of Inyo. The surrounding area, that of "sec-he," was the land of boiling waters, a name JJ assumed referred to the many hot springs that dotted the area. Menily explained that her people were the Gehila, and that her village worshiped the demigod, Tahquitz, "the powerful one who rules." Menily herself was the daughter of the tribes' chief elder and as such bore the name of their female deity, the moon goddess, who together with Tahquitz saw to it that her people flourished. While she provided plentiful wild game, invigorated their crops, and taught them the skills of life, her counterpart, Tahquitz spoke the language of the dead. Whispering to their priests and shamans, he preferred to educate her people in the darker arts of blood and battle, often aiding her people to destroy enemies in times of war.

She and JJ spent the next several hours together, Menily showing him the village and explaining their life and customs. To JJ's utter surprise given the girls initial questioning, the young woman no longer showed any further interest in the details of his life. Whenever he broached the subject, she would politely steer the conversation back toward her people and their culture.

JJ couldn't quite figure out why such a beauty would have any interest in spending so much time with an old man such as himself. Menily's attentions felt misplaced and it worried him to think her interest in him might be anything other than a simple kindness to a grandfatherly figure. JJ had no interest in such things and frankly, the idea repelled him, young women deserving young men and visa versa. This said, as the hours passed JJ became more comfortable with the thought, allowing the distant possibility that the girl might be interested in something more. Would there really be any harm in letting something happen, after all, how could any of this be anything more than a rather complex fabrication of his mind, a "waking dream" as some called it?

In the late afternoon, he and Menily shared a meal together on a nearby hill overlooking the peaceful village and the shallow river that ran off to the north. It was a beautiful setting. The couple spoke at length, each enjoying the other's company as they sat on a patch of cool grass that grew below a majestic ash tree. As the sun began its final drop toward the western horizon, they watched the lengthening shadows spill out across the expansive valley floor below.

JJ sensed distant, long forgotten stirrings arise from somewhere deep inside his being; feelings that he had simply misplaced or perhaps those he intentionally suppressed during his many years of solitary life. As they stood together watching that sunset, JJ found himself quite at home in a way he had never felt before. Menily smiled warmly reaching up with her small hand softly brushing away a small tear that had fallen to his cheek. He looked down into her soft brown eyes and found himself slipping away, slipping away...

The next morning JJ awoke and sat up with a start but found himself safely atop his sleeping bag. Running a hand over his chin he stroked the rough unshaven beard beneath his fingers while glancing nervously about the cave's familiar surroundings until he was sufficiently reassured that he was definitely back where he belonged. If indeed, he had ever been anywhere else.

All of his equipment was in place. His tent, still folded and propped against the far wall, his cooking gear where he had placed it the previous evening, his clock radio undisturbed, its ruby digits confidently stating the time was 8:47 in the am while still sitting upon the small rock beside him. Looking further about the cave, he noted the soft blue-green glow of the cave walls and ceiling still remained but appeared to have dimmed somewhat, likely due to the subdued daylight that streamed in from the entrance way dappling a small section of the cave floor.

He set about the day making extra sure that he did not vary his routine one iota. He began by visiting the resort's dumpster for breakfast, then working the tourist buses at the park before walking over to the golf course parking lot intending to pan handle a few bucks, but as he arrived, JJ felt completely tuckered out. He instead decided to spend the rest of the day dozing in a secluded glade he knew of only a short distance from the twelfth hole. The peace and quiet would allow him to set things back into their proper perspective.

Reaching the glade, he stretched out in the shade upon a bed of cool green turf. The pleasant though disturbing memory of the previous night's dreams faded but stubbornly refused to vanish in the heat of the noon sun that continued to bake the surrounding desert's bone-dry hills and valleys. By mid-afternoon JJ was able to persuade himself that what he had experienced was in fact only a dream, albeit one that seemed incredibly true to life. His understanding of reality was suddenly reinforced as a heavy leather boot caught his leg painfully just above his right knee.

"Up and out of here yah damn niggah!" A lanky thirty-something man with a nasty sneer wound up, then putting all his weight into it, aimed a second vicious kick in the old man's direction. Even as the greens keepers' foot began to move, the old man rolled aside and out of range with a speed that surprised both JJ and the much younger man. Tom Clancy's leg thrust outward sweeping atop the empty spot where just a moment before the old man had lain. Unable to make contact with its target, the greens keeper's leg continued up and outward in a low arc, the momentum of the kick taking Clancy's balance with it causing the man to fall heavily onto his back winding him badly.

Hearing the man wheeze and gasp for breath, JJ decided in an instant that it might be a good time to move along. Rising to his feet, he made off in a dead run crossing a nearby golf green while dragging his pack by one of its straps along on the grass behind him. Several feet off to his right, a golf ball thudded heavily onto the grass surprising him and drawing JJ's attention away from where he was running, a second later his shoulder crashed into the metal flagpole sending him sprawling on the ground. Looking back, he saw Clancy had now risen to his knees. Red-faced and livid with anger the greens keeper spun a string of curses and obscenities that rolled off his tongue in the distinctive drawl of an Alabama cracker. With Clancy now in full pursuit, JJ yelled something back at the man as he picked himself up and ran for all he was worth.

Five minutes or so later, JJ was bending forward with his hands on his knees breathing heavily and keeping a close watch from one of several thickets of dense brush that lined the 12th fairway. He wondered how it came to be that an arthritic old codger like himself had managed to outrun a young buck just out of his prime. Clancy stood in the center of the fairway, hands on hips searching one way and then the other for his quarry. A group of young golfers who up until moments ago had been waiting patiently in their carts for Clancy to leave the course, decided to hurry along his departure with several angry calls. JJ saw the greens keeper begin to open his mouth, obviously intending to trade insults with the young men until Clancy spotted the course marshal's cart that sat only fifty yards further down the fairway. Taking a final look up and down the course Clancy turned about heading back to where his lawn mower awaited him. JJ did not move a muscle until the man and his machine had trundled away out of sight.

Returning to the cave that evening he decided not to chance sleeping inside and risk a repeat of last night's unusual events. Instead, he retrieved his tent erecting it in a flat spot some several hundred yards from the cave's entrance. Unlike the comfortable surroundings the cave afforded, JJ found the long night to be windy and cold. He tossed restlessly, wrapped within a sleeping bag that was simply too lightweight for the chilly mid-October nights. Finally abandoning any hope of sleep, he left the tent to stand alone in the dark predawn hours. After lighting a small fire to warm himself, he stared into the star-studded velvet of the black desert sky, watching the constellations slowly spin westward then disappear in morning's twilight. Later that morning JJ moved back into the cave.

Since moving back into the cave, the strange dreams and the dancing lights on its walls and ceilings had not returned. Each morning he would rise well rested and eager to start his day. Since coming to the Springs, JJ couldn't help but notice his improved stamina. During his frequent trips up or down the series of canyon inclines, he seldom felt himself winded or his heart pound. Better yet, his arthritis symptoms had disappeared entirely; his joints had not ached at all in over a week. It was widely rumoured that the spring waters in the area cured all manner of infirmity and JJ speculated he owed his improvement to the crystal waters of his cave. Still, the old man hadn't managed to shake the uneasy feeling that surrounded him of late. No matter how hard he tried to ignore the odd sensation, he was certain that something else was at work in the background, but as for it being simply innocent and fortuitous or dark and sinister he could not decide.

Ever since arriving in the Springs, JJ had accepted the weather at face value. Each day he would arise to a sunny cloudless horizon, sweat it out in the hot dusty afternoon sunshine, and then be treated to a brilliant western sunset followed quickly by a clear starry night sky. As with most people, JJ thought life in Palm Springs to be typically sunny, hot, and dry, but stay there for a while and you 'd realize the desert wears many faces. It could turn on you, like one of its snakes, something JJ was about to discover today.

He slept in and got a late start. Aside from this minor annoyance, his late October morning had started out pretty much like the others. He began by listening to a twenty-four-hour news channel on his radio, paying special attention to the sports report. JJ washed up and slipped on the cleanest dirty shirt he could find; he would have to visit the coin laundry today, he was starting to offend himself. JJ waited impatiently near the radio, eager to get on with the day but unwilling to forego listening to the announcer provide the results of the Mets / Royals game the night before, his Mets had been just a single game away from losing their chance at the pennant. A nasal and all too cheery voice broke his heart, "There you go folks, five to four in the final inning, well, that's the old ball game for the Mets..." JJ stabbed a finger down atop the power button and the announcer's voice faded out, "And Jesus wept. Damn it boys, the Royals weren't supposed to be that tough!"

The sun was well above the stark horizon as he stepped from the cave. He gave a hard yank on the strap of his daypack that had gotten itself caught up in the clutching brush and brambles that hid the entrance. The pack was much bulkier today having been stuffed with JJ's entire wardrobe along with the water bottle and some leftovers from the previous evenings dumpster raid. He took a deep breath of the warming morning air. "Might be a hot one today old son," he said to himself as he began his march down the broken rocky path that led toward town.

He'd done pretty well with his panhandling lately and had even taken Arnie up on his offer of a cleaning job or two, not that he minded the work. Sweeping up around the kitchen dumpsters hardly put him out of his way at all, seeing how they were already part of his regular route. In the last couple of weeks, JJ had saved up nearly two hundred dollars. He stashed most of it beneath a rock in his cave and carried the other twenty-five bucks in the heel of his runner. JJ figured he was about as rich as he had ever been in the last ten years, except for that time he found two hundred and thirty bucks in a dropped wallet outside a bar back in NYC. Opening it, he discovered it contained credit cards that he could have sold on the street, but he wasn't into that type of thing. He just took the cash and let the wallet drop into a sewer grating before walking into that same bar. He staggered out just six short hours later, drunk as a skunk and broke flat as piss on a plate. That was back in his drinking days, he had smartened up a lot since and now seldom touched the stuff.

Stuffing his load of dirty laundry into a washer, JJ walked across the street to a cafe where he sat nursing a cup of coffee and munching on a donut while keeping a sharp eye on his machine. It was well past noon when he returned to the laundry. He started the dryer and resumed his watch back at the diner treating himself to a tuna on rye and a plate of fries. Finishing off the last fry, he counted out the amount of the bill to the penny leaving it on the countertop and his server glaring at his back as he walked out the door. He paused at the curb for a break in the traffic then crossed over toward the coin laundry feeling a strong gust of hot wind tug unexpectedly at his t-shirt.

Reaching the opposite sidewalk, he glanced up to see the entire northwestern sky stained an ugly gray-brown. The storm cloud was quickly approaching and was already threatening to engulf the noon sun. "Somethin's definitely blow'n in Jeremiah," he muttered as he ducked into the laundry. He quickly folded and stuffed his clothes into the daypack thinking he'd have to make tracks if he was to stay ahead of the weather. Five minutes later when he exited the building, the sun had disappeared and a brisk somewhat cool wind was blowing steadily down the length of the avenue. A few minutes later, strong gusts of wind picked up discarded papers, dust, and even small pebbles; JJ felt the grit pepper his face and bare arms. Squinting his eyes into narrow slits, he bent his head down and headed into the wind, his arms and hands raised to shield his face from the worst of the blow.

The brown-gray of the dust cloud above him was a precursor to the black storm cloud that followed on its heels. JJ could hear the thunderous claps that instantaneously accompanied the bright flashes of sheet lightning that lit up the darkened afternoon sky. He needed to find some shelter before whatever was coming arrived, he could barely see half a block ahead of him. Another several minutes passed and JJ saw he was approaching the Palm Canyon Resort. Breaking into a run, he soon found himself at the back door of Arnie's kitchen. As usual, ever since the air conditioner had packed it in, the door had been propped half open in a useless effort to defeat the heat given off from the ovens and grills. He put a hand on the door and came face to face with Arnie.

"JJ?" Arnie asked, "man alive, what on earth are y'all doin' out there in this here storm?" If possible, the lightning managed an even more intense flash, its blinding radiance making the bright fluorescent overhead lighting in the kitchen appear almost dim by comparison. The thunder pealed above, drowning out the last words of Arnie's question while droplets of rain mixed with hail began pelting down on the asphalt just outside the doorway. Arnie spoke firmly resting a huge hand on JJ's shoulder, "you best come in here old son," leading the old man into the kitchen then shutting the door behind them.

For several minutes, the two men stood watching the sky through a kitchen window as the violent storm ripped through the city. The rain and hail had mixed with the choking dust to become thick black pellets of mud that fell coating the surface of the pavement with a slippery black mess. Standing silent and amazed, JJ had never seen anything like it in all his years and finally muttered in a muted tone, "End o' the world..."

"Huboob" Arnie stated matter of factly.

"What's that?" asked JJ still looking out the window into a storm that seemed to have lost some of its original ferocity.

"Huboob" Arnie repeated, "Huboob is a big dust storm that comes out of the desert. Sometimes they come in dry, other times wet, like this one. It'll take the street crews a couple of weeks to clean up this mess, but at least folks won't have problems with the dust coming indoors like they had when the storm came in dry a couple years ago." The big man shook his head and turned away from the window. "Used to be a rare thing and aside from the weather man, weren't too many folks that even heard of Huboob, now about once a month you got one blowin' inta some town or 'nother. Global warmin' I guess."

"You don't say," JJ replied. The windstorm was quickly blowing itself out. The mud shower had stopped completely and a light rain had started to fall.

An authoritative voice shouted out behind them. "What's this Arnie? We got customers waiting on their orders out on the floor and you're in here entertaining who?"

Arnie spun in the direction of the voice, "Mr. Wallace sir?"

A white-haired man in his early fifties stood in a far doorway, red-faced, and arms crossed, his blustering voice suggested he was fit to be tied. "You're walking on mighty thin ice around here lately; I swear you'll find yourself out on your ass if you keep this up!"

Arnie took a quick glance back at JJ then returned to face his manager. "Why Mr. Wallace, this is JJ." Noting the questioning look on his boss's face, he quickly added. "He's the fella' we hired to clean up the trash in our bins out back on Tuesdays and Fridays."

Wallace scowled, "Looks more like a damned bum to me... anyway why is he in our kitchen," Wallace smirked, his eyes meeting JJ's as he finished the sentence "and not out in the alley where he belongs... with the trash?"

"On account o' the storm sir." He saw the manager pause and consider his words. "Huboob Mr. Wallace, a bad one, couldn't leave him out there?"

The manager paused then relented, "Fine, fine, just have him out of here as soon as the storm ends." Wallace turned about to head back out onto the restaurant floor quickly adding, "and Arnie, don't forget what I said about the orders, we don't want to keep our clients waiting, do we?"

A moment later when Wallace had left, Arnie turned back to JJ. "Dumb ass... don't have no orders waitin'. Guests just come in out o' the storms all; got 'em set up with complimentary coffee and tea." The big man shook his graying head while rubbing his chin. "Pay no mind to him JJ."

"You gonna get fired for having me in here?" JJ asked with a concerned expression.

"Lordy no, besides Wallace can't fire me, that'd be up to Mr. Harrison the general manager and we's good friends, been together at the Palm a long time, yes sir, long time." Arnie paused and looked back at the doorway where Wallace had left only moments before, his face concerned. "Mr. Harrison set to retire next March... Wallace is in line to take over. JJ, my days here are probably numbered."

"I should go Arnie. Don't want to get you into trouble." Arnie and JJ looked out the kitchen window, the storm had blown over and the afternoon sun began peeking out from behind the retreating storm clouds in the distance. The alleyway lay cluttered with strewn papers, disposable cups, wrappers, and drink containers the wind had plucked out of the dumpsters.

Arnie frowned and looked questioningly into JJ's face. "Do me a favor will yah JJ? Would you pick up the trash for y'all go? Give ya a couple of bucks too. Yah know I wouldn't ask but Wallace will be chewing my butt if it stays the way tis."

"Keep your money Arnie. You're a friend, the only one I got now that Credence is back on the pipe and all." He slapped the big man's shoulder.

"Thanks, JJ, appreciate it man." Arnie put a hand on JJ's shoulder. "Take care, now I best be getting back to all those orders." A low chuckle sounded in the man's belly.

It took JJ a full half hour to pick up the wet muddy trash and drop it back into the dumpster. Finishing up, he felt a faint hunger pang and realized he would not be looking into any dumpsters for his next meal, the rain and mud had seen to that. Taking up his daypack JJ checked his jeans finding he still had twelve dollars and change. He would grab a gut bomb at the burger joint on the way home.

The last hours of October 31 were rapidly coming to a close. JJ awoke from a fitful sleep and glanced over at his radio, eleven thirty. Rolling over, he lay on his back staring up at the tranquil glow that played over the cave's ceiling and walls in a gentle oscillating rhythm. JJ began to think back to the dream of a week or so earlier and of meeting the lovely Menily.

He tried to re-imagine her beautiful dark eyes, soft face, and round body. His loins stirred for a moment then quieted, overcome by a feeling of emptiness that crept into his heart. He asked himself "How long have I been alone?" and his mind replied, "Forever!" A hand brushed away a single tear from his cheek and he closed his eyes for a moment. "Oh God!" JJ thought, he had not felt this low in recent memory. "I wish I could see her again...," he said in an almost inaudible voice, "Menily..." Reopening his eyes he saw that the lighting in the cave had begun to change, once again faint ripples of violet, orange and yellow began to brighten with each passing moment. As the light grew stronger, the terrible crush of loneliness and the black weight of his life's regrets begin to vanish in their presence.

Once again, as if magically transported, JJ walked toward the river where he had met Menily during his previous journey to... "To where?" he thought aloud. He had not decided if the village and its people had actually existed sometime in the past or if the entire event was a complete fabrication of his mind. He climbed the final gentle slope that would provide a view of Menily's small valley in its entirety. As before, the shallow river meandered across the valley floor and once again the little village slowly materialized along its banks. Standing atop the knoll, he paused for several long minutes looking down into the vale. Committing the lay of the land to memory, he formulated the intent of revisiting the area when he awoke the next morning and in doing so, JJ had a sudden inspiration.

At the top of the hill, near the side of the trail, a good number of large flat rocks lay scattered about in disarray. Over the next fifteen minutes, JJ spent considerable effort aligning the rocks in such a way so as to fashion a large, if somewhat crude directional arrowhead aimed directly at the village. Feeling about in his pants pocket, he pulled out a coin and held it in his palm while crouching low near the front of his arrow. There JJ dug a small hole, placed the 1995 penny at its base, and covered it with a piece of orange quartzite that had no place among the soft brown sandstone strewn about the hilltop. Satisfied with his work he began to walk toward the village.

Reaching the outskirts of the village, JJ stopped when he saw Menily walking toward him. Stepping close, she cradled his face in her hands and kissed him lightly on the lips, but before his arms could wrap themselves around her, she quickly stepped back. Frowning slightly, she spoke in a soft expectant tone, "I wasn't sure if you would come back to me." She paused, awaiting his response.

"I wasn't sure either. You've got to admit, things are a little strange here; and what with everything I've..." she cut him off as she took his hands into hers.

"But now you are here, that's all that matters." she smiled and their eyes met, JJ had to admit she was right and no longer paid further mind to the circumstances in which he found himself.

The couple sat side by side on a flat outcropping of rock that stretched out into the river dangling their feet in the cool water. JJ looked up into the sky using a hand to shade his eyes from the sun. By his reckoning, it should be well past noon. "Damn strange" he thought, they had been sitting here for several hours in full sunlight and neither one of them had yet to break a sweat. Though the sun seemed as bright as usual, its rays did not burn his skin the way it had back... back in his world. Here the temperature of the air was simply, well comfortable.

He lowered his head and admired the beautiful young woman beside him for several moments then lowered his gaze toward the river. Catching his reflection in a patch of calm water near the outcropping, he spoke aloud in surprise. "It can't be..." his voice trailed off in astonishment as he ran a hand over the dark stubble of his two-day-old beard then through the thick jet black curls on his head. He crouched closer to the water's surface observing the young man who stared back into his eyes in equal amazement. JJ had not seen that face in over thirty-five years...

It took him nearly half an hour to come to terms with the fact that he was, and had always appeared as nothing other than a young man to Menily; at least in this dream or state of consciousness. It was not as if he had never dreamt of being young again. Growing old with arthritis creeping into his joints and limiting his movement, JJ dreamt of running, jumping, and moving about as he had decades earlier, back in his glory days. After all, wasn't this the norm for most of the fifty plus crowd?

What's more, the young woman seemed to have taken all this in stride, almost as if this type of thing happened all the time; perhaps that was the stuff of dreams.

While they sat enjoying the morning, Menily told JJ, she and her people had arrived here years before having traveled from a country that lay many months journey, far to the south. Driven north into the desert they fled the other tribes who took exception to their worship of their lord, Tahquitz, although known by a different name in the south. Arriving in this new land, her people found they were outcasts among the much more numerous Cahuilla peoples. Forced to eke out a hard living in some of the driest parts of the desert, Tahquitz delivered her people from their dire circumstances when he turned a river's course causing it to flow into their remote valley.

Menily told him that Tahquitz was the greatest of the ancient shamans and that her lord was a powerful demigod who had cared for all the people in the old lands far to the south. In return the people worshiped him, placing offerings before his stone alters that rose throughout their many populous cities; some alters so high that they almost seemed to touch the sky. Tahquitz shared the sacred knowledge of life with the Kings and the lesser medicine men, at such times, appearing before them in the form of powerful animals or in dreams where his body coiled above them as a terrifying serpent, his voice like that of thunder in the mountains.

Then the day came when Tamit the sun god became jealous of the people's offerings to Tahquitz and struck out against the shaman. The peoples of the old land chose between those who would follow Tamit and those who would worship Tahquitz. A vicious war erupted and despite their bravery, Menily's people had to flee the dark green jungle forests, their beloved mist covered mountain peaks and lush fields. Tamit broke or corrupted many of Tahquitz' powers, expelling her lord from the light of day, and condemning him to dwell deep within the dark places of the earth. Since that time, her people lived in the desert and here they would remain until Tamit forgot his anger and allowed Tahquitz and his people to return to their paradise, a paradise now so far removed it was, but a distant memory.

Menily slowly turned her head toward the southern slopes of the valley where she watched the horizon intently. JJ's eyes followed her lead and after several moments saw a line of men walking single file down the hills toward the village. Menily stood up on the rock and called out to several other women who were digging shallow culverts in the sandy soil in an attempt to coax small streams of water from the river and into the nearby fields where they would irrigate their meager but hardy crops. Hearing Menily, the women stopped their labors and each in turn took up the call. JJ and Menily left the river arriving with the others who gathered in the village's central meeting place.

JJ watched the village shaman leave the entrance of a large hut as the first of the men came into view. It was obvious to JJ that the medicine man had dressed in his Sunday best. The man's intricate ceremonial headdress, heavy gold and mother of pearl necklace and feathered earplug together with the jet black, short-sleeved tunic and loin cloth the man wore was like nothing JJ had yet seen among the otherwise rather scantily dressed villagers. The shaman spoke quietly with the group of men for several minutes before turning and facing the rest of those gathered. Lifting his arms the shaman spoke unintelligibly in an ugly, guttural-sounding language so completely unlike that of the pleasantly lilting dialect he heard Menily and the other villagers speak earlier. Even so, the others in the village seemed to understand the man perfectly well. When the shaman had finished speaking, the villagers turned and began dispersing while the priest led the men out and away from the meeting place. JJ stood watching the small procession of men leave when he felt Menily's hand tugging on his sleeve and bidding him to follow her.

Menily led JJ to one of the larger grass huts in the village. Upon their arrival, she lifted the buckskin drape covering the entrance and asked him to accompany her as she stepped inside. The hut walls that surrounded JJ were perhaps 15 feet in diameter and some 7 feet or so high. There was a small hole in the top of the roof. Directly below lay a circle of stones containing ash and several small pieces of charcoal that JJ assumed was a small fire pit used for both cooking and warming the hut during the more inclement seasons. A rectangular reed mat covered in a thin layer of straw lay on the hard dirt floor. Atop the bed was a brightly striped cloth blanket with a soft pillow of rabbit pelts at its head. JJ looked back to Menily who had walked over to the far end of the hut and stood in front of a grouping of large woven baskets.

JJ walked over to the girl watching as she removed the covers from atop each basket taking out what he saw were ceremonial garbs that were in every way just as splendid as those worn by the priest in the gathering area just minutes before. As Menily began to prepare, she told JJ of her namesake, the moon goddess of the Gehila tribe.

"Menily and Tamit the sun god share the sky but they are not at peace. Tamit is a jealous god who keeps Menily in her place and while he rules the day Menily must be content to appear in her full glory only during those nights when Tamit sleeps." She paused sweeping her long hair up and across the front of her shoulders tying it in a long ponytail before continuing.

"After Tamit banished Tahquitz, our shaman whispered to Menily during the lonely nights. Tahquitz persuaded the goddess to renew his powers during the darkness promising that his people would worship her beauty in the night just as the other tribes worshiped Tamit who brought forth the day. She agreed and since that time, Tahquitz and his people celebrated and worshiped Menily on each of the thirteen feasts of the year that coincided with the goddess revealing her full glory in the night sky. At these times, Menily returns Tahquitz powers and in turn passes on long life to his followers. Tonight is such a festival."

The girl had slipped off her clothing and stood naked before JJ. "Do you find me beautiful?" she asked, to which he replied, "Oh Lordy yes." She smiled seductively, but then to JJ's disappointment began to dress in the articles of clothing she took from the baskets. "How old do you think I am?"

"Oh oh, here comes trouble." JJ thought to himself, but at least the girl was young and pretty, he would not have to stammer out an obvious lie. "Twenty-one... twenty-two?" he guessed.

She smiled. Menily's costume was resplendent. Her grass skirt was black while the cape she wore draped across her shoulder was the skin of a black jaguar brought with her people when they traveled from the southern lands. Like the priest, she wore an elaborate necklace that draped low and lay upon her breasts but instead of gold, hers was of the purest silver.

Menily looked thoughtful and then replied, "It's been so long... I can't remember my true age but I have lived over two hundred turns of the great wheel." JJ blanched knowing that a single turn of the great wheel referred to the passing of a year. She continued, "JJ, would you like to be truly young once again?" seeing the interest in her face she added, "Join us... and you will live as long as you wish."

The girl picked up her final article of clothing, an intricate and very beautiful headdress from the last of the baskets, placed it beneath her arm then walked out of the hut with JJ in tow. He checked the sky. The sun was setting in the west; it would be dark in several hours.

Menily placed the headdress atop her head then led JJ through the village along a well-worn path that wound back into the hills, the same path that JJ had taken to reach the village earlier in the day. As the couple climbed the hill, other villagers and their children joined them. When they reached the ridge, JJ figured the throng numbered at least several hundred; the whole village must be there. Without pause, JJ looked to his left and saw his stone arrow and the piece of quartzite, he wondered if he would find it tomorrow when he awoke. Menily interrupted his train of thought, tugging his shirt, her other hand pointed to a spot further down the trail where JJ saw the priest and his men were waiting. The men stood before a familiar rocky outcropping; JJ gave an inner shudder recognizing the spot to be the entranceway leading into <u>his</u> cave.

The priest and an older man stood at the entrance. Menily told JJ the older man was her father and the chief elder of the village. Each of the two men addressed the group in the same guttural language he heard the priest speak several hours earlier at the meeting place, but to JJ's surprise, the dialect took on a ring of familiarity, he found he could even understand some of the words. Torches appeared among the crowd as night crept across the desert floor while to the east, the full moon began to peek above the distant horizon. Of the people outside the cave entrance, only JJ, Menily, the priest, and a select group of tribal elders entered.

Inside the cave, two torches blazed on either side of the entrance. Looking about, JJ almost felt as if he had arrived home, with the notable exception of a half-naked man lying flat on his back atop the large flat rock in the center of the cavern; his hands, and feet tightly bound. It came to JJ that the rock must function as an altar of some kind. The priest and his men walked slowly to the far side of the altar then turned, facing toward the entrance they fanned out and stood in silence. Menily took JJ's hand and guided him to the left side of the rock where she turned him about so that he too faced the altar. JJ watched the prisoner at his feet glance about nervously, searching each of the somber faces surrounding him in rapid succession, but finding nothing there to give him hope. Meanwhile, Menily walked to the opposite side of the boulder then faced JJ; each of them stood alone, each before the altar and the hapless soul who lay bound and helpless upon it.

To JJ's left, the priest and the elders remained motionless and silent for several long minutes; God knows how long it must have seemed for the poor fellow tied to the rock. Finally, the priest turned toward Menily and raising his hands upward began to speak in a slow rhythmic cadence, JJ decided his words could only be the ceremonial language of their religion. The instant the priest began his incantation; the temperature within the cave plummeted. When the priest had finished the chant, JJ felt his eyes drawn to the cavern's ceiling where a sudden flash of silver radiance forced his eyes shut; he squinted as he fought to reopen them.

The image of the full moon shone down from the ceiling directly atop Menily, illuminating her body as if caught in a spotlight. The woman's gleaming headdress and silver necklace broke the moonlight into a dazzling display of glints and sparkles that scattered and fell atop the walls and floor of the cave. JJ watched as his lovely young woman transformed herself into an image that bespoke the magnificence of the lunar goddess that could only be Menily.

The brilliance of the incredible scene slowly diminished, although the goddess herself retained an inner radiance that sent muted shards of illumination streaming into the gloomy depths of the cave. The priest now turned toward JJ and once again raised his hands, then in a low voice began a steady chant that steadily increased in volume the longer he continued. JJ looked up. The familiar shimmering lights he had seen before on the cave's ceiling had reappeared, but now their rays and beams were far more vibrant and lively than anything JJ had yet seen. The radiance of the lights flashed in an ever more rapid, brilliant succession as the chanting grew in fever and pitch. The priest's voice became a syncopated series of shouts that accompanied and punctuated each multicolored flash; abruptly the cave fell silent.

JJ stared upward at the ceiling becoming aware that the brilliant flashes of light had not ceased entirely, but had taken on a more somber quality. They began moving together, vague shapes that were slowly evolving into more recognizable forms, forms that eventually became distinct images of men, women, and even children. The beings flowed and glided within, rather than upon, the surface of the rock face above him. As their stately procession continued, JJ could make out the facial features of each individual. In some, JJ could see expressions of surprise or bewilderment, in others that of fear, but the majority wore faces reflecting grief and hopelessness.

JJ heard a distant roar echoing out of the depths of the cavern, somewhere far behind him, but that could not be, since he stood only a matter of feet from the solid rock wall. The bellow sounded again, this time much closer. JJ attempted to turn toward the sound but found he was paralyzed, unable to move a muscle. Instead, he stood motionless, his head and body facing the altar, his unblinking eyes fixed upon the goddess who stood opposite, her face an unreadable mask, her eyes utterly vacant of emotion. The roaring ceased and immediately JJ became aware of a slow ponderous footfall as whatever it was, drew closer. JJ shuddered in response to the pending arrival of its fearsome presence; an evil malevolence accompanied with the promise of violence that began to envelop the very core of his being and force his consciousness from his body.

JJ had experienced a similar event within the cave, that night he had first floated weightlessly above his own body while it remained motionless upon his sleeping bag below. He stole a quick glance over toward where the lunar goddess stood and was shocked to see the spirit of his young woman hovering silently above her own body that now bore host to the goddess Menily. As their eyes met, he immediately understood and looked back to where his body still stood, motionless before the altar.

Horrified yet fascinated, JJ watched as the thing he assumed must be Tahquitz slowly crept the last short distance before reaching his vacant body. As it approached the deity constantly changed its shape, one moment resembling a giant wolf that walked on hind legs, at times a misshapen bear with a wide tooth-studded maw and giant long curved claws, but more often, it was nameless horror that was altogether indescribable. The only feature remaining unchanged and unvaried was its iniquitous eyes. Their red glowing pupils floated within sunken-yellowed orbs glaring out at the world with an insatiable hunger, a longing to consume all that lived.

It stood behind JJ's motionless form pausing for a moment before shooting forward with incredible swiftness, engulfing his body within a heavy mist that quickly disappeared from sight flowing and seeping into every pore and orifice of his body. JJ's apparition continued to hover a short distance away, despairing as he saw a dark shadow sweep across his previously emotionless face. In an instant, his features took on a terrifying grimace of rage-filled hate. JJ's kind, soft brown eyes vanished abruptly, replaced by a smoldering dread that peered out from a death head perched atop an emaciated skeleton bare of skin, revealing only bloody sinew and raw muscle. Its hands were saber tipped claws that clicked and clacked together as they dangled at its sides.

The victim struggled frantically against the bonds that held him fast. Unable to break free he cried out begging for release, begging deliverance from the evil that bowed low then leaned in close. A low moan arose within the beast's chest then increased in pitch and volume climbing in Tahquitz's throat to emerge as an appalling, ghastly laugh as the noisome din passed its lips and rang outward reverberating throughout the rock walled chamber.

As JJ's apparition hovered nearby, he felt a gentle touch as if something was reaching into his mind. That touch became a series of soft tugs soon followed by a much more urgent yank; his soul drew back within his body, back into that living corpse to share a common consciousness with the demon Tahquitz.

A helpless prisoner within his own body, he felt the wicked presence of the shaman, the exhilaration of his power and malice, and its sick thrill as it began to mutilate the victim that thrashed beneath it. JJ sensed something he had not expected, rather than being disgusted and repelled by the feelings of bloodlust that washed over his consciousness, JJ began to enjoy it and then delighted in its terrible fury. He felt himself a willing participant, joining with Tahquitz as the slaughter continued. He felt their powerful claws rip and tear their way into the victim's abdomen then reach upward, probing through gushes of hot dark blood further, deeper into the torso until they found what they sought. The body that lay below them was tight with rigor, the pain, and shock of the attack completely paralyzing and overwhelming the victim's body and mind. As the claws slowly retracted from the body's cavity, JJ both heard and felt a gentle ripping of tissue. The victim abruptly relaxed and went slack. His living heart and dripping bloody lungs were drawn and held out before the goddess who remained motionless before them.

The goddess slowly nodded her head haughtily and vanished, Menily's powerful countenance replaced by that of the simple Indian girl who collapsed in a heap on the cave floor. The cavern lay in darkness, the only exception were the torches that sputtered weakly near the cave's entrance. With the departure of the goddess, JJ felt a renewed strength surge into his soul and he struggled to free himself from the demonic control that gripped his mind. As he struggled, JJ became aware that Tahquitz himself was motionless and still, their eyes were affixed to the dismembered human form that before them.

A faint glow appeared to envelop the corpse and JJ realized that the light originated from within the body itself. The illumination stirred and flowed outward, leaving the ruined body where it lay, gently swirling, it rose toward the cave's ceiling; "Willow o' the Wisp" soft pinks and sky blues accompanied its rise. JJ knew that his... their eyes could not, nor would not look away from the spectacle taking place before them. He watched as the colors brightened then reassembled themselves into the living spirit of the man they had victimized just moments earlier. JJ felt himself and the demon each gasp in unison as the spirit being entered the realm of the dead, itself welcomed by the myriad of other beings of light that slipped and glided within the translucent granite. Tahquitz departed and JJ immediately felt his strength ebb then evaporate with the shaman's departure. In a swoon, he toppled toward to the damp blood soaked earth below him joining the young woman that lay nearby.

Muscles cold and aching, JJ awoke on bare rock. Looking about he found he lay beside the large flat boulder in the center of the cavern. He raised himself onto an elbow and peered about. As usual, his sleeping bag and pillow were lying where they always had, and his other gear was stored away in the far corner where he had left it. The red digits of the clock radio that still sat on the small rock to the side of his bedroll read 8:30 am. Slowly he dragged himself to his feet and sat down on the large boulder using both hands to wipe the sleep from his eyes. Suddenly remembering the terrifying dream from the night before, he shot up from where he sat and spun about to examine the rock.

The surface of the gray boulder was smooth and relatively featureless but the cracks and other small indentations in the stone face were dark and stained. Taking a finger JJ reluctantly rubbed at a dark patch then examined his finger, it had come away clean. "Thank God!" he thought, what would he have done had it been wet with blood.

As was his morning habit, he washed in the small pool. Then a quick thought came to him and he rummaged about in his gear. He knelt again at the pool and taking his flashlight, shone the beam onto his face examining his reflection in the mirror. Turning his face slowly, first in one direction, and then the other, he was unable to detect any difference in the way he looked only the day before. JJ was most certainly not a young man in his twenties or thirties!

He exited the cave striding off in the direction of Menily's village; or more correctly, where he thought it would lie. This morning he moved with purpose, he intended to put these dreams in their proper place, for the last time. It took JJ fewer than ten minutes to reach the small knoll above the wash where the phantom village had appeared. Satisfied he was close to where he wanted to be, he glanced about the ground around him. What he found located off to the right of the path made him blanch.

Walking several yards from the trail, he stood behind an arrowhead grouping of flat rocks that pointed off in the direction where Menily's village should lie. His head suddenly ached and felt heavy as his vision darkened at its periphery and narrowed as if he were looking off into the distance through a tunnel. He stood motionless for several minutes waiting for the sensation to pass. When his head had cleared, he stepped to the arrow's point and bending low reached for a familiar looking piece of rounded orange quartzite. Closing his eyes, he picked the rock up holding it in a hand for several long seconds. JJ gulped, his Adams apple rose and fell in his throat as he opened his eyes staring down into the depression the rock had left. A single copper penny shone in the sunlight as well as something else.

It gleamed and stood out among the small colored pebbles just beside the penny. Reaching down he clutched a fistful of dry sand and raised it to his waist allowing the gravel and sand to pass from one hand to the other, sifting and sorting the mixture until he discovered what had caught his eye.

A silver medallion, perhaps an inch and a half in diameter, lay in his palm glittering in the bright sunlight. For the most part, the artifact was rather crudely fashioned. Its edges were irregularly rounded and the thickness of the disc itself varied considerably. The object had a small hole gouged through the silver, allowing the owner to wear it about the neck as an amulet. He raised the medal closer to his eyes, thinking he could faintly discern something engraved on its face, he spat on the disc using his shirt to wash and polish away the coating of dirt and dust, then examined the object once again.

On one side, he could clearly make out the image of the full moon, complete with the dark Maria or lunar seas together with the major craters visible to the naked eye. Its opposite side featured a coiled snake lying below what JJ thought might represent a jagged lightning bolt. For a long moment, he considered dropping the medallion back into the dirt but changed his mind and shoved the disc into the pocket of his shorts. Maybe he would try to sell it in town.

He swayed slightly as he walked away from the ridge in the direction of his cave feeling almost physically sick. As he walked over the ridge and left the arrow point and the dry wash behind he began to feel a little better. Finding a suitable rock to sit upon he took his water bottle from the pack and poured the cool liquid over his head and face, then took a long drink. There could no longer be any doubt that something very strange was at work here, he shuddered and experienced a sudden urgent wish that he had stayed back in the New York sewers where he belonged.

He slept outdoors in his tent for the next week before a frigid November cold spell drove him back into the cave. While he did not get much sleep those first few nights after moving back into the cavern, he was comforted when nothing else occurred out of the ordinary. The green-blue light in the cave ceiling had not changed color or even flickered and better yet, he had not dreamt about Menily, the village and most importantly the nightmare that was Tahquitz.

He was heading home in the growing dark of an early November evening. The days had grown short, in only another couple December would arrive. Winter was close at hand, but an unusual November cold snap had broken, giving way to some well-appreciated mild temperatures. JJ had spent the afternoon in town where he visited Arnie earning a few bucks cleaning up the alley and scoring a decent dinner courtesy of the Palm. With the approach of night, the golf resorts, stores, and private homes within the valley glittered with every variety of Christmas light imaginable. JJ wasn't much of a fan of the newer types of flashing icicles, stars, snowflakes and the like, preferring instead the older displays that put him in mind of his childhood.

He had to use his flashlight to illuminate the trail on the way home to his cave. It had been dark for nearly an hour when he saw a bright orange disc peeking over the eastern horizon. The moon would be full tomorrow night or the next at the latest... "So what" he muttered to himself. Then suddenly thinking of Menily, the village, the goddess and of course the monstrosity in that particular order he shuddered... "That's what!" his dry voice croaked back at him and he swallowed hard.

JJ stood at the cave entrance and using his flashlight, he carefully inspected the interior of the cave... every inch of it! Stepping just a few feet inside, JJ paused and turned off the flashlight. As usual, the faint blue-green light illuminated the walls and ceilings. Everything appeared in place, nothing out of the ordinary. He turned on his radio finding a station playing some Christmas music and helped himself to a big bag of Doritos he bought earlier in town. It was well after midnight when he turned off the radio and fell asleep.

The next morning he woke refreshed, invigorated, and completely famished. Wolfing down several left over pork chops and a baked potato saved from the night before, he discovered an urgent desire to move. Dressing in a light top, shorts, and runners and clipping a water bottle to his belt, JJ walked toward the entrance before remembering the medallion where it sat atop the radio. He grabbed it and tucked it into his pocket. Ever practicing caution, JJ slowly exited the cave then stood tall in the early light of dawn feeling as though he were experiencing each sensation for the first time. He breathed deep, enjoying the exhilaration as the almost frosty air poured into and filled his lungs. The sun warmed him wherever it struck his bare skin and his ears pricked with the sound of small birds fluttering in the brush. Much more distant, he heard the sounds of Palm Springs as its residents awoke and set about their day.

A simple desire to run came across him and he began a moderate jog along the path that he normally walked toward the golf courses and hotels along Murray Canyon Drive. He enjoyed the way his body moved with a smooth confidence, something that he hadn't experienced in years, no... make that decades. JJ's feet fell in rapid succession atop the dry earth. He began the first of several long steady climbs following the pathway that wound upward along a gently rising ridge. He felt exalted with the newly discovered power that surged within his thighs and calves. Feeling a sudden urge JJ picked up his speed running faster...no faster still, his body demanding it. Upon reaching the top of the ridge, he did not pause but started downward along a much steeper path that whipsawed back and forth falling into a deep gulch where the path ended in a tumble of medium to large boulders that rose perhaps two hundred feet where it met the top of a second though somewhat lower ridge.

Without missing a beat, once again his legs propelled him upward, climbing the rocks as easily as someone would the stairs in their home, his footing as sure as that of a mountain goat, his body as tight and balanced as a professional athlete. Reaching the top of his climb his body finally permitted him a short recess. His lungs revelled as they greedily consumed great quantities of cool desert air while the sweat from his scalp and forehead ran down his face in salty rivulets stinging his eyes and running into his open mouth. The long forgotten taste of youth and vitality returned to him in a torrid rush causing an emotional upwelling deep within his chest that brought forth grateful tears that mixed and fell with the sweat that shone on his chest and dripped from his chin onto the arid dust at his feet.

As he stood atop the ridgeline, he looked back in the direction he had run and was surprised to see he had already traveled what had to be nearly a mile. Less than a minute later, his body had fully recovered from the exercise and a deep sense of satisfaction filled him. JJ quickly surveyed his surroundings and recognized the location where he now stood, the exact spot where he had found himself that first moment when his odyssey had begun. His eyes surveyed the lay of the land as he traced out the shallow river that had run across the dry sand and pebbled wash following the natural curve of the mountain as it gradually descended into the valley. He estimated the location where Menily's small village had sat and the more distant hilltop where they shared their evening meal, as well as something that JJ believed ran much deeper. He walked toward the wash.

The ancient sandbars, water-rounded pebbles, and small rocks strewn along its route easily identified the dry river bottom. JJ walked along the empty streambed as it followed the natural contours of the canyon leading into town. Arriving near a small strip mall, he walked into a pawnshop with the intention of selling the medallion, but at the last moment simply could not bring himself to part with it, instead, he bought a slender length of chain. Threading the metal string through the disc's opening, he placed the charm about his neck.

Again, as with the previous evening, JJ returned to the cave much later than usual and well after dark, but tonight he had no use for his flashlight as the nearly full moon had risen just shortly after sunset. Its silver brilliance flooded the pathway and illuminated the larger rocks, bare trees, and cactus, casting black shadows across the desert floor. Without a thought, his hand reached into the collar of his sweatshirt and grasped the medallion that dangled from his neck. Pulling it from beneath his shirt, he held it out before his face. The medallion whirled slowly on the end of its chain, its smooth surface catching the moonlight and flashing it into his eyes. Letting the disc fall back onto his chest JJ stooped low and quickly entered the cave. Once inside he paused and smiled thinly as he came to the startling realization that he no longer felt any concern with the events of the last several months, none whatsoever.

The next morning found him rested and alert. Leaving the cave, JJ felt terrific as he began to retrace the previous morning's series of effortless runs. Standing on a hilltop that overlooked the north end of the valley, he estimated his cave lay at least a good three miles distant. JJ had hardly cracked a sweat. His breathing was deep but unlabored; placing two fingers to his throat, he found his pulse to be both strong and steady. Without further pause, he continued the exhilarating run that led him down the steep hillside and onto the busy streets of the city, those same streets he remembered exploring when he first arrived in Palm Springs, but on this occasion, he viewed the neighbourhood with a renewed youthful perspective.

No longer just another frightened decrepit old black man, he found himself released from the shadows, alleyways and side streets he had frequented those first weeks. JJ immediately sensed a distinct change in the eyes of the people he passed. Gone were the usual expressions of pity, disgust, or even outright hostility he had come to expect after years of living on the streets. Only minutes later, while running past a series of large sidewalk level windows he caught his reflection in the glass. He slowed his pace to a walk then stopped altogether. Turning to face the window, he found himself staring at a young Cahuilla god who stood in the glass before him.

Everything about his appearance had changed with the obvious exception of his clothing, and his eyes that still bore a look of incredulity if not outright shock. After some study, JJ decided his face still embodied his own unique individuality but came to the unavoidable conclusion that he no longer resembled his African American ancestry. His hair though still jet black had become long and straight extending well past his shoulders while his broad nose had thinned appreciably as had his lips. While considered a good-looking boy in his youth, people had never described him as being muscular or athletic, but now as JJ examined his broad shoulders, corded muscular arms, toned abdominals, and powerful legs he could understand why people took notice of his obvious physical merits.

Just how long he stood on the sidewalk studying his reflection in the central window of the Wells Fargo branch JJ could not say. It was only after a bank guard had approached him and asked him in a sideways fashion if he could provide some assistance that JJ took the hint and moved along. As he continued to make his way down the sidewalk, he noticed that most of the men who passed by would move slightly to one side in obvious deference to his physical size and power. The women were a different matter. Many smile demurely in his direction when they thought he was not looking, but a smaller number regarded him with an unmistakably wanton lust and most of these were of an age he recognized as being more age appropriate to his own advanced, though well disguised years. JJ had to admit, "it turned his crank."

He spent the pleasant sunny afternoon as well as the last of his pocket money drinking beer and conversing with Julie, the middle-aged buxom blonde server who struck up longer and longer conversations each time she brought him another beer or whenever the patio crowd thinned. Always appreciative of curvaceous women, JJ readily accepted her rather forward invitation to accompany her home after shift. It had been many years since he had been with a woman whose attentions he had not purchased and much longer still one who had the means to keep her own apartment.

Arriving at her flat he found himself somewhat intimidated and self-conscious. The old cougar had taken notice of the excited tension that surrounded the handsome young man, who sat quietly in the center of her white leather couch, but rather than suppressing her carnal desires, his sudden timidity had quite the opposite effect and she wasted no time in pressing her home advantage. If nothing else, Julie was adept at placing a man at ease and in return JJ quickly embraced the moment finding himself back in the proverbial saddle once again, and then several more times in rapid succession.

It was almost eight when he took his leave of the very tired but well-satisfied woman in Julie's apartment. The setting sun had already dropped below the taller buildings in the city casting the streets and roadways in light shadow. His body throbbed with vitality, his eyes were clear and bright, his step light and quick. Lost in his own thoughts JJ walked with a casual confidence along the sidewalks heading in the general direction of his desert cave that still lay a couple of miles across the city then another eight or ten more to the southeast. His fingers reached and lightly touched the medallion. Rubbing the metal between his thumb and forefinger, a small voice in his mind softly questioned the amazing transformation that occurred and speculated what might be forthcoming, but as the metal warmed within his touch, he felt the urge to forget the old life and fully embrace the new.

He glanced into the darkening twilight sky and saw a familiar yellow glow. The moon was rising in the east, a full moon, a hunter's moon. The streetlights flickered and popped into life across the city and the number of people strolling along the walkways slowly dwindled. The attention JJ normally gave to his surroundings had made itself absent, and now that the last vestiges of sunset had disappeared and night had taken hold of the streets, JJ found himself a solitary figure walking in an area where individuals shouldn't find themselves after dark. He was smack in the middle of the Gateway Posse Crips turf, hell one of their bars was just up the street! At least the streets were clear, just the odd car passed by.

JJ saw a set of headlights approach and as the distance closed between them the outline of a police cruiser appeared. The car slowed, the officers no doubt giving him a quick appraisal. Just about the time JJ thought they were about to stop the vehicle suddenly sped off, lights flashing and siren blaring, responding to an urgent call. Knowing he should never have been out in the open in this neighborhood, JJ did not hesitate a moment longer and ducked into the next alley.

He spent the next half hour quietly walking past the rundown apartments and houses in the worst part of town. Occasionally he saw a few bums hanging about but none of them presented any threat and only one had the balls to ask him for any spare change, JJ threw him his last fifty cents and carried on. He had arrived within sight of the highway that marked the gang's boundary, just a used car lot to cut through then he would head cross-country, the quickest route home.

A pair of headlights from a car parked to his left flashed on illuminating his figure in their sudden glare. JJ took several more steps until a second set of car lights blazed forth catching him from his right. His eyes temporarily overwhelmed within the unexpected brilliance, his ears found no trouble picking up the clearly recognizable sounds of car doors opening and the rapid approach of footsteps pounding on the asphalt. JJ turned and began retracing his steps toward the alley from where he had emerged just moments before then fell into a dead run.

He was quickly leaving whoever chased him in the dust when he heard several loud pops behind him. JJ felt an intense sting in his left calf; someone had shot him. A few steps later, his left foot dragged on the ground and he knew he had only seconds before they would be on him. He raised his hands above his head and turned to face his attackers. Facing the gleam of the car's headlights, he saw three dark silhouettes approach. One of them spoke up, "Where you think you goin' bitch?" JJ instantly realized the speaker was black. "A little off base huh!" said another then added, "Got some balls cuttin' through our hood, we might just have to cut 'em off." All three men laughed nastily.

JJ heard himself speak out in his own down-home idiom and instantly regretted it, "Yo man, I is no trespass'n, jus goin' to visit my auntie." Now while the gang members wouldn't have given a rat's ass about an old black bum crossing their turf, a buff young Hispanic so obviously making fun of their black vernacular wouldn't be cut any slack. JJ went down under a hail of fists and feet.

Under the onslaught and trying to protect himself, JJ curled up in a ball, his hands atop his head waiting for an opening where he might be able to make a break for it, but a break was not in the cards. If anything the blows were coming faster now, he felt and heard a rib break in his back. A vicious kick caught him in the side of his head stunning him just before another struck him full in the face smashing his jaw and crushing his nose. At that moment JJ knew they would not be satisfied just beating him; their intention was to kill. JJ felt a warm sensation spread out near his groin guessing he'd been stabbed or had simply pissed himself, it didn't matter, JJ could feel himself rapidly slipping away.

Seconds later the punches and kicks were barely registering; he must be in a state of shock. Sensing he was about to die, JJ allowed his consciousness to retreat toward a deep recess in his mind but as he did so he felt something else brush by, something dreadful, very ancient and recently familiar. The shaman's presence welled up and burst to the surface unseating JJ as it took control of his body. JJ sensed its terrible fury and purpose and in a small way almost felt sorry for what was to befall the thugs who were still doing their best to kill him.

The violence of the initial frenzy had left JJ prostrate and unmoving. Now the gang members began taking their time, aiming their kicks where they thought the blows would do the most damage. The gang's leader had even taken a break sitting on a nearby garbage can, huffing and puffing, laughing and still egging on his buddies who were obviously growing tired as well. A few seconds later, the other gang members were satisfied that their victim was out for the count. Their leader stood up from his perch on the garbage can, his hand reaching into his back pocket; it reappeared holding something in its grasp. With a flick of his wrist, the wicked blade of a long gravity knife flashed open and clicked into position.

The gang leader chuckled coldly as he walked over and knelt beside JJ's unconscious form. Guiding the razor sharp blade toward JJ's throat he announced to the others, "Might as well do da man a favor..." The other men stood back several feet waiting for the inevitable gush of blood that would signal the death of yet another of the Posse's victims, their fourth this year. If true to fashion, the gangster would wait for the body to bleed out before reaching up into the wide slash in his victim's neck and up into the mouth, pulling the tongue down and then out, leaving it to hang down below the red gash in the corpse's neck. The Cuban necktie had been one of the Posse's favorite calling cards and would leave no doubt as to who had been responsible for the turf killing.

As in the cave, JJ felt himself leave his body and now found himself hovering in the alleyway, only a matter of feet from where his body still lay crumpled on the filthy asphalt. He watched in fascination as the thug brought the razor sharp knife blade ever closer to his neck. Suddenly JJ became aware of a dark shadow that flooded into the alleyway engulfing the men and dimming the light streaming from the still burning headlights of the gang's cars a hundred yards distant.

Tensing his arm the thug positioned the knife to plunge it's blade into the far side of JJ's throat intending to use all his strength and draw the six-inch blade back toward his chest slicing a jagged path through the tough windpipe, soft tissue and severing each of JJ's carotid arteries. The gangster's arm froze as he saw his victim's eyes unexpectedly snap open, "mother fu..." The gangster would never finish his guttural curse.

A pair of glowing, pale yellow eyes glared out from JJ's broken eye sockets and his bloodied face adopted an incredibly fierce and terrifying grimace. The creature that now inhabited JJ's broken body willed it to rise from where it lay, and rise up it did, though not through any apparently natural means. In a manner that would do any matinee vampire proud, JJ watched as his body slowly brought itself to its feet without having moved so much as an eyebrow. As stiff as a spike in the corpse of Christ, the creature towered above the young thug who still knelt below, immovable and bathed within his abject fear. Ever so slowly, the young man strained his neck, forcing his gaze upward where it eventually met the horror that grinned back in hideous malice.

The two other gang members glanced furtively about the alleyway and then back at one another, the whites of their wide and terrified eyes clearly visible in the enfeebled headlights of their parked cars. Stepping back from the ominous happenings taking place before them, they watched as the creature reached out its arms in slow deliberation toward their still paralyzed leader. JJ heard and felt the broken and dislocated bones within his body snapping back into their proper place. Hot blood rushed in swelling the muscles of his arms, legs, and core. Aware that the flesh of his injured calf was rippling strangely, he felt the muscle squeeze tight about the slug, driving the small bullet from his body as easily as you would pop a ripe blackhead. A sense of unnatural strength pulsed through his body, no longer merely flesh and blood it seemed to have become a composite of granite and liquid steel.

Together with the other two men, JJ's apparition watched in morbid fascination as his body transformed itself into something that fell somewhere between that of a huge bear, boar or maybe a wolf but whatever it was, it bore scant resemblance to the young man that walked down that alley only five minutes earlier. JJ witnessed the ensuing carnage from two simultaneous perspectives, the first where his ghostly consciousness still hovered silently above the alleyway, the second from a much more personal vantage where he and the abomination glared upon the of the gang leader who cowered unashamedly before them. Unwilling to watch but quite unable to block the images being captured within those pale orbs, JJ saw the beasts wicked claws grasp each of the gangland leader's biceps and force the man to his feet. With indescribable force, the beast thrust its arms apart in a wide arc cleanly ripping each of the gang member's limbs from his upper body.

Weaving unsteadily, the gang leader faced the creature, his face wearing a silent scream as his unbelieving eyes roamed from one gaping wound to the other, each limb but an empty socket where a shoulder had hung just seconds earlier. The man's life-blood gushed from his mortal injuries, spurting outward a crimson mist fell across the horrified faces of his companions. For a split second, the remaining gangsters delayed any course of action, their minds still trying to understand what they had just witnessed, but they had delayed far too long.

As before in the cave, unbidden and unwilling, JJ's apparition was violently yanked back into the mind of the beast. An unwilling bystander, he... no they, fell upon the two gangsters in a ferocious wave of violence and malice. JJ heard their body howl in a delight of blood lust while his sharp claws pierced the flesh just below the ribs of the closest man within their reach. Their muscular arm thrust deep, their claws tore and ripped through the soft tissue, probing ever further within their victim. Discovering what they sought, the taloned fist closed tight then swept back in a rush, pulling the victims ruined lungs and quivering heart out and away from his chest to present a macabre display before their owner's incredulous yet dimming eyes.

Abe Jones was the last remaining gang member and at seventeen was also the youngest. His blood running cold, he had watched the systematic destruction of his two friends gripped within a frightened rigor, but as the creature's rabid glare fell upon him his wits quickly returned and he sprinted down the lane in a mad dash towards the nearest of the two vehicles. An up and coming track star before he dropped out of high school, his legs pumped and his heart raced as he ran as he had never run before. Abe felt the balls of his feet barely kiss the earth as he put distance between him and the monstrosity that he knew still pursued him. The headlights of the closest vehicle shone out toward the young man; twin beacons of hope stretching into the dark night, their yellow light suggesting the promise of safety. Ten paces later, he was almost there, "God help me, I'm going to make it!" He jumped and slid across the car's hood reaching the opposite side of the vehicle landing a scant two feet from the open door. Catapulting himself inside he reached toward the door handle in a wild panic. His fingers found and closed about the thin metal lever while he simultaneously pulled the door closed with all his might!

The solid thunk of the closing door was the next thing to heaven in Abe's terrified mind. Stabbing his finger down hard on the door's electric locks, he immediately heard the obedient clicks of the mechanisms locking into place. "Time to leave homeboy!" he grasped for the key that should have still been in the ignition, but discovered its absence. The boy's head whirled like a top as his frantic eyes scanned that portion of that black night illuminated within the car's headlights. Abe plunged his hands downward groping about the floor, searching for the key... "Found it!" As he jammed the key into the ignition, he took a second glance out the windshield, still nothing moved. "Huh, see you in hell you son of a whore...!"

They glided out of the deep shadows near the driver's side door. Their eyes stared, affixed upon the terrified boy who squirmed in the driver's seat. JJ felt his impossibly powerful arms and claws position themselves on the top and bottom of the car's door. Squeezing and digging into the metal, the claws slowly pried the door several inches back from its frame before readjusting their grip. With a single incredibly violent yank, they ripped the door from its hinges tossing it away and leaving it to bounce along the pavement coming to rest some five yards distant.

Knowing what was to come; JJ desperately tried to distance himself from the creature's mind, but found he was unable to break free of the iron grip that joined them. Once again, from this horribly personal vantage, JJ now felt drawn to join with the abomination as they paused for several seconds, sniffing and snuffling, filling their wide nostrils with and reveling in the waves of fear arising from their victim. Tilting their hideous head, first this way then that, their fierce eyes carefully examined the young man with gruesome fascination. Now fully engaged, the thing he had become watched amusedly as the young man descended into full panic mode, now openly weeping and busily pissing and shitting himself beneath the dim glow of the cab's overhead light. Together, they leaned into the car with anticipation and deliberation.

A moment later, Abe's high pitched screams united with JJ's own excited yowls and bellows as his claws and teeth proceeded to tear the young man apart. Hot crimson droplets stippled the inside of the windshield's glass and steering wheel while gouts of bright blood splashed and frothed across the cool leather seat before running to the floor in ruddy torrents, spilling out and pooling upon the dirty floor mat.

At the onset of Abe's first bloody spasm, JJ felt his soul yield to the frantic bloodlust rushing through his veins and in doing so surrendered himself to the overwhelming desire to unite with the shaman's spirit. As one, they turned away from the car and the bloody remnants inside. Their consciousness fully united, the beast that JJ had become ran forward on all fours dashing through the stark light and shadow of the used car lot, quickly leaving the cars and littered corpses in their wake.

Upon reaching the poorly lit, nearly deserted highway that separated the city from the desert highlands, they sprang atop the dark asphalt of the roadway spanning the short distance in a flash. The driver sitting behind the pair of high beams that sped toward them as they crossed would later tell his wife of the odd misshapen creature he witnessed loping across the moonlit highway near Jim Darlings Used Car Emporium. He thought he saw something dangling from its mouth but he could not be sure, it disappeared only seconds later. Whatever it was, it effortlessly climbed the nearly vertical canyon walls without as much as breaking its stride.

Running atop the desert ridges and moving through shadow cast vales they crossed the miles with astonishing speed. Very soon, the beast made out the familiar landmarks as they approached their subterranean lair. JJ felt exhilarated and full of life as they slowed and padded up the trail toward the cave's entrance. As was ever his habit, he now paused, cautiously looking and listening to the sounds of the desert night before entering his den. Bathed in the silver sheen of the full moon he savored the smell of their victim's blood in his nostrils, the taste of it as it lay upon his tongue. Completely satiated in a way he never thought or imagined possible JJ entered the cave.

The ceiling of the cavern danced with myriads of light as JJ made his way toward the altar where Menily awaited him. Reaching the shrine his massive jaws parted, dropping the still dripping meat atop the rock's cool smooth surface. As if on cue, the will o' the wisp that had once been Abe Jones slowly arose from the altar, floated upward and took its place among the ghostly procession that would eternally ply the cold void within the cavernous ceiling.

It was a couple of days into the New Year when Arnie called out to a familiar figure who leaned into the kitchen dumpster at the rear of his kitchen. "Hey old timer!" he yelled out, "y'all can do better than that!"

JJ pulled his head out of the bin then jumped down to the alleyway turning toward his friend with a warm smile, "Arnie... Merry Christmas and a Happy New Year!"

"And to yahself, haven't seen yah in weeks, what yah been up tah?" Arnie ran his hands over his chest and belly brushing some breadcrumbs from his apron.

"Same old, same old. Been hanging out a bit down round La Quinta, good pickin's down there." JJ walked over and took the giants outstretched hand in both of his. "I should have come by earlier, sorry Arnie."

"S'okay old son, but I was gettin a might worried." Arnie grinned back, "Come in I'll fix yah up with a hot coffee and some grub, huh?"

"Sure, be right nice, thanks." JJ followed his friend into the kitchen.

The two spent the next half hour catching up when Arnie seemed to recall something he wanted to ask JJ. "So I guess yah heard 'bout that miss'n green keeper over at Indian Canyon... Tom somethin' or t'other".

"Clancy... Tom Clancy" JJ volunteered. "Yeah, too bad, he'll be rightly missed." He smiled slyly and chuckled to himself.

"Not much and not by many huh?" Arnie added then grew quiet, his mood becoming somber. "Speaking of being missed JJ, ah probably won't be here come next month, Mr. Harrison's leavin' the Palm and Wallace is takin' over... made it pretty clear I'm not wanted."

JJ ran a long tongue over his teeth and lips; "Well ol' son, I wouldn't go countin' those hens just yet."

Author's Note

As a teen and young adult, I remember spending many enjoyable hours reading science fiction stories penned by the likes of Isaac Asimov, Arthur C. Clarke, and Ray Bradbury and horror classics such as those written by Shirley Jackson, Daphne Maurier, Washington Irving and many others. Their novels were terrific, but what I also enjoyed were their shorter stories found within anthologies and less frequently, within the collections featuring a single author. The plots and themes were crisp and clean; but more importantly, the ideas driving the stories forward would take on a life of their own.

Throughout my career as a police detective working within a large Canadian city, I witnessed more than my share of horrors and tragedies and may have developed a natural aversion toward stories based too closely upon the experiences of real life. I suppose this may explain my evolving into a purveyor of escapism, though one not given to truly wild flights of fantasy. Grounded in a slightly bent, rather than a fully warped sense of reality, these stories exude an underlying sense of normality; until they do not.

The nine stories within "And Midnight Came to Call" reflect this preference, often bringing along unexpected twists as they end. It is my genuine hope that you enjoy reading them as much as I enjoyed writing them.

Best wishes,

Stephen Kirk
August 2016